Herbert Durbin

OF LOVE
AND
HEARTBREAK

The Lockhart Trilogy

TATE PUBLISHING
AND **ENTERPRISES**, LLC

Published by Tate Publishing & Enterprises, LLC
127 E. Trade Center Terrace | Mustang, Oklahoma 73064 USA
1.888.361.9473 | www.tatepublishing.com

Tate Publishing is committed to excellence in the publishing industry. The company reflects the philosophy established by the founders, based on Psalm 68:11,
"The Lord gave the word and great was the company of those who published it."

Published in the United States of America

ISBN: 978-1-62902-513-1
1. Fiction / Sagas
2. Fiction / General
13.12.05

To my sister, Barbara Durbin Kenyon, without whose constant encouragement, honest critiques, and occasional language lessons I might never have completed these stories.

THE CABIN ON CHURCH HOUSE CREEK

ONE

It was beginning to look like the afternoon was going to get away from him as he finished the few dishes he had dirtied with his late lunch. His regular Sunday afternoon visit to her gravesite was the only thing left on his agenda for the day. He folded the dishtowel and hung it on the ring glued to the refrigerator and headed upstairs to get his wallet. *She's been gone more than two years now*, he thought. *Why am I still driving out to the cemetery to visit a stone when I know she isn't out there?* Still, he picked up his keys and wallet, went to the closet for his jacket, went back down the stairs and out into the garage.

The cemetery was only about a ten-minute drive from the house, but he had time to reflect on the reasons for his present situation. Her cancer had come on suddenly and been so aggressive that he had not had the time to come to grips with life without her. He had felt lost and without purpose every day since her funeral. He loathed himself for his failure to protect the love of his life from that most horrible and painful death. He had asked himself many times during the past two years, "Why couldn't it have been me?" He was still deep in thought as he turned into the gate at the Heaven's Rest Cemetery.

As he drove up to the section where she was buried, he noticed the late-afternoon sun of the short late-December day was already casting long shadows from the trees and stones. He stood in front of her stone, deep in thought, looking across the fields of dry, dead grass to the stand of live oak trees about a mile away. The gentle slope of the terrain from the edge of the cemetery grounds to the highway just the other side of the trees made the distance seem shorter. As he stood there looking down toward the live oak trees, he noticed that the long shadows caused by the late afternoon sun revealed an exaggerated automobile track in the dead grass. The tracks led from the stand of live oak trees to a cluster of small mesquite trees about one hundred yards to the west of them.

This piqued his curiosity, and he made a mental note to check the area to see why anyone would be driving there. Nothing important, just human curiosity, but it temporarily took his mind off of the unpleasant circumstances of her death.

It was almost dark by the time he returned home. The large, empty house on the hill above the creek that once rang with her laughter now seemed more like an empty church than a home. The house was filled with the ghosts of her memories. Everything reminded him of her. Sometimes late at night, after the lights were out and he was in bed, the emptiness and loneliness of the big old house was almost unbearable. *One of these days I'm going to just pack up and leave*, he thought, as he entered the dark empty house. *One of these days*.

It was the following Tuesday before he remembered he wanted to check on the tracks from the live oak trees to the mesquite trees. In the afternoon, he drove out Highway 16 toward the town of Fairfield where he saw what he thought was the stand of live oak trees on the right side of the highway. There didn't seem to be any way to get to them. A mile farther up the road he turned his SUV around and was headed back toward town when he noticed an old, rarely used cattle guard on the north side of the highway. It was almost completely hidden by a tall stand of dry Johnson grass. He slowed, turned off the highway and crossed the cattle guard. It was then that he saw the faint impression left by a vehicle heading in a slow left turn toward the oak trees. Following these tracks, he came into the grove of oak trees. He continued to follow the tracks as they turned out across the open field and on into the small cluster of mesquite trees.

Suddenly, just in front of him, he saw two small mounds of earth. The earth was freshly turned, and he was certain he had come upon the graves of two small animals. *Someone just burying a couple of pets out here*, he thought, *but why two graves? What if it's not animals, but some missing children?* The thought almost panicked him! *What if someone saw me come out here? One could think I had something to do with burying them. I better get the Hell out of here*!

Slowly he gained control of his emotions. With determined steadiness he climbed out of his SUV and kicked at one of the mounds of earth. It was still fresh and powder like, and the toe of his boot soon dug down and hit something solid. His curiosity outweighed his fear, and he soon uncovered the top of a large plastic cooler. Kneeling down and digging with his hands on one end of the cooler, he found a handle and pulled the heavy cooler up out of its shallow grave. With extreme caution he slowly unlocked the catch and lifted the lid.

It was neither the remains of a child nor those of an animal that he saw. Inside he found layers of bundled $100 bills. They were two rows wide and ten rows long and appeared to be several layers deep. He shut the lid, pushed the cooler out of his way, and frantically dug up the second grave. Here he found another cooler identical to the first. Upon opening it, he discovered it too was full of bundled $100 bills.

He quickly loaded the two coolers into the rear of the SUV and, not waiting to fill in the holes, turned the SUV around and sped out of the cluster of mesquite trees. He continued through the live oak grove, over the cattle guard, and onto the Fairfield highway. Instead of turning left toward town, however, he turned right toward Fairfield and drove as far as the turn-off to the city lake. There he followed the road across the dam. He was taking the long way home, watching constantly to see if anyone was following. Eventually he made it back to his house and into his own garage without ever seeing a following vehicle.

After closing the garage door to make sure no one had witnessed him, he unloaded the two coolers from the SUV and carried them into his living room. He removed the bundles of bills and stacked them neatly on the coffee table. For a while he just sat there staring at all that money. He discovered that there were twenty-eight layers of bundles in each cooler. Simple mathematics told him that two bundles by ten bundles by twenty-eight layers of bundles resulted in five hundred and sixty bundles in each of the seventy-two-quart coolers. Each bundle of $100 bills was worth ten thousand dollars. This meant that each cooler contained $5,600,000. The total of both coolers came out to be $11,200,000.

He had no idea what he should do with all that money. He was hesitant to take it to his bank, as any cash deposit of $10,000 or more raised eyebrows. He assumed it would be dangerous to tell anyone that he had found it. His gut feeling was that it was illegal drug money, or at least the result of some type of criminal activity—otherwise why would someone take the time to bury it? He realized this amount of cash could once again change his life. He left the money stacked on the coffee table, covered it with a tablecloth, then put the dirt-covered coolers in the garage.

He hardly slept during the night, rolling and tossing, drifting in and out of sleep. Early the next morning, while drinking his coffee, he sat and stared at the tablecloth covering the stack of bills. Slowly he began to formulate a plan. He would hide the money in plain sight and use it a few hundred dollars at a time.

He was in good health and had no pressing financial needs, so this money was just a worry. Even if he decided to go on a spending spree which he was not inclined to do, and limited himself to just one thousand dollars a day, it would take over thirty years to spend it.

He waited until the mid-December sun had warmed up the outside air. While he waited he collected three empty soft drink cans from his trash, washed them, and placed them where they could dry thoroughly. He then took the coolers out to the garden hose and washed off all of the soil from their burial site. He toweled them dry but left them in the sun to assure they were completely dry.

For the rest of the afternoon he sat with a notebook and pencil laid out on an atlas and wrote out an itinerary, occasionally looking at state road maps. There were nineteen states that he had never visited. During their marriage they had traveled to thirty-one of the states, visiting some of them many times and only driving through others. His plan was to visit all the remaining states, beginning in the warmer southern states and continuing north as the temperatures got warmer. He would drive no more than seven or eight hours in any one day on roads and highways that saw only light traffic and then stop for a few days wherever fate and the highway took him. He had no plans for what he might do after he had visited the remaining nineteen states, if he was even able to accomplish that feat.

An hour or so before dark he brought the coolers in and stacked them in his kitchen. He glued the empty cola cans into three of the four cup holders in the lid of one of the coolers. *This will be the cooler I work from*, he thought. When the glue had completely dried, he refilled the coolers with all except one of the bundles of money. He laid that one aside for later. He then loaded the refilled coolers into the rear of the SUV, pushing them snuggly against the back of the seat, catch side against the seat. *Could be a couple of coolers full of cold drinks*, he thought. *Who would ever suspect I'm driving around with over eleven million dollars in the back of my car?*

He slid three of the $100 bills from the bundle he had kept back and placed them in his wallet. He then tossed the rest of the bundle into the storage space in the console between the front bucket seats.

The next three weeks he spent getting ready for the new episode that was about to unfold in his life. At forty-two, he suddenly regretted the two years of wasted days and nights pining away for her as if he could somehow bring her back. A man can only love that deeply and completely once in his life. It was over now, and he had to move on. It was as if finding the buried coolers had caused an epiphany. He felt as if his life suddenly had a cause, a purpose, a reason for getting up each morning.

He made plans to close up the house, stop the mail, and have the utilities turned off. At the bank he emptied his safe-deposit box and closed out all of his accounts except the one where his investment dividends and her life insurance annuity were being automatically deposited. He emptied his pantry and freezer and took all of the contents to a mission that fed the poor. He picked over his clothes and kept back only a few pairs of trousers and shirts. An extra pair of shoes, a pair of western boots, his Stetson hat, three belts of differing colors and widths, and two jackets. Everything else from the closets went to Goodwill.

The morning of January 19, the day they were to turn off the utilities, he was up early, showered and shaved. He observed himself in the mirror. He was still fairly young and in very good health, with blue eyes, and blond wavy hair beginning to recede above the temples and thinning in the back. He was just over six feet tall, 185 pounds, and still had a 33-inch waist. In his younger days he was considered quite handsome in the category of a Paul Newman. He finished dressing and loaded the last suitcase into the back of the SUV.

It was almost noon as he drove around the circular drive away from the big house that had been their home for many years. He took one long last look. Strangely, he felt neither sadness nor elation, but more as if he was observing a landmark by the side of the road.

TWO

L eaving the city, he drove south and east on US-84 for a while before leaving it for State highways. He continued in a southeasterly direction for some time, eventually crossing a portion of the Angelina National Forest. He had been driving at comfortable speeds well below the limit in order to take in the winter scenery. Shortly after entering the Angelina National Forest it started to rain softly. The rain grew steadily heavier with each passing mile and he had to drive even slower. Eventually he left the National Forest still driving through the piney woods of East Texas. By the time he reached the little village of Bon Weir, an hour or so later, he was becoming excessively tired from the strain of driving in the downpour.

It was nearing dark when he pulled off the road in front of a small café. He sat in the SUV for a few minutes, trying to relax. The constant sheets of driving rain beating against his vehicle didn't allow him to relax, so braving the elements, he climbed out and hurried inside where he hoped it would be quieter and more restful.

The café was almost empty, so he took a booth away from the windows. He noticed a small girl sitting alone at the counter. She looked to be about six or seven, with hair of tight black curls pulled back in a ponytail. She was totally involved in the drawing and coloring she was doing.

A waitress carrying a glass of water and a menu suddenly entered into his observations. "Hi, I'm Yvette." She smiled, "Do you know what you want, or would you like some time to study the menu?" As she stood smiling down at him, he took in her youthful beauty. She looked to be in her mid-twenties, with tight, curly, coal-black hair and twinkling violet-blue eyes. She was petite in size and very pretty.

He glanced down at the menu, then looked back at her, smiled, and asked, "What do you recommend?"

"The beef stew is always good, and Arty just made a fresh pan of cornbread. Arty's cornbread is the best!"

"Then I'll have the stew and cornbread," he said.

"Anything to drink?" she asked.

"A tall glass of cold milk would be nice," he answered.

"Coming right up," she said, and she turned and walked away.

He watched her walking away and caught himself staring intently at the long perfectly turned legs below the short skirt of her waitress uniform. *Such youthful beauty and charm*, he thought to himself. *Oh, to be that young again.*

"Mommy, I need to go to the bathroom," he heard the little girl say as Yvette went behind the counter to turn in his order.

"Just a minute!" Yvette said.

The little one was obviously her daughter, Jack thought. *Of course, they have the same hair and petite bone structure.* As soon as she had turned in his order, the two of them disappeared into the women's rest room. *That's a cautious mother*, he thought. Yet he couldn't help but wonder why the little girl was sitting alone in this place.

There was a sudden brief lull in the rain, and the three people at the other booth got up, paid their bill, and filed out of the café.

Yvette brought his order. "That your daughter?" he asked, nodding toward the child.

"Yes," she said proudly as she placed his stew in front of him. "That's Juliette. She's 7 going on 17."

"I'd like to meet her. She's as pretty as her mother, if you don't mind me saying it."

"Thank you." She smiled.

He looked at her a for a long moment. She had such an infectious smile on her pretty face, which seemed whiter framed by her raven-black hair. He was touched by the beauty of the moment and drawled, "I came in here to get out of the cold and rain, feeling depressed and sad, but your beautiful smile has warmed my body and soul."

"What a nice complement! I'll be right back with your milk," she said.

She went behind the counter, and he heard her talking to the cook. Very soon a tall, heavy-set man wearing an apron and a ball cap came out of the kitchen area and went behind the counter. "This is Arty," Yvette called to him as she drew the milk.

"Hi, Arty," he said. "I'm Jack. You think this rain will ever stop?"

"Don't look like it," Arty said.

Yvette helped Juliette off of her stool and brought her to his table when she brought his milk. "This is my daughter, Juliette," she said.

"Hi, Juliette. I'm Jack," he said. "Nice to meet you. What is that you're working on?"

Juliette held up the drawing. It was obviously a drawing of the inside of the café and very advanced for her age.

"I'd like to look at it closer," Jack told her. "Could you sit with me while I eat my stew?"

"Uh-huh," Juliette said. "Is it okay, Mommy?"

"Climb in and scoot over," Yvette said, "and I'll sit down for a minute too. We can't go home in this rain anyway."

Jack studied the picture for a while, complimenting Juliette. "You hungry?" Jack asked Juliette. Then, turning to Yvette before she could answer, he asked, "What kind of pie do you have?"

She recited all the kinds of pie and at the end said, "And a strawberry cheesecake."

"Now that sounds delicious," Jack said. "What about it, Juliette? Want a big piece of strawberry cheesecake?"

"Can I, Mommy? Please!"

"Okay," Yvette said, smiling. "Jack, why are you spoiling my child?"

"Why don't you join us?" Jack asked.

"No thank you. Have to watch my figure, you know."

"Why don't you let me watch it for you?"

"Oh, now that's original."

"I'm a bit out of practice when it comes to flirting."

"Didn't sound that way to me," Arty said as he delivered the pie to Juliette and Jack. "Sounded like you was purdy familiar with them there compliments."

"I'm going to get Juliette something to drink. Do you need a refill on your milk?" Yvette asked as she slid out of the booth.

Arty went to the door and looked out into the darkening evening. "We ain't likely to have anymore customers today if this storm keeps up," he said as he turned the sign to closed. "I'm not going to lock the door. Someone might need to get in out of this rain. Hey, Yvette, looks like Charlie's Garage is closed for the day. Did he ever call to say your car was fixed? How are you and Juliette going to get home without your car? Especially in this cold rain. Probably gonna freeze tonight." As he talked he started closing down the kitchen area. Yvette went to help, wiping down the counter and tables.

Juliette ate most of her cheesecake, drank a swallow or two of her milk, and ooched down in the booth, yawning widely. "Somebody sleepy?" Jack asked.

"Mmhmm." Juliette nodded.

"Do you live far from here?" he asked.

"In Bayou Park."

"Maybe, if your mother agrees, I could drop you off on my way to the motel."

"I guess."

"Do you always come to work with your mother?"

"No, the school bus brings me here after school."

"How do you get to school?"

"School bus."

"It picks you up here?"

"No, silly, it picks me up in front of my house!"

"I think I'm beginning to understand."

Jack left Juliette asleep in the booth, gathered up the plates, glasses, and flatware, and carried them to the kitchen. "Caint afford to pay ya!" Arty growled.

"Best stew and cornbread I ever ate!" Jack said. "And the companion or hostess, whichever you call that pretty little thing that you provided, was top notch!"

Jack returned to the dinner area and stood at the cash register. Yvette came over and handed him his bill. "Seventeen eighty-five," she said.

"Here, keep the change," he said handing her a $100 bill.

"Do you realize that is more than an eighty dollar tip?"

"That's for your smile and the loan of your beautiful little daughter for my dinner companion. I understand you two need a ride home? I'd be happy to drop you and Juliette off on my way to find a motel. By the way, she's asleep in the booth back there."

"We don't have a motel in Bon Weir," she said. "The nearest motel is in Jasper, and that's nearly sixty miles away. And good luck finding a vacancy on a night like this. But yes, I would very much appreciate a ride home for Juliette and me."

"How soon will you be ready? I'll go out and warm up the car and bring it right up to the door so the two of you don't drown."

"I'll let you know. I just have to help Arty finish up with a few things."

Half an hour later, he pulled away from the café with Yvette and Juliette. Their conversation consisted mostly of her directions to her home in Bayou mobile home park. After a brief period of silence she took a deep breath and said, "I may live to regret this, but I do have a spare bedroom in my house. You can stay with us tonight if you promise you won't rape me and kill us."

"I don't know…that's a lot to ask of a guy just for providing a dry bed." Jack grinned. Then as he noticed her eyes growing wide he said, "Okay, I promise, I promise."

He turned the SUV into the trailer park and drove up as near as he could to the front steps of the single-wide that she indicated was their home. He opened the car door for her and held his other jacket over her head as she pulled Juliette from the rear seat and carried her under the roof of the porch.

As he entered he noticed everything was very neat and clean. He stood dripping just inside the entryway until she brought him a towel and told him to follow her to one of the small bedrooms. He kicked off his rain-soaked shoes and trailed behind her. The trailer was long and wide—sixteen feet by seventy feet. It had a large master bedroom and full bath on one end, where she and Juliette slept and two smaller bedrooms and a second bath on the opposite end, where she made up a bed for him.

"You can put your things in here and use this bath," she told him. "I'm going to fix something hot to drink. Do you prefer coffee or tea?"

"I'll have what you're having," he said. "Please don't put yourself out. I'll try to be out of your hair early tomorrow."

Yvette put the tea kettle on the stove then went to change into dry clothes and take care of Juliette. Jack had put on his own dry clothes when he heard the old-fashioned tea kettle start to whistle. He entered the kitchen area and found two cups with tea bags already in them. He turned off the fire and poured hot water into one of the cups.

"Do you want me to pour yours now?" he called to Yvette.

"Yes, please," she called back. "There's honey on the bar, or if you prefer sugar I have some little packets in a container in the cabinet over the toaster."

"Honey is fine," Jack called over his shoulder. Then he turned and found her standing right behind him. "You startled me! I thought we were having a long-distance conversation."

She laughed, and then they stood there looking at each other and stirring their tea in silence. *What a beautiful, melodious laugh,* Jack thought. Eventually Yvette took her tea to the living room and sat on one end of the couch, drawing her legs up under her. She was holding the saucer in her left hand and would pick her cup up in her right hand, sip, and then return it to the saucer. Jack sat opposite of her in a recliner. Silence filled the room as they took turns sipping their tea and looking over the rim at one another. *Yvette is one of the most desirable women I have ever seen,* Jack was thinking.

Just then, Juliette came into the living room, carrying a school workbook. She climbed up on the couch next to her mother and asked for help with the book. Yvette showed patience and love as she helped Juliette with her schoolwork. Jack watched without interrupting, although he did freshen Yvette's tea from time to time.

Eventually Yvette put Juliette to bed, and she and Jack were once again alone.

"You haven't asked me about Juliette's father," she said.

"Didn't consider it any of my business."

"I'm going to tell you anyway. He's not in the picture anymore. Actually, he never really was, although we were married for over two years when Juliette was first born. It's the typical story. We were dating in high school. I got pregnant the night of the senior prom. Our parents insisted that we get married. Steve hated me for getting pregnant and not wanting an abortion. He accused me of ruining his life. He resented Juliette. We were divorced when Juliette was about one and a half. He has never tried to contact her, nor has he ever paid a dime of his child support."

"So you have been alone now for what, five years?"

She nodded, and a for a brief moment he sensed her loneliness. Slowly she began to smile again, then said, "So what's your story?"

"My story would bore you to sleep, and it's too early to go to bed," Jack said. "Now, tell me about your car and Charlie's Garage."

"Oh, that. Well, my ex left me with a real piece-of-junk car. Charlie has been keeping it going—barely, mind you—for months now. This morning it conked out on my way to work, and Charlie towed it to his garage, which luckily for me, is just across the highway from the café. He promised to call when he got it fixed. I guess he couldn't bring it back to life this time."

"What time do you have to be at work tomorrow?" he asked.

"Ten, but I have to get up much earlier than that to get Juliette ready to catch the school bus. Would you like me to wake you at any particular time?"

"I'll be up early. Wouldn't want to miss an opportunity to say 'bye' to Juliette."

Their conversation for the rest of the evening was cordial and casual as they got to know more about each other. By the time they retired to the opposite ends of the trailer they were very much at ease with one another.

Jack awoke to the smell of coffee brewing. Although already 6:30, it was still dark outside. He noticed he didn't hear any rain hitting the window. He shaved and showered and dressed quickly. He could hardly wait to get into the other part of the trailer to see Yvette and Juliette. He had been alone so long, and now suddenly two wonderful people who possibly could use his help had suddenly come into his life. He was happy as he went into the area where the two were having breakfast. He wasn't disappointed when he was greeted by Juliette's sweet smile and tiny voice. He had to restrain himself to keep from hugging the tiny girl.

Yvette's warm greeting and lovely smile warmed him, and he felt his heart beating faster as he walked close to her, inhaling her perfume.

"Sit down, Jack." She smiled. "I'll bring you a cup of coffee. How do you take it?"

"Black," Jack replied. "You girls sure do look beautiful this morning."

Yvette set his coffee down and then a plate of bacon and scrambled eggs.

"No man alive can say no to my scrambled eggs and bacon," she said. "Toast will be ready soon. Drink your orange juice, Juli."

"Will you be at the café when I get there today?" Juliette asked Jack.

"I don't know, honey," Jack said. "Do you want me to be there?"

"Yes, I want to show you my artwork. My teacher said it was very good!"

"Then I'll be there for sure. Wouldn't want to miss that!"

He looked at Yvette, who had been shaking her head ever so slightly to indicate that he shouldn't promise her something he wouldn't do.

When Jack returned from walking Juliette to the bus stop, Yvette lit into him.

"Listen," she said, "I don't want you filling my daughter's head with a lot of empty promises like her no-good father did. I've worked long and hard to get her to a place where she can trust again, and you're here less than twenty-four hours, charming your way into her life, and now you'll leave and I'll have to pick up the pieces of her heart. I'm the one who'll hold her tonight while she cries herself to sleep because you just couldn't make it." Yvette's voice was dripping with sarcasm. She turned and went into the trailer with Jack close behind her.

"Wait up!" he said. "I'll be there this afternoon! I will be there!" Jack emphasized. "I wouldn't have made Juliette that promise if I wasn't going to keep it. I'm growing very fond of that little princess. I think I could be fond of her mother too if she'd stop chewing on me." Jack grinned.

"I just can't stand it when my daughter gets hurt. It hurts me too."

"I understand that. Love hurts." Then, after a pause, Jack asked, "Truce?" offering his hand.

"Truce." Yvette smiled.

"Okay, now we have to get your car out of the garage and get you to work. What's Charlie's phone number?"

"Sit your butt down," she ordered. "I'll call him. It's my piece-of-junk car." She was on the phone only a few minutes. When she hung up she turned, took a deep breath, and sighed. "Charlie said he couldn't fix it this time. He told me he'd give me two hundred dollars for it. He thinks he can use it for spare parts and the rest he would sell by the pound. I can't get transportation for two hundred dollars!"

"Do you mind if I talk to Charlie when I take you to work? Maybe he can recommend something."

"It's not your problem," she said.

"But I have all this time to kill before my after-school date with Juliette," Jack teased. "Or I guess I could go to the café and pester you all day."

"Okay." She grinned, her dimples deepening. "Please, go bug Charlie."

They left the trailer in time for a stop at Charlie's Garage. Outside was a nice-looking façade that hid a disorganized and cluttered inside. Parts and tools were strewn about the floor, making it difficult to find space to put a foot down. A counter was stacked high with papers and small boxes of parts, some opened and some still to be opened. They found Charlie in the middle of one of the bays, under the hood of a Ford pickup.

Charlie Poe, a man of fifty-plus years, was a thin man. He was wearing a pair of greasy coveralls and a bill-less engineering cap. His sleeves were rolled up and his hands and forearms were also covered in grease and grime. As they approached, Yvette called out, "Where's my car, Charlie?"

Charlie stood up and pulled a grease rag from his rear pocket. He wiped his hands for a brief moment then said, "I got it out back. This way"—he motioned—"but you can't drive it."

"Charlie, this is Jack," she said. "Jack, Charlie."

Charlie stuck out a greasy paw. Jack hesitantly took it, and they shook hands. They exited through a rear door of the bay, and Yvette went over to an obviously used-up early-model Plymouth Valiant with its hood up. She took everything from the glove box and stuffed it into her purse.

"Are you sure, Charlie? Can't you get it to go just a few more days?" Yvette implored him.

Charlie hung his head and shook it. "No, I'm real sorry, dear, but I can't work miracles. You got nearly two hundred thousand miles on it! That's a lot of miles and a lot of worn-out parts. I'll make you a check for the two hundred dollars I promised if you'll wait a minute."

"I'll pick up the check tomorrow," Yvette told him, "Right now I have to get to work before Arty fires me." She picked up her purse and hurried toward the door. "You coming?" she asked Jack.

"I'll be along shortly," Jack answered, as he pulled the insurance card from behind the driver's-side visor.

As soon as she was out of sight Jack turned to Charlie. "You and me need to talk. That little girl is without transportation, and you add insult to injury by your offer of two hundred dollars. I know you have to make a profit on the parts you sell, but those tires look almost new to me. Surely you can find a buyer who'll give three or four hundred for them. That's a nearly new Interstate battery in there. I know they cost more than one hundred and fifty dollars these days. I think you should make that check for seven hundred and fifty dollars!"

"Now hold on a minute, mister," Charlie said. "You sound like you think I intended to cheat Yvette. I would never do that to her. I've known her ever since she first moved here to Bon Weir with her no-account husband Steve Clarke. She's like part of my family. I just hadn't noticed those things you mentioned. You tell her to come by in the morning. and I'll make her a check for, oh, say six hundred and fifty. I have to make a little on it." He grinned.

"Fair enough," Jack replied, "I'll give her the news."

Jack walked briskly back to his SUV, drove across the highway, and entered the café. He found Yvette and told her about Charlie's re-evaluation. Then he told her he had an errand to run but would be back in plenty of time to meet Juliette's bus out in front of the café that afternoon.

He then went back to the SUV and climbed into the rear seat. From there he could more easily open one of the coolers. He removed a packet of $100 bills and slid it into his front trouser pocket. He got the packet of hundred dollar bills that he had placed in the front console earlier and slid it into his other front trouser pocket. He climbed into the driver's seat and headed up the highway toward Jasper.

It was just before 11:00 a.m. when he pulled into the car dealership. He parked in front and went inside. He was approached by a saleswoman. He told her he was there to buy a used automobile. The third car she showed him he liked very much. It was a fully loaded, two-year-old, midnight-blue Mercury Grand Marquis LS. Jack took it for a spin and was exceptionally impressed with its remarkable new-like appearance and handling. "I'll give you twelve hundred cash right now," he told her, "if you'll throw in a three-year, thirty-six-thousand-mile parts and labor guarantee."

The saleswoman said she would have to run that by her sales manager and she would be right back. A few minutes later she reappeared with a handful of papers, smiling and nodding that she had received the okay.

"I'm buying this for my niece," Jack lied. "I'll need the papers made out in her name."

He gave Yvette's name and the address in Bon Weir that he had gotten from the insurance card. Since it was a cash transaction, there was less paperwork to complete. The total, after taxes, title transfer, and licensing fees, came out to $13,096.25. He placed one packet of hundred dollar bills on the desk and counted out thirty-one more from the second packet. The clerk slowly counted all the hundred dollar bills and came up with $13,100. She then handed him all of the completed paperwork and $3.75.

"They have your new car in 'Make Ready' right now," the saleswoman said, handing him one set of keys. "After they fill it with gasoline, they'll bring it around to the front."

"I have another request," Jack told her. "Is there some way that you could have the car delivered to Bon Weir today?"

"I believe we have a mechanic who lives in Bon Weir. He might be persuaded to leave his own transportation here and drive your car there tonight, provided he can find a way to get back tomorrow morning."

Shortly a mechanic came up to the saleswoman's desk. Pete was the name on his coveralls. He told Jack he would be glad to drive the car to Bon Weir. He said he could have it there about 6:00 p.m. Jack asked him to park the car in front of the café and lock that set of keys in the car. Pete agreed.

Jack asked to use the phone and called the agent's number he had taken from the insurance card. He explained he wanted to remove the Valiant from the insurance and put full coverage on the two-year-old Mercury. He asked for the local agent's address and found the office was conveniently located on the Bon Weir Highway just on the edge of Jasper.

"I'd like to come by your office and pay the difference today if at all possible," Jack told them.

Jack arrived in Bon Weir and drove up in front of the café a few minutes after 3:00 p.m. He sat in the SUV and waited until he saw the school bus stop on the highway in front of the café. He grinned in spite of himself when he saw the tiny second grader jump off of the bus with a stack of papers in her hand. He climbed out and went to meet her. When Juliette saw Jack, she started running toward him. Jack met her about halfway, squatted down, and caught her in his arms.

"Look what I have for you!" Juliette said excitedly. "Do you want to see my artwork?"

"I sure do!" Jack told her. He took the papers, then said, "Let's go inside and say 'hi' to your mommy, and then we'll find a booth so I can take a really good look at them. Okay, sweetheart?"

Juliette took his big hand with her tiny one and skipped along beside him as they went into the café. Inside she let go of Jack's hand and ran to give Yvette a hug.

"I'm going to show Jack my artwork!" Juliette told her.

Jack held up the stack of papers for Yvette to see. Then, taking Juliette's hand, he led her to an empty booth. He spread the papers out on the table in front of them. She excitedly told him about each one while Jack smiled and complimented her. As he watched and listened he found himself drawn ever closer to this violet-blue eyed little girl. He missed the days when he had sat like this with his own daughter. Juliette, however, was young enough to be his granddaughter. *I wish she was*, he thought.

Eventually Yvette got a break and joined them. Jack sat back and enjoyed the happy chatter between mother and daughter. He realized that he had not felt this happy in a long time. He pictured the days when he, his wife, and his daughter had been together and happy. Then realized that this was only a temporary moment of happiness. He had only just met these two, and no matter how much he would have liked to fit in, he realized he had no place in their lives.

"I'm hungry," Juliette said "Can I have a hamburger, Mommy?"

"Okay, Juli," Yvette answered her daughter. Then, looking at Jack, she addressed him. "Can I get you something too?"

"I could use a hamburger. Everything on it. By that I mean mustard, meat, cheese, pickles, onions, tomatoes, and lettuce."

"What you want is a cheeseburger!" Yvette told him.

"I was trying to make it easy so even Arty could understand!" Jack said, raising his voice so Arty could hear.

"Why don't you come back here and show me!" Arty shouted back.

"And a chocolate shake," Jack said, grinning "What kind of shake do you want, Juliette?"

"Strawberry!" Juliette said excitedly.

"Do you have time to eat with us?" Jack asked hopefully.

"No, I have to get back to work now. How long will you be here, Jack?"

"I'll stay here with Juliette until you get off work," he told her. "I have a favor to ask of you anyway. I'll explain fully when you have more time."

Jack and Juliette finished their meals. Juliette bused the table, looking very grownup, then came back to sit with Jack. It was just after dark when Jack saw the lights of the Mercury shine through the windows as Pete parked it out front.

Soon the crowds of people began to leave the café and Yvette was able to take a break and join them.

"What is this favor you'd like to ask of me?" she asked Jack hesitantly. "You know my life is very full with work and taking care of Juliette."

"I considered that," Jack replied. "But I think you can work this into your busy schedule. You see, I bought another car today, and since I can only drive one car at a time, I'm wondering if I can leave it at your house. Of course, I'd need you to start it every day so the oil gets distributed inside the engine. Then I'd need you to drive it every day so the tires don't start to dry rot. Occasionally it will have to be driven at highway speeds for several miles to reduce carbon build up. You know, use it like you would if it was your own car. Would you consider doing that for me?"

"Let me see now, you want me to keep your car for you and use it like it was my own?"

"Well, you'd have to keep gasoline in it and maintain it, so you wouldn't be totally without responsibility. Do you think you could do that for me?"

"I can use it anyway I please?"

"Anyway you please."

"Okay, this can't be good! Where is this mechanical monster?"

Jack handed her his set of keys and told her it was just outside. He explained she could find it easily by just pushing the alarm button on the key fob and it would be the junker that flashed its lights and honked its horn.

Yvette told Arty she was going outside for a minute. She took Juliette, and they went to find the car. Jack followed a few paces behind. He had done this his way, figuring that Yvette would be too proud to just accept the gift of a car outright. He heard the horn honk then the girls' excited chatter as they explored their new transportation. Jack stood back and watched with an air of satisfaction. He took the extra set of keys out of the car and went back inside to visit with Arty.

"So you bought Yvette a new car," Arty surmised. "You know she cain't make no payments. Hell, she barely makes enough here to pay her rent and utilities. If I didn't let her and the little one take most of their meals here, I don't know what they'd do."

"Two things, Arty," Jack replied. "One, there won't be any payments, and two, you know you are never going to let them starve."

"No payments?"

"No, it was a cash deal."

Yvette and Juliette returned about this time, very excited. Yvette rushed up to Jack. "Okay, now what's the catch?" she asked.

"No catch. I even had them put the car in your name to make everything easier for you."

"No! No! You mean you're giving me that car with no strings attached? I can't accept it, Jack! Just what do you want from me?

No one gives something that nice without wanting something in return!"

"Okay, you're right. I do want something from you. I want a big smile and maybe a 'thank you, Jack', but mostly I want to see that smile. That beautiful Yvette smile."

"Are you sure, Jack? No! I can't! Okay, maybe. All right, yes!" She smiled widely, picked up Juliette, hugged her, and spun around. "We have a car that actually runs. Let's go try it out! Wait! Arty?"

"Get out of here!" Arty said, waving a counter rag at Yvette. "But I ain't closing up by myself, so you get back here pronto!"

"It drives like a dream!" Yvette said excitedly as she entered the café a few minutes later. "And it's so quiet! And the heater works too!"

"I have my own armrest!" Juliette said. "And my seat folds down to make a bed!"

Jack took out a small digital camera and recorded their excitement with several shots then, asked Arty to take one of all three of them together.

In the excitement of the day Jack had forgotten to check in at the Jasper Motel. Now it was too late to start out for his next destination. Sheepishly he asked Yvette if he could borrow her spare bedroom for another night.

"Of course!" Yvette assured him. "I wouldn't allow you to do anything else! Uncle Jack will be spending the night again!" she told Juliette.

"I'm glad!" Juliette said, leaning her head against his arm.

Jack was feeling very paternal as he drove Juliette home. She was asleep by the time they got there. Yvette had driven home alone in the new car. He parked the SUV behind the Mercury, leaving his lights on until he saw Yvette open the front door.

Quietly he climbed out, went to the passenger side of the SUV, scooped up his tiny passenger in his arms, and carried her inside.

"Put her down on the bed in my room," Yvette told him in a whisper. "I think I'll let her sleep in those clothes. It's awfully late, and I don't want to wake her. I'll get her up early enough to bathe in the morning."

As they moved into the living room Jack scolded, "I know you can't help it, but it's a shame she has to be at that café every night until ten. A child her age should be in bed by eight." Then, stifling a yawn, he said, "I need to get to bed also. I've got to be on my way early tomorrow. I'll see Juliette to the bus in the morning before I leave."

"Jack," Yvette said, still keeping her voice low, "Thank you again, for…everything."

They were standing close together, and Jack had to restrain himself. He had a powerful urge to once again feel the warmth and tenderness of a female body pressed against his. "It been my pleasure." He smiled. Then, turning toward the bedroom, he said, "I'll see you in the morning."

Jack awoke to the sounds of Yvette and Juliette in their morning routine. He showered, shaved, and dressed quickly in order to not miss walking Juliette to the bus. When he entered the living room area, she was ready for school and greeted him with a cheery smile and hello. Noises from the master bathroom told him where Yvette was.

They walked to the bus stop hand in hand. "I probably won't see you when you get to the café today," he told her. "I have to go away for awhile. I'll try to call you and your mother when I get to my next destination."

As the bus pulled up to Juliette's stop, she hung back, letting the other students get on before she did. She bravely walked to the door of the bus. Then suddenly she turned, ran back to Jack, and lifted her arms to him. Jack bent down and picked her up in his arms. She hugged him tightly around the neck. Then, sliding down, she turned and darted onto the bus. Jack felt a big lump in his throat. "How did I become so attached to that tiny person in the space of just a few hours?" he asked himself.

Jack stood there waving and waited until the bus was out of sight before returning to the trailer. As he entered he found Yvette in the hallway ironing a blouse. She was barefoot, wearing a short half slip that didn't quite reach to mid-thigh and a lacy bra. Jack couldn't avert his eyes, taking in her youthful beauty. Her breasts, barely hidden by the lace, were perfectly proportionate to her petite size. Nothing like the ugly, counterfeit, surgically enhanced things so many of today's women had. "I thought I'd have this finished by the time you got back," she apologized.

"I've got to finish packing," Jack said as he turned and went into the bedroom he'd been using.

"I did your laundry early this morning," she called. "It's on the armoire."

"I found it!" Jack called back. "Thanks!"

As he finished packing his few things he thought about how easy it would be to take advantage of her loneliness while giving in to his own. From their first meeting in the café he had felt drawn to her. Yet he knew it would be wrong on many levels. His maturity finally won out over his desires. He picked up his bags and stepped into the hallway, almost bumping into Yvette as she came walking toward the room, buttoning the freshly ironed blouse. She was still barefoot and wearing the mini slip.

"Did you find everything?" Yvette asked softly.

"Yes, I did."

They stood there close to one another, each looking intently into the other's eyes. Yvette reached up and touched his face tenderly. "I don't want you to go," she said softly. "Can't you stay awhile longer?"

How easy it would be to say yes, Jack thought. "I'm afraid it would only get harder and harder to say good-bye," he said.

She dropped her eyes. "Of course you're right. What will I say to Juliette?"

"I tried to tell her at the bus this morning. I think she understood. I told her I would call her from time to time."

"I'm sure she will appreciate that."

Jack picked up his bags and started for the door, Yvette just behind him. At the door he stopped, put his bags down, and turned back toward her. Without a word she stepped into his arms and they held each other for a long moment. She was still barefoot, and at only five feet four, the top of her head just came to his chin. She rested her head on his chest for the moment. Jack closed his eyes breathing in the sweet aroma of her shampoo and perfume. Yvette slowly drew away, looked up at him, and said, "God bless you, Jack Lockhart. I shall never forget you!"

"I will never forget you either. Or Juliette!"

Jack loaded his bags into the back of the SUV, then retrieved another ten thousand-dollar packet from the cooler. *At this rate I'll have the whole eleven million spent this year*, he thought. It was fate that he had stopped at the café that night. Fate that had brought him into contact with these two wonderful people and awakened his ability to feel alive and needed once again. He wondered if he could possibly fall in love again.

Jack backed out of the drive, but instead of turning toward the highway, he headed down the street to the Bayou mobile home park office. Inside he asked to see the manager. He was ushered into a smoky office where he was introduced to the manager, a short, very fat, balding man with glasses.

"I'd like to pay a year's rent on the trailer in lot H," Jack told him.

The manager pulled a folder out of file drawer behind him and studied it for a while. "That's a rent-to-own. I have a contract here in the name of Yvette Clarke. Is that the one you are referring to?"

"Yes," Jack replied.

"Let me see, the original contract was for twenty-nine thousand nine hundred. She pays three hundred and fifty dollars per month until she either pays it in full or she moves out. She has been paying on it for just over four and a half years now. Her balance at this time is—let me see…ten thousand one hundred. If she continues at her present rate, she will have it paid off in another twenty-eight months. Of course, once it's paid off we will again start collecting the fifty-per-month rent on that space. We waive that fee anytime a resident is buying one of our rent-to-own trailers. Utilities are still the responsibility of the tenant. You say you want to pay a year on it?"

"I've changed my mind," Jack said, standing up. He pulled the packet of $100 bills from his pocket and laid it on the desk. He took another $100 bill out of his wallet to add to it and sat back down. "That should take care of the balance," he said. "I'd like a receipt. And I'd like you to send the paperwork marked paid in full to Ms. Clarke."

"We'll be happy to do that. Remember to tell her, though, she will have to start paying the fifty-dollar-a-month rent on her space," the manager replied.

"Could you include a note stating that fact when you send her the papers?"

"Of course. We just need a name for the receipt."

"Jack Lockhart."

Jack picked up the receipt, exited the office, and looked hopefully in the direction of Yvette's trailer, wanting to get one last glimpse of her. When he didn't see her, he climbed solemnly into the cab of his SUV. He drove to the highway and headed away from Bon Weir. In five minutes he came to the bridge and crossed the river into the adjoining state.

THREE

J ack tried to concentrate on the scenery, but his mind was on a lovely little waitress and her equally lovely daughter. He put a country music station on his radio, but that only made his heart ache worse. When he first planned this trip he hadn't realized how lonely he would be. *Maybe I should just go back and get Yvette and Juliette*, he thought. *No, I can't do that. Juliette is still in school. I'm right—no matter how painful, I have to get on with my life and out of their lives*!

He passed through Merryville and De Ridder hardly noticing them. *This isn't the way I planned it*, he thought. He forced himself to start taking notice of his surroundings. Along the way, properties that had been maintained had huge trees draped in Spanish moss. In other areas the highway right-of-way and the lands just beyond were overgrown with Kudzu.

The traffic was light even though it was a beautiful January day with full sun and temperature in the fifties. He could tell there was hardly any wind since the moss hanging from the trees wasn't moving.

He was down a half a tank when he got to the outskirts of Marksville. It was nearing noon as he pulled into a little convenience store. He topped off, washed his windshield, and went in to pay. "What's that delicious aroma?" he asked the attendant.

"Today's special! Bob-e-cue ribs and pinto beans! Y'all want me to put some in a to-go box?"

"You have a place to eat 'em right here?"

"Yes suh! If ya eat here it's all you can eat fo ten dollars! Y'all want me ta add it to y'all's gas bill?"

"Please!"

Jack paid the attendant, moved his SUV to a parking spot out of the drive, and headed to the room where the attendant had indicated the ribs and beans were being served. The ribs were exceptionally tender and the sauce on them very spicy. The beans had slices of jalapeno peppers floating in them. His nose began to run; his eyes began to water. It was some of the best barbecue ribs and beans he had ever tasted. *Arty should get this recipe*, he thought. He drank two tall tumblers of iced tea before finally resuming his journey.

He departed Marksville a few minutes before 1:00 p.m. He drove along the Mississippi River for several miles before crossing it at Natchez. Outside of Natchez he took the Natchez Trace, North to Port Gibson, then US Highway 61 into Vicksburg.

It was the first motel Jack had been in since he started this journey. It had a five-star rating. The king-size bed had a pillow-top mattress that was, he imagined, like floating on a cloud. He climbed in early but didn't fall asleep right away. He watched the clock, and at 8:30 p.m. when he hoped customers would be minimal, he dialed the number at the café.

"Arty's, what can I do for you?"

"Arty, this is Jack. What's the special for tonight?"

"Stewed rat tails and dishwater. But we don't deliver."

"If you did the cooking I'm sure it's delicious. Can I speak to Yvette?"

"She's busy, but I'll get Juliette for you."

Juliette came on the line and excitedly told him about her school day and making a new friend. She told him she missed him and asked when he was coming back. Jack told her he missed her too. "Mommy wants to talk to you," Juliette said. "I love you, Uncle Jack!"

Yvette's voice was the next he heard. "Jack? That really you?"

"It's great to hear the sound of your voice," he told her. "How is everything?"

They talked for a while, both admitting how each missed the other one more than they thought they would, Yvette asking the same question Juliette had put to him about coming back. Jack talked around it, not wanting to commit to a timetable. Eventually they wished each other well and hung up. Jack smiled, lay back in the bed, and was soon asleep.

It was after 10:00 a.m. when Jack awoke. He wasn't in any hurry, so he took his time about getting cleaned up. He had missed the complimentary breakfast. He dressed and walked across the parking lot to a pancake house and ordered brunch. On his way back he stopped at the desk and told them he would need another night.

Back in his room, he got out his maps and itinerary log and started planning tomorrow's route. He was deeply engrossed in this task when there was a rap on his door and a voice called out, "Housekeeping."

Jack realized he had forgotten to put out the Do Not Disturb sign. He went to the door and invited the housekeeper to come in. He noticed the nametag on her uniform and said, "Hi, Gabriella. I don't need the sheets changed today. I've decided to stay another night."

"Yes, sir," she answered. "Do you want me to vacuum?"

"Not necessary. Who's this?" Jack addressed a small boy with big brown eyes holding on to the housekeeper's cart just outside the door. The boy just stared but didn't reply.

"That's Homer. He's my boy. He's deaf, so he can't talk. He won't be any bother to you."

"He's a cute little guy. How old is he?"

"Almost five. He hasn't always been deaf; it happened when he was a baby."

Jack watched her as she dumped his wastebaskets, took the old towels and soaps, and cleaned his bathroom. She was a very attractive black woman somewhere between twenty and thirty years old. She had a warm smile and a pleasant voice.

"Has he seen a specialist?" Jack inquired.

"No, sir," she replied.

"Do you have such a specialist in mind?"

"Yes, sir. There's one in Atlanta they told me about. He's supposed to be the best at fixing young ones."

"Do you remember his name?"

"I think it was Doctor Samuels or something like that."

Jack got up and walked over to Homer, squatted down, and extended his hand. Homer took a step back and tried to hide behind the cart. Jack leaned to the side, smiling at Homer, then leaned the other way so Homer couldn't see him. Homer moved closer so he could peek around the corner of the cart and see Jack; then tried to hide again. Jack leaned over so he could see Homer and made a comical face, then quickly moved out of sight again. Homer peeked around the corner just as Jack was peeking around it. Their faces almost touched, and Homer broke out in a big smile. Jack extended his hand again, and Homer slapped it, mimicking what he had seen adults do. Jack motioned for Homer to follow him into the room. When he did, Jack motioned for him to climb up on a chair. He put some paper in front of Homer and gave him a pencil. Homer immediately started drawing.

"Smart little tyke," Jack told Gabriella. "If it's possible, you have to get his hearing restored. If not he needs to have special training for the deaf. Are you receiving SSI for him?"

"No, I've never applied."

"I was just thinking that he would have to be tested by a professional in order to qualify for SSI and that would be a good place to start. So you haven't even checked there."

"No, sir," Gabriella said, looking confused. "Do you think I should apply for SSI?"

"I'm not sure of anything." Jack smiled. "Would it upset you if I did some checking? I'd have to know a lot more about him before I got too involved. Like his full name and probably his

Social Security number. Things I don't want to know until or unless they are required."

Gabriella looked at Jack with anxiety and distrust. "We're fine," she said. "We don't need you helping us get SSI or anything else. Is there anything else you need sir?" She took Homer's hand and said, "Come on, Homer. Let's go!" as if Homer could hear her. She left Jack's room, pushing her cart to the next door.

Jack was frustrated that he had upset her. He pulled out the phone book and looked up the address of the local library. A few minutes later he pulled into the library parking lot. He spent the allotted time searching everything he could find about juvenile deafness and copied down telephone numbers of local specialists. He was also able to locate a Doctor Samuels at a hospital in Atlanta who specialized in deaf and hard-of-hearing patients. Jack recorded the number to that hospital's switchboard.

Back in his motel room he started making local calls. He found a friendly ear at a local pediatrician's office, to whom he explained the limited knowledge he had about Homer. She told him the doctor would have to evaluate him before they could make any diagnosis. She was able to set an appointment for him to see the doctor at 9:00 a.m. two days later.

"Now," Jack said out loud, "I have to convince Gabriella to allow Homer to go to the appointment. I wonder if they've left for the day."

He called the desk and asked that Gabriella be sent back to his room. "She's the housekeeper that cleaned my room today, and I'd like to give her a tip. She did such a very nice job. Also," Jack said, "I'm going to need the room for the rest of the week."

A short time later Gabriella rapped on his door and called out, "Housekeeping!"

Jack opened the door and ask her to come in. "Where's Homer?"

"I left him with the other housekeepers, sir. He's okay. Was there something I forgot, sir?"

Jack propped the door open. "Please sit down, Gabriella. Now, I don't know how to approach you, as I don't know you and you don't know me, but please listen to what I have to say. Your little boy really had an effect on me. I want Homer to be able to hear again, if it's at all possible. I spent some time this afternoon researching the area specialists. I was able to get an appointment with a pediatrician at 9:00 a.m. Monday. No cost to you. Please say 'yes' to taking him there. I'll take you if you need transportation."

"I gotta work that day," she said. "What about that?"

"I'll go with you to talk to your supervisor if you'd like. Isn't Homer's hearing more important than anything?"

"Not when you need every dime to pay the bills!"

"About how much will you lose by missing a day? Could you swap days with someone?"

"Sixty dollars! Maybe Mary Nell will swap…"

"Please think it over carefully. See if you can get a swap, and hopefully I'll see you tomorrow when you come to do my room. Oh yes, I wanted to thank you for doing such a great job this morning. Here's a little something extra for your effort." Jack took her hand and placed a tightly folded $100 bill in it. "Give Homer a hug for me!"

Before turning in, Jack again placed a call to Arty's. After a few wise retorts by Arty, he was once again able to speak to Juliette and then to Yvette.

"I received a package of papers in the mail this morning just before I came to work," Yvette explained. "What have you been up to, Jack? You paid off my trailer?"

"What makes you think I had anything to do with that? I've been gone from there for two days now."

"Jack, you have got to stop trying to take care of me. Don't you know I'm an adult? I'll be twenty-five on Valentine's Day!

I appreciate you wanting to do these things for me, but it's too much and you have to stop! Okay, Jack?"

"I'm sorry if I offended you. It gives me a warm fuzzy feeling to be able to do things for you and Juliette. I promise to not treat you like a child anymore. So, Valentine's Day, huh? What do you want for your birthday?"

"Jack!"

They talked for a few minutes more, Jack trying to hide the pain of his loneliness for her. Eventually Yvette had to go back to work and they said good-bye. Jack lay there in the dark and went over their conversation in his head. Eventually he drifted off to sleep.

Jack busied himself the next day shopping for a birthday present for Yvette. He had noticed that the coat she wore was quite old and that the ends of the sleeves were worn. He found a women's apparel shop with a millinery section and was able to find a very attractive coat with matching hat and gloves. He knew Yvette was petite, so the coat size was no problem. He was only guessing at the sizes of the hat and gloves.

"Do you have this same coat in a size that will fit a child?" Jack inquired. "She's about this high and also petite."

"Let's go see," the saleswoman replied.

Luckily, they were able to find a coat in the exact style and color. The hat and gloves were another thing. Jack bought a pair of mittens in Juliette's size and a colorful stocking cap with a large, brightly colored tassel.

In the jewelry section he found a beautiful necklace with matching earrings set with amethyst stones. According to the saleswomen amethyst was the February stone. "I'd like the large coat, hat, and gloves gift-wrapped in one box; the small coat, stocking cap, and mittens gift-wrapped in another box; and the jewelry gift-wrapped in a third," Jack said. "The gift card in the larger box should read 'Happy Birthday' and the one in the jewelry box, 'Happy Valentine's Day.'"

"The gift card to accompany the small coat?" she asked.

"Just say 'I love you!'" Jack said. "It's not for any special occasion. Do you have a shipping service here?"

"Yes, we do!" she smiled.

Jack completed the shipping instructions, insisting that Juliette's gift be sent to her in her name and the two other packages be sent to Yvette. He didn't care about the fact that they would arrive early. He was more concerned that they all arrive on the same day and at the same time.

Jack arrived at the motel midafternoon. He noticed that his room had already been made up and Gabriella's cart was now near the opposite end of the hallway. He briskly walked to that end of the hall and peered into the room through the open door. He saw Homer sitting in the lounge chair playing with a small video game. He could hear cleaning noises coming from the bathroom.

"Gabriella?" he called out from the doorway. "Can I see you a minute?"

Gabriella came to the door. "Yes, sir?"

"I just wanted to know what you have decided about tomorrow morning. Are we going to keep the doctor appointment, or do I need to reschedule?"

"I traded with Mary Nell. I'll be doing seven days next week. I guess we're going to the doctor."

"The office is downtown, and we need to be there a few minutes early to fill out paperwork. Can you meet me here at eight in the morning, or would you like me to pick you up somewhere?"

"We ride the bus. I have to get back to work now, sir."

"Okay, tell you what. Come to my room when you get off today. We'll make a plan then."

Jack and Gabriella agreed that he would take her and Homer home that night so he could see where to pick them up the following morning. It was only a short drive—took less than fifteen minutes—but Gabriella had told him by bus it was forty-five minutes.

The little house just off of Canal Street was small but well maintained. Jack parked in front of their house, opened the car door for Gabriella, and then opened the rear door and lifted Homer out of the SUV. They agreed that he would pick them both up at 8:00 a.m. the following morning.

Everything went according to plan the next morning. Gabriella and Homer were waiting out front when Jack arrived. They found the doctor's office easily and arrived in plenty of time to fill out the required paperwork.

"Would you like me to go in with you and Homer?" Jack inquired. "Sometimes two people remember more of the information they give out."

"I guess so," Gabriella replied. "Are they going to hurt him?"

"No, today is just to determine if Homer's hearing can possibly be restored and what to do next."

"Ms. Williams," the receptionist called to Gabriella, "how will you be paying today?"

Jack put his hand on Gabriella's arm. "I'll take care of this," he said. "You just wait here with Homer."

Jack went to the window and told the receptionist that at the time there was no insurance and that they would be paying cash. "How much will it be? Do we pay now or after the appointment?"

"The nurse will give me a form after the appointment, and you can pay at that time, sir. Routine appointment is one hundred thirty-five dollars. However, we sometimes give a fifteen-percent discount for cash customers."

"And how do we qualify for the discount?"

"I'm entering the information in Ms. Williams's file right now."

Eventually a nurse came and called for Homer. She told them it was okay for all of them to go into the examining room. Jack sat quietly in a chair near the door, observing and listening. The doctor was very thorough taking a long time to look into each of Homer's ears, look into his mouth, and feel for nodules in his neck. Homer sat quietly, holding his video game and staring at the shiny stethoscope hanging from the doctor's neck. As he finished he told them in a positive voice that he could not see any obstructions. He said he would refer Homer to Doctor Harvey, a hearing specialist at the children's hospital, for further testing and evaluation. Seeing the concern on Gabriella's face, he told her to not worry, that at this time everything would be out-patient service. He gave Homer a lollipop, shook hands with Gabriella and Jack, and once again told them to not worry.

At the receptionist's desk on the way out, Jack paid the bill and Gabriella was told as soon as the referrals were confirmed the hospital would call with a time and date for Homer to be seen. Jack gave the receptionist his name and room number as an additional contact in case they could not reach Gabriella. Gabriella gave the motel telephone number as her phone number.

It was after ten in the morning when they left the doctor's office. Gabriella had a worried look on her face. Jack was sure he knew why. *Contemplation of the unknown is very frighteni*ng, he thought. She needed a diversion.

"Let's stop at the Dairy Queen," he said, wheeling the SUV into the parking lot. "Do you ever bring Homer here?"

"No, we don't get out a lot."

Once again Jack opened the door for Gabriella and helped Homer out of the back.

"Does he like chicken strips, hamburgers, French fries, fish nuggets, ice cream, or what?" Jack asked Gabriella "Get anything you want and anything he wants. He was a real trooper this morning. Don't worry, I'm paying."

"I don't know. He does like chicken and French fries."

"What about you?"

"Um, I'm trying to decide. I think I'll have the chicken too, but just a small one."

Jack started turning in the order, getting several different items, wanting to get enough to have lots of leftovers for her and Homer to take home—three orders of chicken strips, two

Hunger Busters, three large orders of fries, two large drinks, and one small drink. They took a table away from the counter and waited for their food.

Homer looked like his head was on a swivel as he looked around the room. Everything seemed to be new to him. His eyes grew wide as he discovered and observed each new thing.

Gabriella still had a worried look on her face and was wringing her hands. Every so often she would stare at Jack when she thought he wasn't looking.

Jack wished he could put her mind at ease, but they were still very much strangers.

"Be truthful with me," he addressed Gabriella. "Are you frightened of me?"

"A little bit," she said. "You just take over! And then I have to do what you say!"

Jack leaned back and sighed. Then he leaned forward toward Gabriella, reached over, and touched her hand tenderly. She pulled it away.

"I'm sorry if I frightened you. I just don't know how to reach you. I wish you would trust me. I mean you and Homer no harm. My objective here is to help Homer if I can. If along the way I can earn your trust and friendship, that's a plus! You are probably suspicious of me because nobody ever helped you before without wanting something in return. You think I must have an ulterior motive. Well, in some way I do. If I can do something to make your lives better I feel good about myself. If I can get you to like me, I feel good about that too. See how that works?" Jack smiled at her.

Their food arrived at that very moment, and Gabriella involved herself with getting Homer fed and getting herself a bite now and then. Jack asked for three to-go boxes.

"You really are a good mother," Jack told her. "Just look how much you've taught him! He'd be an astronaut now if he could just hear you!"

Gabriella actually smiled. Jack smiled back at them while he munched on a piece of chicken.

Shortly, they packed up their to-go boxes and left the Dairy Queen.

"Could you take me to the motel?" Gabriella asked. "I need to check in with my supervisor. I may be able to get some hours today. If I do work, we'll just take the bus home like always."

Back at the motel, Gabriella and Homer went one way and Jack another. He stopped at the front desk and paid for the extra days, which included an additional week. "I have no way of estimating just how long I'll need the room," Jack said. "Can you just leave the ending date open?"

Jack returned to his room, stretched out on his bed, and went over the events of the day in his mind. He had to find a way to earn the trust of Gabriella and Homer. Although it did seem Homer was less afraid of him. "Please God," he whispered, "let that little guy have his hearing restored." He didn't know why, but he suddenly felt exhausted and soon fell asleep.

It was after dark when Jack suddenly awoke. He checked his watch and saw it was already after 7:00 p.m. He got up and washed his face in cold water to revive himself. He checked the mini-fridge and got out a bottled water. He sat down at the desk and pulled out his maps and planned the next leg of his trip. This occupied his mind for half an hour or so. Then he picked up the phone and dialed Arty's Café.

"Arty's, what can I do you for?"

"Got any of the rat tails and dishwater left?"

"No, Jack. For you I made boiled skunk and cabbage! I guess you want to talk to Yvette."

"Let me speak to the princess first."

Juliette's sweet voice was the next thing he heard. "Hello? Is that you, Uncle Jack?"

Jack answered in the affirmative. They went over the school day. Juliette had been asked to a party by a boy. She thought he liked her because he sometimes pulled her ponytail. They continued the small talk for a few more minutes before Jack said, "Your mother said she is having a birthday next month on the fourteenth. That made me wonder why you haven't told me when your birthday is."

"Mine is the next week after Mommy's, on February twenty-first. Mommy said I might get my ears pierced when I'm eight, and that's what I'll be on my birthday. Uncle Jack, I lost another tooth yesterday."

"Did the Tooth Fairy come last night?"

"Oh, I don't believe in the Tooth Fairy, Uncle Jack! Here's Mommy. I love you. Bye."

"Hi," Yvette said in her most seductive voice. "You looking for me?"

"Yes, you sound like the woman I ordered. Can I hear a description?"

Yvette giggled and then asked Jack how he was doing. To which he replied, "Without! I'm very lonely here."

"Why don't you come back? Juliette misses you terribly and talks about you constantly."

"Juliette misses me? Anybody else?"

"Well, I think Arty said something about missing your corny jokes!"

"Oh, now that hurt! You know I'm hilarious." Yvette giggled again, but Jack got serious. "I'm working on a project here that's going to take some time. I don't know how long—at this point there isn't any way to estimate it. Meantime, take good care of my girls. Oh, Juliette says she's getting her ears pierced for her birthday. Is that true?"

"I promised her years ago that she could get them pierced when she was eight. I didn't promise it would be on her birthday, but I guess that's what she heard. Both of our birthdays this year fall on a Monday, so I guess since that's my day off, we could drive up to the Jasper Mall and have it done. Now that I have a car that I can trust to get us there and back."

"Now I know what to get her for her birthday! What do you think she'd say to a pair of four-inch long, dangling diamond earrings?" Jack teased.

"Don't you dare! If you get her any, just get a couple of relatively cheap sets with studs that won't turn her ears green. I've got to go, Jack. Arty is giving me dirty looks. Miss you!"

"Miss you too! Bye now." Jack hung up the phone wishing he had spent his few minutes with her in more constructive conversation. But he realized the levity was to keep them from talking about the real feelings growing between them. "I wonder if you can fall in love long distance," he asked himself.

The trip to Children's Hospital for the scheduled tests didn't take very long, but both Jack and Gabriella made it in total silence, both lost in their own thoughts—Gabriella worried about Homer, Jack worried about them both.

After a preliminary examination it was determined that Homer should be given a CT scan. He would have to be sedated and his head held totally still during the procedure. The scan would take about thirty minutes, and then he would be in recovery while coming out from under the mild sedation. A specialist would read the results of the CT scan and determine how they would proceed.

After Homer was asleep they were told they could leave and that he would be back in his room in about an hour. In the meantime they were told to go to the collections office to set up a payment schedule. Children's Hospital, they were told, would bill them according to their ability to pay.

"We'll pay in full at the time we receive your billing," Jack told them. "You can send the bills to me in care of the motel where I'm staying."

They went back to the waiting area and very soon were told the scan was over, that Homer was back in his room and would be waking up soon.

Homer looked so peaceful and quiet, but soon he began to stir. A nurse came in to check him over, and they were told they could take him home. She told them that someone would be in touch with them regarding the results of the CT scan very soon.

Gabriella picked Homer up and cradled him to her breast as Jack drove them back to their home.

Two whole days went by without any word from the doctor about Homer's CT scan, and Jack was getting anxious to hear the results. Finally, just after noon of the third day, he phoned the hospital and talked to someone in the doctor's office. "We just mailed Ms. Williams a letter requesting she contact us about a follow up appointment. Can she come in this afternoon?"

"What time?" Jack asked.

"As soon as you can. Doctor Harvey is anxious to talk to Ms. Williams."

"Give me thirty minutes," Jack said, "and I'll have her there."

Dr. Harvey explained that they had found blockage in both sides of Homer's ears inside the canal where the eardrum resides that couldn't be seen with standard equipment. He said it appeared that Homer had at one time had a very bad ear infection. The infection had caused his Eustachian tubes to be blocked where they connected to the ear canal and the infected mucus that built up in that area had slowly thickened and hardened and was now keeping the parts of the eardrums on both sides from operating properly.

He explained that there was a new procedure whereby they could insert a tiny tube-like instrument up through the Eustachian tubes, dissolve the hardened mucus, and vacuum it out. This should allow the parts of the eardrum to once again function properly.

The operation would he done in two steps, one side at a time with a two-week recovery period between operations. Homer's hearing would be checked after each operation. His hearing might return gradually, as the eardrum parts may be lazy and need to learn to react to sound. Or his hearing could be instantaneous, in which case Homer might react strangely to the sudden sounds around him. In either case the doctor was positive that Homer's hearing would be at least partially, if not totally, restored. He could hear normally or at worst have to wear hearing aids.

He said he could perform the procedure himself at Children's Hospital and wanted to schedule the operation as soon as possible.

Gabriella, with her same look of concern, had begun to rely on Jack for decisions concerning Homer's hearing, so she looked at Jack for the answer.

The doctor, sensing this, said, "well, Ms. Williams? It's really up to you. Nothing to lose and everything to gain!"

"Will it hurt him?" she asked. "I don't want you to hurt him."

"He won't feel a thing," Dr. Harvey told her. "Once again, he'll be sedated. We have the best anesthesiologists here at Children's Hospital. There are always risks, but they are minimal. Are we settled?"

Gabriella nodded. "Okay, I guess."

"Here, give this to my receptionist. She'll set the appointment for the first operation." He handed Gabriella a charge slip with instructions to his receptionist.

The first operation was to be preformed the following Tuesday. Preparations, sedation, and operation would take about two hours, and recovery another hour. They would keep him in observation for the rest of that day. She could take Homer home the following morning.

On the morning of the first operation all except Homer were nervous with worried anticipation. Jack drove them to the hospital in the predawn darkness. As soon as they arrived and checked in, hospital staff and nurses took over. Homer was wheeled away, and Gabriella and Jack were left to sit in the waiting room worrying.

"Everything will be okay," Jack told Gabriella, placing his hand on her shoulder. "Homer is going to be fine."

"I'm not sure," Gabriella said. "Are you sure?"

"Now what did the doctor say? He said Homer would be fine. Don't you remember?"

Gabriella sat there nodding and staring at the floor.

There was a coffee pot on the opposite wall from where they were sitting. "Do you want some coffee?" Jack asked. "I'm going to get myself a cup."

"No, thanks."

The hands on the clock seemed not to move at all over the next two hours. They sat there mostly in silence, each deep in their own thoughts, Gabriella wringing her hands occasionally, Jack sipping coffee. Finally, after what seemed like an eternity, the door to the waiting room opened and Dr. Harvey walked in smiling.

"Everything went fine," he said. "They're taking him to a room now, and you'll be able to see him very shortly. Once again, everything went fine, and I'm very optimistic your boy will have hearing in that ear when he wakes up. I'll be in to check on him in just a little while. The nurse will come and get you when they're ready for you."

Gabriella looked like she was going to cry when she saw Homer's tiny form on the bed. He looked so little and still. Very soon he began to stir.

Several nurses bustled in and out before Dr. Harvey finally arrived. He checked to see that Homer was awake and then ran a simple test. He softly snapped his fingers close to Homer's right ear. Homer quickly looked to the right. Dr. Harvey then snapped his fingers close to Homer's left ear—no response. He repeated the test again, with the same results. He turned to Gabriella, smiled, and softly said, "I don't know how much hearing he has recovered, but he can definitely hear with the right ear." He left a nurse with Homer and ushered them outside the room. "I wouldn't subject him to any loud noises right away. After the two-week recovery period we'll do the other side. When he's fully recovered he'll need some speech therapy, but we'll deal with that in due course. I think we did well here today." He smiled, patting Gabriella on her shoulder.

"Thank you very much, doctor!" Jack said, extending his hand.

"My pleasure!" Dr. Harvey said with a smile as they shook hands.

The second operation two weeks later was as successful as the first.

The hearing response tests showed Homer had regained over 90 percent of his hearing in the right ear and close to total hearing in his left. Homer began speech therapy a few days later. He became more outgoing, and Jack was thrilled to see him running about jabbering. The change in Gabriella was also very positive, as the burden of Homer's deafness that had weighed so heavily upon her had now been lifted. She seemed to have a new bounce in her step and was much quicker to flash her smile.

Jack made one last visit to Children's Hospital to eliminate all the debt. He paid the speech therapist enough to insure therapy would continue until Homer could speak at age level or better then went back to his room and packed his things. He had been here more than six weeks. *It's time to get back on the road,* he thought.

He had tried to call Yvette and Juliette every night during this time and had only missed them a couple of times. He had talked to both of them on their birthdays. He had sent them both roses on Valentine's Day. Juliette had never failed to tell him she missed him and loved him. It was affecting his decision making.

While he packed he was also remembering how excited Yvette had been to receive the coat, hat, and glove ensemble and how great it was that Juliette's coat exactly matched hers. He recalled her telling him how touched she had been when she received the beautiful amethyst-laden necklace and earring set. And later bubbling on about the tiny amethyst earrings he had mailed Juliette on her birthday. Then he remembered how during every conversation she managed to suggest he return to her and Juliette. *As what?* he thought. *Her good friend Jack?*

He had taken several pictures of Homer and Gabriella, and when he had them developed he found the pictures of Yvette and Juliette and the one with him in the picture. He had the best print of Yvette and Juliette enlarged, and it had been sitting on his bedside table for the past few days. They were the last thing he saw before he turned his light out each night and the first thing he saw each morning. He picked up the picture as the last thing he packed.

Jack looked around the room he had occupied for so many weeks. He pulled out his wallet and left a $100 bill for the housekeeper then picked up his bags and walked to the elevator.

FOUR

Jack's mind was in conflict. He was having an internal mental and emotional struggle with opposing needs and wishes. On the one hand he felt compelled to continue his Samaritan-like journey giving away all the found money. On the other hand he had an overpowering loneliness and need for Yvette and Juliette. The selfish thing, he thought, would be for him to go back to Bon Weir and the inviting arms of Yvette and use the money on himself and his desires. Jack headed the SUV east toward Jackson.

An hour later he picked up the Natchez Trace Parkway heading northeast and followed it the rest of the day. He crossed into Alabama; then half an hour later entered Tennessee. Two hours later he entered the village of Oak Grove adjacent to Fort Campbell in southwestern Kentucky. This was his first time to ever be in the State of Kentucky. He mentally checked it off from his list of states to visit.

The two-story motel situated just off the four-lane was a step or two down from the five-star motel he'd been staying in the past several weeks, but it was clean and the bed looked comfortable. Jack set his bag down, took out his picture of Yvette and Juliette, and placed it on the bedside table. He washed up and decided he would get some supper.

Jack had noticed a bar and grill across the highway from the motel as he turned into the parking area. He crossed the highway on foot and walked into the bar and grill. A number of soldiers in camouflage fatigues were crowding the bar and small tables. Waitresses in tight short shorts and low-cut blouses were walking among the tables with trays of drinks or empties. Jack hesitated and was about to leave when he was suddenly approached by one of the waitress.

"More tables in the back," she said. "Just follow me."

"I was looking for something to eat!" Jack shouted over the din. "Your sign says bar and grill."

She grabbed a one-page menu as they passed the end of the bar and led on through a small door into a room behind it. There were many open tables and the noise was a lot less disturbing.

"My name's Leeza. The pepper cheese steak with onions is a favorite of most of the soldiers. I think you'd like it. It's really good with a cold beer!"

"Okay, that sounds good," Jack replied, "but make it a bottle of water instead of beer. I'm allergic to hops!"

Leeza disappeared into the other room. Jack looked around the room, taking in the décor. A lot of military memorabilia hung from the walls. Pictures of tanks and other assault vehicles covered one wall. A picture of the president hung between the American flag and the flag of Kentucky on another wall.

Several small groups of two and three soldiers, some in uniform and some in civilian clothes, crowded around the small tables, engaged in friendly conversation. Their eyes never failed to follow the movements of the scantily clad waitresses as they moved about in and out of the room.

Jack smiled to himself, remembering his days as a young sailor when girl watching was the most important achievement of the day. He followed their gaze and saw Leeza coming to bring him his food. "You seem to have several admirers," Jack teased her. "Be careful one doesn't try to take you home to show his mother!"

"Already married!" Leeza said, holding up her left hand so Jack could see her rings. "And most of them know my husband, Chris. He's on his third deployment right now. I expect him back in April. Enjoy your steak!" She was gone in a second.

Jack finished his meal, left enough money on the table for Leeza to receive a big tip, and returned to his room in the motel.

He checked the time and dialed Arty's, hoping he would catch
Yvette at a lull in business. After Jack and Arty did their usual
faux stand up comedy routine, Arty put Yvette on the phone.

She was excited to tell Jack that with the money she
had received from the sale of the Valiant, the lower rent, and
inexpensive car, she had for the first time in her adult life, opened
a saving account. "I have three hundred and seventy five dollars
in savings! Aren't you proud of me, Jack?"

"Indeed I am!" Jack assured her. "Are you saving for
Juliette's college?"

"No, not yet. First I plan to pay you back every cent you've
spent on Juliette and me!"

"There's no need to do that. At least don't get in any hurry to
do it. I still have a dollar or two in my wallet."

"Where do you get your money, Jack? Are you an oil man? A
drug lord?"

"Absolutely not! Let's just say the Lord has blessed me. What
is Juliette doing tonight? She is usually the first one on the phone."

"She's doing her homework. Would you rather talk to her?"

"Don't make me chose between the two of you," Jack teased.
"You might not like the outcome."

Yvette and Jack continued the verbal flirting for a few more
minutes, told each other how much each was missed by the other,
and eventually Yvette handed the phone to Juliette. Juliette and
Jack had a short conversation about the day's events in Juliette's
life, missing one another and eventually Jack said good-bye and
hung up the phone. The phone call had done nothing to alleviate
his loneliness but rather seemed to have increased it. He flopped
on the bed and tried to think about tomorrow's travels, but the
pretty face of Yvette filled his mind.

Just after sunup Jack left the little motel at Oak Grove and
drove north toward Hopkinsville. Just south of town he picked
up Kentucky State Highway 80 heading east and followed it for

the rest of the day toward West Virginia, another state he had not yet visited.

He had failed to get fuel in Oak Grove, so he was driving at a moderate speed keeping his eyes peeled for a convenient place to get gas. He finally spotted a station on the opposite side of the highway. Jack made a sharp left turn across the highway, and pulled into the pump area.

When Jack got out he noticed a beat-up early-model Chevrolet suburban just on the other side of the pumps in the lane next to him. He saw a tall, rather plain, blond-haired woman with sad blue eyes and an equally sad looking mouth that turned down at the corners. She was putting gasoline into the suburban. She was dressed in a worn cotton dress and run-down shoes. She shut down her pump when the amount reached twenty dollars.

Jack knew that the old suburban had a forty-six-gallon tank and that six gallons wouldn't get her very far. As soon as she left to go pay for her gas, Jack stepped across between the pumps and opened the filler door on the suburban, removed the filler cap, inserted the nozzle from the pump he was using, and opened the nozzle wide open. The side window of the suburban was open and a boy about ten years old stuck his head out and said, "Hey, mister, whats ya doin'?"

Jack looked into the car and saw four children in the back and two in the front. One of those in the front—a girl who looked to be about fourteen—was holding her youngest sibling on her lap. The girl sitting next to the inquisitive boy looked to be his twin. There were two younger siblings, one probably in the early grades and one Jack guessed to be a pre-school lad. They all were badly in need of haircuts. Their clothes were ill fitting and old.

"I don't have enough room in my tank for all my gas, so I'm putting some of it in your car," Jack explained.

At the sound of his voice, a half-grown blue-tick hound sleeping next to the boy jumped up and began baying and leaping toward Jack, licking him across the face. "That's Rufus," the boy explained. "He won't hurt you."

The gas was pouring into the tank, but not fast enough, Jack thought. He needed to keep the woman away until he had time to finish filling her tank.

"I'm hungry!" Jack said to the boy, "I'll give you a dollar if you'll go inside and buy me a half-dozen candy bars."

"I want a dollar too!" his sister piped up. "Can I help and get a dollar too?"

"Okay," Jack said, "a dollar to both of you. Here's a fifty-dollar bill. Now remember I want six candy bars, and don't forget my change."

When their mother sees them in there, they're going to catch it, Jack thought. *But that should give me time to finish with the suburban tank.*

Jack counted off the gallons—thirty-five, thirty-six, thirty-seven, thirty-eight, ping! The handle automatically disengaged. Jack squeezed the handle a few more times until he could see the gasoline in the neck of the suburban's gas tank. He replaced the filler cap, shut the filler door, and stepped back between the pumps to start filling the SUV's tank.

He was just in time, as the two young ones came running toward him shouting happily and carrying a small plastic bag. Behind them, frowning disapprovingly, walked their mother. Jack took the bag, which also contained his change, and giving each of them a dollar said, "Thank you!" Then, "Wait a minute. This isn't the kind of candy bars I like. They'll have to eat these," Jack said, handing the bag to their mother.

"What's going on here?" the woman asked Jack accusingly. "I've taught my children to not take candy from strangers!"

"You have a couple of cute kids there, and I was just letting them earn a dollar." Jack explained.

"Mom, get in, and I'll tell you everything!" the girl in the front seat called out. "It's okay. Just…can we leave?"

As the suburban pulled away from the pumps, Jack could see the mother looking first at her daughter as the girl tried to explain things and then back at Jack. He hoped he hadn't done more harm than good.

He paid the bill, returned to the SUV, and was soon back on the road.

He drove through areas of freshly plowed tobacco and soybean fields. The farmers were making ready for spring planting. He saw bare places on the hills where strip mines had badly scarred the terrain. He saw the effects of extreme poverty in areas where the mining companies had taken the coal and moved on abandoning whole towns. He drove through the beautiful Daniel Boone National Forest. Just under four hundred miles and seven and a half hours after he left the motel at Oak Grove, Jack pulled into a motel in Ashland, Kentucky, just across the Ohio River from Huntington, West Virginia.

As usual, Jack placed a call to Arty's. When Arty answered, instead of asking to talk to Yvette or Juliette and going through their usual corny greeting, Jack asked him, "How long has Yvette worked for you?"

"Almost five years. Why do you want to know?"

"She ever had a raise?"

"Yeah, every time they raise the federal minimum wage."

"She's been there five years and still makes minimum wage? That doesn't seem right," Jack declared. "Arty, I want you to give her a three-dollar-an-hour raise retro-active to the beginning of this pay period."

"This ain't no Howard Johnson's," Arty explained apologetically. "I can't afford to do that."

"You'll do it," Jack insisted, "and here's the reason why. You are going to start receiving a two hundred fifty-dollar cashier's check every week. You use it to pay Yvette's additional salary. Anything leftover you can use for yourself. That girl spends six days a week, twelve hours a day at your place. Doesn't she deserve a little raise?"

"Sure she does, Jack, and I'd love to be able to pay her more. Where are these cashiers checks coming from?"

"That's to be our little secret. The checks will be coming. As far as Yvette is concerned, you just suddenly got a soft spot in your heart and decided it was time she had a raise."

"I'll be glad to do it, Jack. You coming back this way anytime soon?"

"Not real soon," Jack told him. Then, on a lighter note, he teased, "Maybe you could use some of the leftover money to buy yourself a clean apron."

"Nah," Arty said. "It would just get dirty too! Now, ya want to talk to one of your gals?"

"Of course!"

Juliette's melodious voice came on the line. "Where are you now, Uncle Jack? Mommy has been helping me find the places on the map where you call us from."

"I'm still in Kentucky. The name of the town is Ashland. Can you remember that? How are you? Have you lost any more teeth?"

"No, but my two teeth that are growing in the front are so big that I'm going to look like a rabbit!"

"That's great! I think little rabbits are very cute."

"I don't want to be a rabbit!"

"Don't worry, you won't be! Very soon now your face will grow to fit your teeth and you'll forget all about it. And honey, no matter how big your teeth get, you'll always be my beautiful little Juliette!"

"Thank you, Uncle Jack. Here's Mommy. I love you."

"Hi Jack," Yvette's sparkling sweet voice sounded in his ear. "What's new from your side of the globe?"

"Truthfully? I spent the whole day thinking about you! Are you okay? Arty treating you right? How's the new car? Still trouble free I hope."

"Slow down, Jack! I'll try to answer all of your questions. I've been too busy to think about you. Well, almost," she teased. "I'm fine. Arty knows better than to treat me any way but right, and I love my new car! And really, Jack, if you have all this time to sit around thinking about little ole me, maybe you need to find a job or a hobby. Juliette, on the other hand, asks me every night before bed if you'll be back the next morning. Will you be back some morning so I can tell her yes?"

"Some morning, yes," Jack told her in a voice just above a whisper. "Some morning you'll look up and I'll be standing there."

"Swear it, Jack. Promise me you aren't just saying it to please me."

"Yvette, I swear it. I will be back."

"Have to go now, Jack. Call me!"

The phone line clicked. Jack was still holding the phone to his ear when the dial tone began to sound. A sudden wave of loneliness washed over him. The walls seemed to be closing in, and he was almost overcome by claustrophobia. He picked up his jacket and went outside for a walk to try to shake these feelings. "It's just loneliness" he told himself. "No one falls in love over the phone! We've never so much as shared a kiss! Get a hold of yourself, Jack!"

At a bank the following morning, Jack bought four $250 cashier checks. At the post office he bought four business envelopes that had already been franked. He put one of the checks in an envelope with a short note to Arty then addressed the envelope to Arty's Café and dropped it in the box before leaving the post office. Once Arty established the routine of paying Yvette the additional three dollars an hour, he could start sending the checks in larger amounts that would cover longer periods. *Too large an amount*, he thought, *and Arty might be tempted to spend it on necessary improvements, leaving him short when it came to payroll.*

About noon, Jack crossed the Ohio River and entered West Virginia. It was Wednesday, March 9.

FIVE

It had been ten weeks since he had removed the coolers from their graves. He had spent freely yet hardly made a dent in the piles of cash in the first cooler. As he drove through the outskirts of Huntington, West Virginia, his mind on Yvette, he realized he should be totally honest with her. That would mean he would have to tell her about his discovery of the buried coolers and his involvement in her salary increase. He decided he would call her that night at her home and tell her everything.

As Jack drove along through the outskirts of the city through a residential area, he noticed an elderly woman struggling with raising her garage door. Jack braked to a stop, climbed out, and walked back to help her. An elderly man sat stooped over in the passenger seat of the car. "Could you use a little help?" Jack asked the woman.

"Oh, yes, thank you," she answered. "And once I get it up it's a struggle to get it back down."

Jack raised the old one-piece garage door and waited until the woman drove into the garage. Then, noticing the elderly man was crippled and needing help getting out of the car, Jack assisted the woman with him. The man leaned on his walker with one hand and stuck out his other hand to shake Jack's hand. "Thank you very much, young man," he said. "That was mighty kind of you."

"Jack Lockhart," Jack said as they shook hands. "It was nothing. Can I help you inside?"

"That's okay, I got it now," the man said as he pushed the walker in front of him. "Name's Walter Lloyd. This is my wife, Ginny."

"Very glad to meet you both." Jack smiled.

"Could you use something to drink?" Ginny offered. "Some coffee or iced tea?"

"Sure," Jack said as he followed them into the house. "Whatever you have handy."

Walter went into the living room with Jack following. He backed up against his lift chair and was soon seated. Jack took a straight-backed armless chair opposite of him, assuming the other stuffed chair in the room would be where Ginny sat. Ginny brought a mug of coffee to Walter and asked Jack if he wanted sugar or cream or both. "Just black." Jack smiled.

Walter and Jack discussed the weather and made other small talk until Ginny entered the room and took her seat. Jack took a sip of the coffee she handed him and said, "I recently came into a whole lot of money, and I'd be happy if you would let me replace your old garage door with a new sectional door with an automatic door opener so all you'd have to do is push a button to open it and push it again to close the door. What do you think about that? Will you let me replace it for you?"

Ginny looked at Walter, who was looking first at Ginny and then at Jack.

"You a salesman or something?" Walter asked. "What's the catch?"

"No." Jack laughed. "I'm not a salesman. And there's absolutely no catch or cost to you. Just something I want to give you because you need it."

Tears filled Walter's eyes. "Sorry, I get teary eyed real easy anymore. It sure does hurt me every time I see Ginny struggling with that door. I am very thankful for your concern, Jack. We'd be forever grateful for such a gift."

Jack drank down his coffee. "It might take a day or two to get it installed, but I'll get right on it. Just give me your address and telephone number. Do you have a telephone book I can use?"

"Here, have another cup of coffee," Ginny insisted.

"Thank you, I will."

Jack found a local dealer advertising overhead garage doors and garage door openers. He jotted down the address and got directions to the dealership from Walter and Ginny. He shook hands with them both, thanked Ginny for the coffee, and quickly walked to the SUV. A few minutes later he was entering the building housing the garage door salesroom.

Jack told the salesman what he needed and that he needed it immediately. He was told that they could install the door the following morning. They would send a technician to the house to get the exact measurements and to see if any other supplies would be needed. Jack had to break out another new packet of $100 bills to pay for everything.

He put Walter and Ginny's name and phone number where he could find it and once again headed out of Huntington going north along the Ohio River. Vermont was on his list of states to visit, but since it was only the early part of March and the possibility of snow and ice still existed, Jack decided to head west into Ohio instead of going any farther north.

Jack continued driving along the Ohio River for several miles. Near the town of Henderson, West Virginia, he crossed the Silver Memorial Bridge over the Ohio River into Galipolis, Ohio.

He had not completed as many miles this day as he had at first planned. The events of the morning, although rewarding, had taken a number of hours. He located a nice motel along US-35 and pulled into a spot near the entrance. Luckily he was able to get comfortable, non-smoking accommodations. He dropped his bag on the end of the bed, opened it, and took out the picture of Yvette and Juliette. As he placed it on the bedside table, he suddenly realized that the gnawing in his stomach was not caused by his longing for them but due to the fact he had not eaten all day.

Jack picked up the motel information packet and found that there were no nearby restaurants. He called the desk about room service and was given the name of a very fine restaurant that would deliver. He was told there was a menu in the motel folder on the desk. *Of course,* Jack thought. *How did I miss that?* He looked over the menu, picked up the phone, and dialed the restaurant. "Your order will be there in thirty minutes or less," he was told.

While he waited for his meal to arrive, Jack stretched out on the bed and tried to think of just how to tell Yvette the truth about the money and what he now considered his mission. It might be better told in person, but Jack had determined he had to tell her and soon. He wasn't a very good liar, and although he hadn't exactly lied to her, he had been keeping the truth from her. *More than one truth*, he thought.

He not only wanted to tell her everything about how he had come upon the money, but he also wanted to share the warm feelings that he got from using it to help others who were less fortunate. And of course, he wanted to let her know how he really felt about her. Jack decided this was too important and would take too long to do in the few minutes he would have during her break. He would call her at work and tell her he was going to call her at home after she had put Juliette to bed tonight.

"Room service," a voice interrupted his thoughts. Jack took his order, paid the delivery boy, included a large tip, and spread the meal out on the table. He was famished and ate rapidly.

After eating, Jack shaved then showered, letting the warm water wash away his tiredness. He would stay up late and talk to Yvette later tonight. *With the time difference, it will be an hour later here*, Jack thought. As he brushed his teeth he rehearsed in his mind just what he would tell her. He put on his shorts, sat down at the small motel desk, and dialed the number of Arty's Café.

As soon as Arty heard it was Jack, instead of his usual friendly barbs, he said seriously, "Jack, if you care anything for Yvette you better get back here pronto! There's this dude been hangin' 'round here following her 'round like a hound dog after a bitch in heat! He keeps askin' her out and her bein' so sweet an all, I'm afraid she's a gonna do it! You just cain't allow that to happen, Jack!"

"Thanks Arty," Jack answered, feeling a pang of jealously. "I'll start back first thing tomorrow morning. I'm a good three days' travel away from there, so see if you can keep him away from her until I get back. I need to see just where I stand with her. You know I don't have any claim on Yvette and I never suggested to her that we were anything but friends."

"I know you ain't, but I ain't blind either. I see how she perks up ever time I tell her it's you on the phone."

"Well, tell her it's me now," Jack ordered.

Jack had suddenly decided to not make the late-night call explaining about the money and all of the rest. He would rush back and tell her in person. He tried to hold his feelings of urgency and jealously in check as he waited for her to come on the line.

"Jack," Yvette purred, "is that you? Juliette's asleep. I guess that's why you asked for me first."

"Hi, hon," Jack said softly, trying to show just a little bit of possessiveness. "Yes, it's me. How are you and my princess? Listen, Yvette, I'm coming back to Bon Weir. I've got to see you. I have something I must tell you."

"Really, Jack, you're coming back? How long will you stay this time? Should I tell Juliette, or do you want to surprise her? Don't tease me, Jack. When? How soon will you be here?"

"I'll leave it up to you when to tell Juliette. I'm on the border between Ohio and West Virginia; probably take about three days. I can hardly wait to see the two of you again. As to how long I'll be there this time, it will depend on several things, which we will discuss when I can sit down with you without being interrupted."

"Oh, Jack, there are so many things I want to tell you too, and Juliette has a pile of pictures she's drawn for you, and…well, just hurry and get here!"

"I'll call you from my motel tomorrow night and tell you where I am. See you very soon. Give Juliette a hug for me! Yvette, I lo…miss you"

"Me too!"

Jack pressed the switch hook long enough to break the connection then dialed the motel desk for a 5:00 a.m. wake-up call. As he lay back on his pillow he felt a sense of elation like he couldn't remember having in a very long time. He enjoyed the feeling briefly then sat up and checked his maps. He was more than a thousand miles from Bon Weir. "If I stick to the interstates," Jack thought aloud, "I may be able to save a day of travel."

Jack suddenly awakened. He glanced at the bedside clock and saw it was only 4:17 a.m. He jumped up, quickly dressed, and packed his bag. In the lobby, he filled two cups with coffee just before checking out. It was still a few minutes before five when he wheeled the SUV out of the motel parking lot. He followed the road south along the river for just under fifty miles before finding interstate 64 West.

Jack stayed on the interstate, stopping only at an occasional rest area. At noon when he pulled into a rest area, he found he had traveled 440 miles. The rest area had several snack machines, and he was able to extinguish his hunger and thirst. He was soon back on the road. He continued this pace for the rest of the afternoon, eventually finding a place to get off. It was almost 6:00 p.m. when he parked in front of the motel in Texarkana, Texas. He had traveled more than 800 miles in a little over fourteen hours.

Exhausted, Jack dropped his bag by the bed, pulled out his picture of Yvette and Juliette, and set it on the bedside table. He had some calling to do. First he called the Lloyds. Ginny answered the phone. "Hi, Jack Lockhart here. How are you?"

"Fine!" Ginny answered.

"How's Walter?"

"He doing okay, thanks. They installed the garage door today!" Ginny explained. "It's wonderful! They even put a remote control thing on the front of the garage so I can open the door from there if I happen to be in the yard and need to go into the garage.

There's another button on the wall inside the garage, and I have one inside the car. It's so quiet we can't even hear it in the house. We really love it, Jack! Thank you from the bottom of my heart! Here, Walter wants to talk to you."

Walter and Jack talked for several minutes before signing off. Next Jack called the motel in Vicksburg and after identifying himself, asked to speak to Gabriella. He inquired about her and Homer, and they too talked for several minutes before Gabriella had to terminate the conversation. Then Jack placed the call to Arty's.

After the usual banter between Arty and Jack, he asked to speak to Yvette. When he heard her sweet voice he suddenly didn't feel so tired. "I'm in Texarkana," Jack told her. "I could be in Bon Weir before you go to work in the morning, that is, if I leave here early enough in the morning."

"Oh, Jack, really?" Yvette said. "If you're teasing me, Jack, I'll never forgive you!"

"You're just two hundred seventeen miles away from me," Jack teased, "That's less than four hours. If I leave here at five I could get to your house in time to take you to work."

"I'm going to ask Arty for tomorrow off!" Yvette almost shouted into his ear in her excitement.

"Are you going to tell Juliette? She might not want to go to school tomorrow."

"All I've told her so far is that you are on your way back. We thought you wouldn't get here before late Saturday evening. I think I'll leave it like that and you can surprise her by meeting her in front of the café when she gets off the bus tomorrow. That way she won't miss any school."

"That sounds good to me. I really want some time alone with you to discuss some important things."

"Important things, Jack? You're not thinking of asking for my daughter's hand in marriage are you?" Yvette joked.

"And why not? Am I not good enough for her?"

"No! Not you or any other man!"

"May I at least talk to her?"

"Of course!" Yvette suddenly became more serious and told Jack she could hardly wait to see him and wished him a safe journey. Then she gave the phone to Juliette.

"Hi, Uncle Jack. Where are you this time?"

"I'm in a place called Texarkana. The city actually sits on the Texas and Arkansas border, with about half of the city in Texas and the other half in Arkansas. Have you studied the geography of the states yet?"

"No, just what Mommy showed me."

"Well, have her show you where Texarkana is. I'm a lot closer to you tonight than I was last night, and I'll see you very soon."

"Can you take me to the park when you get here Uncle Jack?"

"I'd love to. I'll talk to you tomorrow. Bye!"

Out of earshot of Juliette, Yvette told Arty about Jack's early return and convinced him to give her the next day off. Arty's sister sometimes filled in for Yvette when she needed some time off, which wasn't often. Arty was sure he could get her to fill in.

Jack turned in early, expecting to be on the road by 5:00 a.m. He rehearsed over and over in his mind just what to say to Yvette. He rehearsed it so much that his dreams were mixed up with worried visions of the three of them. He awakened at 3:00 a.m. almost as tired as when he went to sleep.

He climbed out of bed, took a long shower, shaved, brushed his teeth, and dressed in his finest outfit. He packed his bag, turned out the lights, and proceeded to the check out desk.

It wasn't yet 4:00 a.m. when he wheeled the SUV onto southbound US-59.

The miles rolled by. Jack's excitement turned into nervousness, which grew more intense the closer he got to Bon Weir. What would it be like when he saw her again? He was as nervous as a teenage boy on his first date. Should I bring a corsage? Should I dare try to kiss her? Have I just imagined she cares for me? Jack laughed out loud at himself. "You poor smitten slob! You don't have a chance."

When Jack reached Jasper, he headed for the flower shop in the mall. He had them make up a big bouquet of red and purple flowers laced with white daisies. It included roses, tulips, iris, carnations, purple montecasino, purple statice, and white daisies. He had no idea what kind of flower was her favorite but hoped she would find something in this group she would like. It was a beautiful arrangement set off by a deep purple vase.

He and Yvette had never had a formal date. Jack wanted this meeting to seem like a first date, to be very special. He hoped the bouquet would ease some of the tension he had felt building up inside him over the past couple of hours. He wanted to get to her place in time for a short greeting before she had to go to work.

The sign read "Bon Weir 5 Miles." Jack checked his watch. It was 8:35 a.m. Even with the forty-five-minute stop to buy flowers he was way ahead of schedule. Would he seem too anxious? "Oh, what the hell!" he said. "I am anxious! And excited!" He turned into the Bayou mobile home park, pulled his SUV into the drive just behind her car, and turned off the engine. He took a deep breath, picked up the vase full of flowers, and climbed out.

Jack didn't get to knock. He was about to shift the flowers to his left hand so he could knock when the door burst open and there she was!

Suddenly neither one knew just what to say. Then in unison they both blurted out the first thing that came to mind.

"You're early," Yvette said.

"Flower delivery!" Jack said.

SIX

Yvette took the flowers, hardly noticing. She started talking a mile a minute. "Arty gave me the day off. Juliette is at school. Where did you get these beautiful flowers? You shouldn't have brought me anything. Did you have a good trip? Did you run into any bad weather? How fast did you have to drive to get here this soon? Oh, Jack, I'm so glad to see you." She finally took a breath and set the vase in the middle of the bar that acted as a divider between the living room and kitchen areas. "These are just lovely, Jack. How did you know violet was my favorite color?"

"My turn now?" Jack asked.

Yvette flashed him her famous dimpled smile.

Jack reached out, took her hand, and pulled her to him. She didn't resist. He put his arms around her and pulled her even closer. Yvette lifted her face to look up at him, her violet-blue eyes growing darker with passion. Jack bent and pressed a tender kiss on her willing lips. They seemed to melt together. "I missed that even though it was only in my imagination," Jack whispered. "In my dreams I have kissed you many times. It's so much better in person." He kissed her again, this time longer and with more passion.

"Jack, wait," Yvette whispered as she softly pushed him away. "We need to get some things settled. That was an awfully passionate kiss just to say hello! I'm afraid you may have misread my excited greeting."

"It didn't feel like I was alone just now," Jack said questioningly.

"I know, Jack. Just for a moment there, but really, I don't know anything about you."

"You're absolutely right. Okay, I'll tell you anything you want to know, but first I want to take you to breakfast."

"Oh no, Jack. I just finished breakfast not more than an hour ago. You sit down and let me fix you something."

Jack took a seat at the bar. He moved the flowers over just a bit so he could have an unfettered view of Yvette while she moved about fixing his breakfast.

"Start at the beginning, and don't leave anything out," Yvette teased.

"Once upon a time," Jack joked. He went on to describe his early years growing up on a ranch; his school days; his short tour in the Navy; how he and his wife, Rachel, had met; their happy marriage; his estrangement from his daughter, Rebecca; Rachel's sudden onset of cancer; her terrible suffering and death; and his more than two years of grieving. While he talked Yvette had placed his breakfast in front of him. He ate then helped her clean up everything. Now they were sitting in the living room.

"Before I go any farther in this rather dull story of my life," Jack told her, getting up from his seat, "I want to show you something."

Jack went to the rear of the SUV and pulled out the full cooler. He carried it inside and placed it on the floor in front of Yvette. "Open it," he said, motioning toward the cooler as he sat in the chair opposite of her.

"What's in there, Jack?"

"The rest of my story."

Yvette cautiously unlatched the cooler lid, took a deep breath, then opened it, revealing the stacks of bundled $100 bills. She stared at it for a few seconds before blurting out, "You're a bank robber?"

Jack grinned and stuck out his hand. "Willy Sutton, at your service ma'am," he said. Then, seeing the shocked look on Yvette's face, he quickly and soberly stated, "No, I am not a bank robber!"

He then told her the story about seeing the tracks in the dry grass that led to his finding the two coolers loaded with cash.

"Wait, there's another one?"

"Yes." He explained that he believed it was most likely proceeds from criminal activity. He then tried to explain how he had decided to travel the country finding anyone in need and spending some of it to help them. He told her how their accidental meeting had given him his first opportunity to use the money in a positive way.

"The car? The balance on my trailer?" Yvette asked, beginning to understand.

"And the raise at Arty's."

Yvette looked puzzled. "I don't know what to think right now, Jack. I need some time to absorb all of this."

Jack sighed. "First, let me ask you a hypothetical question. Suppose, although you have suddenly come into millions, you are alone and feeling worthless. Then all at once, into your life come the most wonderful and beautiful people you have ever known, yet they could use a little monetary help. What would you do?"

"I really don't know. I think you should have been honest with me, Jack."

"Yvette, I didn't know you. At that time you were just a pretty little waitress with a million-dollar smile and an adorable little daughter. The hospitality of your home that cold rainy night and your friendship meant a lot to me. It still does! Would you rather I had told you something like, 'I have lots of money; would you like some?' I wouldn't put you in such a difficult and embarrassing position by saying something like that. I was as honest as I could be under the circumstances. I'm being honest now. I've bared my soul here, Yvette."

Yvette sat silent, staring at the cooler full of cash.

"Let me get this out of sight," Jack said, closing the lid and returning the cooler to the SUV. "Would you like me to leave now?" he asked her as he came back inside.

"No! Now I would like to take you somewhere," Yvette said, returning to her usual sparkling, positive self. "We'll take my car and I'll drive. If you have any boots you'd better put them on."

Jack went to the SUV and got his boots. As he put them on he noticed for the first time that instead of her usual waitress uniform, Yvette was wearing form-fitting jeans, a flowery blouse, and a short-waisted denim jacket open at the front. The legs of her jeans were tucked into a pair of attractively decorated knee-high boots.

March in East Texas was usually very pleasant, and this day was no exception. She drove along the river, through the pine trees, going south. She told him they were headed in the direction of the community of Sandjack. They passed under an old abandoned railroad bridge where freight had once crossed the Sabine River. They continued on a winding road for about fifteen miles before she parked near a quaint fishing cabin sitting on a cleared spot in the pines. It was located on Church House Creek just above the point where it converged with the Sabine River. "I played here as a barefoot, tangle-headed girl," Yvette told him. "My father used to bring us here so he could do some fishing. Some of my fondest childhood memories are of the times we spent here. I just love this place."

They got out and walked hand in hand toward the cabin to explore.

"Cabin still in the family?"

"No, Dad sold this place years ago. I was so heartbroken when he did. It doesn't look like the owners use it much anymore." Still holding his hand as they walked along, she turned toward him and asked, "How old are you, Jack?"

"Forty-two. I'll be forty-three in October. I guess that makes me old enough to be your father and Juliette's grandfather. But I'm not too old to fall in love…or to make love, for that matter!"

"I don't see you as that old. Definitely not old enough to be my father."

"Does that mean I have a chance with you?"

"I'll let you know. It's true that my having Juliette has never been a problem to you like it's been with some of the guys I've dated."

"I don't want you to feel like I'm trying to buy your affection. I'm really not, you know. You showed a fondness for me long before you ever saw that cooler of cash. I recall a number of long-distance phone conversations where I detected an interest."

"But not very much earlier than when you gave me the car. I don't know if what I feel is gratitude or true fondness."

"I'll take back everything! How would you feel about me then?"

"I don't know."

"Keep working on it. You'll like me some day."

She had started walking faster, swinging their clasped hands. Soon she began skipping along, tugging on his hand. Looking back over her shoulder, she grinned. "I already like you!" She dropped his hand and sprinted down the sandy path into the woods toward the river. "Come on, old man," she called over her shoulder, taunting him.

Jack broke into a trot and then began to run faster. Unable to catch her in his heavy western boots, he just trotted along behind, watching her young athletic body as she out paced him. That perfect figure, the tiny waist, the flared hips, the bouncing, curly, black waves of hair, a perfect amalgamation of youth and beauty. Jack couldn't deny it any longer; he was in love with her. Yet, at the same time, he realized she was out of his league.

She slowed as she neared the bluff at the edge of the river. He caught up with her on the sandy path and grabbed her hand, spinning her around toward him. Her laughter was like music to his ears, her smile like a magnet to his lips. He pulled her to him as she laughed tossing her head, her hair flying freely about her beautiful face. He bent to kiss her, but she placed the first two fingers of her right hand across his lips. "Not now, Jack."

An hour or so later, they returned to the trailer, arriving in plenty of time to be there when the school bus dropped Juliette off down the block. Jack was there to greet her, and she came running into his arms. He carried her to the trailer before putting her down. Jack and Juliette enjoyed each other's company for sometime. She had stacks of papers she'd drawn. "Just for you," she told Jack.

When Juliette was in the bathroom, Jack asked Yvette quietly, "Am I staying here tonight or will that make you feel uncomfortable?"

"I've already made up your bed for tonight. You're always welcome here, Jack."

"What will the neighbors say?"

"The same thing they said the last time you stayed here. But you know something, Jack? I don't care what the neighbors think."

"Want to drop by Arty's for supper?" Jack asked. "I wouldn't mind going a couple of rounds with the old grouch."

"Could we go somewhere else tonight, please. I'm going to spend twelve hours there tomorrow."

Jack could have kicked himself. *I am so out of touch!* he thought. *Asking her to take a busman's holiday.*

"Sure," he said. "I would be flattered to accompany my two favorite ladies to any public place. Where would you like to dine, milady?"

"I've been dying to go to this new place I've heard about up in Jasper. Family dining, very ritzy, live music, dance floor, and all."

"It may be too ritzy for me. These are my best clothes, and now my boots are rather dusty. Do you think I can get in looking like this?"

"Probably not. We'll save that outing for another day. Can't afford new clothes, Jack?"

"Truthfully, my wife used to buy all of my clothes, and I haven't bought anything other than underwear and socks since she died. I need someone to take care of me, Yvette," Jack said pitifully.

They decided to go to Jasper to a large Mexican restaurant that Yvette and Juliette liked. Juliette sat next to Jack, and Yvette sat across from the two of them. Although Jack would have loved the nearness of Yvette sitting next to him, being able to just look up and see her across the table from him caused him much pleasure. He took long sips on his iced tea so he could keep his eyes on her longer. He watched her eating and listened to her interaction with Juliette while never leaving him out of the conversation. She had a natural rapport with people and her eye appeal didn't hurt.

I'm just a lovesick fool, Jack thought to himself. *I'm a country music song!*

As they drove back toward Bon Weir later, the full moon was just rising. When they reached the village, Jack took the river road that ran behind Arty's Café and was soon parked on a high bank overlooking the river. From here they could all three see the moon. Juliette climbed over the seat and into his lap.

"The moon is beautiful tonight," Yvette said to no one in particular.

"They call that a lover's moon," Jack replied.

"Tell me a story, Uncle Jack," Juliette said as she nestled in his arms.

"Once upon a time, there was this not-so-handsome prince," Jack began, "and he was in love with a beautiful princess who had a beautiful little princess of her own. The prince vowed his love to the beautiful princess and told her he wanted to marry her and take her and the little princess to live happily ever after in his castle far away. But alas, the beautiful princess was suspicious of the not-so-handsome prince and told him she could never marry him. The not-so-handsome prince was very sad, so he went away, never to be heard from again. The End."

"Now tell me a happy one!" Juliette insisted.

Her hair was tickling his chin, and he couldn't get his hand to it, so he tried to blow it away. Yvette seeing his dilemma reached over and tenderly brushed it away. "Thank you," Jack whispered, looking at her with adoration.

Yvette was staring at his face intently. She pursed her lips, squinted her eyes just a little, and said in a whisper, "Umm, not-so-handsome...yes, I'll go along with that."

Jack grinned. "Okay," he said out loud to Juliette. "Once upon a time, in a country far, far away..."

As Jack's voice droned on he soon felt Juliette's body slowly relax as she drifted off to sleep. "Can you trade places with me?" Jack whispered to Yvette. "You'll have to drive us home."

Jack tenderly lifted the young girl in his arms and carried her to the passenger side of the SUV. Yvette went to the driver's side and like a pro, adjusted the seat, steering wheel, and mirrors before backing out and turning around. They were soon pulling into the drive at Yvette's trailer. Jack carried Juliette into the trailer and placed her on her bed.

"Shouldn't you bring your coolers inside?" Yvette questioned him.

"Well, look at you," Jack teased. "Worried someone might want my old coolers." Then he said, "No, they'll be all right out there. Just push the lock button."

Yvette put Juliette to bed. She joined Jack in the living room a few minutes later. "What have you and Juliette planned for tomorrow?" she quizzed him.

"She's asked me to take her to the park. We'll do that and then see what else we can think of to do. We'll probably end up at the café for lunch."

Yvette reached into a small wicker basket on the table beside her, located a key ring with a single key, and handed it to Jack. "That's the key to this house. Be sure you lock up before you drive off."

Their conversation for the rest of the evening was cordial and friendly, Jack, enjoying just being in her presence. As the time on the clock neared midnight, Yvette, covering her mouth to hide a yawn, arose, excused herself, and headed toward her bedroom.

They slept later than usual since it was Saturday. Juliette was the first up and soon had awakened the two of them. Jack fixed everyone breakfast while Yvette got ready for work. "Can't you take the day off, Mommy?" Juliette implored her mother.

"I missed yesterday, and you know Arty is lost without me!" she called from the bedroom. "Besides I can't afford to miss work. You and Jack can have fun without me. Jack told me he is taking you to the park."

They all sat down together to the breakfast Jack had made.

"I didn't know you could cook, Jack. I should tell Arty to hire you!"

"Please don't. I have no desire to spend all my time in a hot kitchen. In that waitress uniform you look just like I remember you," Jack added.

After Yvette left for the café, Jack and Juliette cleaned up the kitchen and made up his bed. They were soon on their way to the park. There were very few visitors at the park this early in the day, so they had no trouble finding empty rides. At the teeter-totter, Jack held one end, pushing it down with his hands and then his foot to raise her high into the air, then letting it go. As she plummeted toward the ground, Jack would catch it just before she hit the ground. Juliette would giggle with delight each time. When she tired of the teeter-totter, she ran to the slide. Jack was able to slide down with her a few times, and then it was off to the merry-go-round. Jack spun her faster and faster while she screamed with excitement. Next it was the swings. Juliette challenged Jack to see who could go the highest. As the swings went back and forth, she pumped her tiny legs vigorously. Jack, who had not been in a swing in a long time, was having a hard time getting started, and she easily beat him.

"I beat you, Uncle Jack," she chortled. "I beat you!"

They continued to swing rapidly for several minutes then let their swings slowly come to a stop. Juliette was chattering on about school, about her friends, and a lot of other things interesting to a child. Jack was nodding and commenting when he felt it important to do so. He looked at Juliette and saw a miniature Yvette. *Yvette, however, knew her father,* Jack thought. *Juliette doesn't know hers.* He suddenly felt the urge to hug his diminutive companion. He picked her up out of the swing, hugged her close, and kissed the top of her head.

It was early afternoon when they stopped in at Arty's to get a sandwich and something cool to drink. Jack lifted Juliette up onto a stool at the bar and called through the window to the kitchen, "Anything eatable in this joint?"

"Jack, you old son-of-a-gun," Arty growled as he came out of the kitchen and grabbed Jack's hand. "Long time since we saw your ugly face 'round here."

"I've been recuperating from the last time I had to eat your cooking!"

Arty stepped closer, leaned so his face was close to Jack's face, and said in a whisper, "That's him." He nodded toward the corner booth. "That's the dude I told you about, the one there in the flannel shirt. I tell you, Jack, I think he's trouble."

Momentarily, Yvette appeared behind the counter and after a cheery greeting, took their orders. Jack turned slightly on his stool and observed "the dude." He was a rather handsome, well-built man, much younger than Jack. Jack also observed that he was a show off, exhibiting boisterous behavior. Jack turned his attention back to Yvette and Juliette.

Yvette placed their food in front of them and walked away. As she passed in front of the dude's table he called out, "Hey, doll face, come here a minute."

Yvette stopped at his table, and they engaged in conversation. Juliette turned to see what was going on, saw the dude, and said to Jack in a very disapproving manner, "That's Roger. I don't like him. He's always staring at Mommy's butt."

Yvette laughed politely at something Roger said then turned and walked away. Jack and Juliette observed Roger ogling Yvette with a twisted, almost evil grin as she walked away from his table to wait on another of her customers.

Suddenly Juliette slid off her stool, and with a deliberate walk she went about halfway to the booth where Roger sat. She put her hands on her hips, bent slightly at the waist, and shouted at him, "Stop staring at my mommy's butt!" Then she repeated it, even louder: "Stop staring at my mommy's butt!"

Yvette stopped and turned around. Everyone in the place was looking first at Juliette and then at Roger. "Shut up, you little twit!" Roger yelled.

Jack quickly slid off of his stool and placed himself between Juliette and Roger. "Don't talk to her that way! You were staring!"

"What's it to you? That's the waitress's daughter, not yours!" Roger said as he stood up. He was over six feet with large muscular arms and chest. He shoved Jack forcefully.

Jack was barely able to keep from stepping on Juliette as he stumbled backward.

"Wanna take this outside?" Roger challenged.

Jack caught his balance and was imagining his epitaph as he said, "Yeah, outside!"

They were almost to the door when Yvette stepped between them, facing Jack. She placed her clenched fists on Jack's chest and braced her toes against the floor. "How dare you two involve my daughter in such boorish behavior? Get out, the two of you, and don't come back in here again!"

"I'm out of here!" Roger shouted as he tried to slam the door against the hydraulic door closer. "You all deserve each other."

Jack looked at the disappointment in Yvette's eyes. It hurt him deeply. He walked back to Juliette, picked her up, and placed her on her stool. "Are you okay, honey? I didn't hurt you, did I?"

Juliette shook her head.

"Eat your lunch now," he said as he kissed her on the top of her head. "I'll see you later."

"See you, Arty," he called, waving at the window into the kitchen. He put a fifty-dollar bill under his uneaten lunch, turned, and walked out of the café.

He drove to the trailer and went in using the key Yvette had given him earlier. He knew he shouldn't, but he took his time packing his few things—things he had thought would be there a while. He put the key by the flower vase. Then he took one last look around, staring a few seconds longer than he had intended on the picture of Yvette and Juliette that sat on the entry table. Sighing deeply, he walked out and locked the door behind him.

SEVEN

Newton, Texas, a small town with a population of 2459, located just eighteen miles northwest of Bon Weir, is the County Seat of Newton County. It was Monday, March 14, just after 9:00 a.m. Jack sat in the records section, poring over the Newton County plat maps. He located the property he was interested in, a five-acre plot located at the convergence of the Sabine River and Church House Creek. In the property listings he found that the site he was interested in belonged to a Wayne and Barbara Landry of General Delivery, Singer, Louisiana. Singer, according to a lady in the courthouse, was about thirty-five miles southeast of Newton. Jack thanked her and left the courthouse.

Less than an hour later he was at the general store and post office in Singer. He got directions to the Landry home and was soon driving into their unkempt yard. He noticed an old johnboat on a trailer that had a flat tire on one side. A welcoming committee of two floppy-jawed, skinny old hounds set up a howling duel as he stepped out of the SUV.

"I'm looking for the Landry place," Jack called out to the elderly man walking out through the screen door.

"I'm Wayne Landry. Can I help you?"

Jack walked up onto the porch, stuck out his hand, and shouted over the noise of the hounds, "Jack Lockhart. Can we go inside?"

Mr. Landry ushered Jack inside and introduced him to his wife, Barbara, as they both looked at Jack with curiosity.

"I'm here about your property on Church House Creek," Jack explained.

"Oh, you're the tax man," Wayne said knowingly. "I apologize about being late, but you see things have been real bad here lately. Get that letter we got from the tax people, Barbara."

"No," Jack said. "You've got me wrong. I'm interested in buying the property if you're willing to sell. If there are some back taxes owed, we can clear that up later. Are you interested in selling the cabin and the land it's on?"

"We should sell it," Barbara said to Wayne, handing him the letter, "we haven't been out there in more than two years and we could use the money toward your operation."

"My doctor's been telling me I need to get a hernia operation," Wayne explained. "We could use the money, but the property won't bring enough to cover an operation."

"It would be a start," Barbara told him.

"What is the property worth to you?" Jack asked Wayne.

"Well, we gave twenty-five hundred when we bought it, but the cabin was in lots better shape then. I doubt it would appraise for that much now. If you could you see your way clear to paying say, two thousand, I might consider it. Back taxes and all you know."

"Sounds like a very good deal," Jack told them. "I'll set everything in motion. You and Mrs. Landry might have to make a trip to Newton or Jasper for the closing, just to sign some papers. Let me have that letter, and I'll take care of the back taxes. Also, I'll need your telephone number so we can keep in touch during the whole procedure. Here, let me give you half as earnest money." Jack counted out ten $100 bills.

"Don't you want a receipt for that?" Barbara asked.

"I believe in a man's word," Jack told her, shaking hands with first Wayne and then Barbara. "Get in touch with your doctor, Wayne, and let me know if I can help you in any way."

"Sit back down and have a glass of iced tea with us," Barbara insisted. "You act like a man whose house is on fire."

Jack sat back down. He and Wayne talked about how good the fishing had been back when he first bought the cabin. How he and Barbara had spent many a cozy day and night there.

"I'm serious," Jack explained as he arose to go. "You need extra money to get that operation, you tell me."

"Sure thing," Wayne said. "Hope to hear from you real soon."

Jack nodded toward Barbara. "Mrs. Landry." He stepped off the porch, waded through the baying hounds, and was soon back on the road to Newton. He paid the back taxes and penalties on the property. He didn't find a real estate attorney in Newton, so drove on into Jasper, locating one there.

Jack explained to the attorney that he was paying all closing costs, title search, attorney fees, etc. The Landrys, he told him, were to pay nothing that wasn't required by law, and should something be required, the cost should be adjusted so that they were out nothing at closing. Jack asked that they use a title company that was fast and thorough and if possible convenient to the Landrys. He gave the attorney a $500 retainer.

An hour later, Jack parked the SUV near the bus stop at Bayou mobile home park. He was just in time to meet the bus. He knew Juliette would be on it because it was Yvette's day off. When Jack saw the bus stop and Juliette get off, he opened his door and stepped out. Juliette saw him and ran up to him. "Where have you been? I've missed you, Uncle Jack."

"I've missed you too," Jack said, hugging her to him. "Did you make me any drawings today?"

"No. I was sad today."

"Why were you sad today? Didn't your boyfriend talk to you or pull your ponytail?"

"Oh, Tommy was okay, but I was sad because you went away and didn't say good-bye."

Jack continued his hug, kissed her on her upturned nose, and released her to walk toward the trailer. He walked part way with her, holding her hand. Then as they neared the trailer, he said, "I don't think your mommy wants to see me, so I'd better say bye now. Maybe I'll see you when you get off the bus tomorrow."

"I ride the bus to the café tomorrow, Uncle Jack," she informed him with a sad face. "Don't forget!"

Jack watched her walk away, turn and wave to him, then enter the trailer. He felt like his world was crashing again. His heart ached. He couldn't have her without Yvette, and he knew he couldn't have Yvette. *I have millions of dollars*, Jack thought, *and I can't buy the only two things in this world that I want.* He kicked a pebble, sending it flying down the street, then marched to his SUV.

Back at his motel room in Jasper, Jack looked at himself in the mirror. "No wonder you can't get anywhere with the ladies," he said out loud. "Just look at yourself, Jack. The way you dress, those overgrown eyebrows—you could use a makeover. And remember if you'd just had a decent suit of clothes when Yvette wanted to go out to that ritzy place you wouldn't have disappointed her!" He dropped on the bed and put his head in his hands and breathed a big sigh.

Jack's dreams that night were filled with nightmares. He was in a house with many halls, right turns, and left turns but no doors. He couldn't find a way out or the way he had come in. He awoke sweaty and tired.

Jack showered and shaved. He checked his eyebrows and decided they would be okay the way they were. After a light breakfast, he drove to the Jasper Mall and found a men's clothier. Two hours later he left with two new suits, each of which had two pairs of matching trousers; four dress shirts; several ties; two new belts; six pair of men's hose; and two pair of dress shoes. One suit was a navy blue pinstripe and the other a brown tweed. One pair of shoes was black, the other brown. *Everything for the well-dressed loser*, Jack thought.

He put all his clothes into the SUV and returned to the mall. He found a store specializing in phones. "I need something that

I can use to call people and they can call me, no matter where on the planet I happen to be," Jack told the clerk.

"You need a satellite phone," he said.

"I'll need two phones with different numbers, unlimited calling, but only one billing address. No extras. I just want to be able to call people whenever I want and talk to them as long as I want." The clerk showed him a variety of phones in many colors. "The one that holds the charge the longest," Jack went on. "I'll need an adapter so I can charge one from my car. I'll take a silver one for me and a pink one for my friend."

Jack's next stop was the barber shop. "Make me as handsome as George Clooney," Jack ordered.

The barber chuckled, "I don't think you brought me enough raw material to work with. Even God only turned out one of them!"

"Just so I don't look as bad when I leave as I did when I came in," Jack replied.

Back at the motel some time later, Jack changed into one of his new suit-and-tie outfits. He stuck a bow on the top of the phone box and carried it with him as he left to go meet the school bus in Bon Weir. He wheeled in just a minute or two before the bus appeared. He got out of the SUV and walked toward the bus as Juliette got off. Even in his new duds she recognized him immediately and came running.

Jack picked her up in his arms, hugging her. She showed him a picture she was holding. She said she had drawn today because she wasn't sad. "I'm glad you weren't sad today, honey." Jack smiled. "I have something for you too," he informed her as he handed her the box.

Juliette quickly opened the box and took out the little phone. "Now you can call me just about anytime you need to talk to me," Jack told her. "Don't ever use it in school or anytime your mommy tells you not too. Otherwise, we will always be connected." Jack pulled out his phone. "See, I have one too. My number is already programmed into your phone so you won't forget it. I have your number in here so I won't ever forget yours either. May I keep this picture?"

"Yes. Let's go show Mommy my new phone!"

"I'm afraid I can't right now. I need to get back to my motel," Jack lied. "Here, give me another hug before I go."

Jack hugged her long and hard, kissed her on the cheek, and told her he would call her on her new phone later that night when he got back to his motel.

Jack was unaware of the fact that Yvette had seen him meet the bus and walk with Juliette toward the trailer on Monday. Juliette had asked her why she was mad at Uncle Jack, and she had assured her she wasn't. She had seen him again today, meeting Juliette's bus. She had watched Jack, in his new suit, give Juliette a gift and had been tempted to go out and invite him in. Arty had explained things to her differently than she had seen them. He had tried to make her see things through a man's eyes.

"I don't think you're mad at Jack for making a scene," she remembered Arty saying. "I think you're mad at Jack for interfering and protecting Juliette, when that's your job. I think your problem is you've been protecting her so long you're afraid someone, Jack maybe, might try to push you out of that position. I think you'd really like to tell Jack you were wrong, thank him for protecting Juliette from that horse's ass, and, that you'd like to have him back in your life. Now that's what I think, but I'm just the cook!"

Back in his motel room, Jack picked up the silver phone and pressed the button for his only previously entered number. It rang only once before he heard Juliette's musical voice: "Hello."

"Hi, honey, it's Uncle Jack. I told you I'd call you. You still at the café?"

"Yes, we still have a lot of customers." she said, sounding very adult.

"What did your mommy say about your new phone? Is she going to let you keep it?"

"She said she was jealous and wanted one too!"

"You tell her to get over hating me and I'll get her one."

"Okay. Mommy!" Juliette called.

"No, honey, not right now! Juliette can you hear me?"

She didn't answer. Jack, frustrated, looked at the phone then put it back to his ear, waiting to see if she would ever remember he was on the line.

"Just what kind of promises are you making to my daughter?" Yvette's musical voice flowed into his ear.

"Uh...hi, Yvette. So very nice to hear your voice. I haven't promised her much, really."

"You just can't leave us alone, can you, Jack?"

"I've tried, but you're right, Yvette, I can't. I realize I'm an embarrassment to you, but doggone it, Yvette, I love that little girl like she was my own and I'm willing to do just about anything, even to wearing a suit and tie, just so I can see her and be around her. What's it going to take, Yvette? Just name it."

"Jack Lockhart, if you make me cry, I'm going to be so mad at you."

"So what's new; you're always mad at me about something. What do I have to do to keep Juliette in my life? Yvette, I'm waiting!"

"Be at the trailer tonight when I get home. We'll talk then."

"I'll be there!"

Jack showered and shaved for the second time that day. He slapped on some aftershave and dressed in his other new suit. He combed his hair over and over again, getting it just right. He even combed his eyebrows. He made the fifty-eight miles to Bon Weir in just fifty minutes. With heart pounding, he parked in front of Yvette's trailer and waited for her to get home.

In just a very few minutes she arrived. Jack jumped out and rushed to help her carry Juliette into the house. Without saying a word he carried her into her bedroom, left Yvette to take care of her, and settled into a chair in the living room waiting nervously.

"Jack, I need to wash up," Yvette called softly from the hall. "Make us some coffee, please." She disappeared into the bathroom.

Jack put some coffee on, got out some cups, put creamer and sugar in her cup just the way she liked it, and waited for the coffee to finish running through the grounds.

She had removed her makeup, taken her hair down, and changed into a robe. Jack, on the other hand, was dressed for church. She took a seat on the couch, drawing her legs up under her like he had seen her do before. He poured their coffee, put a small teaspoon on her saucer next to her cup, and carried the cups into the living room. After handing Yvette her coffee, Jack sat down and they looked at each other. She was just as beautiful as ever. "You know you don't really need makeup. You have what is called natural beauty."

"Thank you for that." She breathed a big sigh. "I'm tired, Jack."

"What can I do to help?"

"Just don't judge me, that's all."

"Judge you? Why would I do that?"

"I don't know. I'm just feeling guilty about something."

"What have you to feel guilty about, Yvette?"

She sighed again and started. "You've made me feel like I'm cheating Juliette by not giving her a father. And I've tried, Jack—I've really tried. I've dated some of the worst scum buckets you'll ever see, hoping to find someone to love her like her father should have. They only want one thing, Jack—to get me into bed. None of them ever gave a whit about Juliette. Now you come along and you say you really care about her, but at the same time you're giving me a full-court press. I can't decide if you really care for her, if you really care for me, or if you're just a better class of scum bucket."

"A scum bucket who loves her," Jack interjected. "I wish for all the world that I could have both of you in my life."

"If I could only believe you have no other motive than the fact you truly care for Juliette, I could, I would, want you back in my life."

Jack stepped across the room and knelt in front of Yvette. He looked into her eyes as he took her hands. "Look at me, Yvette," he said. "I love Juliette. Do I need to say it again? I love that little girl with all my heart!"

Yvette looked into Jack's imploring eyes. "I believe you!" she said finally. "But where does that leave us, you and me?"

"Do you think you could ever love an old scum bucket like me?"

"You're not like them, Jack!" Tears filled her eyes.

Jack stood and taking both of her hands, gently pulled her to a standing position. He turned her face up so he could kiss the tears from her eyes, then her cheeks, then tenderly brushed his lips across her mouth. "Let me love you, Yvette," he begged in a whisper. "Just let me love both of you!"

Yvette put her arms around him, laying her head against his chest. Jack held her to him tenderly for a long time. Then slowly he lowered her to the couch and sat beside her. "If you ever break her heart…if you ever break my heart, I'll never forgive you," Yvette threatened.

"I'd rather die than hurt either of you," Jack whispered, as he cradled her in his arms. "I love you, Yvette."

EIGHT

J ack held the door for Barbara Landry as she climbed into his
SUV. Wayne had climbed into the front passenger seat. They
were on their way to Jasper for the closing on the property on
Church House Creek.

"Heard any more from your doctor about your operation?"
Jack asked Wayne.

"His best estimate, hospital and everything was about fifty-
seven hundred, but you never know," Wayne answered. "This will
give us a start."

They spent the remainder of the trip on small talk. As Jack
wheeled into a parking space at the attorney's office he joked, "I
think the way this works is, the buyer goes in first, gets fleeced,
then the seller and the lawyer split the fleecings."

They all disembarked and ambled into the office spaces.

"Mr. Novak will see you shortly," the pretty little redhead at
the reception desk told them. "Can I get you something to drink
while you're waiting?"

"I could use a bathroom," Barbara said softly.

"Right down that hall, first door to the left."

"Mr. Lockhart," Attorney Novak said, as he entered the
waiting area, "come on back."

They went over the paperwork line by line. Jack was very
pleased to see that the Landrys would not be required to pay
anything. He paid the remaining fees, shook hands with Mr.
Novak, took the deed and closing papers, and left, telling the
Landrys he would wait for them outside.

At the SUV, Jack retrieved another bundle of cash from the
cooler. He counted out sixty bills and put them in an envelope,

sealed it, and wrote across the front of it: "To: Wayne and Barbara Landry." When he saw the Landrys coming out of the building he went to meet them.

"You all want to get some lunch before we head back?" Jack asked them.

They agreed they did. During a pleasant meal and friendly conversation, Jack saw an opportunity to slip the envelope into Barbara's purse. Later, when they were only a few miles from their home, Barbara suddenly asked, "What's this?" She had discovered the envelope.

Jack pretended ignorance.

Barbara and Wayne both took turns looking at the envelope before she tore it open. "Wayne," she said, "look at this!" She handed him the envelope. "There must be a million dollars in there!"

"It's only six thousand," Jack confessed, "enough for that hernia operation I hope. After it's over and you're feeling better, you all have to come visit me at the cabin for a day of fishing and relaxation. I'm planning to fix it up a bit."

Wayne sat in silence for the last few miles staring at the envelope and then at Jack. As they pulled into the Landry's yard, Wayne reached over and slapped Jack on the shoulder. "I don't know what to say!"

"Don't worry about it," Jack told him. "Just get better!"

Back at his motel, Jack asked for the Houston area phone book. He made a short list of home construction companies. After a few calls he was able to locate a builder who could meet him at the café in Bon Weir at 10:00 a.m. the next day.

Pleased with himself for the accomplishments of the day, Jack placed a call to Yvette's new purple satellite phone. "Hello, darling," he said when he heard Yvette's musical voice on the other end of the line.

"Hi," she said. "What have you been doing all day?"

"Missing you!"

"Are you going to be here in time to pick Juliette up and take her home?"

"I won't be able to get there until around four, but I'll take her with me as soon as I get there so she doesn't have to be stuck in the café until you get off tonight. I'll see you in a little while. I love you!"

"Love you too!"

As always these last few days, Jack cleaned up and shaved just before seeing Yvette, even if just for a few minutes. He got to the café just after four. Juliette met him at the door, all bubbly and smiles. She had been so happy the past few days since Jack and Yvette had patched up their differences. Jack picked her up and carried her to his usual table. "Let me talk to your mommy a few minutes, and then we'll go to the park for a little while before I take you home."

Yvette finally got a moment to come over to their table. "Can I get you something?"

"When are you going to tell Arty to get someone else, quit this waitress business, and let me take care of you?"

"Arty wouldn't last a week without me," she teased. "And I've told you before, Jack, I don't need you to take care of me!"

"Well, then come take care of me! You know how needy I am! We're going to the park for a while and then to the trailer. Did Arty fix anything for us to take home for supper?"

"Yes, if you're leaving now I'll go get it." Then, as Jack reached for his wallet, she said, "I've already paid for it."

"What is it?"

"Arty said it was a surprise."

"Oh great, deep-fried scorpion claws probably!" Jack complained.

"I heard that!" Arty called from the kitchen.

"Get your ear away from that knot hole and get back to work, you old coot! You got paying customers out here!" It was obvious to all who knew them that Jack and Arty were actually very fond of each other. The constant bickering was just their subtle way of saying it.

As Yvette set the dinner box in front of Jack, he took her hand and kissed it tenderly. "I love you," he whispered.

Yvette rewarded him with her smile.

Jack stood, and taking the box in one hand and Juliette's hand in the other, they walked toward the door. "Bye, Mommy," Juliette called from the door.

In the park, Juliette and Jack were swinging on the swings, Juliette talking away. "All of the other kids in my class have a mommy and a daddy. I have a mommy and an Uncle Jack. It sounds strange, don't you think?"

"Umm, I don't know. Are you sure you're the only one in your class that doesn't have a daddy?"

"Juan Reyna and Leticia McCutchen don't have real daddies but they have foster daddies. I don't know what that means."

"It means they have a borrowed daddy to love them and protect them."

"Where do you get a borrowed daddy?"

"I think the state provides them. Would you rather have a daddy to love you or an Uncle Jack?"

"I just think sometimes it would be nice if I had a daddy who lived with me and Mommy and would love me and not ever go away."

"Well, until he comes along I'm here to love you and your mommy. Would you like to call me daddy?"

"I think that it would sound funny, Uncle Jack."

They stepped away from the swings and started walking toward the SUV and home. Jack put his arm around her tiny shoulders and said, "I wish I was your daddy. Still, no one will ever love you anymore than I do."

At the trailer Juliette opened their supper box, removed the contents, and heated it in the microwave. She set the table for the two of them while it was heating. Jack sat at the bar and watched.

She seemed so grown up, yet so small. *At only eight she's as self-reliable as her mother,* Jack thought, *and every bit as much of a doll.* His joy at having her back in his life was indescribable.

After supper, Jack did the clean up while Juliette took her bath and got into her night clothes. Then they sat on the couch together and finished her schoolwork. At 8:00 p.m. on the dot Juliette kissed him good night and went to her room. She was allowed to read for fifteen minutes and then, "Lights out," Jack insisted.

Shortly after 10:00 p.m. Yvette came in, tired as usual from here twelve-hour shift. "Juli in bed?" she asked Jack.

"Great to see you too," Jack responded. "Yes, she's been in bed since eight."

"Sorry, Jack, I'm just so tired these days. I think I'm coming down with something."

No! Jack thought. *That's exactly what Rachel said, just before they discovered her inoperable cancer!* "You're not doing that to me again, God," he swore under his breath.

"What other symptoms—other than being tired—do you have?" he asked, trying to show concern while hiding his fear. He placed a hand softly on her shoulder.

"I'm just bone tired, Jack!"

Jack led her to the couch, knelt down and removed her shoes, and began to rub her feet and the calves of her legs.

"Oh, that feels good."

Jack continued to rub her feet and massage her legs for several minutes while Yvette sat with her head laid back, resting on the couch back with her eyes closed and tried to relax. "Now go get undressed and put a robe on, and I'll draw you a nice warm bath. I'll have some hot tea ready for you when you get out."

"You're too good to me Jack," Yvette purred. She disappeared into the bedroom.

Jack fixed her a warm bath with scented bath salts. While she was soaking the long hard day out of her muscles, Jack started the tea then went to her room and picked up her uniform. He removed her nametag from her blouse and placed it on her dresser. He checked the pockets of the short uniform skirt and put the contents next to her nametag. He carried her clothes to the laundry room and started the washing machine. He put her clothes in the machine and checking the hamper added the few clothes that it contained. He took some of Juliette's clothes from her room to round out the load. After he started the washer he called Arty at home.

Arty lived in the back of the restaurant in a very nice, roomy four-room apartment. "This is Jack, Arty. Listen, I have a big favor to ask."

"Sure, Jack, what's wrong?"

"Yvette came home just bone tired tonight. I think she could use some time off. At least a few days if not weeks. Do you think you can find a replacement?"

"I noticed she seemed a little draggy the past couple of days. You ain't done gone and got that girl pregnant have you, Jack?"

"Of course not!"

"Well, I can get my sister to help out for a couple of days, but if it's for very long, I may have to look to replace her."

"Thanks, Arty. I'll owe you one!"

"Think nothing of it!"

Jack looked up to see Yvette in her robe, with a towel wrapped around her head. "Feel any better?" he asked, smiling.

"Much," she said.

"I want you to see a doctor tomorrow," Jack stated authoritatively. "I've already called Arty, and he agreed to let you take some time off."

"Okay, Daddy," she mocked him, mimicking a small girl's voice. She sat on the arm of his chair and mussed his hair.

Jack pulled her down on his lap and kissed her. "I thought you didn't need me to take care of you," Jack teased. Then, in a more serious tone, he said, "I have an appointment at ten in the morning, but I can cancel that and go to the doctor with you."

"Jack, I can't even call for an appointment with a doctor until tomorrow morning, and then it may be days before they can see me. Anyway, I feel a lot better since the bath and foot rub."

"Let me feel," Jack said, poking at her ribs. "I don't think you could ever feel any better to me."

"Stop, Jack." She giggled. "Was that the washing machine?"

"I'm washing a few of my unmentionables," Jack said, using falsetto.

Yvette, totally relaxed from her bath and not having to plan for work the next day, was suddenly in a very playful mood. As tired as she had been just a short time ago, she realized that Jack always made her feel more alive and happy. He was almost always ready to revert back to the child in him. She found it impossible to accept the more than seventeen-year difference in their ages.

"Aren't you supposed to have your unmentionables on right now?"

"Can't mention them."

They laughed and giggled until she thought they might wake Juliette. Finally Jack grew quiet and Yvette looking at his face saw that he had turned serious again. "What is it now, Jack?"

"I'm just afraid I'm too happy. Throughout my life, every time I felt truly blessed and happy, along came something to take it all away."

"Oh, you are such an old pessimist! Be quiet and kiss me!"

"That I can do!"

Jack and Yvette engaged in several minutes of tender and sometimes passionate kissing. He was sitting in the big recliner, and she was curled up on his lap. "We have to stop now," she told him, "before this goes any farther."

They sat like that for a long time, wrapped in each other's arms, Yvette's head on his chest, her hands resting on one of his big hands as it rested on her knees. Finally, Jack broke the mood by saying, "I have to go put your unmentionables in the dryer." Jack lifted her from his lap and put her on the couch.

When Jack returned from the laundry room he told her that her uniform was in the dryer and she would probably need to take it out as soon as the dryer quit so she wouldn't have to iron everything.

"Thanks, Jack. I've only been doing laundry for about fifteen years now."

"It's late, hon. I better be going back to Jasper. I'll call you in the morning to see how you're feeling." Jack bent down and kissed her softly on the cheek. "I'm crazy 'bout ya, baby." Jack turned and pranced out the door.

Jack was up early and knew Yvette would be too since she had to get Juliette off to school. He called her and waited impatiently to hear her voice.

"Hi, Jack. I knew you'd call."

"How are you this morning?"

"I feel fine, Jack. All I needed was a good night's rest."

"You call that doctor this morning, do you hear me? I'm not letting you go back to work until I see a clean bill of health. And maybe not then."

"Okay, I'll call. Gosh, Jack, you sound just like my mother."

"Oh? She has a low-voiced, West Texas drawl? I'll be there in an hour or so. Give Juliette a hug and kiss for me."

Jack dressed and headed for Bon Weir. He stopped at the trailer to be with Yvette for an hour or so before he had to meet the contractor at Arty's Café.

Yvette was in a very amorous mood. As she let Jack in through the doorway, she grabbed him around the neck and kissed him passionately. He enjoyed the moment immensely.

"This does not get you off the hook. You still have to see the doctor."

"All right." She smiled. "But you can't blame a girl for trying." She noticed his Levi's and boots and asked, "Where are you going dressed like that? I thought you had an appointment this morning."

"I'm working on another project that will let me use some more of the found money."

"I'd like to be in on one of your projects. When are you going to tell me more about them and let me help you with one?"

"If you're still at home when I get back from this appointment I'll tell you about all of my other projects up until now. That doesn't include my current one. It's still in the planning stage."

As the hour neared ten, Jack kissed her good-bye and headed toward the café.

The sign on the door of the new extended cab, Ford F-150 pick-up, read KB Construction. The weathered young man, about thirty-five years old, who stepped out to shake Jack's hand, said his name was Kasey Snowden. Jack explained that the job he wanted him to look at was about fifteen miles southwest of where they were standing. They decided that Jack would ride along with Kasey and point the way. About twenty-five minutes later they stopped within sight of the cabin.

"I don't think you'll need any tools other than a fifty-foot tape, a notebook, and pencil," Jack told Kasey.

Jack told him he wanted the cabin restored, as closely as possible, to its original condition. Kasey examined the foundation, the floors, the walls, the partitions, the inside bearing walls, the ceiling, and ceiling joists. He noted the condition of the doors and windows and the old fireplace. They had to go back to the truck for a ladder so he could examine the roof and shingles.

Kasey pushed his cap back on his head, squinted his eyes, then finally spoke. "Probably be a hell of a lot cheaper to just tear it down and build a new one that looks just like the old one. Well, yes, I know it would be cheaper. There's a septic tank here somewhere for that old toilet, but I'll bet it's filled in. We'd need to put in another one. About the only thing that looks like it's stood the test of time is the foundation. They knew they were building on sandy soil, so they went down and found rock."

"Exactly how close can you come to the original using modern materials?" Jack wanted to know.

"You probably won't know the difference. The people who first built it, they would."

"How soon could you start, and how long do you estimate it will take to complete?"

"I can probably start it first week of April. If I can get all the materials and the weather cooperates, two months, maybe ten weeks start to finish. When we leave the job site there won't be a scrap of the old cabin left. We'll haul it all off. I'll magnetically sweep the yard area so we don't leave any nails or metal parts to accidentally hurt someone."

"What about water at the sink and for flushing?"

"I can put in a two hundred-gallon refillable storage tank in the attic above the bathroom and kitchen sink area. It would have to be refilled every so often. If you had electricity out here I could put you in an electric pump and you could use river water. You don't want to go much larger than two hundred gallons because the extra bracing that would be required would take up too much living space. Two hundred gallons weighs more than three quarters of a ton."

"Can you put in sky lighting without taking anything away from the original?"

"Sure can. I was going to suggest that. Let me get my camera and get some shots that I can use when drawing up my plans."

As they drove back to the café and Jack's SUV, Kasey was full of excited ideas. "I've never had anything exactly like this before. I'm anxious to get started so I can show you just what I can do."

"Let me buy you a cup before you head out," Jack offered. "It's a long way back to Houston."

"Sure. Actually, I live north of Houston in the little town of Vidor. It's closer to Beaumont than Houston. I do a lot of work in both Houston and Beaumont."

They had coffee and talked more about what type of furnishings and other possibilities of modern living for primitive locations. Jack gave Kasey his number and took Kasey's card so they could contact one another. Kasey told him he would call him later that day with a ballpark figure and call him the next day with a firm cost if he agreed to the estimate. They shook hands, and Jack watched Kasey drive away.

It wasn't noon yet when Jack got back to the trailer. Yvette was dressed in a cute skirt and blouse and appeared to be ready to go somewhere.

"I have an appointment with a doctor at one this afternoon. I hope you're satisfied."

Jack kissed her hello. "I will be, when he tells me you're okay. Which doctor are you seeing?"

"It's the one in Newton. He's a general practitioner. I take Juliette to him."

"I'll drive you. We can take your car if you'd rather."

"For goodness' sake, Jack, I can drive myself."

"Well, I'm going with you one way or another. Maybe I'll keep your mind off of things by telling you about some of my more recent projects."

The trip to Newton took only twenty minutes, but Jack was able to relate the episode about Homer and Gabriella, the Lloyds, and the others, omitting the Landrys.

"Really, Jack, you filled a woman's gasoline tank? Wow, you're a regular modern-day Jesse James!" Yvette teased.

Dr. Rothstein was a kind, older gentleman, only a few years shy of Social Security. He was considered one of the best diagnosticians in the whole southwest. Jack followed close behind Yvette as she was ushered into the examining room. After hearing Yvette's symptoms, Dr. Rothstein asked her a number of questions. He listened to her heart and lungs, felt her neck to check her thyroid, and performed other medical checks that Jack didn't understand.

"From what you tell me," he said slowly and deliberately, after his examination, "the heavy menstrual periods and your work schedule, I suspect a condition called menorrhagia. This sometimes causes one to develop iron-deficient anemia. I'm going to send you to the lab for some blood work. I should have the results in a few days. My office will contact you after I have gone over the results of the tests. In the meanwhile, I want you to take some time off and rest."

The lab work confirmed Dr. Rothstein's suspicions. He prescribed a tablet containing a mixture of hormones that would reduce the blood loss, iron tablets to replenish the iron in her blood, a reasonable diet with iron-rich foods, and once again stressed to her that she get plenty of rest.

Jack was relieved it was nothing more serious. As soon as the iron was replenished and as long as she stayed on a reasonable diet and reduced the time she spent on her feet, she could soon stop the medications and be absolutely healthy and normal.

Yvette was steadfast in her belief that she needed to continue to work the same number of hours as before. "Because," she insisted to Jack, "Arty needs me! And I need to pay my bills!"

I can fix both of those problems, Jack thought. *Man, she's a stubborn woman!*

Jack began to devise a plan to erase as many of Yvette's burdens as possible. *First,* he thought, *I'll get her hours reduced without diminishing her take-home pay. Then I'll figure a way to get her take home pay increased. The problem of Juliette needing a father, Yvette will have to take care of herself.*

NINE

It was Monday April 11, a beautiful East Texas day. Jack had decided to drive down to check on the progress of the cabin that he hoped to surprise Yvette with very soon. Just two days after she began the medications Yvette had felt so good that she returned to work at the café. Jack was displeased, but he had little or no persuasive power when it came to the strong-willed Yvette.

Monday meant a day off for Yvette and Jack stopped at her trailer before continuing on to the construction site. She greeted him with her warm, cheery smile and a kiss. "Oh, you're wearing the Levi's and boots again. Where are you off to today?"

"Oh, just checking on a few things. Juliette okay?"

"She has a jaw tooth that's about to come out. It's been bothering her. I checked it, and it isn't ready to come out just yet. The way she's been worrying it with her tongue, it won't be long."

"These trips back and forth to Jasper every day and every night are worrying me. When are you going to let me move back in here with you and Juliette?"

Yvette held up her left hand, wiggled her ring finger, and raised her brows as if to say, "You know when."

Jack knew she was teasing. Although he would love to ask her to marry him, he was all too certain she would have an excuse to say no.

"Okay if I stop by later after Juliette gets home?"

"Sure. Plan on staying for supper. I'll fix us all something from my diet plan."

"Can't be too bad for me. Look what's it's done for you! You aren't only beautiful, but now you have a very healthy glow! Hey, do you think it will make me handsome?"

"It's not magic beans, Jack." She gave him her dimpled smile that he loved so much.

"See you around five." He tugged on her hand and pulled her close so he could embrace and kiss her. After the kiss she tried to wriggle away, but he held her, kissed her on the bridge of her nose, whispered, "I love you," and released her.

Before Jack continued to the construction site he wheeled in beside the café and knocked on the door of Arty's apartment.

"Come in," Arty growled. "Door's open."

They said their usual insulting greetings before Jack got serious and to the point.

"I've got a proposition for you, Arty. How would you like to have me as a partner in the café?"

"Never thought about it. I'm doin' okay, no need to complicate things."

"Hear me out now before you say no, old timer. What if I could come up with enough money to give this old place a face lift, hire a couple of new waitresses, maybe keep it open on Mondays too?"

"I'd have to hire another cook. I'm already spending nearly eighty hours a week here."

"Okay, we'll hire another cook, maybe two more cooks if you need them. Plus busboys and as many waitresses as are required so that no one works more than forty hours in a week unless they want to."

"You're worried about that little girl of yours aren't ya? Well, I don't blame ya. Where ya goin' to get all this money, Jack?"

"Don't worry about that. Just think about my offer. If you got your hours down to, say, forty or fifty hours a week, maybe you and me could go fishing."

"I do like the sound of that. You know I'd probably need a manager if I had a staff like you're talking about. That sounds like a lot of bother."

"You should start taking it a little bit easier too, Arty. What are you now, eighty-five, ninety?"

"I'm sixty-one, wise ass."

"Well, give it some thought. I'll drop in on you again this afternoon. By the way, who manages this place now?"

Jack left, driving to the site of the cabin, hoping Arty would think positively about his offer. As he came upon the site he saw that the old cabin had been torn down and carted away, the land had been leveled, a new septic tank had been installed and covered, sewer pipe and other under ground plumbing had been completed, foundation and floors for both the house and pump house had been poured, an electric pole with a meter had been installed, and workers were working on the framing. The old fireplace had been torn down, and all of the stones had been cleaned and saved and were piled neatly waiting for the construction of the new fireplace and chimney.

"You're moving right along," Jack said to Kasey as he came to meet him.

"We're ahead of where I thought we'd be," Kasey bragged. "If this weather holds, and we can get the roof on this week, we can finish up before the end of May."

"If you could have the cabin ready to live in by that time I'd be very pleased."

"This is my brother, Brian. He's the B in KB construction. Brian does the electrical installation, plumbing and sheet metal. I'm more concrete, masonry, and carpentry. Finishing and painting we both can do."

"Pleased to meet you." Jack smiled at Brian. Then to Kasey he said, "I've been thinking I need you to add to what we've already agreed to—a stone pathway from the cabin through the pines, down to the river. Have it terminate at a boathouse and fishing dock combination. Can you get me a figure as to how much more that will cost me?"

"Sure. In the meanwhile, I'm going to need another ten thousand dollar draw today," Kasey informed Jack. "My supplier has the doors and windows in, and I need to pay him so I can pick them up. Also, as you can see, I've got payroll to take care of. Would you like to look at the paneling samples I brought? They stopped making the patterns that were in the old cabin about twenty years ago."

"Can I take them with me and look at 'em tonight?"

"Sure, take your time. I probably won't have to order the paneling before the end of the month anyway."

"I'll have them back to you in just a couple of days. Let me get that money for you."

Kasey went back to his supervising and framing while Jack went to the SUV and fished out a packet of $100 bills. He walked back to where Kasey was busy nailing a window header into the wall they were framing. "Here you go." Jack smiled as he handed him the cash. "Just keep track of all these draws."

Jack stayed over an hour watching the framing continue. Brian came to get a drink of water from the large water cooler in the shade of his pickup. "I've never been afraid of work," Jack bragged with a big grin. "Just look how close I'm standing to this!" Then after a short pause he said, "I'll check back with you tomorrow. I've got another project in the works. May even have a job in it for you and Kasey."

Jack drove back to Arty's and banged on the door. "What the hell do you want now?"

"To pester you some more."

"Ain't ya done enough of that already today?" Arty asked, opening the screen to let Jack in. "I was just about to eat my lunch. You want to join me? I got plenty."

Jack fixed a plate of the fish, country fries, and coleslaw and sat down opposite Arty at the small table. "Well? Are we partners?"

"The last thing you asked me before you left while ago was who manages my place. I hollered after you that I did, but then I got to thinking on it and it came to me that it's Yvette who manages most of it. I'm mainly just her cook. I order what she says we need, I pay the bills, and I cook.

"You know," he went on, "when Yvette first came to me askin' for a job, she was just this pretty little nineteen or twenty-year-old girl carrying a baby on her hip. I tried to say no, but she just started doin' things around here, cleanin' tables and asking people what they needed just so she could get some milk for her little girl. I used to keep Juliette in a swing back in the kitchen so Yvette could tend to her when she got a chance. I think over the years I just got so used to her bossing me around that I didn't realize I ain't the boss anymore."

"What about the partnership? Thought any more about that?"

"It sounds good, the part about me working less hours anyway. Can you write me out a plan, Jack, something that ain't too confusing. You know, kinda like a recipe."

"I'll try," Jack promised as he left his friend's apartment. "I'll bring you that recipe as soon as I can write it up."

Jack called Yvette to see if it was okay for him to come by earlier than he had first planned. He didn't want to be in her way if she was involved in house cleaning or preparing the promised supper. Yvette invited him to come on by the trailer.

"What is that in your hand?" she asked him as he entered.

"Just some paneling samples," Jack replied, holding up the bundle. "I've been talking to Arty about remodeling the café," he continued, as if the samples were for the café.

"Let me see!" Yvette begged as she took the samples from Jack's hand. "If I ever have a stationary house—you know, one without wheels—I'd love to have this in my living room."

"Which one?" Jack asked as he sat down beside her on the couch.

"This one. Umm, no, I think I like this one better. No, that's more for a den or a dining room. This is definitely the living room."

"What about this one?"

"Master bedroom or maybe a guest room."

"And Juliette's room in this dream house of yours, which one for her?"

"You're making fun of me!"

"No, I'm not. Which one for Juliette?"

"This one or this one. I'm trying to imagine how old she'll be."

"It makes a difference?"

"Of course!"

"Okay, which one for my room?" Jack asked with a grin.

"I'm not picturing you in my dream house." Yvette grinned back at him. She got up and started toward the kitchen. "Juliette will be home soon. Do you plan to meet her bus?"

"Yes, I'll just put these samples in the car for tonight. I don't want to forget them." Jack carried the panel samples out the door. At the SUV he made notes on all of her choices before putting them away and walking to the bus stop.

For several days now, Jack had either been meeting Juliette at the school bus stop near her home or meeting her at the café after she got off of the school bus there. On the days Yvette was working, Jack would take Juliette to the trailer, where they would have supper, he would help her finish her homework, and see that she bathed and got to bed by 8:00 p.m. On Mondays he tried to spend as much time with Yvette as possible, but this was her only day off and she spent much of the day doing house keeping chores and laundry.

This day, as usual, Juliette was happy to see Jack and ran from the bus to meet him. They walked hand in hand to the trailer. They entered the trailer, and Juliette and Yvette started their usual mother/daughter tête-à-tête. Jack watched and smiled. Their fondness for each other was obvious. It was almost as if they were best friends, yet Juliette's respect for her mother was just as obvious. Soon after supper, Jack kissed them both good night and returned to his motel. He needed to put his ideas for the café on paper.

The next day was Tuesday, and Arty would be too busy to look over Jack's recipe for their partnership. Jack drove out to the site where the cabin was being rebuilt and invited Kasey and Brian to have lunch with him at Arty's. Jack remained at the site until noon, pleased with the progress. When they broke for lunch they all piled into Jack's SUV for the drive back to Bon Weir.

The café was crowded, but they found a booth that had just become available. Yvette soon approached, giving them all her charming dimpled smile. As usual, Jack took her hand and kissed it whispering, "I love you."

"Who are your friends?" she asked Jack.

Jack introduced them to Yvette. She took their order and hurried off. Jack watched the Snowden brothers as they watched Yvette walk away and said, "This is confidential, but that's the pretty woman you're building the cabin for. Now, are you still certain you're up to the task?" he joked.

"Sure," Kasey said confidently.

"I'll give it my best!" Brian promised, grinning. "That your woman, Jack?"

"Well, I want her to be!" Jack said, "and I'm working hard to make it a reality."

"I wish you the best," Kasey said, "but truthfully man, you don't stand a chance."

"Stranger things have happened," Jack replied. He then went on as if he and Arty had already made an agreement. "Look around this place. The present owner and I have plans to remodel and expand this place. We'd like to seat about three times this many people. We'd like to enlarge and remodel the kitchen, redo the bathrooms, put changing tables in both, etc. There's an apartment behind the café that we would like to extend to include office space and a large comfortable break room. The open field just to the south, between here and the Exxon station, belongs to the café and we want to put in a paved parking area there. Behind that we'd like to put in a play yard. You know a jungle gym-type thing."

As Jack was talking, Yvette came back with their food and drinks. Jack, in his excitement of explaining his latest project, only acknowledged her by patting her hand as she sat his meal in front of him. "Now I'm invisible," she said to Brian as she served him.

"I see you," Jack said, losing his train of thought. "Forgive me for not swooning every time."

Yvette mussed his hair and left.

"This place will be closed next Monday if you'd like to look at it and see what you think. My partner," Jack said assumingly, "will also be available then. He's the one who cooked your lunch today."

"We have an uncle who is an architect in Houston. Maybe I can get him to come up with us on Monday and sketch some designs, get some measurements, and come up with a workable plan for you," Kasey volunteered.

"That would be great," Jack said.

"We should get back to work now," Brian said as he raised himself from the booth.

"I got this," Jack said, placing a large bill under the edge of his plate.

As the three started toward the door, Yvette suddenly appeared. "You all come back real soon!"

Jack dropped the Snowden brothers at the cabin site. He went over his panel selections with Kasey. They decided they would get the crew started Monday morning then meet Jack and Arty at the café around 9:00 a.m.

Arty was pleased with Jack's recipe, which allowed for him to work many less hours. They both agreed Yvette would be the manager, have her own office, and set her own working hours. She would be free to wait tables if she liked. Arty also approved all of the changes to the existing café that Jack and the architect had made. The boys from KB Construction had told them that they could start renovations in late May and the café could remain open for business all but about two weeks in midsummer. After Arty and Jack completed having the partnership papers drawn up, signed, and notarized, Jack informed Yvette about his latest project.

To his surprise, Yvette was excited about the possibility of becoming a manager. She suddenly had a raft of ideas of her own. As she excitedly made each declaration of how she planned to do this or that, Jack would always say, "Which you can accomplish in less than eight hours that day!"

Things were beginning to look good from where Jack sat. He had managed to put in place a plan that would both cut Yvette's hours and pay her a living wage.

TEN

O n Friday, May 20, the week before school let out, Juliette
   told Jack that her school was having an open house and she
wanted him to come to see all of her work that was on display.

Jack dressed in a suit and picked Yvette and Juliette up early
in the evening. Yvette was able to leave work early when Arty got
his sister to work for her. The open house was to last from 6:00
to 8:00 p. m. Jack, who hated to be late, hurried them along and
they were parking in front of the school a few minutes before six.
As they entered the school, Juliette led the way, pulling on Jack's
hand to hurry him. Yvette's heels beat out a fast rhythm of click,
click, click on the terrazzo floor as she tried to keep up. Juliette's
teacher, Mrs. Dela Cruz, ushered them into the classroom and
took them to the area where Juliette's schoolwork was on display.

She had nothing but praise for Juliette and her work, saying,
"Juliette shows a real talent in the area of art! Her perspective,
lines, use of shadow and light, and color selections are way above
her grade level. You should be very proud!"

As Yvette and Mrs. Dela Cruz were discussing Juliette's
progress, Juliette and Jack were slowly walking around the room
looking at other students work.

"That's Tommy's," Juliette informed him. "And that Seth's,
and that's Robert's, and that's Stephanie's and that's…Grandpa!"
she cried. She dropped Jack's hand and darted toward a well-
dressed man just coming in through the door.

He wasn't that much older than Jack, maybe fifty, a handsome
gentleman with wavy salt-and-pepper hair and a thin mustache.
He was accompanied by a very pretty woman who appeared to be

a few years younger and who was also exceptionally well dressed. Jack watched as Juliette hugged and kissed each of them happily.

Yvette, hearing Juliette shout out to her grandfather, excused herself to Mrs. Dela Cruz and walked over to the two and embraced them. "What are you doing here?" she asked.

"I heard there was going to be an open house where my granddaughter's work was on display and lot's of refreshments!" Yvette's father replied.

"I want you to meet someone," Yvette told her parents as she led them toward Jack.

Jack went to meet them, smiling.

"These are my parents," Yvette told him. "This is my mother and my father. Mom and Dad, this is my friend Jack."

"Jack Lockhart, very glad to meet you," Jack said as he pumped Yvette's father's hand.

"Maurice DuBoise. This is my wife, Colette."

"Happy to meet you, Mrs. DuBoise. It's obvious where Yvette and Juliette get their beauty! Juliette's artwork is just over here."

Yvette was walking beside her mother, with Juliette just in front and Jack and Maurice bringing up the rear. As they returned to the area where Juliette's artwork was displayed, Jack hung back, allowing this to be a family affair.

Later at the trailer Colette voiced her suspicions of someone of Jack's age being interested in Yvette. She also noticed the close relationship between Jack and Juliette. When Colette and Yvette were alone in the bedroom, where Yvette was making up a bed for her parents, Colette confronted Yvette. "Are you sleeping with that man? That kind of behavior got you into trouble once before, you know!"

"Not that it's any of your business," Yvette replied, "but no! I am not sleeping with Jack. We are just good friends."

"Maybe that's the way you see it, but I saw the way he looks at you, the way he treats you and hovers over you. He acts like Juliette is his own daughter!"

"And that's a bad thing? I'm glad Juliette has a father figure in her life after the way her own father ran out on us! And yes, Mom, I'm very fond of Jack too. Please, can we just drop it for now?"

Jack told Yvette's parents once again how pleased he was to have met them. He then announced it was time for him to go. As he picked up Juliette and kissed her good-bye he heard Maurice say, "We used to own a cabin near here. Maybe we should drive out there tomorrow morning before we head back to Galveston and see if it's still there. Would you like to go with us, Jack? Yvette, honey, can you get off long enough to ride out there with us? We could take some picnic stuff and make it a family outing!"

This was not how Jack had planned to tell Yvette about the cabin. He had planned a much more romantic way of giving it to her. "Sure, I'd love to go with you," he said. "What time should I be here in the morning?"

They made plans for an early start, Maurice suggesting maybe they could also do some fishing.

Jack took Yvette's hand, pulled her close, and kissed her softly on the cheek. "Count me in," he called to Maurice as he stepped out of the trailer door.

Although the cabin itself was completely finished, the stone masons were still laying the stone for the winding walkway to the boat house and pier, which was also still under construction.

Just after nine Saturday morning they were all seated in Jack's eight-passenger SUV, headed south along the river road toward the cabin on Church House Creek.

Yvette had talked Jack into letting her drive. "You probably don't remember where it is," she told him. "You've only seen it that once."

Colette was seated in the front passenger seat. Juliette sat between her grandfather and Jack in the middle row of seats.

"I have to be at work before the lunch rush starts," Yvette called over her shoulder to her Father. "You all can stay longer if you like. Jack can take me back, can't you, Jack?"

"Sure," Jack promised.

In a few minutes they drove up in front of the cabin. Yvette parked on the new drive. The cabin and surrounding yard were in pristine condition.

"You sure this is it?" Maurice asked.

Jack climbed out, helped Juliette out, then opened the car door and helped Yvette out. Maurice was doing the same for Colette. Jack took Yvette's hand and led her up the path to the door of the cabin. He reached into his pocket, pulled out the keys, and handed them to Yvette. "Try this," he said.

Yvette looked puzzled but did as Jack said. She turned the key in the lock and opened the door. "How did you get the keys? Do you know the owners?"

"Yes, I know her very well," Jack told her. "I'm looking at her right now! Okay, this isn't how I planned to do this, honey. I had planned something more romantic. Everybody come on inside."

Yvette entered the cabin and began to walk through the rooms, observing in stunned silence. As they returned to the living area of the cabin she suddenly blurted out, "This is the paneling you showed me! And this...how long have you been working on this, Jack?"

"Not long. Just since you told me you loved it and loved spending time here as a child. I'm sorry it isn't finished. They still have to complete the walkway and fishing pier."

As the truth and magnitude of the moment slowly began to sink in, Yvette suddenly grabbed Jack around the neck, hugging him enthusiastically. "Oh, I just love this, Jack!"

He held her close, enjoying the moment immensely.

"What's this all about?" Maurice asked.

"You two want to be alone?" Colette asked, sarcasm dripping from her voice.

"Jack just told me this is our cabin again!" Yvette stated gleefully. "Don't you just love it?"

"Let me show you the outside and the section of the path they have finished before I have to take you to work."

"Oh, now I don't want to go to work!"

"I asked them to make the pathway as straight as possible without taking out any of the pine trees," Jack explained. "See the upright poles standing just in the edge of the river? That's where the fishing pier and boathouse will be. They should be here soon. Kasey said they were working today. I guess I should get you to work."

As they drove back to Bon Weir and the café, Yvette suddenly said, "You do so many things just to make me happy! I can't tell you how much I love you, Jack! How can I ever repay you?"

"Marry me!" Jack said seriously. "We love each other, don't we? Will you marry me, Yvette?"

After a short moment of silence Yvette finally said, "Too many things have happened in such a short period of time. I can't think straight. Give me some time to sort all of this out, will you, Jack? Of course I love you, but there is so much to consider."

Jack had his arguments in favor of her marrying him all ready, but he chose not to pursue any of them. He reached over and patted her hand then took it in his hand for a brief moment. "Take all the time you need, hon. I won't change my mind."

She hesitated, Jack thought as he drove back to the cabin. *Is it possible she is really considering marrying me? What if she had said yes? I don't even have a ring.*

"Sorry to leave you all like that," Jack said to Mr. and Mrs. DuBoise as he entered the cabin.

"That's okay," Maurice said. "We were enjoying this time with our granddaughter. Juliette thinks you should have some tall swings out back. Maybe even a trampoline."

"I should have thought of that!" Jack told him. "I'll get right on that, honey," he told Juliette.

"Does this cabin really belong to Yvette now?" Colette asked Jack.

"It will. Just a matter of changing the name on the deed up at the courthouse in Newton."

"And just what do you get out of all of this?" she asked sarcastically.

"I've already received my reward," Jack told her, grinning. "Didn't you see Yvette's face when she realized the cabin was really hers?"

"Ah, leave him alone, Colette," Maurice scolded her. "Can't you see the man's in love?"

"Head over heels!" Jack grinned. "I want you all to know I hope to marry your daughter someday and raise your granddaughter." Then, putting his hand on Colette's shoulder, he said, "I'm like a wart—I'll grow on you."

"Let's walk down to the place where you're putting in the pier," Maurice said to Jack. "You ladies want to come along?"

"I do!" Juliette said. "Come on, Grandma."

They walked down the unfinished path, Juliette skipping along ahead of every one else. They were near the bluff overlooking the spot where the pier was to be built when Jack heard the sound of a vehicle stopping back at the cabin. He could hear voices but couldn't distinguish words.

"I need to check on that," he told Maurice. "You all just take your time."

"It was a hit," Jack told Kasey and Brian as he met them in front of the cabin. "Yvette was out here earlier and saw everything. It wasn't exactly the way I'd planned it, but believe me, it was a hit!"

Both of the Snowden brothers smiled at the compliment. Kasey said the walk and pier would both be complete before the next weekend. A crew would begin construction at Arty's café on Monday, the 23rd.

During the rest of the spring and into the summer months the Snowden brothers of KB Construction, completed work on the walk and fishing pier. They installed a top of the line gym set behind the cabin and were well into completion of the remodeling of Arty's Café.

Yvette, finding her new career both challenging and rewarding, had been in on every aspect of the construction. She believed that as manager, it was her responsibility to ensure that the completed building would house a safe and comfortable environment for her staff. When she found she couldn't devote as much time to the new manager position and still wait on her customers as she loved to do, she interviewed over twenty persons before settling on the girl she finally hired.

The resemblance in attitude and mannerisms between the two was uncanny. Robin was affable, genial, and confident. There was however, a stark difference in their physical appearance. Robin was a redhead in the purest sense. She had azure eyes, and her pretty face was covered with hundreds of freckles. She was shorter than Yvette by two or three inches but just as athletically built. In no time she was a favorite with the customers.

Yvette hired other staff, including dish washers/busboys, and interviewed a dozen or so cooks, all of which Arty, who had the final word, had vetoed.

Arty finally agreed to hire a large black woman by the name of Mable Brown, who brought a sample of her Cajun cooking with her. One taste and Arty was in love. Mable had a small file drawer full of her recipes for Arty to see, but she said she never had to look at them anymore.

As it came near to the time for the grand opening Jack insisted Yvette hire at least a second waitress, as he was certain Yvette would want to spend too much time on the floor with her customers. She hesitantly agreed and eventually hired Sonya, a girl she had interviewed earlier.

Yvette ran advertisements in the newspapers of surrounding towns and bought a spot on local radio that ran for two weeks prior to and two weeks after the opening. To no one's surprise, especially Jack's, the café opened to a total success.

With Juliette out of school and Yvette working only five days a week and more flexible hours, Jack was able to spend some very enjoyable time with the two. They all three spent many a happy hour at the cabin, and when it was impossible for Yvette to be there, Jack would often take Juliette to play on the gym set, fish from the pier, or go boating on the river. Finding time alone with Yvette was another thing entirely.

Jack started purchasing furnishings for the cabin so he could move in and be that much closer to Yvette. He furnished one bedroom for himself, one for Yvette, and one for Juliette should the opportunity ever arise for them to spend a night there. Except for the furniture in his room, he purchased nothing until Yvette had seen it and agreed it was just right for the cabin.

He gathered a large pile of deadfall, cut it in fireplace length, and stacked it near the cabin to use as firewood.

By early June, soon after school was out, Jack had moved out of the motel in Jasper and into the Cabin. Soon Juliette was spending part of almost every day at the cabin with him. He was able to persuade Yvette to come with them after work one Sunday night and spend most of the next day relaxing and enjoying the solitude of the cabin and surrounding area.

Jack purchased a boat with an outboard motor and kept it moored in the boathouse adjacent to the dock. He had only a few opportunities to take Juliette out on the river in it, but he had enjoyed every minute he was with his little friend. "When are we going to take Mommy for a boat ride, Uncle Jack?" Juliette asked him.

"Soon I hope," Jack told her. "She always seems to be at work. Here, you steer for a while. Try to hold it steady. Sharp turns in this current could swamp us. That's right, just like that."

Jack felt a sense of pride as he watched Juliette maneuver the boat. She was growing up so swiftly. "Ease off on the throttle. Now, make a slow turn toward the boathouse. Good. Cut the engine and let her drift into the boathouse. Perfect!" Jack told her as he stepped out of the still moving boat and wrapped the forward mooring line around a cleat. Juliette tossed the after mooring line to him, and after tying it to another cleat, he helped Juliette out of the boat.

"I did good, huh, Uncle Jack," Juliette asked as she danced along the path back to the cabin.

"Yes, I'm very proud of you and the way you handled that boat today!" Jack told her. "You're getting to be quite a young lady!"

ELEVEN

The jewelry store in Houston that Jack was standing in was huge. There were display case after display case filled with wedding and engagement ring sets, along with every other type of jewelry. He spent over an hour with a very patient saleswoman before settling on the ring set he wanted.

The engagement ring that Jack chose had a one carat diamond in the center and a cluster of three smaller diamonds on either side of the center diamond. He purchased three matching wedding bands. A man's ring in size 10 ½ and two women's rings, one in a size 5 ½ and one a size 3.

"She's very petite with small hands, and I want to be sure one of the rings will fit her," Jack informed the saleswoman.

"We can resize any ring, sir. There is no need for you to purchase a second one."

"Well, Houston is quite a ways from where I live. I can always bring a ring back if it don't fit, can't I?"

"Yes, sir."

"Then I'll take all four rings," Jack said, grinning to hide his deceit.

Back at the cabin, he put the wedding bands in a safe place but kept the engagement ring in his SUV in hope that some day soon the opportune time would arise for him to ask Yvette that most important question once again.

In mid-July the remodeling of the kitchen shut down the café for two weeks, and Jack took Yvette and Juliette to the beaches of Mississippi for ten days of fun in the sun.

The hotel was located just across the beach highway from the gulf. Their rooms were located right next door to one another.

The one that Yvette and Juliette shared had two queen-size beds. Jack's room had a single king-size bed. The beaches were white sand and had such a gentle slope that it was ideal for children. Juliette was a doll in her one-piece suit with sun bonnet. Yvette was breathtakingly beautiful in her plain white bikini under a large brimmed white sun hat. Jack just lounged on a beach towel and took in the scenery when he wasn't staring at Yvette. Each night after supper they would all three walk on the beach arm in arm and hand in hand. Sometimes Jack would swing Juliette up onto his shoulders so he could put his arm around Yvette as they strolled down the beach in the moonlight.

They were on such a walk the last night before they were to go back home to Bon Weir.

"It's so lovely here," Yvette said in a whisper as she stopped to observe the setting moon and the slivers of light from it dancing on the waves. Jack stopped and dropped to his knees so that Juliette could dismount. They stayed like this for some time watching the moon slide deeper and deeper into the gulf.

Jack looked at them, mother and daughter standing side by side. *This is the perfect time*, he thought. He was already on his knees. He pulled the ring box from his pocket and reached for Yvette's hand.

She turned toward him. "Yes, Jack?"

"Yvette," Jack started, "you know I love you so very much. Will you please be my wife?"

Juliette started to say something, but Yvette put her hand over her mouth. "Hush now, Juli," Yvette said lovingly to her daughter. "This is important!"

Jack held his breath, opened the ring box, and pushed it toward Yvette.

Yvette's eyes didn't leave his face. She bent over, took his face between the palms of her hands, and kissed him tenderly. "Yes, Jack, of course I'll marry you." Jack slowly arose, removed the ring from the box, and slipped it on to her finger. They embraced, and he kissed her long and lovingly before releasing her so she could look at her ring.

Yvette held her hand up to catch the last glimmer of moonlight on the diamonds. "It's beautiful, Jack," she sighed. "So beautiful!"

Now allowed to talk, Juliette asked her mother, "Are we engaged?"

"Yes, we are," Yvette told her softly.

Jack was so happy he could hardly contain himself. He wanted to run and jump and yell to the whole world that he had finally won the girl of his dreams, the love of his life, the prize of a lifetime. He picked Juliette up and put her on his shoulders. Then he picked Yvette up in his arms and carried them both down the beach, running and turning in a circle every few steps. Suddenly he stepped into a hole and they all went tumbling onto the beach sand in a pile, laughing and giggling like they were all three Juliette's age.

TWELVE

T he wedding was held in the small Bon Weir Baptist Church. Mr. and Mrs. DuBoise drove up from Galveston so Yvette's father could give her away. Her mother, Colette acted as Yvette's maid of honor. The wedding party was quite small. On the bride's side of the dais was the maid of honor and Juliette as one small bridesmaid. On the groom's side were Jack and his best man, Arty.

Jack stood waiting nervously, anxious to get this part over with. When Mendelssohn's Wedding March began, the congregation stood and turned toward the aisle, awaiting the bride's entry. As she appeared in the doorway, Wagner's Wedding Chorus began. Once he got a view of the vision of loveliness coming down the aisle, Jack was unaware of anything else. He could see her violet-blue eyes even through the veil. Her eyes were fixed on him, just as his eyes were fixed on hers. Her slow, deliberate practiced wedding march caused him to become very impatient. He wanted her in his arms immediately. Arty suddenly pushed him forward with his elbow, and Jack remembered he was to go meet her, take her from her father, and bring her the last few steps. He stepped forward to meet them, shook Maurice's hand briefly, took Yvette's elbow, and walked with her up the steps of the dais to the waiting minister.

They recited their vows in front of a small congregation of friends and acquaintances. Yvette Suzanne Clarke became Yvette Suzanne Lockhart. At the point where Jack had just placed the wedding ring on Yvette's finger, the minister paused as Jack stooped and put the size-three ring on Juliette's finger, symbolizing his commitment to her as a father. Yvette pushed the ring onto his finger as a tear ran down her cheek. The kiss they shared at the end of the ceremony was brief yet filled with emotion. Jack had at last fulfilled his dream of having both Yvette and Juliette.

As the rented limousine pulled away from the church, bride and groom in the front seat waving and smiling, Juliette sat in the rear seat, waving and smiling too.

"Juliette isn't going with them on their honeymoon, is she?" someone in the group of well-wishers asked.

"Jack insisted," came the answer.

"That's going to be a crowded bed."

Jack returned the rented limousine to the car rental area at the Houston airport just before they boarded their flight to Buffalo. They had reservations for seven days and nights on the top floor in one of the many honeymoon suites of a five-star high-rise hotel just across the boulevard from Niagara Falls.

Their seats in first class on the airplane were only two seats wide. Yvette sat next to the window and Jack occupied the aisle seat next to her, while Juliette was seated in the window seat just in front of them. Neither Yvette nor Juliette had ever flown on an airliner and constantly voiced their amazement at such things as how tiny the cars seemed to be or the beauty of the tops of the clouds in the bright sunlight. Their chattering back and forth with one another lasted almost the entire trip. Jack was content to listen and watch and squeeze his new wife's hand from time to time. He couldn't remember a time when he had been happier.

Less than five hours later they were checking into their hotel.

"There's a twin-sized bed in the enclave just off of the bedroom in your suit as you requested sir," the concierge told Jack.

The bellman took their things to their suite, and the three of them accompanied him in the elevator to the top floor.

As the bellman opened the doors to their suite, Juliette immediately ran to the windows to look out at the Falls far below them. Jack picked Yvette up in his arms and carried her across the threshold and on into the bedroom and deposited her gently on the heart-shaped bed, all the time with his eyes fixed lovingly on hers.

After completing his chores, the bellman retreated to the door and waited for Jack to tip him. "If there is anything at all that I can do to make your stay more enjoyable, please ask for me, Louie." He half bowed and closed the doors behind him.

All three changed from their wedding clothing into something more casual. Jack ordered room service, a bottle of sparkling water to substitute for champagne so that Juliette could join in the toast. He ordered lobster thermidor for him and Yvette and a hamburger with fries for Juliette.

When their meal arrived, they sat down to the expensively decorated table. Jack made a toast to his new family. "To my lovely new wife and to my darling new daughter."

Yvette made a similar toast. "To my wonderful new husband!"

Not to be left out, Juliette made her own toast: "To the Lockharts!"

As the hour began to grow late, Juliette was first in the bath. She put on her nightclothes and crawled under the covers on the twin-sized bed.

Jack sat on the side of the bed next to Juliette while Yvette went in to bathe. "I love you, my new little daughter," he said as he cradled her small body and kissed her cheek. "Good night and sweet dreams."

Juliette smiled widely. Jack stood up and started toward the bedroom doors. "Good night, Daddy," she said, softly.

Jack's heart nearly burst with pride and emotion. He turned back toward his other prize. "Good-night, Juli," he said. "I love you."

Jack had only been in the bedroom for a short time when his excitingly beautiful bride emerged from the bathroom. Her hair had been combed out and was hanging loosely over each shoulder. She had no noticeable makeup on and was dressed in a form-fitting lavender negligee. It had narrow shoulder straps and a low-cut V neck. It hugged her body seductively to just above her knees.

"I'll be back before you have time to miss me," Jack told her in a whisper. "Don't change a thing."

After showering, he put on his robe and hurriedly stepped back into the bedroom.

Yvette was sitting demurely on the edge of the heart-shaped bed. Jack approached and taking her hands, lifted her to a standing position. She placed her arms around his neck. He kissed the lips on her upturned face. "Would you turn off the lights?" she asked softly.

"Not yet," Jack whispered as he placed his fingers under the shoulder straps of her gown. "I haven't seen all of this prize I won." Slowly and deliberately he slid the straps off of her shoulders and down her arms. Yvette lowered her arms and let the lavender negligee slide unimpeded to the floor.

THE LOCKHARTS OF PINE TREE LANE

ONE

A warm East Texas summer breeze stirred the tops of the pine trees that surrounded the cabin and dotted the five-acre plot of the Lockhart Estate. What once had been a three-bedroom, one-bath cabin on Church House Creek had, over the past seven years, been modified to include another much larger bedroom and another one and one half baths. The kitchen had been enlarged and modernized. The living room had also been made larger and a den with office space had been added. An unattached three-car garage had been added on one end of the cabin with a rather fancy portico between the two. Covered patios ran the length of both the front and back of the now rather large cabin. A lawn covered the cleared area around the cabin and garage. Flowerpots and gardens decorated the outside area in an ordered fashion. Even the stone walkway from the cabin to the boathouse and fishing pier had been lined with an oleander hedge.

Juliette Lockhart sat on the fishing pier that she and her father had used so often over the past seven years. She sat relaxed, knees bent, feet apart with a fishing pole resting against the inside of one knee. Her black curls were tucked into a wide-brimmed straw hat. The young teenage girl, now just fifteen, had grown to be even more beautiful than her mother, though her father always said it was a draw. She was barefoot, dressed in jeans cut off just above the knees, and a summer blouse buttoned with only one button. She had twisted the two lower front halves of the blouse and knotted them just below her bra.

The sixteen-year-old lad sitting next to her was tall and skinny with dark brown hair and brown eyes. He was not at all interested in his fishing pole, but more interested in the exquisitely beautiful individual beside him.

"Stop that, Tommy!" Juliette ordered. "I've asked you to not touch me there. Those are mine, and I'll decide who touches them and when!"

"Ah, come on, Juli. Aren't you my girlfriend? You know all the other kids have gone way past what you let me do. Do you want to be the only virgin in the sophomore class?"

Juliette stubbornly didn't answer. Instead she arose and began reeling in her fishing line. She put her pole over her shoulder and marched up the path toward the cabin.

"Wait, Juli," Tommy McFadden called. "I'm sorry! Are we still going to the movies tonight?"

"Go if you want to. Just don't look for me to be there!"

Juliette and Tommy had known each other since second grade. They had grown up together and been almost inseparable during that time. Tommy was at the cabin almost every day during the summer months and Juliette's parents, Jack and Yvette Lockhart, had shown a fondness for him.

Lately, however, Tommy had begun to have different and deeper feelings about Juliette. Whenever she was near, he felt the urge to touch her. He wanted to know her more intimately. He hadn't kept these feeling to himself. As he and Juliette were such close friends they shared almost everything.

Recently, Juliette had been acting very strange. Like the time she kissed him in the boathouse then slapped him later when he tried to kiss her. He had no idea what he had done wrong. He did know that he didn't want her to be angry with him.

"Please, Juli," he called after her. "If you'll go to the movies with me, I promise I won't even put my arm around you!"

"Then why should I even want to go with you?" Juliette asked in a condescending voice.

Juliette had been just eight years old when her father and mother had married and moved to the cabin. Anytime her grandfather and grandmother, Maurice and Colette DuBoise, visited, her grandfather would tell the story of how her mother and father met in the small café where her mother worked. Because of her father's interest in Juliette, they had become close friends and later married.

Only a few months after they all returned from Niagara Falls the adoption was final and her name was officially Juliette Anne Lockhart.

She remembered the changes in her mother's physical appearance the year after the wedding when she learned she would be getting a baby brother for Christmas. Her brother, Jack Jr., now four, was born just ten days before their second Christmas at the cabin.

At first, she had enjoyed helping her mother with the baby, but later she began to feel jealous of the time and attention her father showed him. Time he had always had for her now seemed to be given to Jacky. When her mother went back to work, where she was the manager of a large restaurant, Juliette had helped her father with feeding, changing, and bathing Jacky.

She loved her little brother, who, like she and her mother, had curly black hair and dimples but lighter blue eyes like her father. What she missed most was the time before Jacky was born when she could demand all of her father's attention while her mother was at work.

She had an exceptionally strong attachment to her father. Although he was forty-nine years old, he was strong and athletic, over six feet tall with deep blue eyes, blond wavy hair, and to her, very handsome.

She remembered his patience while he taught her to play guitar, and how difficult it had been for her to reach around the guitar neck. He never seemed to realize just how small her fingers were.

As she entered the cabin after her argument with Tommy, her father, reading her body language, asked, "What's the problem, Juli?"

"It's Tommy!" Juliette declared. "He's being impossible! He wants me to do things I don't want to do! Physical things, like touching me where I don't want to be touched!"

"I understand," her father said. "He's a teenage boy and that means his hormones are raging. He should be more in control of his actions, but, my sweet, you are a very attractive package. That, I'm afraid, makes it difficult for the members of the opposite sex to control themselves while in your presence. I'm proud of you for being so open and honest with me. Would you like me to have a talk with Tommy?"

"No, Daddy! That would be so embarrassing!"

"The day may come when you find what Tommy is suggesting to be more appealing to you. At that particular moment I won't be around to advise you. What he is asking you to do should only be between two totally committed, adult, married people like your mother and I. However, I'm not so naïve as to believe you won't be tempted to fall for a smooth line, so if you should do something of that nature, I want you to know you can always confide in me. Now, Juli, this is very important, so please listen to me closely. Do not engage in that sort of physical behavior without being totally prepared for the consequences. It's sad to say, but premarital sex is not only sinful, but it can now be fatal as well, should you chose the wrong partner and be unprotected."

"I know all of that, Daddy, but how do I know if Tommy is the right one?"

"I wish I had an easy answer for you, sweetheart. All I know is that you have to follow your heart. When you really love someone, you aren't thinking about yourself. You're wanting to please the other person, make them happy at any cost. That's why it's so difficult to make a clear choice with overactive teenage hormones getting in the way. There is a great deal of difference between love and lust, and even older adults get the two confused. Just don't let anyone ever pressure you into doing something you know is not right. Remember, honey, even if you should make a wrong choice, I'm here for you. You can always come to me."

"I know that, Daddy, but I'm not sure that you've helped me here."

"I have total confidence that you'll make the right decision, if, or when, that situation arises."

"I love you, Daddy," Juliette said, bending to kiss him on his forehead.

"I love you too," Jack said, "since the day I first laid eyes on you. Would you mind watching Jacky for a little while? Your mother will be home soon, and I need to start supper."

Jack Lockhart had long ago accepted his roll in the household. Almost from the very first moment he set eyes on his wife, Yvette, he had been in love with her. Over the years his love for her had only become more enduring. Love, like the love Saint Paul described in his first book to the Corinthians. Unselfish, always protecting and trusting, totally devoted love. He was rewarded daily with the same kind of love from her. Because of this, his housekeeping, cooking, and child-rearing duties weren't really chores, but labors of love.

The past seven years had been some of his happiest. Yvette, now thirty-two, was more lovely then ever. Her glossy black hair of tight natural curls, framing her beautiful face with violet-blue eyes, luscious lips, and infectious dimpled smile, were always a distraction to him. Her model-like figure and engaging personality kept his constant attention.

His daughter, Juliette, had grown into a beautiful and confident young lady. His son Jack Jr., was about to start pre-kindergarten. There was only one thing gnawing at him—the contents of the two coolers in the rear of his closet.

At twenty-five minutes after five, just like every other workday, Jack heard Yvette's car turn into the drive. He wiped his hands and went to meet her at the door. Even after all these years his heart always beat faster when he saw her coming into the house. She placed her keys and purse on the entryway table and greeted him. "Hi, Jack. Where are the kids?"

"Hi, sweetheart. They're both out back. How was your day?"

Yvette kissed him hurriedly. "Oh you know, same old things. I want to say hello to Jacky and Juli. What's that your fixing for supper? It sure smells good. I'll be back in a minute."

Jack stood there feeling as if he was missing out somehow. He remembered when her kisses were heartfelt and tender, not just distracted ricochets. He wondered if her passion for him was waning. He knew he still felt the same passion for her as the day he said I do. He finished setting the table and called to her and the children. "Time to wash up for supper."

After their meal, Yvette and Juliette cleared the table and cleaned up in the kitchen while he and Jacky took a walk down to the boathouse and pier. Within minutes the girls joined them. They all stood and watched the river as it went rushing by.

A heavy, early summer rainstorm north and west of Bon Weir had caused a lot of runoff. As the river began to rise it also began to move more rapidly.

Jacky was riding his father's shoulders and Yvette automatically stepped close to Jack as they stood near the water's edge. Jack put an arm around her in a protective posture and pulled her even closer to him. Juliette stepped close to her father's other side, and Jack put a protective arm around her.

The rushing waters had a mesmerizing effect. They stood there for several minutes, watching in silence.

The sound of a motorcycle approaching disturbed the solemnity of the moment.

"It's Tommy," Juliette said. "He's here to take me to the movies. Do you think I should go, Daddy, after what he did this afternoon?"

"What did he do?" Yvette wanted to know.

Just then, Tommy appeared at the top of the bluff. "Hi, Mr. and Mrs. Lockhart. Nice night, isn't it?" He continued down the path toward them.

"Hi, Tommy," Jack answered. "Yes, it is. Did you come to talk about the weather?"

"No, sir. Juli promised to go to the movies with me tonight. I've come to pick her up."

"Is that right, Juli?" Jack asked. "I don't recall you saying anything to me about it."

"I haven't decided whether to go or not!" Juliette stated cheekily. "Why should I?" she asked Tommy.

"Please, Juli," Tommy begged. "Here, I brought you a flower."

"You got that from my mother's garden!"

"But the sentiment is the same!" Tommy pleaded pitifully.

"Oh, all right, but you have to ask my dad!" she said, raising her nose slightly in the air.

Tommy collected all his courage and asked Jack if he could take Juliette to the movies. Jack gave a stern warning about motorcycle safety, told him to have her home as soon as the movie was over, and no later than 11:00 p.m. regardless. "And," Jack told him, "you treat her like the lady that she is, or this will be the last time she will go anywhere with you!"

"Yes, sir," Tommy said. "We'll be back by eleven o'clock."

As the two young people ran to the motorcycle, put their helmets on, and rode off, Yvette again asked Jack, "What did Tommy do?"

"I'm not sure just what he did. Some inappropriate touching is all she would say."

"And you let my daughter leave with him? Go after her right now!"

"Our daughter," Jack corrected her. "I don't think I'd like to embarrass her like that. She's got a mind and a will of her own, Yvette. We just have to trust her to do the right thing."

Like I did? Yvette thought, with a feeling of compunction.

Later that same evening, Jack was sitting in the den looking at an old very worn highway atlas. Yvette had just put Jacky to bed. As she entered the den, Jack looked up at her and sighed. "Do you still love me, Evie?"

"Now why would you ask me a thing like that?"

"Well, for one thing, that glancing kiss at the door today, and for another the way you and Jacky ran off and left me on the path tonight!"

Yvette smiled at him. "You never could keep up with me, old man." She took his face in her hands and kissed him tenderly as she lowered herself onto his lap. "Of course I still love you, Jack."

"I've always felt you might think that you had to settle for me just for Juliette's sake. I have, after all, done all of the pursuing."

"We've talked of this before, Jack. Yes, I was conflicted for a while and your devotion to Juliette did play a big part in my decision, but believe it or not, I really do love you." She kissed him again.

Jack held her on his lap. "I guess I'm like an old comfortable pair of shoes; you don't get excited about old shoes, just the new glittery ones in the store window. Well, I still get excited about you, Evie! Every time I hear your car turn into the drive, every time I see your lovely self come in that door, I get excited!" He dropped his voice to almost a whisper. "I'm excited now! Your nearness always gives me the libido of a young man."

"I know, but maybe later. I have some calls to make, staffing problems." She kissed him hurriedly, stood up, and went to her desk.

Jack picked up the atlas, thumbed through it absentmindedly, then got up and went to take a shower. It was still an hour before Juliette was to be home. Although the shower felt good, he still wouldn't be able to relax until he knew she was home, safe, and in her room. Suddenly the shower door opened. "Scoot over, old man," Yvette said coquettishly as she joined him.

Overnight, the rains had moved farther south. Jack suddenly awakened to the sound of nearby thunder. He could faintly hear what appeared to be heavy rain on the roof of the cabin. A flash of nearby lightening lit up the room and he saw Yvette was also awake. "Reminds me of the night I first saw you," Jack said as he squeezed her hand softly. "What time is it?"

"Almost six. Time for me to get up anyway. I think I hear Jacky, could you—"

"Already on my way."

The sudden noise had awakened and frightened little Jacky. He was sitting up and sobbing softly into Juliette's shoulder as Jack entered his room. Jack sat down beside them and wrapped his arms around both of them. "I should have known you would be in here with him," he told his daughter lovingly. "It's okay Jacky," he said. "Thunder is just noise. It won't hurt you."

"I'll take care of him, Daddy," Juliette told him. "He's okay now."

Jack felt a real sense of pride in his daughter. He recalled she had always had an air of maturity about her. It was often difficult for him to remember that at just fifteen, she herself was still just a child.

He fixed breakfast for just the three of them. Yvette never had anything other than a cup of coffee before going to work. She always ate a midmorning snack at the restaurant.

The rains gradually became less intense and it was only sprinkling by the time Yvette was ready to leave for work.

"I'm going to take the kids all day tomorrow so you can have a day off," Yvette told him as she passionately kissed him good-bye. "Was that better?"

"I'll hold on to that kiss all day," Jack told her.

"Oh, will you two grow up!" Juliette scolded.

TWO

The next morning, a Saturday, as promised, Yvette loaded her two children into her sedan and took them to the mall in Jasper for the day. She said they had some shopping to do, would get something for lunch, then take in a movie before returning.

Jack was left alone with his thoughts. He took a cup of coffee out onto the patio and sat down in a lounge chair. Lately he had been thinking about the contents of the two coolers that were hidden in the very back of his closet, the coolers that he had found buried in a field in Central Texas nearly eight years ago. It was his attempt to dispose of the contents that had led to his meeting Yvette and Juliette. The meeting that had subsequently led to his marriage and thus delaying, for the past several years, his disposal of said contents.

One of the coolers was still completely full and the other still had more than half of the original cash. He estimated that he probably still had close to nine million of the original eleven million, two hundred thousand dollars, remaining.

"I need to formulate a plan that will allow me to dispose of the contents while still allowing me the maximum time with my family," Jack mused.

His thoughts were suddenly interrupted by the sound of a motor vehicle coming up the drive. Jack looked up and saw Arty's old rust-colored Jeep pickup as it rumbled to a halt. "Get out and sit a spell. Would you like a cup of coffee?"

"That what you're callin' that tar you brew?" Arty growled. "Yeah, why not? Looks like I need to put on another pot. I need to show ya how to make good java anyway."

Arty, a tall, heavy-set man in his mid sixties with tufts of gray hair showing below the ball cap he always wore, was Jack and Yvette's partner in the Blue JAY Restaurant. He was also the lead chef. He had once owned, operated, and been the cook in the tiny eight-stool, seven-booth café where Jack had first met Yvette and Juliette one very stormy January night many years ago. When the three of them became partners, they had tried several combinations of their initials before coming up with the name Blue JAY Restaurant. Finally by using the first initial of their first names they arrived at the JAY Restaurant. Eventually they added the Blue and had Juliette paint the likeness of a blue jay, a bird common to that part of Texas, on the restaurant sign.

Jack and Arty sat for a long while on the patio discussing the weather, the rising river, and the fact that it wasn't a good time to go fishing. They discussed Jack's children, the oldest of whom Arty had a part in raising, and finally, Arty got around to the reason for the visit.

"Well, Jack," Arty started, "I've been thinking. I'm going to be sixty-eight here in a couple a weeks. The restaurant is makin' us all a good livin' now, and I've got more time in behind that grill than most people my age have in just blinkin' their eyes! I think it's time for me to just chuck it all in and go fishin'. What do ya think, Jack. You think Vet could get along without me?"

Jack looked at his old friend and partner. "It's about time you stopped poisoning the dining public," he teased. Then, laying his hand on his shoulder, he told him in his most sincere tone, "It's going to be very difficult for her to get along without you. No one could ever replace you! Still, after she tries to talk you out of it, I'm sure she'll be, as usual, very understanding."

"Would y'all want me to move out of the apartment so the new chef can have it?"

"That sounds like something for the partnership to decide," Jack told Arty, "and since the two of us form a quarm, why don't we just put it to a vote right now? All in favor of Arty staying in the apartment say 'aye,' those opposed say 'no.'"

Arty half-heartedly said, "Aye."

Jack enthusiastically said, "Aye! The ayes have it. Guess you're stuck there." Jack grinned. "At least you'll be close to Mable and her cooking."

Mable Brown was another chef at the Blue JAY Restaurant. Arty had been instrumental in her hiring, and she was Arty's favorite. She could cook anything Cajun, but her specialty was shrimp Creole.

"Vet gonna be mad when she hears she didn't get a vote?" Arty asked.

"If she is, I'll tell her it was your idea. What are you going to do with all this spare time?"

"Don't know. There has to be something goin' on besides breakin' eggs and burnin' hamburger meat. I ain't seen much past the end of my arms now since Houston beat Santa Anna! Well, you know how that goes. One thing for sure, I'm gonna take some time to go visit my sister and her husband out in Albuquerque. You remember my sister Stella, don't ya, Jack? She used to fill in for Vet ever once in a while."

"Sure I remember Stella. When was it they moved to New Mexico? Three, four years ago?"

"Somethin' like that."

For more than two hours they continued their conversation before Arty stood up, picked up his cup, and carried it inside and rinsed it out as he was in the habit of doing. "So long," he said. "Better hit the trail."

"Come and go fishing with me sometime," Jack offered as he waved good-bye.

Jack watched his old friend drive off and felt a sort of sadness. Arty hadn't retired just yet, but it wouldn't be very long. He knew this would cause Yvette some emotional distress. She and Arty had been together for more than twelve years, sometimes more than seventy hours in a week. They could almost read each other's minds. He wondered if he should, or was it even possible that he could, somehow prepare Yvette for this. Jack's instinct to always protect his love from any kind of hurt was very strong.

In the late afternoon Yvette's sedan rolled into the yard, and Jacky was the first one out of the car after it stopped.

"Look what Mama bought me!" he yelled as he came running to Jack.

Jack stooped to pick him up, listened while he told all about the toy, then put him back down so he could play with it. As Juliette walked by him, Jack reached for one of the bags she was carrying, asking, "What kind of toys did you get." Juliette jerked the bag away and went hurriedly into the house. "What did I say?" Jack asked with a puzzled look on his face as Yvette approached.

"Feminine things!" Yvette told him quietly while raising her eyebrows and rolling her eyes cutely. "Mysterious feminine things."

"Can I help you with your bags, or are they a mystery too?"

Yvette gave him a flirtatious grin as she handed him her bags. "I'm afraid you already know all of my mysteries." He followed her into the house and put the bags on the end of the bed where she directed. They exchanged kisses before she shooed him out of the bedroom.

"How soon should I start supper?" he called through the door.

"Let me fix it tonight," she called back. "I never get to cook anymore. Could you please just watch Jacky?"

"Sure." Jack followed the sound of the happy chatter to where Jacky and Juliette were now playing together. Jack joined in the fun, momentarily reverting to his childhood. Yvette came out, sat in the patio swing, and watched her family playing together for a few minutes before going to prepare their evening meal.

When Jack joined her a few minutes later to help out, he found her happily smiling to herself. "Can I get in on the secret of your happiness?" he asked.

Yvette gave him a quick hug and a tender kiss and said, "Oh, I'm just happy!"

"Let me make the salad," Jack offered.

The two of them worked around one another preparing the evening meal, engaged in relaxed conversation. Their fondness and respect for one another was obvious.

Within a week after his retirement party, Arty showed up at the Lockhart cabin. Jack heard the old pickup coming and met him as he parked.

"Thought I'd take you up on that fishin' offer," Arty said as he untied a long cane pole from the side mirror of his truck. "Ya got time ta drown a few worms?"

"Sure, you go on down to the pier without me," Jack told him, "Me and Jacky will be down in a little while. You need to get a head start on Jacky anyway."

"That boy good at catchin''em?"

"He's caught quite a few. I need to go put his life jacket on him and get him ready."

Arty, Jack, and little Jacky spent a quiet few hours on the pier, during which time Juliette joined them. Arty told Jack he planned to leave early the next week to go to Albuquerque. He thought he might spend two or three weeks with his sister and brother-in-law, Stella and Lonny Burkett, who now lived in Sombra Del Monte, a suburb in the northeast section of Albuquerque. During the conversation Jack questioned the reliability of Arty's old truck and insisted he take Jack's SUV.

"I insist," Jack told his old friend. "The SUV has just been sitting in the garage collecting dust and needs to be driven. Besides, it has less than fifty thousand miles on it. It may be almost ten years old, but it beats that thing you're driving. Isn't that the truck they brought over on the Mayflower?"

Arty took a nice-sized large-mouth bass off of Jacky's line and dropped it into the live pail. "If you're sure it wouldn't put you out none. It would be kinda nice to drive in the rain once without it wetting me down on the inside of the cab."

"Then it's settled. Just park your truck in back of the garage and take the SUV with you when you leave today. That way you can get used to driving it before you start that long trip."

Soon the fishing party had pulled enough fish out of the river to make enough for the five of them. As they cleaned the fish and cut fillets, Jack asked Arty to stay for supper.

"Only if you let me cook 'em," Arty offered.

"Yvette will be so pleased to have some of your cooking again!" Jack said enthusiastically. "I'll make the coleslaw. I've got a fresh head of sweet purple cabbage in the crisper and some large juicy carrots."

"You put some chopped shallots in there too, don't ya?" Arty asked, trying to be helpful.

"Never have before. Why, does that make it better? You haven't ever tasted my coleslaw!"

"Might not want to! You got any shallots, Jack?"

"No, but I'll be sure and have some the next time you come to supper. Be sure and warn me ahead of time!"

"Would you boys please play nice," Juliette said authoritatively.

Yvette was excited to see Arty's truck sitting behind the garage as she turned into the drive. She had seen very little of him since his retirement. As she entered the house she could smell hot cooking oil and fish.

Jack met her at the door, wearing an apron and a big grin. "Hired a famous chef to cook supper for you tonight, my darling," he bragged. "Arthur 'Arty' Carmichael!"

Yvette dropped her purse and keys on the entry table, kissed Jack, hugged her children, then hurried into the kitchen to give Arty a big hug.

"I knew you'd end up cooking somewhere." she smiled. "I'm just happy it was here! What's that? Hush puppies? Mmm, smells good."

"I don't know what Jack told you, Vet, but this ain't a permanent arrangement. Juli and Jacky and me, we all caught a mess of fish, and Jack not knowin' how to cook, an' all, I just volunteered to do it for him."

"Well, I'm just happy you're here. I'll change and help set the table. Be right back."

Jack followed Yvette into the bedroom while she changed. "Arty plans to leave for a trip to visit his sister in a few days. I've loaned him the SUV. I just couldn't imagine him driving his old wreck all that way. Here, let me help you with that zipper."

"I think that's a splendid idea, Jack. You don't drive it that much anymore. So you all went fishing today. How did Jacky do?"

"He held his own. Juli caught about as many as I did. Arty was so busy taking fish off of Jacky's line he kind of fell behind. It was a fun day. Would have been perfect if you'd been here."

Yvette finished changing, kissed Jack tenderly, and headed for the kitchen to help Arty.

Just like when I first met them, Jack thought.

THREE

Jack looked up from his hedge trimming chore as he saw a vehicle approaching. At first he didn't recognize that it was his own SUV pulling into the drive. "Has it already been three weeks?" he asked himself as soon as he recognized the large form of Arty behind the wheel. He did not recognize the smaller person beside Arty. He unplugged the hedge trimmer and placed it where little Jacky couldn't reach it. Jack walked over to meet the approaching SUV.

Arty climbed out, went around to the passenger side door, and opened it. "Hi, Jack," he said.

"How was the trip?" Jack asked him. "How is Stella these days?"

"This here's Shannon," Arty said as a girl approximately Juliette's age stepped down from the SUV.

Shannon was thin, about five feet, six inches tall, with long blond hair. Her blue eyes were staring out from a face almost completely covered with a head scarf. Her hair was parted in the middle and hanging over the sides of her face, almost totally covering her eyes.

She was dressed in tight-fitting jeans with holes in the knees and a denim vest over a white and yellow polka dot, peasant blouse. She was also wearing running shoes that had once been white but now showed where someone had tried to change the color to yellow using a marker. She was carrying a large denim purse.

As she hesitated by the side of the SUV, Arty told her, "It's all right. This is my friend Jack that I told you about."

"Come inside out of the heat. I was about to have a glass of iced tea. Would either of you care for a glass, or a soda maybe?"

Jack said, smiling. Then he addressed Shannon. "I have a daughter about your age."

"I'll take you up on that iced tea," Arty said. "How about it, Shannon? Would you like something?"

Shannon nodded as she walked hesitantly beside and slightly behind Arty. Juliette and Jacky, hearing voices in the front of the house, came around to see who was there. Just as they arrived in the yard, a sudden whirlwind blew Shannon's hair and scarf in such a way as to uncover a portion of her face, revealing many large angry looking scars.

"Did you hurt your face?" Jacky asked innocently.

Shannon quickly hid that part of her face.

"Hi, I'm Juliette. This is my little brother, Jacky. Please excuse his rudeness. He doesn't know any better."

"This is Shannon," Jack said, "My daughter, Juliette, and my son, Jacky."

They all sat at the dinning room table and Jack and Juliette fixed each a glass of iced tea. Arty and Jack discussed Arty's trip and his visit to his sister's.

Juliette and Shannon engaged in teenage girl talk. As Shannon became more at ease, Juliette took Shannon's hand and asked if she would like to see her room. She led her away, followed closely by Jacky, who wanted to know more about her face. Shannon let him touch and feel her scars.

"Does that hurt?" he wanted to know.

Shannon slowly began to let down her guard in the presence of the small boy and eventually removed the head scarf. She and Juliette continued to talk about girl things and Jacky, soon bored, went to climb up on his daddy's lap.

Arty told Jack that he was on his way back, driving through the Sandia Mountains of New Mexico, when he saw Shannon walking along the side of the highway. He was just on the east side of the town of Tijeras. It was cold up there in the mountains that day, and he said he just couldn't let her walk. All she had with her was that small bag, and he didn't think she was going very far. Arty explained how she told him that she had been in foster homes since she was four and had just reached sixteen years of age and had been what she called 'emancipated'. She just wanted to get as far away as possible from the hurt and disappointment of living in foster homes.

She told him her mother and father had been killed in the same automobile crash where she received all of her facial scars. She had been in so many foster homes she couldn't remember them all, but without exception, she had been taunted because of her looks and had even been abused because of them. She recited to Arty many of the names she had been called. She didn't know her last name, and at one of the earlier foster homes, she had been dubbed Shannon "Phantom" by some of the older children. Now, that was the only last name she knew.

Arty said he had planned to only take her as far as Lubbock before dropping her off. When he got into Lubbock, however, and discovered she had no money and no place to stay he just rented a room with two beds and they stayed there together the first night. They spent a second day driving across Texas and stayed in a similar motel in Tyler the night before. He told Jack he had grown very fond of Shannon during their almost three days together, but he had no place for her to stay, so of course he thought of Jack and Yvette's place.

"What do think, Jack? Do you think you and Vet could let her stay here for a while?"

"If she was running away when you found her, she might just run from here too. No guarantee she'll stay, but I'm sure Yvette will be okay with it. We've got a spare room, or if they want, Juliette and Shannon could bunk together."

"I appreciate it, Jack," Arty said as he arose from the table. "I'll just go say adios to Shannon before I go."

Yvette was as warm to Shannon as she was to everyone. The girls wanted to sleep in the same room. Shannon had never had her own room and Juliette had never had a sister. Soon the girls were the best of friends. It wasn't long before Shannon began to feel at home and only showed signs of self-consciousness due to her outward appearance when strangers were around. It hurt Yvette to see this, and she discussed it with Jack.

"Jack, honey," she said as they lay in bed one night, "Shannon tries to hide every time we have any company. She's even more self-conscious when Tommy comes around. I wish there was something we could do for her. She's really very sweet, if people would just look past the scars."

"I've noticed that too. We have all done our best to show her we accept her as she is, but maybe there is something that can be done about her outward scars. Maybe if she saw herself to be as beautiful as we all think she is, it would help to heal the inward scars as well. I'll look into it."

The following night, as Jack and Yvette were once again lying in bed just before falling asleep, Yvette addressed Jack. "All day today, when I had a minute to myself, I thought about what we talked about last night. You know, fixing Shannon's scars."

"I've been thinking about that too," Jack said, "I was on the Internet today checking out scar removal. There are a number of procedures available, but we really need to get her to a plastic surgeon to find out what's best for her."

"Can you find out what degree of pain is associated with each procedure? It may be too painful and risky to chance getting her hopes up. And also there's the cost."

"Have you forgotten my coolers?" Jack asked. "I think it's time to put them back into action."

Yvette rolled over on her stomach and propped herself up on her elbows, looking at Jack. Then smiling at him, she said, "You have been waiting for something like this for a long time, haven't you, Jack? I'll bet you can't wait to get started."

"You know me so well, my sweet. Now, I've located a doctor, a specialist in scar removal, at the large hospital complex on the University of Texas campus in Houston. I'm just waiting for the right time to talk to Shannon about it before I call for a consultation."

"Oh, let me do it, Jack," Yvette begged. "Let me talk to her. If she agrees we'll all go to Houston together, but after we all agree on what steps will be required, I want to be in on the whole thing. I'll take some time off from the restaurant and everything. Oh, this is so exciting! I want to go wake her and talk to her right now."

"You just want to get your hands into my coolers," Jack teased. "Okay, Evie, this one is yours. When you talk to her don't get her hopes too high. I want to hear what the plastic surgeon has to say before we commit to anything."

"I love you," Yvette said as she plopped onto his chest and kissed him. Then she flipped back onto her back and entered into deep thought.

Shannon was at first hesitant but eventually agreed to go to Houston and hear what the surgeon had to say. Jack did the calling to set up the first appointment then allowed Yvette to take on the remainder of the project.

As Juliette and Jacky sat in the ornate waiting room in the university hospital, Jack, Yvette, and Shannon met with the surgeon. He took a close look at Shannon's scars, nodded a few times, then finally addressed them.

"No scar can be removed completely," Dr. Julian Kolb told them. "Plastic surgeons can often improve the appearance of a scar, making it less obvious through the injection or application of certain steroid medications or through surgical procedures known as scar revisions. I would recommend a combination of procedures. Z-plasty to improve the hypertrophic facial scars and some laser skin resurfacing. Possibly some steroid injections. Fortunately for you," he addressed Shannon, "the scars aren't deep enough to require shin grafting or flap surgery. After your face has completely healed and all of the reddening has vanished, a thin coat of makeup in your skin tone and color and no one will be able to see where you once were scarred.

"Are these procedures painful?" Yvette asked.

Doctor Kolb nodded toward Yvette but addressed Shannon, smiling. "There is a small amount of discomfort. In some cases more than in others. However, we use every precaution to ensure that our patients experience the least amount of discomfort. I think Miss Lockhart is the perfect candidate for us."

No one tried to correct the doctor's use of Lockhart as Shannon's last name.

Yvette and Shannon went to the offices to check in and set up a payment schedule. Jack took his children to the hospital cafeteria to get a snack and to wait to hear the next step. He picked a table and waited for Yvette to find them. Jacky finished his meal, accompanied Juliette to the restroom, and was now fast asleep on the seat next to Jack.

Finally Yvette arrived. "She's all checked in and up in her room. There is a place for me to sleep in her room. I just need our overnight bags and my small suitcase from the car, and you can all be on your way back to the cabin. I'll stay here with Jacky and Juli while you run and get them. Thank you for this, Jack. I just know she's going to be beautiful."

Jack went to the car for the bags. When he returned he asked Yvette for the room number so he could take the bags up and say good-bye to Shannon. "I put three packets in your overnight bag," he whispered into Yvette's ear just before he went up to Shannon's room.

Jack sat by the bed in Shannon's room. He took her hand and asked, "Are you frightened?"

"It's more like worry than fear," she said. "I can't wait to have a new smooth face, yet at the same time, I wonder if I should want to change the face I've always had. But if you're asking if I'm afraid of the pain, then it's no."

"Mrs. Lockhart will be here with you throughout the whole thing. I'll be just three hours away should you need me. Best of luck. Now give old man Lockhart a hug."

Back in the hospital cafeteria, Jack and Yvette said good-bye. Jack gathered up the sleeping Jacky in his arms, and he and Juliette walked to the distant parking garage.

"Shannon will be okay, won't she, Daddy?" Juliette asked. "Can they really give her a new face? Will she be beautiful?"

"I'm certain she'll be fine. Your mother will see to that. I already find her to be beautiful in many ways. The only reason your mother and I looked into this is because of Shannon's self-esteem issues. Here, take the keys and open the door for me."

Jack buckled Jacky into his booster seat, and they were soon on their way back to the cabin. As he drove along he was happily engaged in back-and-forth banter with Juliette, who was very good at teasing him in retaliation.

They were only about five miles from Bon Weir when Jack noticed the rear of his SUV was not trailing properly. He pulled onto the shoulder so he could use the levelness of the lane entrance. He found that the right side rear tire was almost totally flat and was losing the remainder of its air rapidly. He told Juliette to awaken Jacky and that the two of them should then walk up the lane a safe distance while he changed the tire.

Jack was in the midst of changing the tire when he saw the car with the sheriff's emblem on the side make a U-turn and pull in behind the SUV. The officer left his flashing lights on to warn traffic from both directions and climbed out.

"Need any help, Jack?" Newton County Sherriff, Thomas E. McFadden asked.

"No thanks, Tom. I'm almost through here. How's Karen?"

"Oh, she's fine, just fine. How are you this fine day, Miss Juliette? That Jacky is sure getting to be a big boy."

"We haven't seen much of Tommy these past few weeks. Is he working somewhere?" Jack asked as he tossed the flat tire and jack into the rear of the SUV.

"No, I don't know what he's up to these days. I know he starts two-a-days next week. Want me to follow you a ways to make sure everything is okay?"

"Thanks, but I think it's okay. I'm just going up to Charlie's. I'll have him put his pneumatic wrench on those lug nuts when I drop off the tire. Nice to see you again, Sheriff. You and Karen come see us sometime."

"We'll do that." He turned his patrol car around and sped away.

After leaving the tire at Charlie's Garage and having the lug nuts checked for snugness, Jack turned the SUV toward home. "So Juli, what's with you and Tommy?" he asked.

"He doesn't like to come over to our house because he feels uncomfortable around Shannon. I told him I won't go anywhere with him if Shannon can't come along with us, so now he's mad at me. He called Shannon a freak!"

"Not to her face, I hope!"

"No, but if that's the way he feels, he might just as well have said it to her face. That's what his actions say!"

"You are very wise, my darling."

Jack wheeled the SUV into the garage at the cabin. He watched while Juliette got her brother out of his booster seat. "I'm going to have to rely heavily upon you for whatever time it takes for Shannon's procedure and recovery. Your mother wants to be there to support her all the way. It's just you, me, and Jacky for a while."

"Don't worry, Daddy," Juliette said, patting him on the shoulder. "I'll take care of you and Jacky."

It was the first time in almost seven years that Jack had slept alone. The bed seemed larger and colder. He traded his pillow for Yvette's so he could breathe in her lingering aroma as he drifted off to sleep. He shifted his thoughts from Shannon's ordeal to missing Yvette and then…it was morning.

Just after ten, Yvette called. "Her first procedure went fine. Shannon said she felt more pain than she thought she would, but she endured it without crying. She was in surgery for about three hours, from six to nine this morning. We can come home today, but she'll have to be back in three days to have the stitches from the Z-plasty removed. She will need several more Z-plasty surgeries and follow-up appointments to correct the lesser scars, but in nine months to a year, Dr. Kolb thinks the redness will fade and there will be no noticeable scars remaining.

Because of her youthful immune system, Shannon's healing process was rapid and remarkably worry free. After her stitches were removed, she had to return to the hospital for three more z-plasty surgeries and several times for laser skin resurfacing and steroid injections. Shannon's last trip was merely so Dr. Kolb could marvel at his own handiwork and assure himself that there was no further need for his expertise. As the redness slowly disappeared, Shannon, with the help of strong sun-block creams, was able to get out of doors more often. By her seventeenth birthday, June sixth of the following year, only those who knew where to look could see even the faintest remainder of a scar. She was, in the words of Jack Lockhart, "A vision of blond loveliness!"

In early September, when school started, Juliette entered her sophomore year and little Jacky was off to pre-kindergarten. As Yvette left him for that first day of school they both shed a few tears.

As part of her emancipation, Shannon had been required to take and pass the GED test, so she stayed at the cabin and helped Jack while everyone else was either going to school or working. Shannon enrolled in some online college courses, studying toward a nursing degree. She also took a class in dermatology and some early childhood development classes. Jack gave her a top of the line laptop computer to aid her in her studies.

Tuesday evening, September 18, was the date of Jack and Yvette's wedding anniversary. Jack had been planning a romantic evening out for him and Yvette for some time.

He knew that for this anniversary the flower was jack-in-the-pulpit, the stone was onyx or golden beryl, and the gift was copper or wool. Jack placed a potted jack-in-the-pulpit in the center of their dinning room table so Yvette would see it as soon as she entered the house. In the bedroom he hid a beautifully wrapped gift in his closet. Inside the box was a plum-colored negligee. It was a long gown with plunging neckline, revealing side slit and lace insets. In his jacket pocket he had a boxed bracelet and earrings set of hand-crafted copper, set with onyx and golden beryl stones. He had reservations for 8:00 p. m. at Yvette's favorite restaurant. Jack contacted a friend, a violin player, who knew their favorite tune and who agreed to play it for them when Jack gave him the signal. The restaurant manager was glad to be in on the romance of the evening when Jack gave him a large tip.

Jack watched from the window in anticipation as 5:25 neared. His heart beat faster as he saw Yvette's car turn into the drive. Juliette was the first into the house. She kissed Jack on the cheek and hurried to find Shannon and Jacky. As Yvette came in through the door that Jack was holding for her, he grabbed her and kissed her lovingly. "Happy anniversary, Evie darling. How was your day?"

Yvette put her things down on the entryway table as always and hugged and kissed her husband. "You remembered! What's this?"

"Believe it or not it's known as jack-in-the-pulpit. I thought it would remind you of me when I start telling my parables and stories. I have reservations for eight this evening at La Boheme.

"Oh Jack, you know how I love that place. I hope I can find something to wear."

Two hours later, Jack and Yvette left little Jacky in the care of his sister and Shannon. Their night out was everything Jack had planned and more. Their meal consisted of breaded, broiled abalone, artichoke in a light cream sauce, brown rice, and a garden salad. As the violinist played Reginald De Koven's "Oh Promise Me," Jack led Yvette onto the empty dance floor, where he held her tightly to him as they moved to the music. Yvette had her eyes shut part of the time and a dreamy smile on her face. As the music stopped, Jack kissed her softly and led her back to their table. After a dessert, he placed the small gift box on the table in front of her. Yvette opened the box and seemed very pleased. She placed the bracelet on her wrist immediately.

"Do you think it goes with this dress?" she asked Jack.

"Perfectly," Jack told her.

They arrived home a little past eleven. Yvette went to check on her children and Shannon. All were asleep except Juliette. "How was your night?" she asked her mother.

"Wonderful! You know your father. He hired a violinist and everything. Get some sleep now. I'll tell you all about it tomorrow."

While Yvette was in the bathroom getting ready for bed, Jack opened the door just far enough to slip the box containing the negligee into the room with her. He heard her delighted sounds when she saw the gown. Eventually she appeared in the doorway dressed in it. As they embraced Jack remarked in a voice barely audible, "Seems like such a waste of time to put on something as beautiful as this just so I can take it right back off you."

As they kissed, Jack could see her eyes growing darker with passion. Afterward as they lay in bed together Yvette whispered, "I have never loved you more Jack. You never disappointment me." Jack smiled as he fell asleep. It was an anniversary that he would not easily forget.

FOUR

The fact that Shannon did not know her last name seemed to constantly gnaw at Jack. He determined that if it was at all possible he was going to find her last name and heritage. There should be a record of her birth if he just knew what town and state she was born in. If all attempts failed, Jack and Yvette would adopt her and give her the Lockhart name.

While he and Shannon were at lunch one day he asked her a series of questions regarding this. Shannon did not know where she had been born. She could not remember her mother and father. For some reason she thought her last name started with a D. She did not remember the crash that had taken her mother and father. She didn't remember when she had learned about it. She did remember it was snowing the day she left the hospital for the Children's Protective Services shelter. She recalled the names of the towns where the last few foster homes were located. All in all, that conversation rendered very little.

Jack began to put some things down. Somehow the people at CPS knew Shannon's birthday was the sixth of June. She had been four at the time of the accident. She had apparently been released from the hospital in the winter months. The foster homes that she could remember had all been in or around the towns of Bernalillo and Rio Rancho in Sandoval County, New Mexico, an area just northwest of Albuquerque. Jack decided to look for automobile accidents in the archives of the *Albuquerque Journal* starting in the early spring of 1996, the year Shannon turned five, and going backward in time until her fourth birthday, June 6, 1995.

The roar of Tommy's motorcycle broke the afternoon silence. "Juli home yet?" he asked Jack as he braked to a stop.

"You know she walks to the restaurant everyday after school and rides home with her mother. She'll be here in about an hour."

Shannon had gone with Jack to pick up Jacky at pre-k and was in the backyard swinging him when they heard Tommy's motorcycle come into the yard. Jacky jumped out of the swing and ran around to see what the noise was. Shannon followed closely behind him. Jacky ran to his father and jumped up into Jack's arms.

Tommy had not seen Shannon since her facial scars had been removed and didn't recognize her. "Hi, I'm Tommy McFadden." He smiled. "You aren't from around here, are you? Are you a friend of Juli's?"

Shannon just looked at him for a few minutes. Then, smiling, she walked over to him, offering her hand, and said demurely, "Hi, my name is Shannon. I live here."

Tommy's mouth dropped open. He blushed then finally found his tongue. "Shannon the..." He put his open hand near his face and made a circular motion. "I mean...wow, you're beautiful!"

"Thank you."

"I thought you would be at football practice this afternoon," Jack said to Tommy.

"Eh, I wrote a low score in English and Coach benched me till I get my grades back up. If I'm not going to play, I'm not going to practice!"

"You know what, Tommy," Jack said, "I detest that kind of attitude. Why don't you just take your motorcycle and go somewhere else. Come back and visit after you've grown up."

Tommy, embarrassed at having Jack dress him down like that in front of Shannon, revved the engine on his bike and sped away, leaving a black streak on the driveway.

"I don't see what Juli sees in that boy!" Jack said to no one in particular as he watched Tommy speed away.

"I think Juliette has outgrown him," Shannon said to comfort Jack. "She hasn't mentioned him in a long time."

Sometime later, Yvette and Jack were in the bathroom preparing for bed. Jack was at the sink brushing his teeth as Yvette stepped from the shower, drying her hair. "Jack," she said in a whisper. "This is what Juli told me on the way home today. There's a new boy at school. He's so hot! All the girls think so. His name is Greg. He's a senior. His locker is right next to Juli's, so he has already been talking to her. They have two classes together, chemistry and band. She thinks he's going to ask her out."

"You are really enjoying this aren't you?" Jack teased Yvette. "Living vicariously through your daughter."

"You never ask me out anymore, Jack. Why is that?"

"You wanna go out with me?" Jack asked, "Wanna get a cherry coke at the drug store? Wanna see my tattoo?"

"Yes, yes, and yes!" Yvette teased him.

"Truthfully, I don't get to take you out nearly as often as I'd like. I really enjoyed our anniversary soirée."

"I did too," Yvette said, smiling.

Juliette and Shannon were already in bed but were not asleep. "Tommy was here today," Shannon whispered.

"What did he want?"

"To see you."

"Oh, he is such a bore. He's stuck in puberty! Now Greg, this new boy I met at school, he is much more mature than the jocks like Tommy, and he's really hot. I wish you could meet him! Well, maybe not. One look at you and he'd never ask me out."

"Now you're being silly. You are much prettier than me!"

"No, I'm not! Believe me, Shannon, you are very pretty! I've always thought so. Even before your surgeries. Like I've heard my dad and mom say, you are a beautiful person."

"Thank you, Juli. I think all of you are beautiful people too. So tell me more about this Greg."

"He's tall and very good looking! He has blond hair and the sexiest brown eyes! He's a senior and very serious. He isn't stuck up at all. He started talking to me the very first day. I'm hoping he'll ask me out."

"We better get some sleep now before we wake Jacky."

"You're right. Good night, Shannon."

"Good night, Juli."

Jack had been looking at the *Albuquerque Journal* newspapers online for days, searching for automobile crashes where adults were killed and a child survived. He was puzzled by the fact that there was no corroborating information. For instance, if Shannon had survived a crash where her parents died, why didn't the authorities just look for the next of kin to give the baby to? Why didn't CPS have records of her last name and the names of her deceased parents? How was it they knew she survived a crash when they had no other information? Jack decided to hire a private investigator.

The P.I. Jack located in the Albuquerque area said his name was James Stockburger. He had been a detective on both the Las Cruces and Santa Fe Police departments before retiring and moving to Paradise Hills. Here he had opened his own practice, a two-person office, his secretary and himself. Jack explained he just wanted to find the last name of a person. Mr. Stockburger agreed to take the job for two hundred a day plus expenses.

Jack gave him the timeframe of the accident and told him that he only knew the first name of the child involved. He told him he thought the parents had been killed outright and the child had probably been thrown free. Jack explained that Children's Protective Services had taken custody of Shannon probably in the winter of 1995-96. He also gave him the names of the foster parents that Shannon could remember.

Mr. Stockburger said there had been many accidents and multiple car pileups on the stretch of Highway I-40, once route 66, coming down from the Sandia mountains into Albuquerque. It was an especially bad section of highway in bad weather. He recalled one accident, about eight or ten years back, where a fully loaded gasoline tanker coming down in a snowstorm hit some black ice, slid sideways, and flipped on the top of a passenger sedan, trapping the occupants. This pileup then involved other vehicles. The tanker caught fire and the occupants of one vehicle and the truck driver were burned beyond recognition.

"Sometimes they pull so many casualties from the multiple-car pileups they lose track of which vehicle they pull them from," James Stockburger said. "Let's go over the information one more time. Female, approximately four years old. First name of Shannon, last name possibly starts with a D. Accident victim sometime in mid to late 1995. Hospitalized till late 1995 or early 1996. Left the hospital with multiple facial scares. In care of CPS and foster care facilities until Summer 2007. That about it?"

"Just that she is sure her parents were killed in the same accident."

"Right. Well, I'll see what I can find out."

Jack hung up the phone with a feeling of hope.

The next day, Jack asked Shannon if she would like to accompany him on an errand. They drove into Newton, where Jack wire transferred a substantial amount of money to the James Stockburger Detective Agency.

On their way back to the cabin, they stopped off at the Blue JAY Restaurant for lunch and to pass the time until they could pick Jacky up at pre-k. The lunch crowd always included a group of students from the high school, and they were soon joined at their booth by Juliette and her new friend Greg.

Greg was tall, like Juliette had said, over six feet, athletically built, with a pleasant smile and the rugged good looks of a healthy seventeen-year-old male.

"This is my father and my friend Shannon," Juliette told Greg. "Daddy, this is Greg Wilson." Jack and Greg exchanged handshakes and greetings.

"Please join us," Jack said.

Juliette slid in beside Shannon, and Jack slid over so Greg could sit beside him. "So you're Shannon," Greg addressed her. "Juliette has talked about you in such flattering terms, but I must say, even with her advanced knowledge and command of the English language, she didn't do you justice!"

Shannon looked down at her hands on the table, blushed, and mumbled, "Thank you."

Jack laughed and addressed the group. "I used to think I could spread it on pretty thick, but Greg here just topped anything I've ever said."

They ordered sandwiches and drinks. When their waitress, Molly, asked if there was anything else, Jack told her he wanted to speak to her manager. When Yvette saw who had asked for her, she explained something to the young waitress and Jack could see the relief on Molly's face.

"Jack," Yvette scolded him as she stopped at their table, "stop tormenting my help! Oh, I see you've met Greg. Hi, everyone. What are you doing here, Jack?"

"Couldn't live another minute without seeing your pretty face!" Jack commented then continued, "Shannon and I just came in a little early today so I could take care of some business. We're here passing the time until we go get Jacky. Can the manager eat lunch with us?"

"Not this time. Besides, where would I sit? I'll see you at home later. Nice to see you again, Greg. I'll see you at home, Shannon. Juli, just come on back to my office when you get here after school. Now remember, Jack, no more tormenting the help!"

Jack's eyes followed her every move until she disappeared into her office.

"Daddy," Juliette said, snapping her fingers, "you can come back to earth now!"

The conversation at that point was mostly between Greg and Juliette, though Greg often addressed his comments to Shannon. It was obvious to Jack that Greg was more than a little bit interested in her. He watched his daughter's body language and listened to her words and saw and heard a lot of teenage competition. It seemed that Juliette was desperate to keep Greg's attention. Still, she didn't want to leave Shannon completely out of the discussion.

"Daddy, Greg wants to be a doctor," Juliette addressed Jack.

"I'm glad to hear that." Jack looked at Greg and continued, "What schools have you applied to?"

"Just a couple so far. There's the problem of tuition. I have the grade point average—no problem there—but I've been having a difficult time obtaining scholarships due to a problem with transfer of grades. You see, my father is the new pastor at the Pentecostal church here. Our family has moved so many times during my school days that some of my records have been lost. Even if I can get them all together I will probably only be able to get a two-year scholarship. That leaves at least four more years unpaid. I'm sure I'll have to work my way through medical school. That could delay my internship by two or three years. But I'm going to do it. I am going to medical school!"

"It's all he ever talks about!" Juliette said to Shannon.

As the teens got up to leave, Jack extended an invitation to Greg to visit their home on Saturday. "If you come around noon or before, we'll do some fishing and have a cookout. The girls might even take you out on the boat."

Before he and Shannon left, Jack called the little waitress back to his table. Trying to keep a straight face, he said, "Just one more thing, young lady!" He watched her grow tense then took her hand and pressed a big tip into it. "Just keep up the good work, Molly!" Her smile was quick.

As Juliette and Greg walked back to the high school campus, Juliette said to Greg, "You seemed to have made a big hit with my dad. Are you going to come to our house Saturday?"

"Will Shannon be there?"

"Yes, as I've told you, she lives with us."

"I'll try to be there." Greg smiled. "I usually have to help my folks get the church ready for Sunday worship. If we get finished in time I'll call you."

On Friday, just like every other school day, Jack and Shannon went to pick up Jacky from pre-k. Shannon buckled Jacky into his booster seat and climbed into the back with him. She was growing very fond of the little guy, and he showed a deep fondness for her. They had been home less than an hour when Jack got a call from Jim Stockburger.

"We won't be able to get any information from Children's Protective Services," he told Jack. "Those people are entirely incompetent. First of all, each caseworker has two or three times the case loads they can handle. Records are missing or incomplete. If they do have records of twelve years ago it would be nearly impossible to ever find them. Because of the disorganization I found there, the States Attorney General is about to launch an investigation!

"I've been looking at this from another angle," Jim went on. "There was an accident on November 27 of '95, two days after Thanksgiving. That's the one I thought happened eight or ten years ago—the gasoline truck and the sedan. The coroner had the charred bodies for several months before disposing of them. He was able to get enough tissue from each body to determine one was a male and the other a female. He also was able to get sufficient tissue for DNA analysis. They need someone from the family to come forward with their own DNA sample to determine the identity of the deceased. They are as yet still unidentified.

"It won't help identify the victims, but we could eliminate them as our client's parents if we could get a DNA sample from her. If she could just go to the criminology lab in Austin and let them take some hair and saliva samples from her, they could extract her DNA and then we can compare. My contact there is Dr. Marsha Gooding. She'll be waiting for your call."

Before hanging up, he gave Jack a telephone number where he could reach Dr. Gooding so Jack could set up a time and a date for them to obtain the DNA samples.

Shannon had given Jacky a snack and they were playing on the gym set out back when Jack went to find them. He rough housed with Jacky until it was time for him to start the evening meal. "Come on, you guys," he said. "Shannon, you can make the salad. Jacky, you and me need to wash our hands and then you can help me set the table."

FIVE

A trip to Austin from Bon Weir requires one to drive on farm
to market roads and state highways for about one-third of
the 325 miles. Jack figured the required time for them to travel
that distance safely was about six and a half hours. This meant an
overnight stay in Austin. Jack wanted to take the whole family,
but that would mean missing school and work. He planned to
drive down one day, spend the night, then after the DNA samples
were taken, drive back the following day.

Jack told Shannon the DNA samples she would be giving
could help them discover her last name. Shannon was anxious
to help.

"I can either get a room with two beds or I can get two rooms.
Do you mind sleeping in the same room as an old man," Jack
asked her.

"I'd rather not sleep in a hotel room all by myself," Shannon
replied. "I'd feel safer if I was in a room with you."

"Okay, I'll reserve us a room with two queen-size beds."

Their appointment with Dr. Gooding was at 9:00 a. m. on a
Monday. On Sunday he and Shannon drove about halfway across
the state to Austin, checking into their hotel room just as the sun
was setting. They dined at a spaghetti house restaurant for supper.

Later, back in their room, Shannon confided that she had
never had a foster family treat her as nicely as his family did. "You
and Mrs. Lockhart have been more like parents to me than any of
the foster families I stayed with. I feel as if Juliette and Jacky are
my real sister and brother."

"I'm glad you feel that way, Shannon, because I've become
very fond of you also. You are like a daughter to me. If we don't

figure this thing out, you will always have a home with Yvette and me."

At the lab the next morning everything went swiftly. The white-coated technicians took several strands of hair, a blood sample, and several saliva swabs. Dr. Gooding told them she would ensure that Detective Stockburger received the results immediately after they were obtained. Jack and Shannon were on their way home within the hour.

"Shannon, dear," Jack addressed her as they rode along, "I wish you would call me something besides Mr. Lockhart. That just seems so formal. Do you think you could call me Jack?"

"I don't think I should call you Jack; that just seems disrespectful. I'd like to call you Daddy, like Juliette does, but that might cause Juliette to be uncomfortable, like I was trying to steal her daddy or something."

"What about a compromise. How do you like the sound of Daddy Jack?"

"Let me try it. Daddy Jack, can we stop at the Dairy Queen? I like it."

"So do I," Daddy Jack replied. "To the Dairy Queen!"

Although Shannon had protested that she did not want it or deserve it, Jack had been paying her a small salary for her help with Jacky and other housekeeping chores she performed around the house. It was slightly more than Juliette got for her allowance. However, Jack was putting a monthly amount into savings for Juliette and Jacky. As they sat in a booth at the Dairy Queen, Jack suggested to Shannon that she too put some of her salary into savings. "I'll take you by my bank tomorrow so you can get started," he told her. "Would you like me to do that?"

"Yes, and could you teach me to drive so I can get my license?"

"Of course. Juliette's going to be sixteen in about four months. I can teach you both at the same time. How does that sound?"

"Great! We can get our licenses together."

"Then I guess you'll both want a car," Jack said, feigning dejection. "It never ends."

Thursday evening, three days after the DNA samples had been taken, Jack received a call from Detective Stockburger.

"Mr. Lockhart, Jim Stockburger here. I've been swinging the net a little wider. I've found a missing person case up in Los Alamos that looks interesting. A family of three—a father, mother, and small girl didn't return from their Thanksgiving vacation in November of 1995. This would put their going missing at about the same time as our client's being in the hospital. The missing couple are Eldon and Beverly Deweese. The report indicates that the girl was approximately three years old. The missing persons report was initiated by Mr. Deweese's employer, a brokerage firm, where Mr. Deweese was a senior partner. Its coincidence to the time and resemblance to our client's family makeup is what piqued my interest."

"I have received the DNA results from the Austin crime lab and the crime lab here is comparing it to the DNA obtained from the charred bodies. I should have those results in two or three days. Meanwhile, I'm searching for next of kin of the missing Deweese family. That case is still open, but no one has worked it in years. I'll keep you posted and inform you as soon as I hear from the lab here on that DNA."

On Saturday, October 20, Jack was allowed to sleep an extra thirty minutes so Yvette could fix him a birthday breakfast. When he arrived in the kitchen area, the whole family was there to wish him a happy birthday.

In the evening Arty drove up, followed closely by Sheriff and Mrs. McFadden. Yvette's father and mother, Maurice and Colette DuBoise, had arrived midday. Several other of Jack and Yvette's friends soon arrived. Jack spotted Greg and Tommy among the guests. When Yvette brought out the sheet cake that would be served to the guests, Jack noticed it had the single obligatory "Over the Hill" candle, shaped like a tombstone with the number

50 molded into it. After he blew out the candle and everyone sang "Happy birthday, senior citizen," he endured several minutes of jokes about senility, baldness, and adult diapers.

Eventually the happy crowd broke up and everyone went home. Juliette and Shannon helped Yvette clean up. Soon the cabin grew quiet again and Jack and Yvette sat alone on the patio swing.

"October sure is a beautiful time of year here in the piney woods—not too hot, not too cold," Yvette said softly as she nestled against Jack. "Did you notice how much attention Greg showed to Shannon today? I could see it hurt Juli. But Greg is interested in medicine and Shannon is taking the nursing courses. It gives them something in common."

"I saw Tommy and Juli talking together," Jack stated. "I don't especially like that boy. What were you and Karen talking about?"

"Tommy. Karen said he's been showing an interest in law enforcement. He's even been on some ride alongs with his father on routine patrol. He's also been talking about joining the Marines or Navy."

"That might grow him up a little and change my opinion of him. The armed services have made a man out of many a boy. I assume our conversation here is about Juli's pick for her future mate. Well, she could do worse than a marine or sailor. I just hope whoever she chooses has some aspirations toward a college degree."

"Jack, she's fifteen. Why don't we let her grow up before we marry her off?"

"We all want our children to do better than we did. Of course that's impossible from where I sit. I won the jackpot. You, on the other hand—"

"Won the Jack!" she joked, finishing his sentence.

"You know what I mean. I want Juli to have everything. The storybook, happily ever after life with Prince Charming, and that certainly isn't Tommy."

"Maybe he is in Juli's eyes."

"No, I think that's Greg."

"Well, whoever it is, you'll just have to accept her choice."

Jack groaned.

Monday afternoon, Jim Stockburger called Jack again. "The DNA results confirm a relationship between our client and the deceased female whose charred remains were taken from that car. It doesn't prove they were mother and daughter, only that they were close relatives. The results of the DNA comparison also confirmed that our client was not in any way related to the deceased male from that accident. We still don't know who the couple in the car were, but we can almost certainly say that this was the accident that resulted in our client being in the hospital."

"In my attempt to tie this accident to the missing Deweese case, I've been interviewing people in the neighborhood where they lived at the time of their disappearance. One neighbor, an elderly woman who has lived many years in the house next door to the one they occupied, remembers them very well. She described Eldon Deweese as a large, dark-haired, swarthy man much older than his wife. She said that Beverly Deweese was a rather young, very attractive, blond girl. The baby had blond hair and blue eyes like her mother. She said they seemed to be a very odd couple because of the great differences in age. She thought, from the clothes they wore and the expensive car he drove, that they were among the many millionaires living in Los Alamos. I've not been able to verify that fact, but it wouldn't be unusual since there are more millionaires per capita in Los Alamos than any other city in the United States. I'm searching for a relative of the missing couple. When I get more information I'll be in touch."

Jack thanked Jim for all of the information before hanging up.

Maybe the D Shannon remembered was Deweese, Jack thought. *Should I try it out on her or wait for conformation?* He decided to wait.

On Sunday morning, just after church services, Greg joined the Lockharts and Shannon for a boat trip down the Sabine River. They picnicked on one of the many sandy beaches that have formed on either side of the river during the hundreds of years it had carved the border between Texas and Louisiana. Because the river was down, the beaches were wider. Jack picked a spot where the river bed was wide and the slope of the sand into the river would be safer for Jacky to play. They pulled the bow of the boat up onto the sand and secured it by dropping the anchor onto the beach.

Yvette, dressed in a light yellow short-sleeved blouse and white denim cuffed Bermuda shorts, was lovely as always.

Juliette and Shannon, each dressed in an open blouse over a bikini top and shorts, were vying for Greg's attention.

Greg, in tennis shorts and tee shirt, enjoyed every minute of it. Jack was almost jealous of his youth and vitality. They played a game of volleyball in which the girls were on one side of the net and Greg and Yvette were on the other. Jack tried to keep score and referee when he wasn't chasing Jacky away from the river.

When they tired of chasing the ball, had burned sufficient hot dogs and marshmallows, drank up all of the tea and most of the colas, they headed back up the river.

Shannon had not kept her face covered properly the entire day and her face was beginning to turn red and blotchy as they approached the boathouse. Yvette brought this to Shannon's attention as she applied another coat of sunscreen to Shannon's face. As they disembarked, Shannon, embarrassed, tried to outrun the rest of them. Greg easily caught up with her and put his arm around her, trying to ease her embarrassment.

Juliette felt terribly jealous. She took Jack's hand as they all went up the path toward the cabin and told him, "I hate Shannon!"

Yvette and Jacky were just ahead of them on the path. Jack held Juliette back for a few minutes, letting the others get some distance away. He looked at his lovely daughter, who now had tears in her eyes.

"No you don't, Juli honey. I know you. You don't really hate anyone." He hugged her to him and let her cry for a few minutes. When she had gained her composure he gave her his handkerchief. "Here, wipe your eyes, blow your nose, and smile. We have to go say good-bye to Greg."

Juliette was a gracious hostess, accepting Greg's compliments of satisfaction, for the great time he had. She smiled prettily as she waved good-bye then excused herself early to clean up and go to her room.

Shannon was just a little sunburned, so her dual-colored skin could easily be hidden by makeup. "You were warned this might happen if you got too much sun," Yvette scolded. "You'll have to stay inside as much as possible for the next few days. Why didn't you keep your hat on?"

"And play volleyball?" Shannon asked. "I couldn't do that!"

"Of course, you couldn't. I'm sorry I even suggested it. You should get cleaned up and ready for bed now."

Jack had put Jacky to bed and was now sitting with Juliette in the room she shared with Shannon. "Remember, Juli," he said, trying to comfort her, "it isn't Shannon's fault that Greg chose her over you. She has done nothing to cause you to want to end your friendship with her."

"I know, Daddy, but it still hurts."

"Does it help at all to know I still love you very much?"

"Maybe a little."

Jack leaned over and kissed Juliette on her cheek just as Shannon came in from the bathroom. "Good night, sweetheart," he said. "Good night, Shannon."

"You are so lucky," Shannon told Juliette after Jack shut the door behind himself, "to have a father who loves you like Daddy Jack does. I wish I had a father to love me."

"He is special," Juliette said. "My mom has always said so."

Early in the following week, Jack received an update from Jim Stockburger. "I was able to locate a partially burned license plate in the evidence box in the pending files of the Albuquerque Police Department. The box contained the few items that were gathered at the scene of the accident. I was then able to trace that plate to one registered to Mr. Deweese. I'm now ninety-nine percent sure that the woman in the car was Mrs. Deweese. That still doesn't confirm Deweese to be the last name of our client, but I think we are getting close to a solution. When I have more information I'll get back to you."

Juliette and Shannon both began to take the online driver's education course, studying together before completing and passing the written test. Jack had been giving both of them driving lessons in the SUV. When he felt they had mastered that, he borrowed Yvette's sedan and let them practice in it. By mid-November they were both ready to take the behind the wheel, State's driving test. To no one's surprise they both passed and got driving permits. Since she wasn't sixteen yet, Juliette's license was an instruction permit that required her to have an adult licensed driver with her in the car anytime she drove. Shannon, already sixteen, was limited to a daytime curfew. As Jack had predicted, the girls began to lay heavy hints on him about needing their own transportation. Jack began to search car dealerships online for an idea about cost, quality, and efficiency of the new cars. The ones he saw that he thought would be reliable transportation drew negative comments from the girls. The ones they found to be hot, he thought were too sporty and way too expensive.

Jack was at the computer doing one of these auto searches when he received another update from Jim Stockburger.

"Through inquiries made to the Missing Persons Bureau about Mrs. Deweese back in 1996 and again in 1997, I was able to track down an elderly aunt of Mrs. Deweese, who now lives in Florida. This maternal aunt, who asked to remain anonymous, gave me the following information. It may be enough to give you and Miss Shannon the information she needs.

"Beverly Lynn Kaiser was the great-great-granddaughter of German immigrants Hahn and Gretchen Kaiser. Her father and mother, Phillip and Shannon Kaiser, are still alive and living in Atlanta, Georgia. Beverly was married in June of 1990 to Erick Mikkelsen, a supervising foreman in the shipyards in the Pascagoula, Mississippi, area. He was killed in an industrial accident shortly after their baby girl was born. This was about a year after their marriage. Soon after the death of her husband, Beverly left Mississippi with her baby daughter, headed for the West Coast. There she met up with an older man who was taking care of her and the baby. The last anybody heard from Beverly was a letter she wrote to her parents in 1994, post marked Los Alamos, stating she had moved to New Mexico with her male friend when he was transferred by his company.

"I think we can safely say that Shannon's last name is Mikkelsen. There is a record of a marriage between Beverly and Eldon Deweese, but no record of an adoption. I'm sending you a copy of a birth certificate showing a baby girl by the name of Shannon Renee Mikkelsen, born June 6, 1991, in Pascagoula, Mississippi. Shannon may want to contact her grandparents to let them know she's alive. I'll close out this account as soon as I have obtained adequate information about her paternal grandparents.

"Now that the authorities are positive of the death of Mr. Deweese his files have been reopened and the attorneys are pouring over the details to see what assets he left and if he left a will. In the final package I mail to you, I'll include the attorney contact information. Miss Mikkelsen might have some inheritance coming to her that he bequeathed to her mother."

Jack thanked Jim Stockburger, hung up the phone, and leaned back in his desk chair in deep thought. He had only told Shannon he would try to find her last name. This information could be overwhelming to her. He was tempted to keep the information to himself until Jim called with the information on her paternal grandparents. Finally he decided he would share it all with her, if Yvette agreed with him.

After everyone except he and Yvette were in bed that night, Jack and Yvette were sitting together in front of the fireplace. Jack got up, stirred the fire, then came back and sat where he could look into her eyes. "Evie," he said, "I need your advice. I found out today what Shannon's last name is."

"Great, what is it?"

"Wait, it isn't that simple," Jack explained. "She has living relatives in Atlanta and Florida and probably in Mississippi. Her mother and father are both dead; that we have confirmed. But her father wasn't the man with her mother in the accident where Shannon received her scars. That was her stepfather. There's more to it, but that's the essential points. I need your help in deciding when and how to tell her."

"Well, what is her name?"

"Jim Stockburger is mailing me a birth certificate with the name Shannon Renee Mikkelsen. Do you think we should wait until we get the birth certificate to tell her? Jim is still in search of her paternal grandparents, her father's parents."

"I know what paternal means, Jack," Yvette told him with a grin. "You are so serious! Relax, Jack. Shannon will take this news very well. Look at all she's been through!"

"Exactly, Evie. I don't want to add to it."

"That's the very characteristic that made me fall in love with you Jack, your overwhelming compulsion to always protect everyone from any kind of hurt. Do you know how much I love you right now?"

"Then you think it will be all right to tell her right away, tomorrow even?"

"Yes. Why don't you do it when the two of you are alone in the morning, after we have all gone? I think you'll be surprised at how well she handles the information that her Daddy Jack uncovered for her."

Jack reached over and pulled Yvette closer to him. "Let me show you how much I love you right now!" he said as he kissed her passionately. As the fire died, he helped her off of the settee and to their room.

SIX

"**S**hannon, dear," Jack called, "when you have some time I need to talk to you."

"What is it, Daddy Jack?"

Jack poured himself a cup of coffee. "Would you like something? This may take a few minutes."

"I've got it," Shannon said as she poured herself a cup of coffee and sat down opposite of Jack at the breakfast table, smiling.

Jack took a sip. Then, looking very serious, he began. "I received the information about your last name that we have been waiting for. First of all, you were born Shannon Renee Mikkelsen." Jack paused here to let her absorb that.

"Shannon Renee Mikkelsen. I wonder why I've thought all these years that my last name started with a D."

"That's probably because the last name of your stepfather was Deweese. Let me explain all that Detective Stockburger uncovered." Jack went on to tell her as much of her family tree as he could. He explained that there was still a search being conducted for her father's family. He skipped over the more gruesome details.

"Shannon Renee Mikkelsen," she repeated. "It sounds so strange," Shannon mused, "but now I do have a last name!" She jumped up and hugged Jack. "Thank you so much, Daddy Jack. You'll never know how much this means to me. Can you get me the address of my grandparents, the Kaisers? I want to write to them. I'll send them a picture of me with my new face."

"And I worried that the information might upset you," Jack said, showing relief in his voice. "We'll be receiving a whole package of paperwork from Mr. Stockburger very soon that will contain all of the information I have given you, your birth certificate and more. I'll call his office right now and get the Kaisers' address and telephone number for you. I'm sure they will be overjoyed to hear from you."

While Shannon went through her pictures to pick out just the right one and tried to find just the right words to put in her letter, Jack called the office of James Stockburger in Paradise Hills. Jim's secretary gave him the desired information—an address and telephone number in an Atlanta, Georgia suburb.

Just as he hung up, the telephone rang. "Did you tell her yet?" Yvette wanted to know. "How did she take it?"

"Better than I expected, Evie. Right now she's in her room picking out pictures and writing to her grandparents. I am so relieved."

"I thought she might take it that way. You, my darling, worry too much."

"We may see you for lunch. I'm sure Shannon will want to mail her letter right away."

"Oh, please do. I'll arrange my schedule so I can sit with you. I'd like to be in on her excitement."

"Then it's a date," Jack promised her.

Jack and Shannon arrived before the noon rush of high school students. Yvette joined them shortly, rewarding them with her smile.

"Well, Shannon, I heard you got some news today."

"Yes, thanks to Daddy Jack I now have a last name! It's Mikkelsen. Do you like it?"

"It suits you, Shannon Mikkelson. Yes, I like it."

"Shannon Renee Mikkelsen to be exact," Shannon said, tossing her head proudly.

"What are you grinning about?" Yvette addressed Jack. "Really proud of yourself, aren't you?"

"Just happy," Jack answered.

Just then, Juliette entered the restaurant accompanied by Greg and Tommy. Seeing her mother and father sitting with Shannon, she approached their table, followed by the boys.

"Come over here," Jack addressed Greg and Tommy. "I'd like to introduce you to someone. Ladies and gentlemen, may I present Miss Shannon Renee Mikkelsen!"

"You found out your last name!" Juliette shouted, reaching to give Shannon a hug. "That's wonderful news. I'm so happy for you."

Greg and Tommy both congratulated Shannon. Then Greg asked if he could sit with Miss Mikkelsen. Juliette and Tommy took the booth behind Jack.

"What's new?" Jack asked Greg. "How is the college application situation?"

"I've been able to get everything together, and I've applied to Baylor College of Medicine in Houston. BCM has everything I need, and it's also very close. They have a very good nursing program in clinical anesthesia that you should encourage Shannon to look into."

"You sound very excited. How are you going to pay for all of this?"

"During Christmas break I plan to go down to Houston and look into the job market. Maybe I can find a job that will let me mesh school hours to fit my work schedule. Meanwhile, if I can keep my grades up here, I can qualify for some scholarship funds."

"Good luck, Greg," Jack told him, "I hope you are able to find something. If you need help with writing your résumé, you should asked Mrs. Lockhart. She's very talented in that area."

"Sure, Greg, I'd be glad to help," Yvette said.

Juliette was sitting in the booth just behind Jack, and as there was now a lull in the conversation he could hear Tommy's voice. "It's just a school Christmas party, Juli. Who else am I going to ask? You've always been my first choice!"

Jack couldn't hear Juliette's answer.

Yvette stood up, said she had to go back to work, and left them to go back to her office. The high school students soon left, leaving Jack and Shannon sitting alone in their booth. "Miss Mikkelsen," he said, "let's go pick up little Jacky."

Within a week Jack and Shannon received their information packages from the Stockburger Detective Agency. Jack's was a duplicate of Shannon's, except his had a line item expense account with a final charge slip.

Shannon found she had many new relatives. On her father, Erick Mikkelsen's side of the family, she found she had two new uncles, three aunts, grandparents, and several cousins. On her mother, Beverly Kaiser's side, besides her grandparents, she found she had an aunt, an uncle, and her great-aunt, Kathryn Cox, of Miami Beach, Florida.

Shannon learned that when her mother, Beverly, had "run off to marry that Mikkelsen guy," her aunt Kathryn had been her only contact with the family. When Beverly stopped contacting her around the holidays in 1995, she had contacted missing persons in 1996 and again in 1997. It was these contacts that led Jim Stockburger to Shannon's great-aunt Kathryn and eventually to the truth about her last name.

SEVEN

Jack was working on a promised gift for Jacky's fifth birthday, December 15th. There were only a few weeks remaining before he would have to deliver on that promise.

Jack had been raised on a large cattle ranch in Brewster County, the largest county in Texas. It had been many years since his boyhood days on the family ranch. The arid landscape and wide-open spaces were home to Texas Longhorn cattle, and more recently to large herds of Black Angus. Jack could still remember how exhilarating it was to be alone in the saddle beneath the wide-open Texas sky. He had told Jacky many stories about those days, and Jacky had asked him for his own pony.

In Angelina County, up near Lufkin, Jack had located and purchased a gentle three-year-old female riding pony, tack, and trailer. The mare had been bred and was expecting to foal in the spring. She was all black except for a white spot on her face that resembled an elongated hourglass, reaching from between her ears, to the bottom of her upper lip. The rancher who Jack was now paying to board her had promised to deliver her tack and trailer, when Jack had her corral, stable, and shed finished.

Jack was in the rear of the cabin digging postholes for the corral fence when he heard the sound of a vehicle stop out front. Laying down the digger and taking off his gloves, he wiped the sweat from his forehead and walked to the front of the house. Juliette was just getting out of a partially primed 1969 Ford Mustang convertible being driven by Tommy McFadden.

"Does your mother know that you're not coming home with her today, Juli?"

"Of course, Daddy."

"What's that you're driving?" Jack asked Tommy. "Looks like a pile of work."

"Tommy's restoring it!" Juliette volunteered. "Isn't it great?"

"I need to apologize to you, Mr. Lockhart," Tommy said seriously. "I've been a real jerk lately. I hope you'll accept my apology."

"All right, son," Jack said, shaking Tommy's hand. "We'll start new today."

"I would like to talk to Shannon too, if it's all right with you, Mr. Lockhart. Is she here?"

"She's in the house, I think in the laundry room. Come on in, and I'll help you find her," Jack told him as he held the door for Juliette and Tommy.

"I wonder if I could have a minute of your time," Tommy said to Shannon when they found her, in the laundry room as Jack had said. "I need to say something to you. I'm sorry for the way I treated you when you first moved here and the unfair things I said about your looks. Can you ever forgive me?"

Shannon looked at the sincere expression on Tommy's face. She had already forgotten the cruel things he'd said. "Of course I forgive you, Tommy." She dropped the dishtowel she was folding into the clothes basket and gave him a friendly hug.

"I think this calls for a celebration," Jack told the three. "Who wants a cola or a glass of iced tea?"

"I do, Daddy," Jacky said. "I want a cola."

Tommy and Jack had a long conversation while the girls watched Jacky and finished folding the laundry.

Tommy said he had quit sports so he could concentrate on his new chosen career path, mechanical engineering. He planned to change some of his school courses at the beginning of the next semester to fit that goal. He was working part time after school and on weekends for Charlie Poe. Tommy said he had really been trying to clean and straighten up Charlie's garage.

"You can see the counter top now and even get from one end of the garage to the other without tripping or stepping on something! Charlie's letting me use all of his tools and equipment to restore the Mustang. Just one more very important thing, Mr. Lockhart," Tommy said. "I'd like your permission to take Juli to a school-sponsored Christmas party up in Newton on Friday, December 21. It won't be over until midnight, but I promise I'll have her home as soon as possible after the party."

"I'll check it out and let you know later," Jack told him, "If there's going to be alcohol or drugs there, I can tell you right now the answer is no. Who are the chaperones?"

"I'm not sure. I'll get you the names. I really have to go now, Mr. Lockhart. Charlie is expecting me."

"Drive safely."

Yvette was planning a Thanksgiving special at the restaurant and a big family Thanksgiving at the cabin. "How are you going to pull all of this off?" Jack wanted to know. "Who have you invited to the cabin? Couldn't we all just eat our Thanksgiving meal at the Blue JAY, let the cooks fix it and the cleaning staff take over after the meal? Spare you a lot of grief."

"And what will I be doing all of this time while someone else is cooking our meal and cleaning up afterward?"

"Walking around looking gorgeous?" Jack offered.

"I want to have my mom, my dad, and Arty. Shannon wants to invite her grandparents and her great-aunt Kathryn. Do I have to give you a list right now?"

"What's my part in all of this?" Jack asked warily.

"I want you to make a large container of your famous potato salad. Arty's going to bring a large pan of his cornbread, walnut, chopped apple, and cranberry stuffing. I'll do two smaller turkeys instead of a giant one so we can have one on each end of the table. Your potato salad will go with the leftover turkey sandwiches later on. We'll have mashed potatoes and turkey gravy with the main meal. You'll see, we'll have a great time. Now go worry some other place while I plan this."

Jack went to finish the corral fence, connecting the last rails to the back wall of the horse stall and shed. He was almost ready for Jacky's surprise. He wanted to get some feed stored in the shed first. He still had over three weeks until Jacky's birthday. He wanted to put some hooks in the ceiling of the shed so he would have a place to hang a bridle and rope. He had already purchased a saddle rack and placed it in the shed.

"What are you building, Daddy?" Jacky asked. "Can I help?"

"I'm building a corral fence. Yes, here, put a washer on this lag bolt then put it into that hole in the plank. Now step back while I set it with my hammer. Here you want to tighten it? You have to turn the wrench this direction. That's called clockwise."

Jacky, at almost five, was curious and eager to learn. Jack tied a nail apron around him and filled the pocket that hung down in front of him with lag bolts and washers. Jacky painstakingly placed a washer on each lag bolt before placing it in each hole that he could reach. For the higher rails, Jack picked him up so he could reach them.

Later at supper, Jacky announced to everyone, "Me and Daddy are building a corral fence."

"What's it for?" someone unwisely asked.

"I don't know," Jacky told them. "What's it for, Daddy?"

"We'll need a corral if we ever get that pony you want," Jack told him. "It would be sad if one day a pony showed up and we didn't have a place for it to live. It might just go away and find another little boy."

"We'll build it a home, huh, Daddy?"

"We sure will!"

In the morning Jack took a long distance call for Shannon. The voice on the phone identified herself as Marissa of the law offices of Keller and Caruso of Los Alamos, New Mexico. She wanted to talk to Miss Shannon Mikkelsen. Jack called Shannon to the phone.

Shannon listened attentively while making some notes. When she hung up she turned to Jack and told him she had been talking to the attorneys that were taking care of her late stepfather's estate. They were sending her an overnight package of papers that she had to sign in front of a notary and send back. Something about an inheritance and trust.

The next day when Shannon received the papers, she and Jack went over the information before taking them to his bank to have her signature notarized. After totaling all of Eldon Deweese's assets and investments, including interest that had been accruing and reinvestment of dividends for the past twelve years—and after the attorneys had taken their bite—Mr. Deweese had left his wife and by stripes, Shannon, just over six million dollars. This was to be held in trust for Shannon until her twenty-first birthday. The papers were signed, dated, notarized, and returned.

Jack advised Shannon to seek investment advice before she reached twenty-one and started withdrawing her funds. He believed that during the four and a half years before she turned twenty-one her dividend reinvestments could earn her an additional one point five to two million dollars more. He suggested that at that time she might be able to live off of investment dividends, which are taxed at a much lower rate than income.

Shannon had one more request of Jack. "Daddy Jack," she began, "I want to find out what they did with the bodies of my mother and Mr. Deweese. I think they should have a proper burial."

"I'll find out for you if I can, dear. You might want to get in touch with your grandparents to see how they feel about it. Maybe they have a family plot where they would want their daughter to be buried."

Jack placed a call to Jim Stockburger. He was assured by Jim that he would get the information from the coroner and get back to him ASAP. "No extra charge, Mr. Lockhart," Jim said. "I should have included that information in my report."

Jim returned the call in less than an hour. "Unfortunately, Mr. Lockhart," he said, "since the bodies were never claimed, they were cremated. However, the ashes are being kept in a special vault at the crematorium where next of kin can claim them. I'd need a power of attorney from a family member before they could release them to me. Here's the crematorium's name, address, and phone number. Let me know what you decide."

"Thank you. We will."

Shannon called her grandparents to see what they thought about funeral arrangements for her mother and what should be done with Eldon's ashes since no one had come forward to claim them. Grandma and Grandpa Kaiser both were on extensions and she was able to talk to both at the same time. She told them that she had found a picture of her stepfather in the papers she had received and it had evoked pleasant memories. They all agreed that instead of scattering the ashes, both urns should be buried, after a graveside service, in the Kaiser family plot, which was located near the Chattahoochee River.

Shannon thought it would be simpler and a lot less expensive for her to send Mr. Stockburger a power of attorney than it would be to fly to Albuquerque and back. The urns arrived via registered mail within the week. Shannon packed her bags for a two-week stay with her grandparents and flew to Atlanta.

It was cold and rainy during the graveside services. Shannon stood between her grandmother and grandfather as her Mother's and Eldon's urns were buried. A small stone was ordered that would be set within a month.

When she returned just two days before Thanksgiving, she was accompanied by Mr. and Mrs. Kaiser and her great-aunt Kathryn Cox.

The day before Thanksgiving, Yvette's parents, Maurice and Colette DuBoise, arrived. Jack said Yvette was as happy as a chicken making a nest as she fussed around making room for everyone to have a bed and a room. Jacky would move into the room with Jack and Yvette. Great-aunt Kathryn would take his room, and the Kaisers would use the guest bedroom. Shannon and Juliette would sleep on the foldout couch in the den, and Mr. and Mrs. DuBoise would sleep in the girls' room.

When Arty arrived early on Thanksgiving Day there were so many cooks and supervisors in the kitchen it was a miracle that anything got done. However, at 1:00 p.m., when Yvette called everyone to the long Thanksgiving table, it was an aromatically delightful and beautiful sight.

They held hands and prayed over the feast, and then each gave thanks for something special the past year.

When it was Shannon's turn, she said, "I don't know where to begin. There's Mr. Carmichael, who picked me up by the side of the road; there's Mrs. Lockhart and Daddy Jack, who have done more for me than I can ever repay; there's my best friend, Juli, and my little brother, Jacky; my grandparents and my great-aunt Kathryn. I thank God for all of you."

EIGHT

By Friday, December 14, the day before Jacky's birthday, Jack had the corral finished and the horse stall and shed completed and stocked with oats and hay. He placed a call to the horse ranch where Jacky's horse was being stabled and made arrangements for the pony to be delivered midmorning the next day.

When the horse and trailer arrived, Jack took Jacky with him to watch them unload his pony. He sat Jacky up on the top rail of the corral fence near the gate and told him to just watch until the pony was unloaded. As the shiny black mare backed out of the horse trailer, Jack loosely holding the bridle rope, Jacky said loudly, "Blacky." He had just named his pony.

After unloading, the horse trailer was backed into a spot near the rear of the shed. Jack and the ranch owner had a few quiet words then shook hands before he drove away. While Jack got the saddle, bridle, blanket, and a brush from the horse trailer he let Jacky sit on the top rail and talk to the mare. She was curious of her new surroundings and nuzzled the legs of her new owner.

Jack went into the corral, took the halter off of her and brushed her down. He put a saddle blanket on her and then the little saddle. As he cinched it up he realized that although it was a child's saddle, the stirrups hung too low for Jacky's feet. Jack had not yet put a bridle on her, yet she was so gentle she just stood there unflinching while he saddled her. He scratched her between the ears as he placed the bit between her teeth and stretched the bridle over her ears. Again she allowed this without resistance. Finally he lifted Jacky from the corral fence and placed him in the saddle. Blacky raised her head as if to ask "Which way?" Jack told his tiny son to hold to the saddle horn as he led them out of the corral and up to the back door of the cabin. He opened the door and called for everyone to come outside.

Even the excited happy chatter of the three females and Jacky didn't frighten the mare, and Jack knew he had gotten just what he'd paid for—a very gentle pony.

"His feet don't even reach the stirrups!" Yvette said. "Don't you let him fall off of there, Jack."

"I'll fix them to fit him later," Jack told her. "Right now they need to get acquainted."

The girls each took turns holding the reins and leading Blacky around the yard.

"We have any apples or carrots?" Jack asked Yvette. "I want to let Jacky try giving her a treat."

"Both," Yvette answered. "Which do you want?"

"Let's try one of each."

"Do you want to ride Blacky?" Jacky asked his sister, who was holding the reins and leading the pony around the yard.

"Maybe later. You enjoy your birthday present today."

As they came back to where Jack and Yvette were standing, Jacky stuck his arms out toward his daddy and said, "I want down now."

Jack lifted him off of Blacky and placed him on the ground near him. He took the reins from Juliette in one hand and Jacky's hand in his other and led them both into the corral. He took the bridle off of Blacky and handing Jacky the big juicy carrot, said, "Here, give her a reward for taking you riding, Jacky."

As Jack took the saddle and blanket off and brushed her down, he watched the delight in Jacky's eyes as his pony enjoyed the carrot. "Here," Jack said, handing Jacky the apple. "Now give her some dessert." After finishing the apple, Blacky snorted, shook her head, and turned to go to the corner of the corral to the watering trough. Jacky trailed along behind her.

"Watch she doesn't step on you, son. She can't see behind her. You need to stay where she can see you at all times. She's very gentle but she is also much larger than you, and could accidentally seriously hurt you!"

Jacky went to the edge of the trough and watched her drink. Jack took a bale of hay out of the storage end of the shed and popped the wire off of it, letting if fall loosely into the feed trough. "Come on, Jacky. It's time for our lunch too."

They ate only a light snack, as Yvette planned to serve cake and ice cream a little later.

Jack fashioned a pair of stirrups nearer to Jacky's size out of one of his old western leather belts, attaching the loops to the saddle tree in the same slot the other stirrups occupied. He tied them with leather thongs so they could easily be removed when Jacky got bigger.

At 2:00 p. m. the kids from Jacky's pre-k class and other small folks began arriving. Jack tried to stay out of the way and let Yvette, Juliette, Shannon, and the few mothers who stayed organize the fun and games. Then Jacky announced that he had gotten a pony for his birthday and everyone ran to see. Jack had to saddle Blacky and lead her around the yard for the next two hours until everyone had a turn. It was a fun time for everyone.

Later that night, after Jack had seen to it that Blacky was settled in the horse stall, he joined Yvette in front of the fireplace. "Tomorrow you have to cut me a nice Christmas tree," she told him. "It's only two weeks until Christmas, and I need to get started on my decorating. You know Shannon won't be spending the holidays with us, don't you? She's decided to spend Christmas with the Mikkelsens and New Year with her great-aunt Kathryn."

Jack pulled Yvette close to him. "Where do you get all this energy? You just entertained a jillion little curtain climbers, and now you're ready to start decorating for Christmas! Save a little of your vitality for me."

"Don't worry," she said, getting up and heading for the bath. "I've saved your entertainment for later."

"Wait for me!" Jack called, getting to his feet.

Jack had finally consented to let Juliette go with Tommy to the school-sponsored Christmas party when he learned that Greg and Shannon would be going too. As promised, Tommy had provided the names of the chaperones and Yvette had approved of each.

Tommy had completed much of the restoration of the Mustang and had the top up to protect the hairdos of the ladies.

"Wow, you look breathtakingly beautiful tonight," Greg told Shannon.

"You too," Tommy told Juliette.

"I'll be sitting here with my shotgun in hand if you boys try to bring these two beauties home any later than one a. m. tomorrow morning!" Jack warned Tommy and Greg. "And absolutely no drinking!"

"Yes, sir," Greg addressed Jack. "I don't drink, and I would never do anything to hurt either Shannon or Juli! You have my word, sir!"

"The same goes for me, Mr. Lockhart," Tommy said, looking at his shoes.

"Up here, Tommy," Jack told him. "Look me in the eye and tell me you'll take the best possible care of my daughter!"

"Yes, sir," Tommy said looking squarely at Jack.

"Okay then, you kids go have a good time."

"Do you think you scared the boys sufficiently, Jack," Yvette teased him as they watched Tommy drive cautiously away.

"I hope so. Maybe he'll think twice before speeding or doing some other foolish teenage male prank. I was a teenage jerk myself once, Evie. Teenage boys aren't to be trusted!"

"Are you really going to stay up until one? You know you have to get up early to drive Shannon to Houston to catch her flight."

"I won't sleep until I see them both back here safe and sound."

Jack sat alone in the den in front of the fireplace and enjoyed a cup of hot chocolate. It was just after midnight when he heard the car drive into the yard. He heard the car doors slam and the two girls came hurrying inside out of the cold. Jack met them in the hall as they were about to enter their room.

"You're home earlier than I expected. Did you have a good time? Was Santa Claus there?"

"Oh, it was all right," Juliette told him.

"Yes, it was okay," Shannon said.

As Jack quietly slipped into bed a few minutes later, Yvette asked him, "Was that the girls? Is everything all right?"

"Yes, they're home. I didn't receive the glowing report I expected. Must have been a boring party."

The night passed too quickly, and soon Shannon and Jack were on the road to George Bush International airport, just north of Houston.

"I'm apprehensive about meeting all the new relatives," Shannon told him.

"You'll do just fine," Jack replied. "Do you have enough spending money? You might find a newly discovered cousin that you need to buy a gift for. Here, let me give you some extra cash. Now you call us every night and let us know you are okay. You know how Mrs. Lockhart worries about you."

"Thank you, Daddy Jack," Shannon said as she hugged him and kissed his cheek. That's my flight number."

"Have a good flight," Jack called after her.

Christmas at the Lockharts was quiet that year, just the four of them around the tree while Jack played Santa and passed out gifts. First everyone watched as Jacky tore into his gifts. Then they got to ooh and ahh as Juliette opened her gifts. Next Yvette, and finally Jack. The only gifts left under the tree were Shannon's.

Jack sat sipping a big mug of eggnog and watching Jacky playing with his toys. His gaze slowly went to Juliette, who was cheerfully engaged in conversation with her mother, and finally to his pretty wife sitting on the end of the couch, legs drawn up under her like he'd so often seen her, smiling that adorable smile of hers. Jack Lockhart was a happy man.

NINE

When school started in January right after the Christmas break, Shannon enrolled in some high school classes to pad her academic record. Her goal was to more easily get into Baylor College of Medicine so she could attend at the same time as Greg. She was considered a part-time student, and as such she had freedom to enter and leave campus at irregular hours. Her classes did, however, make her eligible to attend the junior/senior prom. Although he hadn't asked her, everyone took it for granted that Shannon and Greg would be going together.

A new junior on the high school campus at the beginning of that semester was seventeen-year-old Robert "Bobby" Wayne Miller. He had a driver's license and drove his own four-year-old very shiny pickup. His parents were the new owners of the Bayou Mobile Home Park.

Juliette and Tommy were friends again, but Juliette had made it clear they were only friends. The Christmas party just two weeks earlier had ended badly when Tommy tried to get intimate. Greg had to step in and she had ridden home in the back seat of the car with Shannon while Greg rode up front with Tommy. Although Juliette shared almost everything with her father, she had not told him about this. He already had a low opinion of Tommy McFadden. She did, however, tell her mother.

"Tommy can be so sweet at times, and then he'll do something like that and it just makes me so mad! Why can't he be more like Greg or Daddy?"

"No two personalities are the same, sweetheart. But believe me, as sweet as you think your daddy is, there have been times when he made me mad too!"

"But you've kept on loving him. Has he ever done anything to test your love for him?"

"No. Every day just seems better than the day before. I pray that someday you'll meet someone just like your daddy. He has a capacity for love greater than anyone I have ever known. You've felt his love for you and you can see it in the way he treats Jacky. He has a special love for Shannon. You add all of those feelings to the passionate love he has for me, and you see what I mean."

"He really does love you. I can see that. And you totally love him. You are so lucky, Mom."

"So are you! Now, I don't keep secrets from your daddy, so if he asks me about this I'll have to tell him. I won't volunteer anything. Eventually you may want to tell him yourself. He'll grouse about it, but he won't really hurt Tommy."

Greg Wilson became a regular at the Lockhart home, taking some of his evening meals there. He spent hours in Shannon and Juliette's room studying with Shannon. Eventually all the studying paid off in exceptionally high college-entrance exam scores for both of them.

Both Tommy McFadden and Bobby Miller were infatuated with the exquisite Juliette and were in constant competition for her attention. Juliette, on the other hand, seemed to not know they existed. She was also studying hard and working on her design art, hoping to get into one of the colleges of art located in Austin, Dallas, or Houston.

It was Valentine's Day—and Yvette's birthday—before Jack had even gotten used to the new year. On Wednesday, the day before her birthday, he asked Juliette and Shannon if they would take Jacky for a little while on Thursday and be sure they were all out of the house when Yvette got home. "Here," Jack said, handing Juliette a $100 bill, "you all eat at the restaurant tomorrow and be sure to take your time. Get Jacky a dessert or two. I want some alone time with your mother!"

"He is such a romantic!" Shannon said, grinning as she drove the SUV to the restaurant on Thursday. "He's still wooing your mother after seven and a half years of marriage."

"Sometimes he's so embarrassing," Juliette said. "The way he flirts with her all of the time!"

"Oh, I think it's cute, and your mother seems to thrive on his attention."

Jack put two thirty-two-inch tall vases, each with two dozen long-stemmed lavender roses, on either side of the front door. He scattered lavender rose petals from the front door to their bedroom. He placed her birthday gift on the bed and made a heart-shaped ring of rose petals around it. He showered and shaved. By 5:15 he was waiting impatiently for Yvette, just inside the front door.

At 5:25, like so many times before, Jack watched her turn into the drive and felt his heartbeat quicken. It didn't make any difference how many times he had watched her come home, he always got excited like it was his first. He met her at the door, pulled her into his arms, and kissed her tenderly. "Happy birthday, my darling, and happy Valentine's Day."

Yvette returned his kiss then pushed him gently away. "May I please get into the house before you accost me," she asked, smiling. Then seeing the vases of flowers, she said, "Oh, Jack, they're beautiful."

"Follow the trail of petals," he instructed her. He followed closely behind her until she entered their bedroom. Once inside he watched her open her birthday gift. Her delightful girlish sounds caused him to believe he had done well. As she went into the bath to freshen up, Jack closed the bedroom door and brushed the rose petals off of the bed.

A week later, February 21, Juliette turned sixteen. Yvette hosted a birthday party for her in the party room at the restaurant.

The party was in full swing when Jack drove up with a new deep-sea blue BMW 650i series convertible and parked it out front. He opened the trunk and got the giant plastic bow and ribbon and placed it on the hood. He put the keys in a small gift box he was carrying and slipped it into his coat pocket.

When Jack entered the party room, the band, having been alerted to the fact, suddenly stopped the tune they were playing and started playing the Neil Sedaka song "Sweet Sixteen." Juliette rushed over and grabbed his hand. As the dance floor cleared, she pulled him out onto the floor to dance with her. As Jack held his lovely sixteen-year-old daughter in his arms and moved around the floor with her, he was overcome with emotions as memories of the past eight years flooded into his mind. From the darling little seven-year-old fatherless child he had discovered on a counter stool in a tiny café, through all the years up to this very day, he had loved her unconditionally. As he spun her at the end of the dance and they both took a bow, he was as proud of her as any one has a right to be. Before he left her to go find Yvette, he hugged her tightly and kissed her lovingly with a father's kiss upon the lips. "Sweet sixteen and now you've been kissed," he whispered to her. There was a mixed reaction from the crowd.

The gift opening had been near the beginning of the party, so Jack had to find an opening near the end of the party to give Juliette her gift.

He found Yvette in her office. "Why are you hiding in here, Evie?" he asked. "Did my dancing embarrass you?" Then he noticed the tears. "What's wrong?"

"Nothing is wrong, Jack. I'm crying because of what I just saw on the dance floor. That was so very touching and moving. When I realize that my little girl isn't a little girl anymore. Do you realize she's almost as old as I was when I found out I was pregnant with her."

Jack hugged his wife tenderly, kissed her tears away, and gave her his handkerchief. "You better freshen up, Evie. The party's winding down, and people are going to want to thank the hostess. I'll go run interference for you."

Jack found Juliette in the company of Bobby Miller and some of her other friends. "I guess you didn't find a gift in that pile from me," he told her as he pulled her away from her friends. "That's because I forgot and left it in my pocket. Here, it's just a little something to remind you every day how much I love you, Juli."

Juliette opened the box, expecting some earrings or an engraved necklace. "What's this?" she asked. "Are these car keys?"

"Take a look outside," Jack told her. "I hope you like the color."

Most of the group of teenagers followed Juliette out of the party room and outside into the parking lot in front of the restaurant. Those who hadn't been following what was going on suddenly looked up and wanted to know where everyone had gone. Only a few people were still in the party room when Yvette returned.

"Where is everybody?" she asked. "What did you do, Jack?"

"Why do you always assume I did something?" Jack wanted to know.

TEN

February turned into March, and as April approached, the wildflowers began to bloom in the open areas along the Sabine River. Blacky had begun to show the unmistakable physical features of a mare about to foal. Jacky just thought she was getting fatter, as his legs stuck out farther when he tried to ride.

Yvette always took Juliette and Jacky to school on her way to work. Shannon, who went to school later in the morning, drove the SUV with the booster seat in the rear and brought little Jacky home with her when her classes were over. Consequently, Jacky grew very fond of Shannon, and the fondness was mutual.

Jack saw the SUV with Shannon at the wheel and Jacky in the rear come into the yard. He remarked how the SUV seemed to fit her. Shannon, whose father had been a very tall man, had grown over the last few months to a height of over five feet seven inches and still seemed to be growing taller.

"Oh, I love driving this car," Shannon told him as she helped Jacky out of the back seat. "I like being up where I can see around me. And you're right, I feel comfortable in it. I think it just fits me."

"Then it's yours," Jack told her while picking Jacky up for a hug. "The first day you have off we'll go up to Newton and change the title into your name."

"I couldn't do that. What would you have to drive?"

"Let me worry about that. I'd still want you to pick Jacky up after school, so we're doing each other a favor."

"When I get my inheritance, Daddy Jack, I'm going to pay you back for everything," she said, hugging him around the neck.

"No need to do that, honey. It's just an old car."

Supper over and the cleanup finished, the girls were off to do homework and talk girl talk. Jack and Jacky went to finish up the chores outside. By this time Jacky knew just how much oats to put in the feed trough. He made sure the water trough was full, but he wasn't big enough to spread the hay.

After chores Jacky ran inside to spend time with his mommy. Jack remained outside for a while, watching a full moon rise. He noticed Blacky seemed restless. He went into the horse stall and talked to her soothingly for a short time while patting her on the neck.

Jack slept fitfully that night, awaking early. He'd had half a pot of coffee by the time it was light outside and Yvette came into the kitchen.

"What time did you abandon me this morning?" she asked as Jack fixed her a cup just like she liked it.

"I'm not sure. I just didn't sleep much last night. Guess it's time to start breakfast for everyone. Think you could eat with us this morning?"

"Maybe a scrambled egg and a piece of toast. I'll do the toast. Is something bothering you, Jack?"

"Not that I know of. Must be the full moon."

As everyone got up and ready for school, Jacky went out, like every morning since he got his pony, to say hello to Blacky. In two minutes he came back in yelling, "There's a baby horsy in the stall with Blacky!" The whole family ran outside to see the baby horsy Jacky was telling them about. Sure enough, like most horses, Blacky had given birth during the night or early morning hours and now, standing in the stall beside his mother, was a male foal.

He was all black except for his legs, tail, mane, and face. On his legs, which seemed uncommonly long, he had white stocking like markings from his knees to his hooves. His mane and tail were white, and like his mother, he had a white blaze down his face.

"He's just adorable," Yvette said, trying to get a closer look.

Juliette and Shannon were leaning on the corral fence, looking at the foal with big smiles on each of their faces.

"Stay back, Jacky," Jack cautioned his son as Jacky started into the corral. Mother horses are very protective of their young. Let them have some time together. I'll introduce you to him after school today if Blacky will let me. Why don't you try thinking of a name for him today at school? Maybe the other children can help you."

As the young foal began to nurse, Jack reminded everyone that they still needed to get breakfast and get to school.

When the house was quiet, Jack went out into the corral and talked softly to Blacky and tried to get close to her foal. At first it shied away, but soon curiosity got the best of it and Jack was able to make its acquaintance. In just a little while it was following him around the corral. Blacky came with them, and if she thought the foal was getting too close to Jack, she would nudge it away with her nose. By the time Jacky and Shannon returned from school, Jack was certain that Jacky would be safe from Blacky's maternal instincts. Jack squatted in the corral and watched for several minutes as his son interacted with his pony and her new foal. Jacky wanted to give the foal some oats, and Jack explained to him that a new foal didn't eat oats. "He drinks milk from his mother's teats," Jack instructed him. "It will be ten days or maybe two weeks before he will be interested in hay or oats. When he's ready you'll see him trying to eat his mother's feed."

After many a family discussion, where names like Luna and Lunar and Full Moon were tried, they all came to the conclusion that the foal should be named Apollo. It was based on a number of things. The moon had been full the night of his birth, the Apollo moon landings, and someone thought the little stud looked like a Greek god. In due course, Apollo would be weaned, grow to be taller and a lot friskier than his mother, and be broke to saddle.

Jack realized he was once again in need of personal transportation. The SUV was the only vehicle that had a trailer package, and he needed to take the young colt to the veterinarian for shots and physical check up. He went online and in a few hours had found a new fully loaded metallic-silver 2008 Ford Expedition. It had twenty-inch wheels and came with a trailer package. It had nineteen actual miles. The dealer, located in Jasper, could deliver it to Jack's home the very next day.

Meanwhile, high school graduation grew near. In early May, plans were being made for the junior/senior prom. When Greg finally asked Shannon to go with him, Juliette was feeling left out. She and Shannon had shared so much over the year. Shannon was only a few months older than she and yet, by a twist of fate, was eligible to attend the prom while she wasn't.

The date of the prom was May 23, just two weeks before the June 6 graduation, which was Shannon's birthday. While Yvette was busy getting Shannon ready for the prom, Jack and Juliette were setting up a cookout for several of Juliette's friends and classmates, most of whom were looking forward to being juniors the next school year.

When Greg arrived to pick up Shannon, who was a vision of blond loveliness, Jack and Juliette were still in the house to wish them well and take some pictures. "Have her home at a decent hour!" Jack told Greg. "And drive carefully."

"Yes, sir," Greg replied.

Yvette and Jacky joined Jack and Juliette for a hot dog and a cola before she took Jacky back into the cabin to get him ready for bed. Soon the teenagers began to arrive, and among the group Jack saw Tommy. Juliette introduced Jack to Bobby Miller, who, although he was a junior, had decided to attend Juliette's party rather than go to the prom. He was carrying a guitar case.

During the evening, the shy Bobby was talked into opening the case and taking out his beautiful old Martin acoustic guitar. As the teens encouraged him to play something, he was hesitant to even strum a few chords. Finally, in frustration, Juliette took the guitar and began to play and sing. Bobby started to sing along with her in two-part harmony. As Bobby moved closer to Juliette so their voices could blend, everyone realized that they were both gifted singers. The way their voices complemented one another was extraordinary.

A little after 11:00 p.m. Jack broke up the party and sent every one home. As soon as Juliette went into the house, Yvette joined Jack outside. Jack was just watching to make certain the fire went out. They sat together under the stars holding hands like teenage lovers far into the night as they waited for Greg to bring Shannon home. Finally, Yvette left him to go to bed and to sleep. It was well after two in the morning when Jack saw the headlights of Greg's family station wagon approaching. He sat in the porch swing in the dark and waited.

As the station wagon turned into the drive, Jack was directly in the glow of the headlights for a few seconds. He got up and went to meet Shannon. She hurriedly got out of the car without waiting for help and rushed inside without a word to Jack. Jack noticed that her hair was mussed and her dress wrinkled. He was about to go speak to Greg, but he backed the station wagon hurriedly down the drive and sped away.

Inside, Jack went to the closed door of the girls' room and called softly to Shannon. "Anything you want to talk to me about, sweetheart?"

He heard a muffled, "No. Good night."

Jack went into the master bath and quietly showered the smoke smell off of his body and out of his hair before sliding into bed beside Yvette. He was sure something had happened and he didn't want to think about what it was.

Shannon didn't have to wait for graduation to get the results of the extracurricular courses she was taking. For the last two weeks of school she didn't need to attend. She still made the journey to pick up Jacky from pre-k every school day.

On graduation night, as Jack and Yvette were about to take the family to see Greg graduate, Shannon announced that she didn't feel well and wouldn't be going with them.

"What is it, dear," Yvette asked.

"I just don't feel like going. Greg won't miss me. If you want, you can leave Jacky here with me. I won't mind at all."

As Jack drove away from the house with Yvette and Juliette he asked his wife, "Lovers quarrel?"

"I don't know. Shannon has been acting strange for days now. She may be anticipating their separation when Greg goes to Baylor this fall."

June 6 was Shannon's seventeenth birthday. Yvette had planned a big party, but because it conflicted with Greg's graduation, she decided to move it to Saturday the seventh. Once again the party was given in the restaurant party room, with much of the same group that had attended Juliette's party.

The party room was decorated in yellow balloons and streamers, Shannon's favorite color. Even her dress was a light yellow color with white lace inserts. She was wearing white gloves that came to the elbow and white pumps. Juliette had fixed her hair for her. She was very lovely.

When the teens let Jack and Shannon have the dance floor, Jack moved her gracefully around the floor while a recording of Dean Martin singing "Amore" played.

"You look especially beautiful tonight, Shannon," he told her. "It's amazing how many wonderful things have happened to you in the past year since you came to live with Yvette and me. My birthday wish for you is that you have the brightest future and happiness always." As the dance ended he brushed her cheek with a fatherly kiss and whispered into her ear, "I love you."

Jack's gift to her was in an envelope in his inside coat pocket. He wanted to wait for the best time to give it to her. He had spent countless hours on the phone and in travel to and from Baylor College of Medicine in Houston, making arrangements to pay for both Shannon's and Greg's tuition, books, housing, and other expenses. The authorization was in the envelope. He had hoped to present it to her in the presence of Greg, but for some reason Greg did not show up for Shannon's party.

He waited until she had opened all of her other gifts before handing it to her. "Now you and Greg can attend college together!" Jack told her excitedly. "Isn't that what you wanted?"

"Yes," she answered, "but I'm not sure that's what he wants anymore."

"Where is he tonight?" Jack asked her. "Did he know that you were having your birthday party tonight?"

"I don't think he cares."

Jack had a penchant for interfering in the lives of those he loved any time he felt they had been treated unfairly. Sunday afternoon he put in a call to the church parsonage. He asked Reverend Wilson if he could speak to Greg. When Greg picked up the receiver Jack asked if he could come out to Lockhart Estate and see him.

"Why?" Greg wanted to know.

"I need to give you your graduation gift. Besides, there's a pretty blond here who'd like to see you."

"I'll see if I can borrow the car."

"Don't disappoint her, son. Get yourself on out here. If you don't have a ride, I'll come and pick you up."

Greg finally arrived at the Lockhart house about 3:00 p. m. He was hesitant to approach the house, but Jack went out and invited him in.

"Sit down," Jack told him. "Would you like something to drink? Iced tea, cola?"

"No, thank you."

"Well, I'll get right to it then. In this envelope is your graduation present. Go ahead, open it."

Greg slowly opened the envelope and began to read a portion of each page. "What does this mean? I get a free ride at Baylor College?"

"I thought you could do a better job of studying if you didn't have money worries."

"Wow, I don't know what to say, Mr. Lockhart! Thank you, thank you!"

"Don't let me down, son. I'm counting on you to make us all proud. Now, Juli, would you ask Shannon to come out here, please?"

Momentarily Shannon appeared. "Yes, Daddy Jack?"

"Sit down with us a minute. Why don't you tell Greg here what I gave you for your birthday? Then, Greg, you can tell Shannon what you got for graduation. Juli and I will be just outside on the patio."

Yvette, who had been watching Jacky ride Blacky, came around the corner of the house just then, trailing the two.

"Jacky, ride out front here where we can see you," Jack called. Come sit down by me for a while, Evie. I need your company."

Inside, Greg and Shannon were talking. "What's up with you, Greg? You get what you want and then you treat me like you don't know me? Why haven't you called? Why didn't you come to my birthday party?"

"I've just been feeling so guilty. That's not the way I was raised. I didn't plan that to happen, Shannon. We just went too far. I'm so sorry. Although I don't remember you saying no or stop, I don't blame you for anything. Are you okay? Do you think you could be…you know?"

"It's still too early to tell."

"You know I love you, Shannon, and I'll stand by you no matter what."

"You say that now. We'll see what you say if I am. Let's change the subject," Shannon continued. "I've had time to look into housing at BCM, and the dorm where I'll be staying is only about four blocks from where you'll be. The library is convenient to both. We can study there together. When do you think we should go down there?"

They continued to make plans, eventually finding their way out onto the front patio, where they joined the Lockharts.

"So, have you two settled your differences?" Jack asked as he noticed they were holding hands.

"Just a little misunderstanding," Shannon told him. "We appreciate the gifts so very much, Daddy Jack, although we really haven't had time to absorb all that it involves. I still plan to pay you back every cent some day." She bent and kissed him on the cheek.

It was just a few days later that Yvette noticed that Shannon was not wearing a bra around the house. She found her alone and asked her why she had not worn a bra to supper. "Are you out of bras? Have you out grown all of yours?"

"They irritate me. For two or three days now, my breasts have been so sore and tender and my nipples are sore."

"Shannon, is there any chance you could be pregnant? When was your last period?"

"I don't know. I don't remember. Yes, it's possible." Shannon began to cry.

Yvette hugged her, saying, "Here, now that won't help. You'll come with me in the morning. We'll get a pregnancy test from the drug store and figure out what to do from there. Greg?"

"Yes."

"If you are—and we don't have any proof yet—it's not the end of the world."

The test showed a positive reading, and two days later they were in Dr. Laura Mueller's office. Dr. Mueller was considered the best obstetrician in the area. She finished her tests and examination with one word: Congratulations!

Shannon didn't know if she was happy, sad, or just scared. She felt a little unsteady as she and Yvette left the doctor's office.

"Does Greg know about this?"

"No, no one but you."

"Do you plan to tell him?"

"Yes, I need to know how he'll react. I need to know if I'm going to be alone in this."

"Oh, you aren't alone, honey, believe me. When Jack hears about this, he'll be stuck to you like glue until the baby comes and after. And you have me and Juliette and don't forget your best bud, Jacky. He'll be there for you no matter what. But I understand you want the father to be there beside you all the way. How do you plan to tell him?"

"I need to do it in person. I'm supposed to see him tonight. I'll tell him then. What do I say?"

"You'll know what to say when the time comes and the two of you are alone. Just talk to him like you always do. Here's something to think about as you tell him. If he truly loves you, he'll be happy before the magnitude of the responsibility hits him. If he starts immediately bemoaning how this will affect him, he isn't the right one to be a father. I'm speaking from experience."

"I appreciate that. I think it's all right for you to tell Daddy Jack. I know you don't keep secrets from each other."

"I won't rush to tell him, but if he suspects something and asks me, I'll have to tell him at that time."

Greg was later than usual and didn't get to the Lockhart home until nearly eight. The summer sun was just about to dip below the pines when he drove up. Shannon was dressed neatly as if going for an interview instead of a date. When Greg came to the door, she greeted him and asked if they could sit in the patio swing for a while and watch the sun go down. She had fixed them both some tea to drink.

As they sat on the swing watching the last few rays of the sinking sun, Shannon turned toward Greg, taking his hand. "Greg," she said, breathing a big sigh, "I have something to tell you. I went to the doctor today. She confirmed it. I'm pregnant. You and I are going to have a baby!"

Greg sat looking back at her lovingly while she waited for his reaction. Finally he spoke. "Shannon, darling, I know this isn't the preferred sequence for things, but you are the only one I would ever want to be the mother of my children! I think we should be married right away. Marry me, Shannon. Marry me tonight so I can take care of you and little Greg Jr. or Shannon Jr. for the rest of our lives. I love you, Shannon," he whispered as he pulled her close to him.

Shannon was crying so hard from happiness she couldn't get any words out. Finally she blurted out, "Yes, Greg, yes. I love you too. Yes, I'll marry you!"

Jack, hearing the last few words, peered out through the screen, asking, "You kids okay? Do you need anything?"

Shannon dried her eyes and dragged a shy and grinning Greg into the house. "Greg just asked me to marry him!" she announced to everyone.

"What did you say? Yes, of course! Let me see your ring." Juliette said excitedly.

"Of course I said yes!" Shannon answered excitedly. "But no ring yet."

"Well I-I, hadn't planned on asking her until later," Greg stammered. "I haven't been anyplace to buy a ring just yet."

"All the better," Jack told him. "Let her pick it out and you can't disappoint her, son. I was wondering when you'd get around to popping the question. I thought I was going to have to ask her for you. When do you think you'll be getting married? Before you go to Baylor or sometime later?"

"Soon, very soon," Greg told him.

"There's still two weeks of June left," Yvette said. "If we try really hard, you could have a June bride, Greg."

"I'd like to take Shannon to my house now to tell my parents. Thank you for everything, Mr. and Mrs. Lockhart. I'll have Shannon home before eleven."

They watched as Shannon and Greg drove away. "Shannon gets everything," Juliette said, smiling happily.

"Come here, old man," Yvette said taking Jack's hand and pulling him into the bedroom and closing the door behind them.

"Young love make you feel amorous?" Jack asked her hopefully.

"You have to help me plan and pull off this June wedding!"

"Of course, if that's what they want, but it seems to me that the idea originated with you, Evie."

"Jack, what is the usual reason for a rush wedding?"

"Sailor is leaving in the morning for a long cruise."

"Jack!"

"Okay, I was making light of the situation. How far along is she?"

"Just a few weeks. I'll call Mrs. Wilson after she's had time to get over the initial shock and let her help plan the reception. And I'll ask for their church on Sunday afternoon June 29. You know the bride's father pays for the wedding, don't you? Well, Daddy Jack, break out your wallet."

When Greg and Shannon arrived at the Wilson home, Mrs. Wilson made Shannon comfortable, while Greg, who had asked his father for a private consultation, was ushered into his father's study.

"What's this about, Greg?" Reverend Wilson asked.

Greg took a deep breath and began. "Father, I'm going to be a father."

Reverend Wilson looked at his son for several seconds before saying anything. "What have you decided to do about it?"

"Accept my responsibilities. I love Shannon very much, Father, and I've asked her to be my wife. We'd like to be married as soon as possible."

"Then I think we should take this conversation into the dining room and join the ladies."

"Carolyn," Reverend Wilson said, addressing his wife, "I believe these young people have an announcement to make."

"I love Shannon very much, Mother. I've asked her to be my wife and she's consented. We want to be married right away," Greg told her.

"And we're to be grandparents!" Reverend Wilson added.

Shannon blushed and dropped her head, as she felt she had disappointed the people who were soon to be her mother and father in-law. "We didn't plan for this to happen," she said softly.

Mrs. Wilson busied herself smoothing out the tablecloth and filling everyone's glass. Finally she spoke. "Where are your parents, dear? Shouldn't we be meeting them? Are they aware of all of this?"

"Shannon's parents are dead, Mother," Greg told her. "She's been staying with Mr. and Mrs. Lockhart."

"Just how soon do you wish to be married?" Mrs. Wilson asked them. Then addressing Greg she asked, "Do you still want your father to marry you? That's what you've always said you wanted."

"We haven't had time to plan that as yet," Shannon smiled. "Greg just asked me to marry him this evening. Could we be excused? We need to talk about that and other things."

The next day, as Yvette and Shannon were in full preparation for marriage mode, Jack talked to Greg.

"Here you were about to go off to medical school, and I was about to erase the last obstacle. You had plenty of time in the future for marriage and starting a family. What were you thinking, Greg?"

"I wasn't, sir. We were kissing like so many times before and then…it was too late."

"You were waiting for Shannon to stop everything."

"Yes, I guess I was."

"That was your responsibility."

"I know. I wish—"

"You know by now how I feel about Shannon. Since fate brought her to my door, I've learned to love her like she is my own daughter. You treat her fairly. Don't ever hurt her, or you'll have me to answer to."

"You have my word on that, sir. I already hurt her once, and I don't ever want to see her hurt again."

"I wish I had counseled you early on how Shannon is new to real love. She has been constantly abandoned, mistreated, and abused most of her life. Her parents died and left her when she was very young. Foster parents often withhold their love to protect themselves from pain at the time of separation, or they aren't the loving kind. Foster children, many of them having no example of love in their lives, are often cruel to one another. When she came here, not just her face, but her psyche was extremely scarred. She was starved for true, unconditional love, making her vulnerable to even the smallest acts of affection and attention. A probable reason for her not stopping your advances and taking the chance of losing another important person in her life."

"I'm just beginning to understand," Greg answered. "Yes sir, I wish you had made me more aware. But I'm not blaming you. I blame only myself."

"Now that you are about to take a wife and be a father," Jack went on, "let me tell you two other important facts I've learned. First, you will always come second to Shannon's children. A mother loves her children first, then her husband. That's just how it is. You'll have to accept it. Second, it's just the opposite with us men. Sure we love our children, we'll give our lives for them, but we hold their mothers in much higher esteem. You'll see."

Although it was a lot to accomplish in under two weeks, Yvette pulled it off. Shannon and Greg were married in the Pentecostal Church with Greg's father officiating.

Jack was as proud as Shannon's own father would have been as he walked her down the aisle. Her hand was resting on his forearm his hand on hers. Occasionally he would glance at her and smile. Near the altar he took Greg's hand and placed it on Shannon's elbow as Greg led her the rest of the way to where his father waited for them. Jack then took his place beside Yvette.

In the congregation on the bride's side, were the Lockhart family, Mr. and Mrs. DuBoise, the Kaisers from Atlanta, a group of Mikkelsens from Mississippi, Great-aunt Kathryn, and Arthur "Arty" Carmichael. The groom's side was equally well attended.

After a well-attended reception in the church antechamber, the couple honeymooned on Padre Island before moving into married couples housing on the campus of Baylor College of Medicine in Houston.

The Lockhart home suddenly felt a little less complete—Juliette and Jacky missing their best friend, Yvette and Jack missing a daughter.

As Jack and Yvette lay in bed one night, Yvette sighed. "I wonder if Shannon is all right. I wonder if she's having morning sickness; is the pregnancy interfering with her studies?"

"You have their phone numbers, Evie. Why don't you just call her and stop all the worry?"

ELEVEN

It had been over ten years since Jack last saw his daughter Rebecca. His first wife Rachel, died not knowing the whereabouts of her daughter. The blond, blue-eyed Shannon had often reminded him of his daughter in the days just before Rebecca left home. Rebecca too had blond wavy hair like Jack and the same blue eyes. Maybe it was because she would be turning twenty-nine in just a few days, that she had recently invaded his thoughts. He began to remember the day he last saw her.

Shortly before her eighteenth birthday, Rebecca had become upset with her mother and father because she found their rules were much too strict. She had demanded that she get her own way, and when she didn't she vowed to leave as soon as she became eighteen years of age. Her exact words were, "When I'm eighteen, I'm out of here!"

On the morning of her eighteenth birthday, while the ailing Rachel was preparing a birthday cake, Rebecca, making the excuse she needed to run to the store for some feminine hygiene products, walked out the door and was never seen again.

Jack had exhausted most of his savings at the time trying to find her, to no avail. Now, as he felt the empty space left in his life by the departure of Shannon, he realized how much he also missed Rebecca. *I need to try once again to find her*, he thought. *But where do I start?*

He wondered if Jim Stockburger could help him. In this case, however, he had nothing but a ten-year-old picture and her name. Her looks would have changed with age, and she could have changed her name by marriage or in order to continue hiding from him.

Jack looked in some old papers from his previous searches and found her social security number, her high school graduation photo, and the number of her 1995 Texas driver's license. He also found the envelope holding the pictures of her that he had been keeping. A deep sadness enveloped him as he looked at her pictures. The ones when she was a baby, through the toothless-smile era, the awkward early teen years, up to the last one of her smiling happily in her cap and gown. For the first time he realized how much she resembled Rachel.

Jack placed a call to Jim Stockburger. Jim's secretary, took the call and assured Jack that she would have Mr. Stockburger return his call at his earliest convenience.

It wasn't until the next day that Jack received a call from Jim Stockburger. "Mr. Lockhart," Jim began, "how can I help you?"

Jack explained that this time he was looking for a missing person. He gave Jim as much information as he had.

Jim said he thought it might be a relatively easy case if Rebecca had not changed her social security number or moved out of state. He asked Jack to send him a copy of the latest picture and promised to give Jack at least a weekly update.

That evening at 5:25, Jack haunted the front entry way as usual, impatiently waiting for Yvette to come home. He was soon rewarded by the sight of her sedan driving into the garage. As he kissed her hello he could tell she had something on her mind. Yvette seldom brought her work home, but tonight seemed to be different.

"What's up, Evie?" Jack asked.

"Oh, just some stuff at work."

"As a partner, albeit a silent partner, I have a right to know these things."

"It's nothing, Jack, really."

Jack stood, hands on his hips, blocking her way, grinning.

"Oh all right! We are having constant supply problems with our present restaurant supply company. I've decided to find a new one to replace them as soon as the present contract expires. I'm going to start in Beaumont interviewing restaurant supply companies until I find one I'm satisfied can fulfill our needs. I could do it all by phone, but I want to personally see what kind of layout they have and how much product they keep on hand. That way I will know what they tell me is true. I only have six weeks before the present contract expires, so I may have to make one or two trips a week until I find the right one. If I can't find one in Beaumont I may have to go to Houston, Galveston, or Lafayette."

"I'm sure you'll find the right one. Need me to ride along with you?"

"No, I'll be okay. You have your hands full here with Jacky and Juli."

Within a week, Jim Stockburger called. "Think I've got something for you, Jack. A Becky McKenna, with a Corpus Christi address, has been using the social security number you gave me. I'm going to fly down there in a couple of days to interview her. If it is Rebecca Lockhart, how much information am I allowed to give her?"

"Whatever you need to tell her to get her to contact me. If it's her, I'd like to get together with her as soon as possible."

"Okay, Jack, I'll call you later."

Jack hung up the phone with mixed emotions. He wanted to jump for joy, but he knew this could be an imposter. This could just be another dead end like he had found during his search for his daughter several years before. Jack still held to a glimmer of hope.

Yvette's first exploration to a Beaumont restaurant supply company turned out to be unsuccessful. She said there were two more suppliers on US 86 just north of Beaumont in the area where all the new chain motels were locating. She planned to make another trip next week. She was hopeful one of them could fill the restaurant's needs.

In bed that night, Yvette asked Jack, "What's wrong, honey? You have been so quiet and distant lately. Is it me?"

"No, Evie. I've just had a lot on my mind lately." He kissed her tenderly and rolled onto his side.

The next day Jack kept Jacky all day while Juliette went to a skating party in Jasper with Bobby Miller and other friends. Bobby's pickup and Juliette's car were loaded with teens. Jack gave a stern warning to them all about highway safety and cautioned them against illegal drinking. Jack watched as they drove away. He always worried anytime Juliette was out of sight and didn't rest easy until he saw her safe back at home.

Jack got the boat out, and he and Jacky went up stream a little way to where the river had once cut a nice horseshoe-shaped cove, a spot where Jack had pulled out a few very large catfish. He showed Jacky how to bait his hook with stink bait, and they sat waiting for the first fish of the day. As usual, as Jacky's bait was the first in the water; the little five-year-old caught the first fish. It was a channel cat about fourteen inches long. By now Jacky was good at landing a fish into the boat, but Jack still had to take it off of the hook. When they had their limit they started for home. Jack still had to clean and cook them.

"Did you like the fish I caught for you, Mommy?" Jacky asked Yvette at supper.

"Yes, very much," Yvette told him. "Did you help Daddy cook them too?"

"Mmmhmm, and I put the raisins in the salad."

"You are getting to be as good a cook as your daddy," she told him, giving him a hug. "Now you take Daddy and Bobby outside while we girls clean up the supper dishes."

Jack sat in the porch swing and Jacky climbed up beside him. Bobby sat in a lounge chair silently. He was one of the shyest boys Jack had ever seen. Jack began to swing is small arcs. Jacky, tired from a big day and with tummy full, soon found the rocking motion too much and fell asleep. Jack carried him in and put him to bed. He then went to the kitchen, where Yvette was wiping a few last dishes and putting them away.

"Do you want some help," Jack offered.

"I'm just finishing up. You can go run me a bath if you want."

Jack did as his wife suggested. He was sitting on the edge of the tub testing the temperature with his hand when she came in, undressed, and stepped into the tub. He excused himself and closed the bathroom door behind him as he left.

Now I know something is wrong, Yvette thought. *Jack hardly noticed me get undressed! Am I getting fat?* She stood up and tried to see her posterior in the mirror.

After her bath she slipped into a sexy nightgown and sat cross-legged on top of the sheets and waited for Jack to come to bed. She heard him shower, and soon he came into the room wearing pajama bottoms like always. He bent over and kissed her tenderly, but distractedly, and crawled into bed.

"Are you okay, Jack?"

"Yes, I'm fine. Good night, Evie. I love you."

The call that Jack had been waiting for finally came. Jim Stockburger had been to Corpus Christi and met with Becky McKenna. "It's no doubt this is your daughter, Mr. Lockhart. She said she was born Rebecca Marie Lockhart. Her mother's name was Rachel and her father's name was Jack.

"She has also been looking for you. She said she returned to your home six or seven years ago to find the house empty. She then spent several days looking for her parents and only found where her mother was buried. She is married and has two children, a boy and a girl. She is anxious to meet with you, Jack, but thinks the first meeting should be somewhere neutral, just the two of you."

"How does she look? Is she healthy? Are her children healthy? What do they look like?"

"All in due course, Jack. Do you want me to set up the meeting?"

"Yes, of course, as soon as possible. I'll meet her anywhere, at anytime!"

"Then I'll set it up and get back to you. And yes, you have a very lovely daughter. I didn't meet any other members of her family."

It was Tuesday the next time Jim Stockburger called. "It's all set up," he said. "Mrs. McKenna will fly from Corpus Christi to Beaumont Wednesday afternoon. She has a room booked at the Hilton Garden Inn for Wednesday night. She will meet you in the Hotel dinning room Thursday morning. She'll be wearing a bright red scarf so you will be able to recognize her. I suggest you wear a bright red handkerchief in your jacket pocket to make it easier for you to be recognized. Good luck, Jack. I hope everything works out."

Two more days, Jack thought. *Two more very long days.*

Wednesday night he hardly slept, realizing his long lost daughter was only eighty miles away. What would it be like? What would he say to her? She was his flesh and blood and yet a stranger. His tossing was disturbing Yvette's sleep. He took his pillow and moved to the couch.

On Thursday morning Yvette left early, telling Jack she had to meet with another restaurant supply company. Jack left Juliette in care of Jacky and was soon on the road to his rendezvous with his daughter.

He was apprehensive about meeting her. She had been just a girl when he last saw her more than ten years ago. Now she was not only an adult, but a married woman and a mother. He was extremely nervous as he entered the dinning room a few minutes before ten. He didn't have to search for her at all. His heart beat faster as he saw, sitting alone at a table facing the door as he walked through it, the likeness of his sweet Rachel sitting there with a red scarf around her neck, smiling widely. He covered the rest of the space between them in record time. Instead of the awkward postering he had imagined, she stood and embraced him as readily as he embraced her.

For the next two hours they caught up on highlights of the past ten years. During their talk they left the dining room, walked slowly around the outside of the motel, stopped for a while at the swimming pool, sat under one of the poolside umbrellas, then went back to the dining room for something to drink and more conversation.

Soon after leaving home, Rebecca had joined a group of other youths that she had graduated with, traveling around the US. She and one of the young men in the group, a man by the name of Sean McKenna, had become lovers and eventually married. After they married, they left the group and Sean entered Corpus Christi State University to study marine biology. She went to work to support them while he was in college. He now works for the Texas State Aquarium. After Sean went to work, she was able to get some college courses but was still a few credits short of a degree. One summer, between semesters, they went back home and tried to find Jack but found the house closed up. They visited her mother's gravesite before returning to Corpus Christi. She didn't ever expect to see her father again. Rebecca shed a few tears of regret for running away and asked for his forgiveness. They embraced for a long minute.

Rebecca gave him pictures of his grandchildren—Kevin, age seven, and Rachel, age five. Jack was overjoyed to know that he was a grandfather and expressed his desire to meet them soon.

He gave her his address, drew her a map, and gave her an open invitation to visit anytime. He told her just how much she looked like her mother. He told her he had never stopped loving her and hoping for this very day.

Eventually Rebecca said her flight was leaving soon and she would have to call for the airport limousine. Jack offered to drive her to the airport, but she told him the limo could take her right to the door. She accompanied him to his car and there beside the car they embraced again for another long minute. Rebecca then lovingly kissed her father before smiling, turning, and walking away.

Yvette was sure she had finally found a supplier who could meet her needs. She inspected their warehouse, and when she was satisfied that they kept sufficient product on hand to keep her supplied, she signed a contract. She shook hands with the manager, and they walked out into the noonday sun. As she said good-bye and walked to her car, she noticed just across the street in a motel parking lot a man who looked very much like Jack. He was standing by a Ford Expedition the same color as Jack's, embracing a very pretty young blond woman. As she watched, the blond gave him a kiss and was smiling and laughing as she moved away. As the man turned to get into his vehicle, she recognized it was without a doubt Jack. Her heart almost stopped. *So,* she thought, *that's the reason Jack doesn't seem to want me anymore. Another very young woman. A midlife crisis.*

Jack was elated that he had finally been reunited with his daughter. They had exchanged telephone numbers, and Jack couldn't wait to tell Yvette, so they could plan a family get-together. He drove swiftly back toward Bon Weir, taking the cutoff to Pine Tree Lane just above Church House Creek. He arrived home a little past 2:00 p. m. He hadn't felt this good since he first contacted Jim Stockburger. At first he had been tempted to tell Yvette about his search, but he decided it would be better to wait and see if there was anything to tell.

He picked up Jacky as he came through the door. "Guess what, Jacky? You are an uncle. Uncle Jacky!"

"What's an uncle?" Jacky asked.

"It's like when your sister has children. You are then an uncle to her children."

"Where are Juli's children?"

"Eh, okay never mind. I see I'm in over my head here. Did Juli let you ride Blacky today?"

"Uh-huh. But she wouldn't take me for a ride in the boat."

"Juli isn't supposed to take you out in the boat unless Mommy or me is with you. Where is Juli?"

"Right behind you, Daddy," Juliette answered for her brother.

Jack gave Juliette a hug and thanked her for watching Jacky.

"Did you get your business taken care of today?" Juliette asked her father.

"Yes, I did, thank you, and I can't wait to get the whole family together to tell them about it.

Yvette drove back to the restaurant at Bon Weir slower than usual. She was heartsick and fighting back tears. All the years that Jack had promised he would always be true, that he would never do anything to hurt her, all lies? She would never have believed it, but she had seen it with her own eyes. Jack embracing a young, blond woman, and that woman had kissed him in a very familiar way. She had never seen Jack kiss anyone other than Juliette or Shannon, and those were fatherly kisses. Could she have been wrong all this time? She told herself it was only a kiss, no harm done. But look where they were. Outside a motel! And they were obviously leaving! Jack had the perfect setup for cheating. She was at work all day. He could easily get Juliette to watch Jacky. She wondered how long this had been going on. She tried to think back to the last time she had denied Jack's advances. When did he first become distant? Had she done something to drive him into the arms of another woman? Hadn't he recently said he always became excited when he saw her? Maybe all young women excited him.

As she arrived at the restaurant, she hurried into her office, gave orders that she was not to be disturbed, and locked herself inside. Yvette began to cry like she had not done since finding herself alone with two-year-old Juliette just after her divorce from Steve Clarke. She sobbed out the hurt and disappointment, the difficulties of being a mother and wife. The fears of bringing up children in this crazy world. The frustrations of being a manager. Finally, she had no more tears to cry. She washed her face, put on fresh makeup, forced a smile, and went back to work.

Jack had supper planned and in the preparation stage when he noticed it was time for Yvette to come driving into the yard. He positioned himself at the door so he would be the first one to get her smile and her kiss and waited and waited.

Something was wrong. She was never late. He went out onto the patio and listened for automobile engine noises. Nothing. He turned the fires down under everything he was cooking and called her. It rang, but she didn't answer. Jack was starting to panic. Should he call Sheriff McFadden? Should he turn off everything and go look for her?

"Juli," he called, "your mother is late, and she isn't answering her phone. Can you drive up the highway and see if you can see her? I'll call the sheriff and…never mind, there she is!" Jack stated, letting out a sigh of relief.

Yvette drove slowly up the driveway, not really wanting to face Jack, but knowing she still must. She would take her time and find the right time and the right words. She must not upset her children. She walked slowly and deliberately to the door. Jack, all smiles, opened it for her.

"You had me worried sick, Evie! What happened? You're never late."

Yvette stepped past him, picked up Jacky and gave him a hug and a kiss, greeted Juliette, and went to her bedroom and closed the door behind her.

Jack stood there with his mouth open. *Uh-oh*, he thought. *That time of the month again. I better be on my best behavior.*

He walked to the door and called through it, "Evie, can I get you something to drink? Draw you a bath?"

"No thank you," she answered coldly.

"If you need me for anything just let me know," Jack offered as he turned to go back to his cooking. "Supper will be ready in about forty-five minutes."

No one saw Yvette until Jack called everyone to supper. She ate only small bites, forcing herself to swallow. She talked to her children and Bobby but acted as if Jack did not exist. Jack tried a few times to enter the conversation so he could announce his good news, but he was unable to.

Later, Jack entered the bedroom to find Yvette already in bed. She was lying on her side, facing away from his side of the bed. He tried to kiss her good night, but she turned her face away from him.

"Now, doggone it, Yvette, what have I done to make you so angry with me?"

"You know what you did," she told him in a cold and indignant voice. "And who you did it with!"

"Now you're not making any sense," he told her, resting his hand on her arm and gently trying to get her to turn toward him.

She pushed his hand away and Jack laid down beside her in temporary confusion. *Maybe after she's had a good night's sleep*, he thought. He was about to relax when she got up, picked up her pillow, and left the bedroom. He followed her into the den, where she was trying to open the foldout couch.

"Come back to bed Evie," he begged.

She looked at him with a cold stare.

"Okay, if someone has to sleep out here, I'll do it."

Jack opened the foldout bed, put some sheets on it, got his pillow, and went dejectedly to his punishment. He hoped tomorrow she would let him know just what he was being punished for.

The next morning things had not changed with Yvette. She was as loving as always to her children but cold and indifferent toward Jack. After she left, he finished cleaning the breakfast dishes. Juliette was outside playing with Jacky, so he went to his desk and checked his calendar for the past several days to see if he had missed some important date. Finding nothing, he sat pondering the situation for a few minutes before shrugging his shoulders in defeat. He dialed the number Rebecca had given him and waited to hear her voice.

"Hello," the male voice on the other end of the line said.

"Hello, Jack Lockhart here. I'm looking for Rebecca McKenna. Have I reached the right number?"

"Oh, hello, Mr. Lockhart. I'm Sean McKenna. How are you?

"Fine, fine. Please call me Jack, Sean. How are you?"

"Very well, thank you. Hold on a minute and I'll see if Becky can come to the phone."

Very shortly Rebecca picked up the phone. They had a pleasant conversation. They made plans for her family to come to the cabin in two weeks when Sean started his vacation. "He gets two weeks, and we'd like to spend the first few days with you, getting acquainted with you and the rest of your family. You should have heard what Sean said when I showed him your picture last night. He said you didn't look as old and mean as I had described you." She laughed.

"Wait until he sees me in person and learns how really old and mean I am!" Jack laughed. "I can't wait to see all of you. Looking forward to spoiling those grandchildren. I love you, Rebecca. See you very soon."

Since a good night's sleep hadn't changed Yvette's mood, Jack decided to move his things into the guest room. He would give her some space while trying to remember what sin he had committed that made her this cold toward him. While he tried to figure that out, he would try to woo her once again. He called the florist and had a dozen violet roses delivered to Yvette at her office. The message on the card read, "Wherever I went wrong, please help me make it right. My love forever, Jack."

Yvette accepted the roses and read the card. *He knows what he did wrong*, she thought. *He just doesn't know he got caught. Well, until he confesses and begs my forgiveness…and even then I may not be able to forgive him!*

When the roses didn't work, Jack tried being pathetic. He sent a single white lily and the poetic lines of a troubadour from the nineteen sixties:

> I've been accused, convicted and condemned
> My trial's over and now I face the end
> Is this your way of telling me we're through?
> When all I'm guilty of is loving you.
> You were the judge, the jury, all in one
> You found me guilty and now my term's begun
> I must confess I've never been untrue
> And all I'm guilty of, is loving you.

Even these heartfelt words of supplication didn't affect Yvette's determination to make Jack pay for his perceived indiscretion. The cold in the Lockhart house continued for days. Each night, Jack went to serve out another lonely night of punishment in the guest room. When Shannon and Greg called he just left Yvette a note on her desk. Jack would have found his life meaningless if it wasn't for his children and the upcoming visit from Rebecca and his grandchildren. He had tried to tell Yvette about it, but she wasn't interested in anything he had to say.

On Friday after work, the McKennas took a flight from Corpus Christi to Beaumont, where they rented a car and drove to the same motel where Rebecca had stayed when she and Jack met. The next day they drove the remaining eighty miles to the Lockhart Estate, arriving just after ten in the morning. Jack, who had been playing with Jacky and keeping an eye out for them, saw their car turn into the drive and hurried to greet them.

Yvette, hearing the commotion, looked out the window from the den just in time to see Jack embrace Rebecca. *That brazen hussy,* she thought. *And the nerve of Jack having her come here!* She went angrily out onto the patio to give Jack and his mistress a piece of her mind. She arrived just in time to see that a man and two children had also arrived in the car with the young woman.

The man had dark hair and deep blue eyes. The little boy had blue eyes and dark hair but not as dark as that of the man. The little girl had blond hair and blue eyes like the woman.

"Evie," Jack called, "come and meet my daughter Rebecca and her family!"

Yvette stopped in her tracks then hesitantly walked toward the group. Jack was still being introduced to everyone himself. As she drew near she saw that Jacky had already introduced himself to the children.

"This is my wife, Yvette," Jack said, "and our children, Juliette and Jacky."

"Evie, this is my daughter Rebecca, her husband, Sean, and their children, Kevin and Rachel. My grandchildren!"

Yvette was feeling a mild case of nausea as she realized that what she had put herself and Jack through over the past several days, had been totally unnecessary. How could she have been so wrong? Why had she ever doubted Jack? As she looked at Rebecca she could see the family resemblance. Her hair and eyes were the exact colors of Jacks. Even the shape of her chin showed a family resemblance. She went about her hostess duties without a hitch. She fixed a pitcher of lemonade and one of iced tea and invited everyone to help themselves.

After greeting Rebecca and Sean, Jack took stock of his grandchildren. Five-year-old Rachel had her mother's wavy blond hair and blue eyes. Her little upturned nose had a row of freckles that spread out onto her cheeks. Seven-year-old Kevin had dark hair and blue eyes and also had the freckles across his nose. "They're adorable, just beautiful!" Jack told his daughter.

Jacky took his neice and nephew to show them Blacky and Apollo then came running back to ask his Daddy if they could all ride Blacky. Jack said he would saddle her as soon as he got the okay from Kevin and Rachel's parents. Rebecca and Sean went with Jack and the children to see just how dangerous the situation was.

"Kevin, Rachel, have you ever ridden a horse?" Jack asked his grandchildren. He helped Kevin into the saddle first, as Rachel showed some fear. The children all got a turn on Blacky, got to interact with Apollo, and finally discovered the gym set. Meanwhile Jack and Sean were getting to know one another. After a while, Rebecca went to look for Yvette.

The noonday sun drove all the adults inside, and they were sitting in the den. "How long can you stay?" Jack asked Rebecca.

"Two or three days if you can find room for us."

"That's no problem at all," Jack told them. "There are bunk beds in Jacky's room where Kevin can sleep. Juliette has two beds in her room, so Rachel can sleep in there. That couch makes into—"

"Jack likes to joke," Yvette interrupted. "Of course you'll sleep in the guest room. Come let me show you, Rebecca."

Jack played host while Yvette made a large plate of sandwiches for their lunch. As she called the children inside, Jack made the comment that instead of anyone having to spend time in the kitchen later they should all go to the restaurant that Yvette managed.

"Do I have to go too?" Juliette asked Jack, "Bobby and I were planning to go to the movies."

"No, you go ahead with your plans. Your sister and her family will be here tomorrow."

"Sister," Rebecca said. "I have a little sister and a little brother. Just sounds a little strange but exciting!"

"And," Jack interjected, grinning widely, "your brother is the same age as your daughter."

At the restaurant later they were able to get one of the long tables so everyone could be seated together. Yvette sat next to Jack, and he presumed she was pretending nothing was wrong for the sake of the guests. As their waitress brought them menus, she acknowledged Yvette and Jack, saying, "Good evening Mr. and Mrs. Lockhart."

It was then that Jack recognized the back of Arty's head in a booth with Mable Brown. He decided to go over and interject himself into their evening. "Good evening, Ms. Brown," he said. "Is this old coot bothering you?"

Arty grabbed Jack's hand. "Jack, you old hound dog, what's ya up to."

"I'd like to introduce y'all to some relatives of mine."

Arty stood up and helped Mable up from her seat. As they approached he said, "Now, who are all these good-looking people. Cain't be kin of yours, Jack."

"Folks," Jack said, "this is Ms. Brown and a good friend of mine, Mr. Arty Carmichael. This is my daughter Rebecca, my son-in-law Sean McKenna, my granddaughter Rachel, and my grandson Kevin. You know Yvette and Jacky."

"Glad to meet all of you," Mable told them sweetly. "My, what beautiful children."

"Glad to make your acquaintances," Arty said. Then, motioning toward Jack, he said, "I feel sorry for you if you're kin to this one!"

"Would you care to join us?" Yvette asked them.

"No, we wouldn't want to horn in on your party," Arty told her.

As they turned to go back toward their table, Arty winked at Yvette and put a friendly squeeze on Jack's bicep.

Back in the cabin much later that night, as everyone except Jack had gone off to bed, he searched to see where Yvette had put his pillow and other things so he could make the foldout couch into his bed. Finding nothing, he tapped lightly on her door. "Evie," he called quietly. "Where did you put my pillow?"

"It's in here," she said, opening the door for him.

"Can I get it so I can go to bed?" he asked.

"Wouldn't you rather sleep in here with me?"

"You mean it's all right? Please don't tease me, Evie. I'm pretty bruised up from your treatment of me the past several weeks."

"Come in here, Jack. Now hold me. No, Jack, hold me like you mean it."

Slowly it all came back to him. The tenderness of her kisses, the softness of her body, the heat and the passion. Apparently whatever she had been punishing him for, his sentence had been commuted. He slept better than he had slept in weeks.

The McKennas stayed much longer than they first planned. With boat trips to both fishing and beach areas, pony rides, and gym set fun, the excellent food, and socializing, they really hated to leave. Jack was also sorry to see them go. Soon the Lockhart Estate was quiet again. As everything returned to normal, Jack was still curious about his crime never being explained to him but wasn't about to ask. Yvette was being very nice to him and he did not want that to stop.

Juliette was feeling some new and strange emotions. She confronted her father. "Do you love Rebecca more than me because she's your real daughter?" she asked.

"Of course not! You are as much a daughter to me as Rebecca. I love you both."

"You spent a lot more time with her than you did with me. I felt left out and jealous."

"Oh, Juli honey, I'm sorry you felt left out. I spent more time with her because I knew our time together was limited. Come here and sit beside me. I'll tell you one of my stories."

Jack told the one about seeing the pretty little curly headed girl on a stool in a café and falling in love with her. And just to prove he loved her he'd given her a ring on his wedding day. Juliette always liked that one. She kissed her father and told him she was feeling a lot better.

"Just think," Jack told her, "when school starts and they ask you what you did over the summer, you can now brag that you have a new sister, a new brother-in-law, a niece, and a nephew."

"Speaking of school," he went on, "Jacky starts kindergarten this year. I'm going to miss Shannon driving him home every day."

"Kindergarten will be all day this year. I'll be able to take him to school with me and bring him home."

"My children are growing up and leaving me," Jack lamented.

Jack was enjoying being able to once again sleep in his own bed with his wife. He made it a point to be as unselfish and attentive to her needs as possible. Yvette had been extraordinarily attentive to him, also. It was like they had started a second honeymoon when she finally got over whatever it was that had caused her to be so cold toward him. He didn't even mind waking up some nights with his arm asleep because Yvette was sleeping on her side, with her head on his chest, her hair against his chin, her arm extended across him, her body partially on his arm and body. Sometimes he would lie there for hours just listening to her soft breathing and inhaling her aroma. He derived extra pleasure from slowly moving his hand softly down her ribcage and feeling her tiny waist and then following the sharp upward curve as it flared into her smooth rounded hips. They would soon be celebrating eight years of marriage, and Jack was as much in love with his bride as he had ever been. He placed his open palm gently on her bare shoulder. A smile of peaceful contentment filled his face as he drifted off to sleep.

TWELVE

The hot August days had warmed the waters of the gulf, which lay some eighty-five miles to the south of the cabin on Church House Creek. On August 23, two days before school started, a seasonal hurricane entered the Gulf of Mexico about midway between Cancun, Mexico, on the Yucatan Peninsula and the Florida Keys. It was now on a path to hit the coast of the United States in the Beaumont, Lake Charles area. The storm had slowed overnight and was now intensifying over the warm gulf waters. It was still more than three days away from landfall, but the outer rings were already bringing intermittent rains at the cabin. The predicted rains in the area, if the storm stayed on track, could be as much as fourteen to twenty inches in a twenty-four-hour period. The area between Lake Sam Rayburn on the Neches River to the West and Toledo Bend Reservoir on the Sabine River to the North, an area that included Bon Weir and the Lockhart Estate, was mostly flat, sandy loam soil dotted with farms and timber land, small streams and creeks. That much rain in such a short period of time would surely cause at least some severe local flooding. Although the cabin was on higher ground, it was also precariously situated close to Church House Creek on the south and the Sabine River to the east. The only road to the house, Pine Tree Lane, was an improved gravel road just on the north side of Church House Creek.

For two days the rains were intermittent and growing stronger. There was a lull in the rains as Yvette left for work and the children left for their first day of school. An hour later heavy rains began to fall and steadily got more intense. The winds were blowing from east to west and getting stronger. All day the rains continued with only a few periods where it would let up. With each hour Jack grew more concerned. By mid afternoon Church House Creek was running just below flood stage and still rising. He called Yvette at the Blue JAY and discussed the situation with her.

"I don't think you can get home tonight, and I'm not sure I can get out. What does it look like where you are?"

"We are still high and dry here, but you are right. A trucker just stopped in here and said about two miles of FM 1416 just this side of Church House Creek is under water. School let out early, and Juli and Jacky are here at the restaurant with me. We can bunk in with Arty. Are you going to be all right, Jack?"

"Not until I see all of you are back here with me safe and sound! Don't worry about me and the ponies. This is the highest point in the five acres. We'll be fine. Call me every hour or so and let me know you are all okay. I love you, Evie."

All night and into the following morning the rains and winds continued. Then about noon they suddenly stopped, the skies cleared, and the sun came out brightly. Jack had hardly put fresh hay in the horse stall before the clouds returned and the rains started again. This time the winds were out of the west blowing easterly. Jack realized that the lull had been the eye of the tropical storm moving almost directly overhead. The rains continued for another eight hours before tapering off and becoming intermittent showers. By now Yvette and her children had found other shelter in Jasper and had purchased additional clothing and other needed supplies. Yvette called Jack several times during the day and night.

After more than thirty hours the heavy rains had continued, with only brief periods between downpours. The rivers, creeks, and streams were all over their banks. The rising waters had not yet reached the cabin, but most of the yard surrounding the house was under water. The boathouse and pier were near the top of their mooring pilings and Jack feared they would soon be washed away, boat and all. He made his way down to the boathouse and piloted the boat up near the house, tying it to a nearby pine tree.

The corral and horse shed now had several inches of water in them, so Jack put halters on both ponies and led them to higher ground to keep their hooves dry. He used several long ropes tied between trees to form a makeshift corral. He carried a bale of alfalfa hay out to the horses breaking it into two piles. He tore the lid off of a large cooler and placed it in the roped in area and filled it with tap water.

Next he placed a call to Yvette. "How are you all doing, Evie?" he asked. "Do you have everything you need?"

"We're fine, Jack. How about you? You have enough supplies to hold out?"

"Don't worry about me. Let me talk to Jacky."

Jack told his young son that he had moved the ponies to a safer place and that they were okay. That he missed him and loved him and would see him as soon as he could. He then told him to put Juli on the phone.

"Hi, Daddy," Juli said. "Are you okay? Is everything still dry inside the house?"

"I'm fine. Yes, we are still dry so far. The water doesn't seem to be rising so fast. I hope it peaks and starts to recede soon. How are you all doing?"

"We are bored!"

"I miss you all and love you, Juli. Let me speak to your mother."

Yvette told him that she had been in touch with the highway patrol and been told that US Highway 190 from Jasper to Newton was open but down near Bon Weir, where the highway crossed the river there were places that the water was still over it. She'd been in touch with Arty, and the Blue JAY was still dry. She missed Jack terribly and was anxious to get home to him.

"Stay there as long as it takes. I want you all to be safe. I think the river and creek have about reached their crest. I miss you like crazy. I love you, Evie!"

The next day the waters had receded far enough that Yvette and the children could get to Bon Weir but no closer to home. Jack filled the gas tank for the boat, put an extra five-gallon can of gas in the boat, made sure there was a life jacket for everyone, and headed up the water-covered lane and highway by boat. Where the water had receded enough that the highway was dry, there was still sufficient water in the road-side ditches to float the boat. But it was sometimes so shallow he had to walk along on the highway and pull it along beside him. He was able to get as close as one quarter of a mile from Bon Weir by boat. He tied the boat and walked the remainder of the way to see his family.

Jacky was the first to see his father as he neared the restaurant. He pushed the door open and went running into Jack's arms. After a happy reunion with the rest of his family, Jack drove everyone to the boat in Yvette's car. Then while they waited at the boat he drove her car back to the Blue JAY and trotted back to the boat.

Home at last, Jacky ran immediately to see that Blacky and Apollo were okay. Juli wanted to wash up and put some old familiar clothes on. Yvette wanted to get into her kitchen and fix a real meal. Jack just wanted to hug every one and relax now that he had his family around him again.

Over the next several days the waters slowly receded, the school reopened, and Yvette was able to get back to work. The ponies returned to their corral and stall. The boathouse and pier began to move back down their mooring piles.

The river was still above normal and running very rapidly, causing bank erosion. Floating in the rolling torrents were a lot of up-rooted trees and other debris. Jack went down to see if the boathouse and deck were still intact. When Jack heard voices above the roar of the river, he looked up river and saw four figures on the roof of a submerged house. Jack quickly put his boat into the water and gave chase. As he came alongside he could see there was a man, woman, and two small children on the roof. He tried several times to get along side the roof edge before he was able to toss the man his bow line.

When the man looped the bow line around a vent pipe, the boat swung rapidly around with the bow now pointing up river. A small spotted Jack Russell terrier came over the crown of the roof just then and joined the group, wagging its tail. Jack helped the girl, then the boy, the small dog, and the woman into the boat. The man then gradually eased himself down the roof, holding to the bitter end of the bow line until he could jump into the boat before releasing it. As soon as he got onboard he grabbed the line and coiled it up.

With everyone aboard, Jack revved the engine to pull away from the house only to find he was making no headway against the rapid current. As he dodged tree limbs and other debris, he turned the boat back down stream looking for a cutout or cove of some kind. He was able to get close to the bank when he suddenly found himself in an eddy. As the boat began a slow spin, the stern came close enough to the bank that Jack could toss the anchor and line up onto the river bank.

With the aide of the rescued man he was able to pull the boat up onto the river bank where they all disembarked. As they caught their breath and gave thanks for solid ground under their feet, Jack stuck out his hand.

"Jack Lockhart," he said with a smile.

"Oh thank you, Mr. Lockhart!" the woman said. "We thought for sure we were goners."

"Buford Thibodeaux," the man said as he shook Jack's hand. "My wife, Olla Mae, my boy, LeRoy, and my daughter, Bernadette. Thank you for coming to our rescue!"

"You're completely welcome," Jack told them. "What happened?"

"Our house used to be about a tenth of a mile from the river. During these rains and runoff the river split and cut a new path on the front side of our house. We were surrounded by water for two days. I couldn't get to work and the kids couldn't get out to go to school. Then a little while ago the whole house fell into the river. We were lucky to be able to climb out onto the roof."

"My house is about a mile or two from here," Jack explained. "There's more water we'll have to cross before we get there, but we have dry clothes, food, and water. When we can walk, we'll need to drag the boat along behind us. When the water is deep enough, we'll all get in and ride."

Jack took out his pocketknife and cut the anchor line and placed the anchor in the boat. He knotted the end of the line and handed it to Mr. Thibodeaux. He picked up the bow line and tossed it over his shoulder. "Come on, Mr. Thibodeaux," he said. "Let's get to mushing."

Most of the time there was enough water or wet land for Mrs. Thibodeaux and the children to ride in the boat, Jack and Mr. Thibodeaux digging their shoes into the wet ground, leaning into the ropes, and at other times rowing or using the oars as poles in shallow water to push the boat along and occasionally being able to start the boat motor and ride. After about an hour they arrived at a wide place in Church House Creek that didn't seem to be running as rapidly.

"If we put in here," Jack told them, "I think I can take us right to the driveway to my house located on the other side of this creek."

A few minutes later, six cold, wet bodies were standing at the Lockhart back door. "Come on in," Jack told them, "and make yourselves at home. Mrs. Thibodeaux, you and the children can clean up in here. I'll see what I can find for you all to wear. Mr. Thibodeaux, you can use the shower in the guest room. I'll get you some of my clothes to change into."

By the time Juliette and Jacky got home, Olla Mae had the washing machine going and with Jack's help had fixed everyone a sandwich and a drink for lunch.

Jack introduced his guests to his children. Jacky immediately wanted to play with Tahyo, the spotted puppy. When asked about the puppy's name, LeRoy told Jacky it was a Cajun word meaning "hungry dog." He told him his mother had named her that because she was always hungry.

Juliette was immediately attracted to the diminutive Bernadette and they were off to Juliette's room.

Yvette soon came driving into the yard, and as usual, Jack positioned himself to be the first to greet her. After a quick hug and a kiss Jack introduced her to her guests. He followed her to the bedroom and assisted her with her change from her work clothes to her casual clothes, all the time talking nonstop in his Texas drawl.

"I found them on the top of their house as it went floating down the river this morning, Evie. I let Olla Mae look through your closet and drawers for the things she's wearing. I knew you wouldn't mind. They don't fit her right, but I'm going to take them all to Jasper in the morning to get some things in the right sizes."

"I'll go with you. Juliette and I can help Olla Mae and Bernadette pick out some things while you gents go shopping in the men's stores."

Jack and Buford put the table leaf in the dining room table, and Jack got four extra chairs. They hadn't had this many people at the table since Thanksgiving Day.

"What do you do for a living?" Jack asked Buford.

"I'm a crew supervisor for Layfayette Construction. We've been missing a lot of days because of the rains, and then I got completely cut off by the river and haven't been to work in over a week. I talked to the boss yesterday and he understands, but in construction work if you don't work you don't get paid."

"That house, were you renting or did you own it?"

"We were buying it. I don't know if 'washed away by heavy rains,' is something our insurance covers," Buford joked.

"And the land," Jack asked seriously. "How much of that washed away? How many acres did you own?"

"Three. You're right, half of our three acres may be silt on the bottom of the river. Well, as Job in the Bible said, 'The Lord giveth and the Lord taketh away.' I guess we shouldn't question the Lord."

"I commend your ability to make light of your situation," Jack observed.

"Well, the Lord sent you to rescue us. So I'm going to keep on trusting him to take care of us."

"You can stay here with us as long as it takes for you to get back on your feet," Yvette chimed in. "We have plenty of room."

"This is some of the best chicken I've ever tasted," Jack observed. "Evie, you need another great cook at the Blue JAY?"

Saturday morning the two families headed for the mall in Jasper. They needed both vehicles so they would have access to both booster seats. While the females and the children did all of the clothes shopping, the males took a ride to Jack's favorite automobile sales room. Jack was carrying several packets from the coolers.

Buford didn't want to look at new vehicles but found a three-year-old four-door Ford F-150 with a locking toolbox already installed that he really liked. It was low mileage and priced very reasonably. Jack tried to talk him into getting a new truck, but Buford told him he could more easily pay Jack back if he got the used one. He thought his insurance would probably pay for most of it. And he was really pleased with the fact that he wouldn't have to purchase a toolbox. In about an hour they left the dealership in two vehicles, returning to the mall. They found the ladies loaded down and still shopping.

As they approached the group Jack heard Yvette say, "Oh! This would look so cute on Bernadette!"

To which Olla Mae replied, "We already have way too much. Please, Mrs. Lockhart, we will never be able to pay you back for all of this!"

"Nonsense!" Yvette said. "You're not going to pay me back a dime. I love doing this!"

"We're going to go look at some Craftsman tools," Jack told his wife. "Mr. Thibodeaux lost all his tools when his truck went into the river yesterday. Let's meet at your car about one, Evie. We'll take a break and eat lunch at Spanish Uno. I'm hungry for a California taco."

After lunch they all piled into the three autos for the drive back. The trunk and part of the back seat of Yvette's car was full of clothes, shoes, and even a few toys. Olla Mae rode back to the Lockhart Estate with her, and Jacky rode along with his mother. Jack had a few of the larger tools in the back of his car, and Juliette and Bernadette rode with him. Bernadette, who always wanted to be with Juliette, used the booster seat in Jack's car. LeRoy rode in the new truck with his father.

By Monday the waters of the Sabine river had receded sufficiently that the five-mile stretch of US 190 between Bon Weir and Merryville and the bridge over the river on it were determined safe for travel. Buford Thibodeaux was able to return to work and with the loan of Jack's Expedition, Olla Mae was able to take her children to their school in Merryville and to visit her folks.

Over the next few days the Thibodeauxs were able to file insurance claims, move into a rented house close by Olla Mae's parents, and put a down payment on a lot in a new development. Buford had plans he had drawn up and soon started building them a home in his spare time. Somehow they still found time to visit the Lockhart Estate occasionally on a Sunday afternoon. When they received their insurance money for the lost pickup truck and tools, and the house and all its contents, Olla Mae insisted Jack and Yvette be paid back everything.

Finally everything was as back to normal as it would ever be. Jack and Yvette were relaxing together on the front patio one night.

"Next Thursday will be our eighth wedding anniversary," Jack commented. "Is there anything special that you want to do? Somewhere special you want to go?"

"Yes," Yvette answered him. "I want to spend a quiet night here at home. Just the four of us. After the kids go to bed we'll pretend it's just the two of us. Nothing special, Jack, okay?"

"If that's what you want. Can I ask you a question, Evie? Something that's been on my mind a long time."

"Sure Jack, ask away."

"It would sure make me feel better if I knew what I did to get you so riled up at me just before Rebecca and her family came to visit."

"Okay, let me ask you a question. What day did you first notice I was angry with you?"

"That's easy. The day I first saw Rebecca. I came home all excited to tell you about it and got cold shouldered!"

"Do you remember where I went that day?"

"I'd have to think about that. To work, I guess. I remember you were late getting home that night and I was pretty worried about you."

"Okay, you're never going to get it. I went to Beaumont to interview a new restaurant supplier."

"Oh, yeah. Now I remember. You never did tell me how that came out. You weren't speaking to me."

"The company where I went to interview is directly across the street from the Hilton Garden Inn. I was coming out of my meeting with the CEO of the company at exactly the same time you were kissing Rebecca. I had no idea who she was. I just saw my husband, who had promised to always be true, kissing another very young, very attractive woman."

"You mean that's it? You put me through that hell because you caught me kissing my daughter? That would be funny if it hadn't hurt so much. Why didn't you just come right out and accuse me of having an affair? At least give me the chance to deny it and explain? Well, come to think of it, that would have been kind of hard to believe. A daughter I hadn't seen in eleven years and there I am kissing her and at a motel. I can see where you could get the wrong idea. It's nice to know you care enough about me to get that upset."

"You probably won't remember this either, but just a few days before that you made me a bath. I came in and undressed in front of you, climbed into the bath, turned and faced you before I sat down, and you acted like you didn't see me. Three or four days later I see you at a motel with another woman!"

"No, I'm not buying that. Not possible."

"Oh, it happened! So I wasn't feeling all that attractive a few days later when the now-famous kiss took place."

"I'm sorry, Evie. I guess I deserved having to sleep on the couch."

"No, you're not supposed to be apologizing. I'm just trying to explain the circumstances that contributed to my totally misjudging you."

"Then I guess you need to apologize to me." Jack grinned.

"I'm sorry, Jack."

"For what? Come on you can say it."

"For your poor eye sight! I'm sorry you can no longer see well enough to notice when I'm nude!"

"That's not what I meant and you know it," Jack said as he made a playful grab for Yvette. She jumped up and darted away. He chased after her, caught up with her, and she pretended to try to get away before surrendering to his advances.

They returned to the porch swing where they sat close together under the stars until late into the night. Shortly after midnight, Jack picked her up in his arms and carried her to their bedroom.

Peace and tranquility had again returned to the cabin on Church House Creek.

WHAT ABOUT SUNDAY?

ONE

At thirty-five years of age, Yvette Lockhart was a strikingly beautiful woman. Her raven-black hair of tight natural curls framed a face of natural beauty. She had a lovely, infectious, dimpled smile, full mature lips, perfect white teeth, and violet-blue eyes.

She was the manager and CEO of the Blue JAY Restaurant in Bon Weir, Texas, a position she had held for the past several years. Yet as she drove slowly home this day, she felt as if her life was meaningless. Every day she did the same things. She got up at six, went through her toilette routine, drank a cup of coffee, hugged her children and kissed her husband good-bye, then drove the eleven miles to the restaurant. There, she spent another boring day doing the same things she did every day.

Her husband, Jack, at fifty-two, was already showing signs of aging. He now had love handles and a slight paunch, his waist having grown from thirty-three when they married to thirty-five. His once blond, wavy hair was now thinning and turning silver. He had a bald spot on the back of his head that was growing larger and was always visible unless he was wearing his Stetson.

Although he was still very attentive to her needs in the bedroom, his lovemaking had become routine, predictable, and less frequent. Even there it was difficult for her to continue to give her best and not show her boredom.

Yvette herself was in the prime of her life, while Jack, it was sad to say, was years past his prime. She hated the fact that he was slowing down. He had been like a hero to her when they first met. He was tall and strong and ruggedly handsome. Although he was much older than she, he had courted her and wooed her in such a way that she had finally said yes to one of his many proposals. She had been very fond of him and was flattered by his constant attention and his deep affection for her daughter, Juliette.

Although because of this she loved him dearly, it was not the kind of deep passionate, stimulating, erotic love between a man and a woman that she had read about and would often hear people speak about. She wanted to experience that kind of exuberant, ebullient love. She also wanted to feel alive, feel the freedom of not having any responsibilities. She had known nothing else since she became a mother at seventeen.

Now, even the drive home was boring. The house, the yard, the trees—all boring. She felt like she needed something more in her life. *This can't be all there is*, she thought. *I want and I need an immediate change.*

She pulled into the garage, turned off the ignition, and sat there for a few minutes, gathering her strength to face another boring evening at home. She knew exactly how it would go. Jack would be just inside the door to greet her. He'd follow her like a puppy dog to the bedroom, where he'd help her change clothes while asking her about her day. They'd have supper, and later he'd fall asleep while watching the evening news. She breathed a big sigh, picked up her purse, and went into the house.

"Hi, Evie," Jack Lockhart greeted his wife enthusiastically. "How was your day?"

They touched lips in a routine, casual way. "Same as always," Yvette replied. "Something smells good. Where are Jacky and Juli?"

Jacky was Yvette and Jack's eight-year-old son, Jack Jr., and Juli was their eighteen-year-old daughter, Juliette. Juliette had just graduated from Bon Weir High School and would soon be going to the University of Texas in Dallas, where she planned to study toward a PhD in art and technology.

"Jacky's out back with his ponies. Juli went to visit Tanya. I'm here missing you and your gorgeous smile," Jack answered while trying for a more meaningful kiss.

"Don't, Jack. I'm trying to change clothes!"

Jack felt the hurt of yet another rejection, but he smiled and gave her some space. "I need to check my sauce," he said, departing for the kitchen. "Please let me know if I can help you with anything."

Jack did not work outside of the home. Instead, he was the family cook, housekeeper, child care provider, launderer, and yard man. "Labors of love," he called them. He had been doing these things since their marriage. He was blindly, unconditionally, head-over-heels in love with Yvette and had been for more than ten years. He thought about her every moment he was awake and dreamed of her often when he was asleep. There was nothing he would not do to please her.

His only involvement outside the home was as a partner in the Blue JAY Restaurant with Yvette and his best friend, Arthur (Arty) Carmichael. His income was derived from one-third of the profits from the restaurant, some interest on deposits, and dividends from income investments, all of which were directly deposited into his and Yvette's joint accounts.

Yvette changed into some casual slacks and a peasant blouse. She took off her heels and slipped into a pair of loafers. She sat for a moment massaging her calves before joining Jack in the kitchen.

"Spaghetti," Jack announced. "With my famous sauce. Would you like to help me make the salad?"

"No thanks," she told him. "But I could sure use a glass of chilled chardonnay."

Jack picked up a wine glass and poured a generous amount of the white wine into it and handed it to his lovely wife. "I was thinking more along the lines of a red burgundy, with the pasta," he said, "but whatever you wish, My Liege."

"I must compliment you, Jack," she said condescendingly. "No matter how many times you fail, you never give up trying to be humorous."

"Oh? Have I hurt your feelings?" Jack asked. "I was referring to your status in this house and in my heart."

Yvette just looked at him then turned and took her wine to her desk in the den and began going over some work-related scheduling for the weekend.

Jack had noticed that Yvette didn't seem very happy anymore. She didn't want him in the bedroom with her when she got home today, and now she was putting him down for not being funny. Jack began to worry about his wife. He wondered what had caused her to suddenly turn cold toward him. He didn't believe he was being less attentive to her needs. *It must be work related,* he thought.

When Yvette, Jacky, and Jack sat down to supper, they ate in silence for a while. Finally Jacky broke the silence. "Mommy, how come you never go fishing with us in the boat anymore?"

"I'm just too busy with work. Doesn't your father take you fishing?"

"Yes, but I want you to go!"

"Maybe in a couple of weeks. We'll see."

"Why don't you take two or three weeks off this summer, Evie?" Jack asked her. "You should relax, get away from all the repetition and drudgery of the restaurant! We could go down to the gulf beaches and enjoy some time together. You know what, Jacky? The gulf beach is where I asked your mother to marry me back before you were ever born."

"Really? What did you say Mommy?"

"Well, I thought about it, and I thought about it, but I said yes anyway." Yvette smiled at her son.

"Oh, that's how it's done!" Jack teased her. "That's how you make something humorous!"

Even with the lighthearted banter at supper, Jack did not find things in the bedroom any different than the several nights before. He made many tender, romantic overtures, only to be rebuffed by Yvette. He fell asleep early in the morning still worrying about how he could help to make Yvette happier.

Yvette often walked around the restaurant during the noon rush to observe her staff at work and answer customer questions or just to nod and smile at her regular patrons. Today as she was at this task, she noticed a very expensive sports car pull into a parking spot just outside the window, near to where she was standing. An incredibly handsome young man wearing a very expensive suit climbed out. He removed his jacket and placed it on the back of the seat. As he turned to come inside, Yvette noticed he was wearing a tight-fitting short-sleeved Polo shirt stretched over bulging biceps and pectoral muscles and rock-hard abdominal muscles. She was immediately attracted to this handsome stranger and went to meet him at the door. She showed him to a seat and introduced herself as the manager. She called for Molly, one of her favorite waitresses, to wait on him. Yvette noticed he was not wearing a wedding ring.

Soon after he was seated, Yvette returned to her office to continue work on the weekend staffing schedule.

At the end of his meal, the handsome stranger requested that Molly find the manager so he could have a few words with her.

Molly stuck her head into Yvette's office. "The hunk at table fourteen wants a word with you," Molly told her.

"Thank you, Molly. Tell him I'll be there in just a few minutes."

Yvette looked down at her hands, which were trembling slightly. She noticed her rings and quickly slid them off of her hand and put them in her top desk drawer. Then, smiling her prettiest, she walked out and over to table fourteen.

"How can I help you?" she asked while looking into the sparkling brown eyes of the stranger.

"Can you sit down a minute and talk?"

"Sure, for a minute or two."

He took out a business card and handed it to her. "My name, as you can see, is Rex Colt. I make the trip between Shreveport and Houston about every other week. I hate to fly, so I always drive when I can. I was trying out a different route when I saw your place. I really enjoyed the meal, the atmosphere, and meeting the exquisitely beautiful and sexy, manager. Could I have your card so I can call ahead the next time I'm coming this way? Maybe we can spend a little more time together. I'd love to get to know you."

He told her he was thirty-seven and owned his own company, a world-wide online Internet company. He told her he would be coming back through Bon Weir in two days and would like to see her again at that time. They made a tentative date to have lunch together upon his return. He paid his tab and left a generous tip for Molly. Yvette watched him as he walked away and out of the restaurant. She couldn't help noticing how his trousers tightly hugged his muscular buttocks.

Yvette went back to her office, feeling a twinge of guilt. She opened her desk drawer and put her rings back on. "What am I doing?" she asked herself. She noticed her heart was still pounding and her hands were still a little shaky. She sat for a while and thought about Rex. He was approximately six foot three, which made him almost a foot taller than she. He had dark brown, almost black hair, sexy brown eyes, and a disarming smile. Suddenly she thought of Jack. There was no comparing boring old Jack to the young and excitingly sexy Rex.

The rest of that day, during the evening, and all the next day, Yvette found her mind often wandering to Rex and she became excited in anticipation of his return. Yvette could not remember being this captivated by any man. During those two days she found excuses to keep Jack away from her any time he wanted to physically show his amorous nature.

When Friday finally arrived Yvette was extremely nervous as she prepared for work that morning. She wore a form-fitting purple dress with a deep square-cut neckline, showing just enough cleavage; the hem of the skirt came to mid-thigh. Around her tiny waist she wore a wide black belt. She was wearing dark pantyhose and black suede, open-toed pumps with three-inch heels. Juliette fixed her hair for her in a cute style with a broken part near the middle of the top of her head and cascades of black curls hanging down over each shoulder. When Jack remarked how thrillingly beautiful she was, she told him she had an important meeting at the restaurant.

It was just after eleven in the morning when Molly knocked on Yvette's office door. "The hunk is back and asking for the manager," she told her.

"Tell him I'll be right out."

Yvette's heart was pounding. She removed her wedding and engagement rings and placed them in the drawer as before. She checked her makeup in her office mirror, smoothed her dress, and smiling broadly, she walked out to where Rex was waiting.

For the next two hours they sat talking and laughing and getting more acquainted. Rex tried several times to take her hand, but she always withdrew it. "Not while I'm at work," Yvette said, implying that anywhere else would be okay.

Rex was insisting on a more physical relationship. "God, you're gorgeous today!" he told her. "I'd like to take you somewhere away from here, where we can be alone!"

"Maybe someday," Yvette said, fantasizing about the two of them.

As Rex prepared to leave, she told him that she didn't want to meet him at her workplace anymore. The next time he came this way she would meet him in Jasper up on US highway 96.

"They have many fine restaurants there, and it's just an hour drive from here."

"I'll call you," Rex said as he took her hand and kissed it in a gallant gesture. "We can set up a date and a time for our next rendezvous."

Yvette was feeling many new, strange, and different emotions as she watched the handsome, sensual Rex leave the restaurant and climb into his Ferrari. Although she had only sat and had lunch with him in her restaurant, in full view of all of her employees, she still had feelings of guilt. It wasn't so much for what she had done, but for her thoughts of what she possibly could do.

For the next two weeks Yvette thought of little more than the next time she and Rex would be together. She continued to push Jack away every time he tried to be affectionate. Jack was as patient with her as he had always been, but sometimes when they were in bed together he couldn't keep his hands off of her. When she resisted his attempts to arouse her sexual desires, numerous times, Jack begged for an explanation.

"What's the matter, Evie?" he asked. "Are you ill? You haven't wanted me in weeks. Have I done something to hurt you? Please, just tell me what's wrong."

"I'm tired, Jack. I want to go to sleep now."

"Okay, hon," Jack whispered as he kissed her cheek and rolled over on to his other side.

Morning dawned, and soon Yvette was off to work with hardly a notice of Jack. Her good-bye kiss was cold and impersonal. Jack now felt older than his fifty-two years. In just a few weeks they would be celebrating their tenth wedding anniversary, and she no longer thought of him as a lover. Just a comfortable old teddy bear to sleep next to.

He decided that their tenth wedding anniversary would have to be one of their best. He would take her back to Niagara Falls and the honeymoon suite. Maybe if he got her away from work and the rut of everyday living and back to a place with such great memories, he could get her into a happier and more affectionate mood.

He picked up the phone and made a call to the Niagara Falls Hyatt on the Canadian side. He reserved a honeymoon suite for five days, September 16-20. He asked that several vases of fresh lavender gladiolas and roses, lavender being Yvette's favorite color, be placed throughout the suite. He reserved a window table at 8:00 p.m. on September 18, the actual day of their anniversary, at a high-end restaurant overlooking the falls.

He called Juliette at the University of Texas at Dallas where she was now enrolled, to let her in on his plans. She told him she would be happy to take care of Jacky while they were gone.

Jack made a trip to a jeweler in Beaumont. The necklace he purchased had two entwined hearts of white gold, inlaid with two carats of small diamonds, hanging from a braided white gold chain. Realizing Yvette would say she had nothing to wear with it, Jack purchased a lovely dinner dress in her size and favorite color. He had the two gifts wrapped separately and hid them in his closet.

A week before his next visit, Rex called Yvette at work and they worked out their next meeting. He would be in Jasper at 10:00 a.m. on August eighteenth, on his way to Houston, and again about noon on the twentieth, on his way back to Shreveport. Yvette promised to meet him for a two-hour lunch on each of these days at a restaurant on the ground floor of the Hampton Inn.

"I can hardly wait to see your lovely face and figure," Rex said seductively. "Wear something sexy!"

"I'm anxious to see you too," Yvette told him, "I'll be coming from work, so I'll be wearing my work clothes. I hope they are sexy enough for you."

The week went slowly by, Yvette thinking of the rendezvous and keeping Jack at bay. She even had a dream about Rex in which they were in a heated embrace. She awoke, her clothes damp from perspiration, quietly showered, put on fresh clothes, and returned to bed. Jack stirred, reached out and pulled her close to him. She let him hold her like that until she was sure he was asleep again before turning back on her side away from him. Yvette didn't understand her own feelings, but she knew she suddenly didn't want to sleep with this old man she had married almost ten years ago. She had to find a way to tell him.

Yvette was nervous and excited and almost to Jasper when she noticed she had not taken her rings off. In struggling to remove them, she almost drove off the highway into a speed limit sign. "I'll take them off when I get to the Hampton Inn," she told herself.

As she pulled into the parking area just before 10:00 a.m., she noticed Rex's Ferrari was already there. She quickly removed her rings and put them in her purse before getting out of her car.

Rex met her at the door, gave her a friendly kiss and hug, then led her to his table. They had hardly ordered their drinks before he took her hand and said, "I've got to see more of you! I'll meet you here every Wednesday and Friday. Two weeks is too long to go without seeing you! I've never before met such a gorgeous woman."

"Thank you. I think you're gorgeous too!"

"I mean it! I think of you night and day."

They sat and looked deep into each other's eyes, Rex still holding her hands tenderly in his. They were interrupted by the waiter bringing them drinks and menus. Yvette's stomach was full of butterflies, and she only picked at her food. Rex, noticing this, pushed his plate back and asked her if she was feeling all right. For the rest of the two hours, they made small talk to keep from mentioning what was really on their minds.

For the next few weeks they met secretly every Wednesday and Friday for a two-to three-hour rendezvous. Their embraces and kisses grew more passionate with each parting. Finally, Rex decided to take their romance to a new level.

"Do you think you could go away with me for a couple of days?"

"I don't think so."

"Think about it. You and me on a beach somewhere together, no one around to bother us. Come on, you're the manager. Give yourself some time off! I promise you we'll have fun."

"I'll have to think about it."

"What's to think about? You do want to be with me, don't you?"

"I have to tell you something, Rex." Yvette paused, took a deep breath, and stated, "I'm married."

"I thought as much. No gorgeous female like you should be running around unattached. What kind of dope are you married to! Why is he letting you out of his sight?"

"Jack is no dope. He's just very trusting."

"It doesn't bother me at all that you're married. I still want you to go away with me for a few days. Look, I have a beach property in the Bahamas. We can fly down one day spend a couple of nights and fly back. You ever been to the Bahamas?"

"No. But I've heard it's a wonderful place to vacation."

"Listen, I'll treat you like a real lady. If I try to go too far, you just say stop and I'll stop. Strictly platonic, if that's what you want. I'm telling you up front I want more, but I won't push you into anything you don't want. Come on, you'll have a great time. We'll fly down after your work on Friday, spend Friday and Saturday nights there, and fly back on Sunday. I have a private jet and pilot. We can fly out of Jasper County-Bell Field an hour after you get off work. It will only take two and a half hours to get there."

"Okay, I'll think about it. What kind of clothes does one pack for a trip like that?"

"I'd say you're already thinking about it. Sun dresses, bikinis, and an evening gown. But we can purchase anything you don't have or you forget. They have great shopping there."

Before they noticed it, the two hours had passed and Yvette had to get back to the restaurant. Out at her car, she allowed herself to be kissed and found herself enjoying and returning his kiss with a lot of passion. She didn't want him to stop kissing her, but both knew they must.

On the way back to Bon Weir, Yvette talked to herself seriously. "What am I doing? I'm a married woman with children. What will Jack do if he finds out I have been kissing another man and I'm considering going away with him for a weekend?"

Over the next few days Yvette thought first about going with Rex and then about not going. As the date grew closer, she decided she had to go. If she didn't she might always wonder about what might have happened if she had gone. She phoned Rex to let him know of her decision. He was delighted with her decision. She also told him she could arrange to meet him at the air field earlier in the day on Friday as she had arranged her schedule to be off as early as nine on the morning of the seventeenth.

Once Jack had everything arranged for their tenth wedding anniversary, he waited for the right time to tell Yvette about his plans. On Friday Yvette came home very happy. He decided that this would be his best chance, while she was in such a good mood.

"Evie," he began as they sat at the table that night, "I've got wonderful news. I've booked the same honeymoon suite we had ten tears ago for our tenth anniversary next weekend. We can fly up on Thursday the sixteenth and fly back on Monday the twentieth. We'll relive old times. Put some spark back in our marriage. You can get some much-needed rest. Juli said she'd come home to take care of Jacky while we're gone. What do you think?"

"Huh? Were you talking to me, Jack?" Yvette asked him absentmindedly.

"Yes! I just asked you if you want to go to Niagara Falls with me next weekend! Where are you tonight, Evie?"

"Next weekend, Jack? Oh, I'm afraid not. I have to be out of town that weekend. Restaurant manager thing. It just came up. It's too late to try to get out of it now."

"I was just thinking about you and how tired and overworked you've been lately," Jack said, trying to keep his disappointment from echoing in his voice. "You really need to take some time off. Seriously, honey, I'm worried about you!"

"Mmmhmm." she answered.

After kitchen cleanup Jack went to his desk in the den. He called all the places in the Niagara Falls area where he had reservations and canceled them. He called Juliette to tell her his plans had been canceled and she didn't need to make the trip back home unless she wanted. Jack was disappointed, but he understood that Yvette was under tremendous pressure to keep the Blue JAY a successful business. Maybe he left too much of the responsibility to her. He wondered how he could intervene to lighten her load. Worry kept him away from the bedroom until late, and Yvette was fast asleep when he climbed into bed sometime after midnight.

The private jet with Yvette Lockhart and Rex Colt landed in the Bahamas midafternoon on Friday. The villa belonging to Rex consisted of several bedrooms arranged in a semicircle around a large pool that lay between the villa and a wide, tapering beach to the ocean. The grounds were dotted with palm trees. Rex and Yvette had adjoining rooms. Their first evening they spent unpacking, having a leisurely meal, and sitting by the pool talking until early morning. Rex took her to the door of her room, kissed her passionately, and asked if he could come in.

"Not tonight," she told him.

On Saturday they slept late. It was already past noon when Rex knocked on her door. "Hey, beautiful, I have something for you," he called.

"I just got out of the shower. Please give me a minute," she answered.

She opened her door barefoot and in her robe. She had no makeup on, and her hair was wet and wrapped in a towel.

"God, you get more gorgeous every time I see you," Rex exclaimed, pulling her into his arms and kissing her passionately. "Here, this is the gown and jewelry that I want you to wear tonight. We will be dining on my yacht. There will be a lot of well-heeled people there. Now, get dressed in something casual and light, and I'll meet you by the pool. I'm going to take you to a place where they serve breakfast twenty-four hours a day."

Rex was dashing in a casual suit of white. Yvette, dressed in a figure-revealing tri-colored sun dress, was a delight to his eyes. They ate leisurely, enjoying tropical fruit and other delicious morsels. Yvette was so involved in falling in love with the strikingly handsome Rex that Jack and the fact that this was her tenth wedding anniversary didn't enter her mind.

They were chauffeured around the island, first in a limousine and then in a horse-drawn carriage. Rex made a pretense of showing her the sights when in fact he was just grateful to be alone with such a prize and be able to hold her close without interruption. Yvette felt such pleasure in his caresses and constant attention that she did not discourage his advances.

Later they sat by the pool, Yvette in a skimpy, two-piece lavender bikini and Rex showing off his firm, muscular, tanned body in white swim shorts. In the late afternoon, Rex left her at the door of her room, telling her he would be by for her at seven thirty for their trip to the yacht.

Shortly, a hair dresser arrived and put Yvette's hair in beautiful cascades of curls. Yvette dressed in the strapless gown, shoes, and jewelry that Rex had provided. There was also a small matching bag and shawl.

As promised, Rex came for her at seven thirty. He took in a sudden breath as he saw her total loveliness. She was equally impressed with Rex, in his expensive form-fitting suit.

They dined and danced amid men and women dressed in expensive evening clothes. There were many young women dressed in low cut backless gowns with plunging necklines and breasts pushed up until they almost popped out of the top, but Rex could only see Yvette. He took every opportunity to get her on the dance floor so he could hold her sensual body in his arms. Yvette showed no hesitation as she let him embrace her each time. As they danced close together, it seemed there was no other person on the yacht, on the island, or in the world. They were in a dream world all their own.

On the boat ride back to the island, they sat so close together they were like one. Yvette didn't remember the walk from the boat landing to the villa, but suddenly they were in the hallway near their rooms.

Yvette was walking closely to Rex leaning on him as they reached her room. He looked at her to see if she would want to stop there. She let him lead her on to his room. He opened his door, and they both stepped inside. Once the door was closed Rex turned toward her. She faced him, turned her face up toward his, and standing on her tiptoes, let him kiss her feverishly. She returned his kiss with the same intense emotion. He was slow and tender yet deliberate as he undressed her, removing one piece of clothing at a time and then taking in her loveliness before removing the next. They shared a night of unforgettable passion locked inside each other's arms.

Yvette now believed she had at last experienced the kind of passionate all-consuming love she had been missing. Toward morning they slept, Yvette's small, soft, supple body pressed tightly against the rock hard muscular body of Rex.

TWO

Jack sat alone in the pre-dawn hours of Saturday, September 18. It was their tenth wedding anniversary, and Yvette was not there to share it with him. He waited until 8:00 a.m. before trying her phone. No answer. Now Jacky was up and he fixed him breakfast.

"Can we go out in the boat today, Daddy?" Jacky asked him.

"In a little while. I want to call your mommy and wish her a happy anniversary first."

Shortly, Juliette called from her dorm in Dallas. "Happy anniversary, Daddy!" They passed a few pleasantries and talked about her college classes. "Let me talk to Mom, now."

"She isn't here right now. She had some kind of job-related thing that took here out of town this weekend. I'm sure she'll be disappointed that she missed your call."

"Tell her I miss her and I love her. I miss you and Jacky too. I love you, Daddy."

Jack placed another call to Yvette's phone. Still no answer. He got the same message about the phone being turned off or the customer having traveled out of the covered area. He got himself ready to take Jacky on a boat ride and placed his phone inside his shirt pocket.

While Jacky piloted them up and down the river, Jack made many other attempts to reach Yvette by phone, always with the same result. When Jacky grew tired of boating they returned to the house.

In the late evening, Jack gave up trying to reach Yvette by phone. He was saddened that this would be their first anniversary away from each other. He sat alone in the dark, missing her painfully until long after the eighteenth had turned into the nineteenth. He felt such dejection because he had not been able to take her away and revive her spirit and vitality. Jack loved her more than life itself. Her happiness was his only purpose, yet he couldn't seem to find the right things to do for her to bring back the joy he had once witnessed. Toward dawn, he finally fell asleep.

The private jet owned by Rex Colt touched down at Jasper County-Bell Field just before dark on Sunday September 19. Yvette gave Rex a lingering kiss at the door of the plane as she disembarked. The small suitcase that she had taken had been replaced by three larger ones filled with the expensive clothes Rex had bought for her. As the skycap wheeled her bags away, she stood on the tarmac and waved at the departing Rex. An hour and fifteen minutes later she drove into the yard at the Lockhart home.

Jack and Jacky both went out to meet Yvette at the car, Jacky receiving the warmth and attention Jack was so sorely in need of. Yvette hardly let him hug her and received his kiss by turning her cheek to him. Jack noticed she was dressed in a neat suit with skirt and matching blazer. Clothes that he had never seen before. As soon as he could draw her away from Jacky, he took her into the bedroom and handed her the gifts he had purchased to give to her on their anniversary.

"Happy Anniversary, Evie darling. I've missed you terribly!" he said, trying to caress and kiss her.

Yvette pushed him away and sat down on the end of the bed, holding the gift boxes on her lap. "Sit down here, Jack," she told him, patting the bed beside her.

Jack sat down beside her, putting his arm around her to pull her close to him. She pulled away.

"There's something I have to tell you, Jack" she said soberly, looking him in the eyes. She took in a deep breath and let it out noisily. "I've met someone, Jack. No, not just someone," she corrected herself. "A very special someone. I've fallen in love with him, Jack. I haven't been on a business trip. I've just spent the last three days with him."

Jack's mouth was open as if he wanted to speak, but no words came out. He searched his wife's face for signs she was jesting, but he could see she was being painfully truthful. Slowly the devastating reality began to erode his usually logical mind. He had dozens of questions to ask her, some requiring a simple explanation and some that would be hurtful and carnal. Slowly he stood up and turned to look at her face. She was looking at him with an expression not unlike a naughty child begging for understanding and forgiveness.

Finally Jack found his tongue. "I've got to give this some thought, Evie." He turned and walked out the door, closing it softly behind him.

Jack wanted to be angry with the man who had stolen from him, but logically he hadn't stolen her if she went willingly. He walked down to the corral and stood between the ponies. Horses, who didn't have to contend with human emotions, always seemed to calm him. After about an hour of deep thought and horse patting, he returned to the house and found Yvette with Jacky. He had been keeping some homework for his mommy to help him with.

Jack fixed a pot of coffee in preparation for a long night. When Jacky went to bed Yvette joined him in the den. "Would you like a cup?" Jack asked his wife.

"No, thank you. My nerves are jittery enough. I think a glass of chardonnay might help them."

"Let me get it for you." Jack said getting up. He poured her a tall goblet of wine, freshened his coffee, and returned to join her.

"What have you decided?" Yvette asked as she accepted the wine.

"To give you whatever you want and need to make you happy. You know I'd give my life just to see you happy, Evie."

"Don't talk like that, Jack. We have some serious things to discuss."

"I am being serious." He paused and looked at her, the hurt evident on his face. "Okay, I guess you'll want a divorce. You hire yourself a good lawyer to make everything legal and proper. You can have everything except Jack Junior. No one is going to adopt my son and pretend to be his father! What's the name of this Bozo anyway?"

"Rex is not a Bozo, Jack!"

"No, Rex is just a lowlife, back-stabbing, sneaky little, wife-stealing son-of-a—" He paused "Sorry, Evie, maybe I shouldn't be drinking the coffee either. Where did you meet this slime ball, anyway?"

"Maybe we should do this another time. I can see this is upsetting you, Jack."

"No, it's okay. Maybe I should just shut up and listen to you."

"First, I think we should find separate living arrangements," she said matter-of-factly. "I'll do as you suggested and contact an attorney. I want us to still be friends, Jack. I want you to be a part of Jacky's life."

"What am I going to tell Jacky? I'm not going to live here anymore? He's only eight! How's he going to cope with that when I can't figure out how I'm going to cope with it? Are you absolutely sure this is what you want? Does this, what's his name, Rex, mean that much to you?"

Yvette took a long sip on her wine, leaned back against the back of her chair, closed her eyes, and sighed heavily. Finally she opened her eyes and said, "Yes, Jack, I'm sure. Yes, he does mean that much to me."

"Then I guess we're through here. I'll sleep in the guest room tonight, and tomorrow I'll find a more permanent arrangement. As long as we are in agreement about Jacky, I won't contest the divorce. That way you can have me out of your life sooner." Jack stood up and looked at Yvette with such hurt in his deep blue eyes that she had to avert her eyes.

Although Jack was in the guest room bed, he did not sleep at all that night. Before it was light he was up, showered, shaved, and dressed. When it was time for Jacky to get up, Jack got him up and dressed for school. As they sat at the breakfast table, Jack told him he would be going away on a long trip soon. "I'm going to start sleeping away from home too, but I'll come back each morning to take you to school for a little while. I won't be able to do that when I take my long trip."

"Why do you have to go on a long trip, Daddy?" Jacky wanted to know.

"Well, it's something your mommy and I decided on. It's to make her very happy. You want your mommy to be happy don't you, Jacky?"

"Yes, sir."

"So do I. You know I'd do anything to make your mommy happy, don't you, Jacky?"

"Yes, sir."

"Someday, when you are all grown up, I want you to find someone as beautiful and special as your mother for you to marry."

"Okay, Daddy."

Yvette came into the kitchen about then, picked up the cup of coffee Jack had prepared for her, and said hello to Jacky. She took a sip, looked at Jack over the rim of her cup, and asked, "Everything okay in here this morning?"

"As okay as it ever will be," Jack answered her. "I'm about to take young Jack here to school now. I guess I won't see you tonight when you get home so…this is goodbye. Do I rate a hug?"

There was actual sadness in Yvette's eyes as she gave Jack a friendly but loveless hug. Jack fought the urge to carry the hug farther, turned, and walked out the door behind Jacky.

Yvette thought Jack's shoulders seemed to have a little droop to them. His step was a little slower.

After dropping Jacky off at school, Jack drove back to the house. He passed Yvette on the lane just about halfway to the house as she was on her way to work. They waved and smiled in the friendly Texas fashion as they passed.

Inside, he went to his desk and removed several of his more important papers. He was especially interested in the partnership papers. In the bedroom he noticed that the two gifts he had given Yvette for their tenth wedding anniversary were lying next to the bed unopened. "I guess she doesn't want them. They probably remind her of the fact she was out betraying her marriage vows when she should have been here celebrating the joys of marriage," he said out loud to himself. He packed two suitcases with his clothes and put them into his car. He then took the two coolers from the back of his closet and loaded them. Before he left he made sure the ponies had plenty of food and water, breaking a fresh bale of alfalfa hay into their trough.

At the home offices of Rex Colt Enterprises, Rex was sitting in his spacious office with several of his male subordinates. "Look at this picture!" He laughed. "It shows her figure really well. We were by the pool. Her bikini is wet and leaves very little to the imagination. Here, look at this one of her in the pool! I told you clowns, no woman can resist the Rex Colt charms. This one is married and still she came along willingly!"

"You hound dog!" one of the men exclaimed. "How do you do it? That's the fourth one this year."

Rex stood up and took a bow. "I'll give you guys one of my secrets. It's the most important one. You make her believe that you believe that she is the most important person you have ever met. That she is the only person in the room no matter how crowded it is. Don't let anything distract you. This one is a little more special than most. I think I'll keep her on the hook for a while longer. She is exceptionally good in bed! I think someone has been teaching her. Probably that old fool she's married to. She rang my bell a number of times!"

Just then the phone rang. He picked it up and recited, "Rex Colt, how can I help you? Oh, hello, beautiful." He nodded toward his friends, pointed to the phone, and to the picture on his desk of the bikini clad woman. "I'm missing you too. Wednesday at the usual place? Sure. Only this time I'll get us a room. Can't wait. Me too. Bye." He stood and took a high-five from each of the men before telling them to get back to work.

Yvette entered the restaurant and went immediately to her office. She had left work early on Friday and needed to see what the receipts were for all three days and catch up on anything else outstanding. She called in all three weekend managers one at a time to get a verbal report to go along with the written log. At nine o'clock she dialed Rex at his office. She was anxious to tell him that Jack had agreed to a divorce but didn't want to tell him over the phone. When he answered, they only talked for a few minutes. He told her he missed her, would be there Wednesday, and instead of lunch, he would have them a room reserved. She felt a blush touch her cheeks and ears as she thought about it.

Jack headed his car for Newton. The attorney who had drawn up the original partnership agreement was no longer alive, so Jack met with a younger attorney. He had his name removed from the partnership agreement and Juliette Anne Lockhart's name put on the agreement in place of his. He signed all the necessary documents and paid the attorney fees. The attorney told him he would need to meet with Miss Lockhart and get her notarized signature before it would be official. He let Jack know he would send copies of the new partnership agreement to all three partners as soon as he had finalized the paperwork.

Jack drove back to Bon Weir in time to pick up Jacky at grade school. He drove him to the Blue JAY Restaurant.

"You'll be riding home with your mother from now on," he told Jacky. "I'll still be there to take you to school for a while yet and drop you off here after school. You can't spend time at the house alone."

"Okay, Daddy," Jacky said as he picked up his things and went into the restaurant.

Jack wheeled out of the drive and headed to Jasper to find lodgings for the night.

Yvette looked up from her desk as Jacky came into her office. "What are you doing here?" She smiled.

"Daddy said you are going to take me home with you tonight."

"Oh, yes, that's right. Do you have any homework?"

"No, ma'am, not today. We had a substitute."

"Okay then, how would you like to fill napkin holders?" Yvette stepped to the door and called to the nearest wait staff person she saw. "John, how busy are you right now?"

"Two tables, one about to finish."

"Will you please show Jacky how to refill the napkin holders? Put him at a booth near my office and get him started. Check back on him from time to time. Thank you, John."

At 5:00 p.m. Yvette took Jacky and drove to the quiet, empty house that had so recently been a home. As she parked and headed for the door, Jacky went running to care for his ponies. Yvette almost expected Jack to greet her grinning that boyish grin and grabbing for her as she entered the front door. When it didn't happen, she felt a sudden twinge of regret. She put her things on the entryway table and headed for the bedroom. No one wanted to help her change her clothes. No one had laid out a change for her like Jack always did. She felt another small twinge of regret. She picked up her phone and dialed Rex. She got his answer machine. "Hi, it's Yvette. Just missing you. Call me as soon as you can."

Yvette now realized she had not fed Jacky at the restaurant and would have to make them something to eat. Something else Jack always did. She found all of her things she had put in the clothes hamper when she returned from her trip were still there. Jack had not done laundry before he left.

Jacky came in, washed his hands, and began to set the table. "Oh," he said, "we only need two places tonight."

Yvette began fixing sandwiches for their supper. She poured Jacky some milk and noticed they were low on both milk and bread. Since Jack did most of the cooking he always did all the grocery shopping.

"Are you happy now, Mommy?" Jacky asked her.

"Yes, of course!" Yvette smiled at her son. "Why do you ask?"

"Daddy said he has to go away on a long trip to make you happy. If you're already happy, he doesn't have to go!"

"Part of the trip is to make him happier too."

"But Daddy is always happy and smiling and singing. He gets real happy when you get home from work. He's funny. Sometimes he dances when you come home."

"I've never seen him do that."

"He does it while you're still outside the door." Jacky laughed.

At eight thirty Jack called to remind Jacky it was bed time. "It's bedtime, young man," he said. "Is your mother okay? Does she need anything?"

"Bread and milk. She said we are low on bread and milk."

"Okay, I'll bring some tomorrow. I'll see you at seven fifteen tomorrow morning. Now turn off your light and get some sleep."

Next, Jack called Juliette's phone. "Hi, sweetheart, how's my girl?"

"Hi, Daddy. What's up?"

"Just called to see how you are doing. Are you planning to come home for a visit anytime soon?"

"Probably not until Thanksgiving. You all could come up here and visit me you know."

"I'd like that. I don't think I could get your mother to come with me, however. Do you want me to come by myself?"

"That might be a lot of fun, me and my Daddy on a date just like when I was a little girl."

"You remember that? I was having to court two women at the same time back then. In some ways it seems so long ago and in other ways like it was just yesterday. Those days are so special to me! When would be a good time for you? Don't forget I have to drive Jacky to school every morning."

"Anytime, Daddy. Just call before you come so I can be sure to be here to meet you."

"I'll do that. Now call your mother, honey, and let her know you're all right."

"Okay, but why don't you just tell her?"

"She'd rather hear it from you. I love you, Juli. Bye."

Juliette did as her father had instructed and called her mother. They talked for a few minutes, Juliette assuring her she was doing fine. She asked about Jacky. She told her mother that when she had talked to her father earlier he said some strange things. "Is he feeling all right," she asked.

"I just think he's got a lot on his mind right now. You know your father. He can only obsess over one thing at a time."

"Okay, Mom. I love you."

Yvette had not anticipated the loneliness of the quiet house without Jack. She had, however, initiated his moving out and had to be tough in the face of her loneliness. She bathed and did her nighttime toilette ritual, put on a sexy nightgown, crawled onto the bed, and dialed Rex's cell phone number. For the second time she got his voice mail.

"Rex, darling," she purred. "I'm so lonely tonight and missing you terribly. Please call me as soon as you get this."

Rex still had not returned her call when she fell asleep hours later.

Jack rolled into Bon Weir about 6:00 a.m. He picked up a gallon of milk and a loaf of whole-wheat bread at the all-night convenience store. He was sitting in front of the cabin at six thirty. He knocked, and when no one answered, he let himself in. "Milkman!" he shouted to alert Yvette that he was in the house.

Yvette stuck her head out of the bedroom. "Jacky is outside doing his chores. He's running late because I didn't get him up on time. Can you please fix him a breakfast, Jack?"

"It's going to have to be cereal this morning," Jack told her. He poured a bowl of cereal and went outside to find Jacky, who was struggling with the wires on a bale of hay. "Go eat your cereal, son," Jack told him. "I'll finish up out here."

They were about to leave when Yvette came into the kitchen. "No coffee?" she asked.

"I guess not this morning." When he reached the door and Jacky was sprinting to the car, Jack turned to Yvette and asked, "Who's going to spread the hay for the horses when I'm gone? Lover boy?"

He saw the redness caused by anger start rising up her neck and into her cheeks. Before she could lash out, he quickly apologized. "I'm sorry Evie. Damned jealousy, I guess. I'm going now. I love you."

Yvette hated to admit it, but she couldn't imagine Rex out spreading hay for the horses. Or fixing Jacky's breakfast. Or running to the store for milk and bread. What she could imagine was his rock-hard, muscular body as he held her in a romantic embrace. That image pushed all other thoughts from her otherwise organized mind. But, she recalled, he had not yet returned her calls. As she made a last-minute look around to make sure she hadn't left anything, she noticed the gifts Jack had given her Sunday night. A feeling of regret once again passed over her. She put the still unopened packages in an empty space in what had just recently been Jack's closet. "Now," she said, "I won't be reminded of that again."

At work, Yvette finally did what she had promised Jack she would do when they talked Sunday night—she called a divorce attorney. She made an appointment for 11:00 a.m. that same day. The attorney asked a lot of questions that she didn't like answering, but she got through it.

"If it's, as you say, a friendly non-contested divorce, it will cost you very little and I can get it on the docket right away. The minor child will be a problem, however, and we will have to have a specific plan for custody before we can take it before the judge."

"Joint custody with equal time and visitations. We don't want our son traumatized."

"In the matter of division of property, what assets do you want to retain and which do you want your husband to have?"

"He said I could keep everything except Jack Jr."

"I'll still need to have a list of them. Does your husband have any personal assets that we should list?"

"His car, but I don't want that."

"Any personal income?"

"I don't think so. He doesn't work outside of the house. We are partners in a business, and his profits are deposited into our joint accounts."

"You might want to think about freezing all withdrawals until after the final decree. If he has access to all of the family funds, he could legally withdraw all of them before we can freeze them."

"Jack would never do that."

"You never know what a man will do when he's pushed to the limit, Mrs. Lockhart. I'll get a preliminary agreement typed up for your husband to sign. What address is he using?"

"He still gets his mail at the same address as I do."

Jack dropped Jacky at school and told him he would be there to pick him up at three. He then drove the fifty miles to Orange, to a Honda motorcycle dealership. Jack purchased a six-cylinder blue and silver Goldwing Honda touring bike and a motorcycle trailer. He was in front of the elementary school as it let out.

"Whose motorcycle is that?" Jacky asked his father.

"Right now it's mine. But when I'm through with it, if you want it, I'll give it to you. It's for that long trip I'm going to be taking soon.

Jack drove Jacky to the restaurant and dropped him off. He towed the motorcycle to Jasper and found a large storage space to rent. He left the bike on the trailer and left them both in the storage space. At his hotel room later he made the nightly calls to his children.

"Bedtime very soon, Jacky. How is your mommy?"

"She seems sad. We ate supper at the restaurant today so she wouldn't have to fix sandwiches."

"Did you feed and water your horses tonight?"

"They had plenty of everything. I'll check them again in the morning. Guess what, Daddy? Mommy bought me an alarm clock so I can wake up on time every morning because you aren't here to wake me up anymore."

"That's very good. Did she show you how to work it?"

"Yes, sir."

"Good night, Jacky. Lights out. I love you."

"Good night, Daddy."

The conversation with his daughter lasted much longer. Juliette told him her mother thought he was obsessing over something.

He laughed it off. She told him about one of her classmates who was, in her words, "a doll" with long eyelashes, big blue eyes, and blond hair. His name was Rolf Olsen. They had gone out a few times. She was sure Jack would like him. "He's taller than you, Daddy, and a lot thinner," she teased. "Maybe you'll get to meet him when you come up to visit."

Early the next morning Jack drove into Yvette's front yard. He went into the back and found Jacky struggling with a hay bale. Jack cut the wires on three bales. "How much can you pick up Jacky," he asked. He kicked the top of the bale with his boot heel, knocking off a chunk about a foot thick. "Can you toss that in the trough? Good boy." Jack went into the shed and got his hand axe. "Here Jacky, take this axe and chop the bale into pieces that you can easily handle. Yes, just like that. Have you had your breakfast yet?"

"No, sir."

"Let's go see what your mommy has fixed for you. Evie," Jack called out as they entered the house.

"In here, be out shortly," she answered.

Jack noted that nothing had been fixed for breakfast again. He checked his watch, and seeing they had plenty of time, he put on some coffee and scrambled some eggs while the toast was browning. He poured Jacky some orange juice and scooped the eggs onto a plate for him while he buttered the toast.

"Aren't you going to eat with me, Daddy?"

"Not today, son. Okay, now go brush your teeth and get your homework."

As Jacky hurried off to brush his teeth, Yvette came out of the bedroom dressed in a new, very sexy outfit. "Oh, you made some coffee. Thank you, Jack."

"Where are you going looking like that? Don't you have work today?" Jack asked her indignantly.

"Not that it's any of your business, but I have a date for lunch!"

Jack bit his tongue. His opinions no longer mattered to her. He wondered what he had done to cause her to suddenly, at age thirty-five, start acting like a heartless, sex-starved tart. His heart was breaking. *I haven't neglected her needs in the bedroom*, he thought. *It has to be that I'm just too old and ugly.*

When Jacky came out with his homework and they started to leave, he hugged his mother good-bye. Jack rinsed his coffee mug and put it in the dishwasher. He took a long last look at the woman Yvette had become. He did not like the image she portrayed. Without another word, he turned and walked out behind his son.

Yvette assigned a temporary manager. She told him she was leaving at nine and that she would be back before three. Excitedly she drove to the Hampton Inn in Jasper, making record time. She had been there only about ten minutes when she saw Rex's Ferrari come wheeling in. She checked her makeup before stepping out to meet him. Rex was very complimentary about her looks, her dress and sexiness. They checked into their room and were soon in each other's arms. Later, as Yvette was dressing, she asked Rex why he had not returned her calls.

"I was very busy and I get so many voice mails, I rarely check them anymore. Was it something important?"

"Yes," Yvette said, smiling. "I wanted to tell you how much I missed you and needed you! Our exercise has made me hungry. Put your clothes on and take me to lunch."

As they dined Yvette looked into Rex's eyes. "I've asked Jack for a divorce," she told him seriously. "He said he won't contest it. I contacted an attorney yesterday."

"Whoa! Aren't you moving a little fast?" Rex asked, trying to not show too much apprehension.

"No, I don't think so. I've found what I want, and Jack no longer belongs in my life. Don't you want me, Rex?"

"Of course. But I have to tell you, I'm not looking for marriage and a family. What we have here, this torrid lovemaking every time we can get together, that's all I can promise you. If you have to have more than that, I'm the wrong guy."

"No, Rex, you're the right man for me. I want you, however you want it to be. I'll meet you anytime, anywhere, only just don't ever say it's over. Promise me! Say you love me, Rex!"

"Of course I do," he replied.

After a light meal they returned to their room for more afternoon play.

Jack picked up Jacky from school at three and took him to the restaurant.

Not seeing Yvette's car in her space, he went in with Jacky and headed for Yvette's office. Mrs. Lockhart isn't in, Mr. Lockhart. She called a little while ago and said she would be back by three thirty." Jack took a seat in a booth with Jacky and waited. At 3:45 he said, "Come on, Jacky. Let's go check on the ponies."

While Jacky was out with the ponies Jack went into the house, cleaned up the kitchen, and started supper. When he had to make a bathroom call and was returning, he noticed his closet door was slightly ajar. Looking inside, he found the still unopened anniversary gifts he had given Yvette. He was overcome with anger, picked up the gift boxes, and took them to throw them in the trash then thought better of it and just tossed them into his car.

It was almost six when Yvette came in. Jack looked at her disapprovingly. "Did you forget you have a son to take care of?"

"You are not my father! Don't try scolding me!"

"No! If I was your father, I'd turn you over my knee and spank you soundly!"

"Oh, you'd love that, wouldn't you?"

"I'm very disappointed in you right now. When a man acts like this, they say he's thinking with some other part of his anatomy other than his head. Well, in your case you are thinking with your hips. You're better than that, Evie! Where's the sweet, beautiful, level-headed girl I married? I want to talk to her."

"She grew up!" Yvette said as she stomped off to the bedroom.

"Are you trying to prove you can't take care of Jacky so the judge will award custody to me?" he called after her. "Do you want me to counter sue?"

Jacky came in about that time. "Wash up for supper, Jacky" Jack told him. "Your mother is home now, and I have to leave. I'll pick you up in the morning. If you need anything before then, call me. I love you, Jacky."

"Okay, Daddy. I love you too."

Before going back to his room in Jasper, Jack stopped off to visit his old friend and partner Arty Carmichael at his apartment behind the restaurant.

"How are you, Arty?" Jack asked as Arty met him at the door.

"I'm afraid to check! Afraid to check! Get in here, Jack, you old son-of-a-gun," Arty greeted him. "I ain't seen you in a coon's age. How y'all doing? Here, have a cup of java."

Jack took the coffee, took a big swallow, sighed, and sat down across from Arty. "Yvette and I have split the blanket."

"Well, I been hearing rumors. What happened, Jack? She really been seeing that scalawag everybody's been talking about? Mable told me she's been out of her office a lot while she's been out gallivanting around with him."

"I guess it's mostly true, but my problem is with Jacky's welfare. I've moved out. I have a room up in Jasper. Jacky gets out of school at three. She's supposed to be keeping him here until she goes home after work, but she isn't thinking straight and forgets about him. He can ride the bus here each night if I had someone to be here for him when he gets here. Could you see your way clear—"

"Of course, Jack," Arty interrupted. "Tell the little tyke to come on back and spend the time with me. What do you plan to do about Vet, Jack?"

"Well, I'd like to spank her butt! But since that would be considered assault, I'm just going to give her everything she wants and let her sink or swim on her own. You know I still love her so much. This is killing me, Arty." Jack choked on his words and tears filled his eyes.

Arty patted Jack on the shoulder. "You'll get through this."

"Knowing you'll be looking out for Jacky is a load off of my mind," Jack said. "Great coffee. I'll be going now. Say hello to Mable for me."

On Thursday morning when Jack took Jacky to school, he went to the school cafeteria and made arrangements for Jacky to eat his breakfast and lunch at school. He paid for the remainder of the semester. He stopped off at the principal's office and made arraignments for Jacky to ride the bus to the restaurant every evening.

"That's bus number three," Mr. Jenkins told him. "Will he need a ride in the mornings too?"

"Not just yet," Jack told him.

"Well, when he does, he'll need to be at the bus stop on the highway at the end of Pine Tree Lane by seven each morning. That's bus number seventeen."

"Thank you very much, sir." Jack stood and shook hands with Mr. Jenkins.

With the assumption that Yvette would not run off and leave Jacky unattended on the weekend, Jack made arrangements to meet Juliette in Dallas on Saturday. As they sat on a park bench under an enormous live oak tree eating ice cream cones, Juli laid her head on her father's shoulder and asked, "What's wrong, Daddy? You seem so sad. You've been sighing every two minutes since you got here."

"I'd like to tell you that it's because I'm tired, honey, but you know I've never lied to you and I'm not about to start now." He took a deep breath, exhaled noisily through his mouth, and began. "Well, I've gotten so old and ugly that your mother doesn't want me around anymore."

"Quit teasing, Daddy. Really, what's wrong?"

"I'm not teasing, honey. She filed for divorce last week."

"You are joking! On what grounds?"

"I really didn't ask her that. I don't know what technical terms they used, but I told you the real reason. She's thirty-five and more lovely than ever, and I'm a hundred and two and about as sexy as a worn-out sneaker. She asked me to move out, and I did."

"I don't understand! She's always told me she loved you and that I was so lucky that she found you because you loved us too."

"I'm trying to understand it too. I still love all of you. You and Jacky and yes, even your mother. You can't kill that kind of love. I'm a little bit put out with her right now, but I'll always love her no matter what she does to me. I've decided to not contest the divorce. The lawyers would just try to verbally crucify everyone. I don't want to put your mother through that."

"I'm going to call her and give her a good talking to!"

"Don't do that, Juli. Don't take sides. Just love her and listen to her and try to understand what she must be going through. You can call her and tell her you know she's filed for divorce and then listen and try not to be too judgmental. She's going to need you, Juli. She won't be able to lean on me this time."

The rest of the day Jack enjoyed the company of his darling daughter, who so much reminded him of the younger Yvette. On Sunday, just after noon, as they sat on a bench on campus in front of the wing that housed both male and female students, they were suddenly joined by a very tall and very handsome young man. "This is Rolf!" Juliette told him excitedly. "Rolf, I want you to meet my dad."

"How do you do, Mr. Lockhart?" Rolf said, extending his hand.

"Please, call me Jack. Mr. Lockhart makes me feel as old as I am." Jack smiled at him as they shook hands. "Is that a Scandinavian accent I'm hearing?"

"Yes sir. I'm from Trondheim, Norway, here at the university on an academic scholarship. I believe Trondheim is a little larger than Bon Weir." He smiled, his perfect white teeth showing. "Juliette and I had plans for later in the evening. Maybe you would like to join us? Or would you prefer to cancel?" he asked Juliette.

Jack could see why Juliette thought him to be a doll.

After receiving Juliette's assurance that she would meet him later, Rolf said good-bye to her and Jack and headed off to the dorm entrance.

"Rolf is studying for his PhD in physics," Juliette told him proudly. "He is so intelligent, Daddy."

Jack and Juliette discussed school and friends and old times when Juliette and her mother lived in the trailer park. As the afternoon wore on, Jack had to say his farewells and head back to Jasper.

With Jacky's meals and ability to get to school and back home taken care of, Jack had only the horses to worry about. He called an old friend who lived in Merryville just five miles East of Bon Weir over in Louisiana.

"Thibodeaux residence, Buford speaking,"

"Hi, Buford, Jack Lockhart here. How are you? How are Olla Mae and the kids?"

They continued pleasant conversation for a while before Jack finally came to the point of his call. Jack told him he was going to be gone for a while and although his eight-year-old son did a very good job of taking care of the ponies, he wondered if LeRoy would want to earn a few dollars for checking on them every two or three days.

"I'm sure he would. LeRoy just got his driver's license and it has a motorcycle stamp on it so he's been looking for a reason to drive or ride his motorcycle. I'll send him over after school tomorrow, and you can show him what he needs to do."

The next day after school, Jack picked Jacky up at the restaurant after telling both Arty and Yvette he would be doing so. They met LeRoy Thibodeaux at the house, and Jack and Jacky explained to him what needed to be done with the ponies. Jack told him to keep track of his time and he would pay him ten dollars an hour. By the time LeRoy and Jacky had finished, Yvette was home. This time she had remembered to bring Jacky's supper with her.

Jack went to meet her, smiling. "Hi, Evie. You okay?"

"Yes, fine."

"You look fine! I've hired young LeRoy Thibodeaux to help with the ponies. You remember LeRoy, don't you?"

"Yes of course. How are you, LeRoy?"

"Fine, thank you, Mrs. Lockhart."

"Jacky will still be responsible for the ponies, but LeRoy can do the tougher chores until Jacky gets big enough to do them on his own. Anything else I can do for you, Evie?"

"No thank you."

Jack stayed until LeRoy left then told Jacky good-bye and headed back to Jasper and his lonely room. The next morning he was back at the house in time to walk Jacky to the bus stop. As they waited for bus number seventeen he told Jacky he was going away soon and he would have to start catching the bus here from now on.

THREE

Jack Lockhart sat in the hearing room and listened to the attorney go over the division of property. The house and land had always been in Mrs. Lockhart's name and would remain so. She would also retain all furnishings. The joint accounts would be divided equally. Jack could retain his Ford Expedition.

"As to the minor child," he continued.

Suddenly Jack was paying attention.

"Since the father has shown no visible means of support, having recently transferred ownership of his one-third of the Blue JAY Restaurant to his daughter, and furthermore having no permanent residence, we are petitioning the judge to give full custody of the minor child to the mother as custodial parent. The minor child is already in residence in her home. We shall further petition that liberal visitation rights be granted to the father. The petitioner has requested that she be allowed to retain the use of her maiden name, DuBoise.

He passed the papers to Jack, stating, "As soon as you sign these, I'll be able to take them before the judge for his signature. As soon as the judge signs, the marriage is over."

"What do you mean by liberal visitation rights?"

"This decree will name Mrs. Lockhart, the mother, as custodial parent, and the visitations will depend on what she and the judge decide."

Jack turned to Yvette. "This doesn't sound like what we agreed to. Are you trying to take Jacky away from me?"

"Sir, please address your questions to me," the attorney admonished.

"I'm not in love with you and I'm not married to you, so if you don't mind, I'm talking to my wife. Evie, are you trying to take Jacky from me?"

When Yvette just sat there looking at her hands and refusing to look at Jack or answer, Jack tossed the papers back at the attorney.

"I'll sign only when I see joint custody with both parents having equal and same visitation rights. Don't try to tell me because I don't work a nine-to-five and live in a suburban home that I can't take care of my children, you pompous ass!" Jack stood up so vigorously he knocked his chair over. He kicked it out of his way as he stormed out of the room.

"This is why we like to have an attorney to represent the other side," Yvette's attorney told her soon after Jack left the room.

Jack drove to Bon Weir, parked in front of the restaurant, and went inside. He had not turned over his keys to either the restaurant or the house, so he let himself into Yvette's office and sat there waiting for her to come in.

As she came through the doorway, Yvette looked at him with anger in her eyes. "What do you want, Jack?"

"First, I'd really like to see you happy and smiling again. I haven't seen you smile in weeks, Evie. How can I make you smile again?"

"You could leave!"

"I will soon enough. Look, honey, can't you get that lawyer of yours to fix the papers so we both have a say in how Jacky is raised?"

"Don't call me honey!"

"Okay, slip of the heart. I'll try not to do it again."

"Good!"

"Look, all I'm asking for is equal time with Jacky and equal say in how he's raised. I don't want that upstart boyfriend of yours, who's afraid to look me in the eye, having anything to do with my child. Don't make me have to counter sue. I don't want them using your behavior to beat you over the head with. Then everyone, including the children, will know about it, and what will that do to them?"

He could see Yvette's jaw tighten, so he quickly calmed his voice. "Come on, Evie. You've always been logical. At least for a girl." He grinned.

She glared at him for a few seconds then said, "Okay, I'll talk to the attorney. Do you think you can behave at the next meeting?"

"I'll try, but no promises. A man can only stand so much heartbreak at any one setting. I'm going now, Evie, but I want you to know I still love you and I'll take you back into my arms and into my heart whenever you say the word."

Yvette continued to stare angrily at him. Jack walked out, closing the door behind him.

Yvette called Rex's cell phone. She needed a sympathetic ear. She got his voice mail. Maybe this time he would call her back. "Rex, darling, I need you. Please call me as soon as you get this," she pleaded.

It would be two more days before their regular Wednesday morning rendezvous. Yvette needed a friendly ear now. She felt so alone since she had asked Jack to move out, and Rex could only be counted on for one thing. She didn't need anything physical. Right now, she needed a friend. She picked up her purse and went through the kitchen to Arty's apartment.

Arty heard the knock on the kitchen door and expected to see Mable carrying his lunch. When he saw the small figure of Yvette he smiled his big friendly grin and said, "Well, to what do I owe this great honor?"

Yvette suddenly broke down in tears. Arty wrapped his big arms around her and pulled her into his apartment. They sat down on his couch and he rocked her back and forth like rocking a small child while she cried into his chest. He handed her tissue after tissue. Finally she gained her composure.

"What's wrong, Vet?" he asked her.

Arty could shoot the breeze with the best of them, but he was out of his league when it came to comforting females.

"I just needed a friend," she said. "Someone who won't judge me."

"Been a lot of that goin''round?" he asked.

"Yes, but most of it from me. I think I've ruined everything." She sighed.

"Now why would you say that?"

"I've been so selfish thinking about what I want and not thinking of anyone else. I've lost my family."

"They ain't lost, Vet. I saw Jack and Jacky just today."

She smiled and brushed a tear away. "Thanks, Arty, I feel a lot better now. I better get back to work."

"Sure, Vet, you can come cry on me anytime!"

Yvette went back to her office and to work. She was trying to keep busy so she could keep her mind off of her personal life. It didn't work. She knew she could not make a life with Rex the way things were. Should she resign her position and go live with Rex? He hadn't asked her to. He had never even told her he loved her or wanted her like she wanted him. Was this all in her head? She would confront Rex at their next meeting this Wednesday.

Just after three Jacky came into her office, hugged his mother, and went to Arty's apartment. Jacky loved to listen to Arty's stories of the olden days way back in the 1970s. Arty had learned to cook when he was a sailor aboard a war ship during the Vietnam War. He had pictures of strange places and odd things.

As Yvette was preparing to go home for the day, her phone rang. She grabbed it, hoping it was a return call from Rex.

"Hi, Mom," Juliette said. "How are you?"

"Oh, Juli, it's you. How are you, dear?"

"Who were you expecting? Daddy?"

"No, no one special. So how are things at school? Will you be coming home anytime soon?"

"Yes, I thought I'd take next week off so I can be home for Daddy's birthday. Are you planning anything special?"

Yvette sighed. "Juli, I've been meaning to tell you this. Your father has moved out."

"I know that, Mom. Daddy told me. And I know you asked him to move out. Why Mom? What did he do?"

"He didn't do anything. It's just that…we've grown apart. It happens. People change."

"He told me he's still crazy about you. Don't you love him anymore?"

"Not in the way I used to. It's hard to explain, Juli."

"Mom, have you fallen for another guy? My friends think that's the only reason you would ever dump Daddy."

"I'll not discuss that with you!"

"Then it's true! Mom, how could you? Where is Daddy now?"

"He doesn't give me that kind of information. I think he has a room in Jasper. You can always reach him on his phone."

"I'll be coming home this Friday evening. I'll try to talk some sense into you then. I love you, Mom."

"I love you too, Juli."

Yvette tried one more time to reach Rex by phone. This time she was successful.

"Hello, beautiful. I've been meaning to call you. I've just been so busy. Listen, beautiful, I can't make our date on Wednesday. I've got to fly to New York for an important meeting. I'll try to be there on Friday if I can force myself to stay away from you that long. How are things with you?"

"Oh, Rex darling. It's so great to hear your voice. I've had such a terrible day. I've been missing you dreadfully. Could I drive up to Shreveport and accompany you to New York? I could make your nighttime much more exciting! I just can't wait until Friday to see you. I need to be with you right now!"

"No that wouldn't be wise. I'll be tied up in meetings all day and you would just be bored. We'll just have to suffer until Friday. Sorry, beautiful."

When the conversation was over, Yvette had a feeling of rejection. It seemed to her that he really didn't care whether he saw her or not. She was all the more determined to press him about their relationship when she saw him on Friday.

There was, in fact, no Rex Colt Enterprises private jet that flew out of Shreveport bound for New York City on Wednesday. Actually, Rex was entertaining the newly hired twenty-something redhead from accounting in his apartment that night. Rex never spent a night alone. Meanwhile, Yvette was spending all of her nights alone except for the company of her small son.

When Friday finally arrived, Yvette could hardly contain her urgency to see Rex. She was dressed in her sexiest clothes. She had to watch herself to keep from breaking the speed laws. They met outside the motel and were soon in their room. Within seconds they were entwined in each other's arms, Yvette giving herself completely and unrestrained to the man of her dreams.

"Love me!" she whispered to Rex. "Just love me!" Later as they lay on the bed, exhausted, she asked Rex, "Do you love me?"

"Of course," Rex replied.

"Then why don't you want to make me your wife? I'd make you a very good wife. And every day you could come home to this. Wouldn't that be wonderful?"

"I told you I'm not looking for a long-term commitment. Don't press me on this, beautiful, or I'll have to stop seeing you."

"Oh, don't say that! Okay, I'll stop pressing. But I love you so very much, Rex. I die every day that we are apart. When will I see you again?"

"Hush, now let's enjoy the rest of our time together."

They spent the remainder of the afternoon in bed, causing Yvette to return to the restaurant late. She had not heard Rex say what she wanted him to say. Yvette was beginning to feel like Rex was taking advantage of her. Since the day she told him she had asked Jack for the divorce he had seemed somehow different. She was determined that, come what may, she would win his total love and commitment.

Yvette was able to have the corrections that Jack insisted on made in the divorce preliminary papers. Jack hesitatingly signed them and a few days later received his summons. Jack sat in the courtroom looking at Yvette, who refused to return his gaze. The judge read over the terms and asked Jack if he agreed. Jack said that he did. He asked Yvette if she agreed; she said that she did. The judge signed the decree and declared their marriage void. Jack felt like he was too heavy for his legs as he forced himself to stand. Yvette still wouldn't look at him. He dragged himself slowly to his car. He watched as Yvette DuBoise, in the company of her attorney, left the courthouse. He started his car and drove back to his room.

Jack would be fifty-three in just a few days, yet he flopped on his bed and wept like a small child. When he had expended sufficient tears, he sat up and began to take stock. He hadn't lost everything this time; he still had all of his children. He had to find a way to deal with the hurt, his anger and hatred of Rex, the frustration of losing control of his life, and find something to fill the enormous hole in his heart. He would say good-bye to Juli and Jacky for a time and go somewhere to try to heal. He felt a deep-seated urge to be alone and in the saddle again.

Jack called Juli and found she had taken a week off and was now at home. He asked her to stop by the school and get Jacky and for the two of them come to see him in his room at Jasper Courts. "I'll take the two of you to supper."

They arrived at Jack's at 4:00 p.m. Jack had washed his eyes and recovered from his cry enough that it wasn't apparent. During their dining, Jack told them he was going to take a trip and be gone for several weeks or maybe even months.

"Is this the one to make Mommy happy?" Jacky asked. "She is very sad, isn't she, Juli?"

"Yes, she is," Juli answered him, patting him on his head.

"I hope this will make her happy, but I'm not sure. I really don't know what I can do to make her happy, but you kids can. You can help out around the house. Be diligent in your good behavior, Jacky, and tell her every day that you love her."

"I will, Daddy," Jacky said. "I wish I could go with you."

Jack hugged him then told him he couldn't take him because he now was the man of the house and had to take care of his mother and the ponies.

Back at his room, Jack talked in private to Juliette. She was so angry with her mother. "She is acting like an out-of-control teenager," Juli stated.

"Don't be too hard on her, Juli. She had you when she was a teenager, and maybe she needs to go back and pick up the years she missed."

"Well, she just makes me mad. How can she do this to you?"

"You and Jacky too. If I have anything to be angry about it's the way this affects the two of you. Look, your mother is just a human, with all the emotions and faults that come with being human. Just keep on loving her and try to be forgiving. You know I'll always love her and I've already forgiven her. Just wish this awful heartache would end."

As dark fell, Juliette and Jack Jr. left Jack's room and headed for the cabin.

On Wednesday, October 20, Jack's fifty-third birthday, he got up early. He went to the storage unit and hooked the motorcycle trailer onto his car. He closed out the rental on the unit and went back to the Jasper Courts. After removing all of his belongings from his room to his car, he went to the office to settle his bill. At ten past ten he drove out of the Court's driveway, heading northwest on Texas State Highway 63 toward Lufkin and points west. By late afternoon he was pulling into the central Texas town that had been his home for so many years during his first marriage.

He stopped at the flower shop and bought a small pot of bluebonnets.

"We haven't seen you in here in a long time, Mr. Lockhart," the clerk said.

"I moved to Bon Weir several years back," Jack answered. "I'm just passing through. I want to get some flowers for Rachel's grave. How have you been, Mrs. Webb?"

"We had quite a bit of excitement here since you've been away. Big murder trial! Bob was on the jury!"

"Is that right? What happened?"

"Well, it seems these two drug runners got into an argument. One pulled out a gun and shot the other. He's up in Huntsville now. The argument was over some drug money they buried out on the Segovia Ranch just south of the Cemetery. According to Bob, when they went out to dig it up, it was gone. Each blamed the other for stealing it."

"Did the guy say how much money they buried?"

"No, but Bob said the rumor is it was millions."

A few minutes later Jack was pulling into the circular drive of the old house he had abandoned almost twelve years ago. He took time to put the Expedition up on jacks so that the tires didn't touch the floor of the garage. In an adjoining garage stall he drove the Honda off its trailer and stuffed as many packets of bills as he could into the saddle bags. He tied the weather-proof duffel bag containing three sets of his clothes behind the seat. Jack put on his leathers, gloves, and helmet. He picked up the pot of bluebonnets, straddled the Honda, and headed for the cemetery. In ten minutes he was rolling up to the section of the cemetery where a headstone with his name and that of his first wife were located.

He stood with helmet in hand and stared first at the stone and then at the surrounding countryside. He noticed the slope of the terrain and then noticed the familiar stand of live oak trees and the group of mesquite trees where he had dug up the treasure that sent him on his journey so many years ago. He looked back down at the stone and began to talk to Rachel as if she were standing right there.

"Hi, Rachel honey," he said as he placed the flowers on her headstone. "I'm sorry it's been so long. I brought you a pot of your favorite flowers. A lot has happened since I last visited you. I think you'd like to know I found Becky. She's still very beautiful. She's happily married to a very good man by the name of Sean. You have two gorgeous grandchildren. A boy, Kevin—I think he's about ten—and a beautiful little girl, Rachel, about eight. Becky named her after you. When you first left me, I was so lonely I wanted to die. After about three years of heartbreak and grieving, God gave me someone to help me get over it. She is beautiful like you. We have two children. A girl, Juliette, eighteen, and a boy, Jack Jr., who's eight. You're wondering about Juliette's age. Well, she is the daughter of Yvette, my latest love. I adopted Juli when we got married.

"Now, God is testing me again. Recently I lost my new love. Not like you. I know you didn't chose to leave me. She just stopped loving me. I don't know why, but the loneliness and heartbreak feel the same. It seems no matter how hard I try, I just can't keep the love of a good woman. I miss you, Rachel. The twenty years that I shared your love has turned out to be the longest love I'll ever know."

Jack put his helmet back on, straddled the Honda, and slowly exited the cemetery. An hour and a half later he was checking into the Hampton Inn in San Angelo. He tossed the duffel bag on the suit case holder, sat down at the motel desk, and called Juliette.

"Happy birthday, Daddy," she said cheerfully. "Are you okay?"

"I'm fine. How are you and Jacky? Is he taking my leaving okay?"

"He's been a little down all day, so I made him a cake in your honor. I even let him blow out some candles."

"That was very sweet of you. Is your mother okay?"

She lowered her voice so Jacky couldn't hear. "She went to meet with her new beau and hasn't got home yet. I think there may already be some trouble there. She seemed absentminded this morning before going to work."

"Well, take care of her if you can, Juli, and call me if you or Jacky or…if any of you need me. Is Jacky handy?"

Jack consoled his young son and talked to him for several minutes. He signed off after telling him to take care of his mother.

Jack didn't sleep very well. The hole in his heart had not even begun to heal. *Tomorrow and each day after that it will get better,* he thought. *It has too. It can't hurt any more than this.*

Wednesday October 20, at 9:00 a.m., Yvette left the restaurant for another rendezvous with Rex. She had dressed in her sexiest dress and underwear. Today she would change Rex's mind about wanting her all of the time. Their meeting went like always, an immediate heated sexual encounter. As they lay on the bed catching their breath, Yvette, with her beautiful smile, turned to Rex and said, "Now, isn't that what you want every day and every night for the rest of your life?"

Rex got up without answering and went into the bath. In a few minutes she heard the shower running. When he came out a few minutes later, he was toweling off. She watched him with anticipation and apprehension. He began to dress.

"Rex, darling, what's wrong?"

"I have to go."

"But we just got here!"

Rex continued his dressing. He tied his own tie, pushing her away when she tried to help. "It's been a lot of fun, beautiful. I won't be back this way again, ever. Lose my phone number, will you?" He walked out the door.

Yvette spent the next few hours crying or feeling like dying. She cried because of her bruised ego. Then, as nausea set in, she cried from the hurt and realization that she may have thrown away the best thing she had ever known for a few tawdry moments in a motel room. Between bouts of crying, she called the restaurant and told them she would not be back today. It was after dark when she finally had the strength to return home. She hoped it would not be too evident to Jacky and Juli that she had spent the past several hours crying.

The big Honda Touring bike was like riding a cloud. It was quiet and powerful. It was hard to keep it down to the seventy-five-mile-per-hour speed limit on Interstate 10. Often Jack glanced at the speedometer and saw he was making eighty-five miles per hour. By late afternoon he was sitting in front of a motel on the outskirts of Las Cruces, New Mexico. He checked in and called his children.

Jacky was, as usual, very low key. He had his daddy's temperament, which meant he rarely got overly excited about things. Jack assured him he loved him and missed him before he handed the phone to his sister.

Juliette said she was heading back to Dallas the next morning since part of the reason for her taking a whole week was to celebrate his birthday with him. She told him that her mother had not returned until late last night and when she did get home, it was evident she had been crying.

"Let me talk to her, Juli."

Yvette came on the line. "Hi, Evie, how are you?"

"Oh, I'm okay."

"Jacky doing okay?"

"Yes. Sure. He misses you, but he's okay."

"I miss him too and Juli, but most of all I miss you!"

"Don't start, Jack!"

"You mean you don't miss me just a little?"

"If that's what you wanted to talk to me about, good-bye."

The line went dead. *At least I got to hear her voice*, he thought.

Jack hadn't eaten all day and suddenly he felt some hunger pains. He left the motel and rode down the avenue to a bar and grill. It was early and the bar was almost empty. There were many very small tables with only two chairs. He asked the bartender if he could get a sandwich and a cola. As he sat down he noticed a female on a bar stool at the very end of the bar watching him closely. Jack smiled and nodded in her direction.

She slid off of her stool and started walking slowly and seductively toward him. She appeared to be in her late forties but was still rather well maintained. She had a nice smile on a face that showed many character lines. Her larger-than-average breasts were pushed up high and tightly together. Her tight skirt revealed a figure, although not perfect, at least well proportioned. By the time the bartender delivered his sandwich and drink she had reached his table and said softly, "Want some company?"

"Not really, but that chair is empty and you can sit down there it you want."

"My name is Laney. Do you wish to be alone?"

"No. Please don't take offense, Laney, but you just aren't the person I wish was sitting there."

"None taken." She smiled. "That's a very attractive wedding band. Where's the bride tonight?"

Jack took a big bite of his sandwich and looked at her but didn't answer.

"Oh, trouble in paradise?"

Again he just chewed his food and didn't answer.

"Would you like to buy me a drink?"

"Not especially," Jack answered, "but if you'd like one. Bartender," he called, "give the lady her usual."

The bartender placed a small colored drink in front of her and told Jack it would be ten dollars.

"How long have you been a B-girl?"

"How did you come to the conclusion I was a working girl? Was I that obvious?"

Jack smiled. "I spent some time overseas in the Western Pacific back when I was just a kid, and in the Navy. Aren't you a little old for this profession?"

"My aren't you truthful?"

"I try to be," Jack answered.

"Well, I didn't get into it until late. I got nothing from a bad marriage and an even worse divorce. I live with my bedridden mother, who's addicted to prescription pain medications, and I have no marketable skills. I can pick up enough to pay my bills this way. I get five dollars from every drink I can get you to buy me. There now, how's that for honesty?"

Her smile was actually very pretty and warm. He could see how she would be attractive to lonely males on the prowl. Jack pulled out a $50 bill. "Bartender, five more drinks for the lady." Then to Laney he said, "What is your price for an all-nighter?"

"That depends on what you want."

"Your top price, everything included!"

She looked at him, sizing him up. Rugged good looks, clean shaven, clean clothes, well built. "I like you." She smiled charmingly. "I'll let you spend the night with me for three hundred."

Jack took three hundred dollars from his wallet and passed it to her. "How much of that does he get?" Jack indicated the bartender.

"Half."

Jack had finished his sandwich. "Put it all in your purse and wait here for me," Jack told her. "I'll be right back."

He pulled several napkins from the holder on the table and stuck them into his shirt pocket. He went out to his Honda and got a packet of $100 bills from one of the saddle bags and wrapped it in the napkins. When he returned he stood in front of Laney, blocking the bartender's view.

"Open your purse," he ordered. She did as he requested, and he dropped the bundle into her purse. "Close it, and don't open it again until we get out of here! Now come with me."

Jack tossed $150 on the bar. "The lady is checking out for the night," he told the bartender.

The bartender picked up the two bills, grinned, nodded, and put them in his pocket.

"You owe me for six drinks," Laney told the bartender. He hit the cash register and gave her thirty dollars.

Outside, Jack ask her where she lived and how she got to work each night. She pointed to a trailer behind the bar. "Don't worry," she told him suggestively, "my mother doesn't hear very well and her room is on the opposite end of the trailer."

"You know." Jack smiled. "I really am tempted. You are very attractive. But no thank you. I'm madly in love with the mother of my children. I just bought you out of that place so you won't have to work tonight. Now go home and spend some time with your mother."

"Are you for real? If so, you are some kind of special! What did you put in my purse? Drugs?"

"No, nothing like that." Jack laughed. "It's a gift. Look at it when you get home. If it's something you don't want, just toss it. Good-bye, Laney. Best of luck."

"Wait, what's your name?"

"Jack." He grinned. "Tonight's John was a Jack!"

She stepped close, stood up on her toes, and kissed him on the cheek. "Good night, Jack."

Jack straddled the Honda, put his helmet on, and rode to his motel. As he lay there trying to go to sleep, he remembered Juli had told him Yvette had been crying when she came home from her last date with Rex. He recalled the lines of an old country song. "If he ever breaks your heart, if the teardrops ever start, I'll be there before the next teardrop falls." Jack thought about heading back to Yvette as fast as the Honda would carry him. Then, he realized she didn't want him. His heart ached all night. He slept very little and felt tired when he awoke.

He headed north from Las Cruses, took it easy on the Honda, and only made it as far Las Vegas, New Mexico, that day. Once again he called his children. After talking to Jacky he asked him to put his mother on the line.

"Yes, Jack, what is it?"

"Hi, Evie. How are you?"

"I'm fine."

"Everything okay at work?"

"Yes."

"Jacky doing okay in school?"

"Yes."

"Juli make it back to school okay?"

"Yes."

"You still love me?"

"Stop that, Jack!"

"Well, I was getting a lot of yes answers and was hoping. Do you need anything, Evie? Are you sure you're okay?"

"Yes, we are just fine. I don't need anything from you, Jack."

"Okay, I love you."

"Good-bye, Jack!"

He had tried and she didn't sound so hostile this time. After he had eaten supper and returned to his room and he was sure Jacky was in bed asleep, he dialed Yvette's phone once again.

"What is it this time, Jack?"

"Remember when you told me you wanted us to remain friends?"

"Yes."

"Well, this is your friend Jack. Is this my friend Evie?"

"I guess it is."

Jack thought he heard a smile in her voice. "Are you as lonesome as I am tonight, friend?"

"Probably. Why are you doing this, Jack?"

"Okay, promise you won't hang up?"

"I don't know."

"Promise!"

"Okay, Jack, I promise."

"Because I love and I miss my friend."

"Okay. But you know this can never lead to anything, don't you?"

"Is my friend already in bed?"

"Yes."

"So am I. I wish…good night, friend."

"Good night, Jack" she said. Her voice seemed softer and almost tender.

Jack slept better than he had slept in weeks.

Yvette hung up the phone and began to sob quietly into her pillow. She wanted to believe Jack could still love her, but how could he after what she had done to him, their marriage, and their family. She had pushed Jack away so that she could selfishly have Rex, and now Rex didn't want her. She felt nauseated and went to throw up, but nothing came up. She had not eaten in almost three days. She continued to sob into her pillow on and off for the rest of the night. Both Saturday and Sunday she spent almost the entire day in bed while Jacky made himself microwave meals. Sunday afternoon, although weak and lethargic, she forced herself to call Molly and ask her to fill in for her at the restaurant for a few days. By Monday her crying only brought sounds. She did not have enough moisture in her body to make tears. She just didn't want to live anymore.

Jack continued his aimless journey for several days, stopping every four hundred to five hundred miles, spending lonely nights in motel rooms in places he had never seen before, handing out packets of bills anytime he thought he had found a need. He called every night to talk to his children and when possible to Yvette.

One night he was in Ft Morgan, Colorado. The next day he crossed into Nebraska and followed the Platte River into Eastern Wyoming. He headed north at Douglas then up to Gillette, east on I-90 to Spearfish, South Dakota. Taking state highways and staying west of the Cheyenne Indian Reservation, he arrived in Lemmon, South Dakota. He continued north on state highways until he reached Richardton, North Dakota, located on I-94. He then headed west across Montana, staying one night in Stanford, Montana. So it was that he arrived in Coeur d'Alene, Idaho, the day before Halloween.

The air was cold and brisk with just a hint of snow. Jack decided he had gone about as far north as he wanted to go this fall and planned to head southwest the next day, through Washington, Oregon, and northern California. He took a room in a very nice hotel, ordered room service, and placed his calls.

He had noticed that lately some of Yvette's conversations with him seemed strangely calm and pointless. He had asked Juliette if she thought her mother was taking tranquillizers. Juliette thought not, but she had also noticed her strange conversations.

This night when Jack called Juliette she was at a filling station near Lufkin and would soon be home, in time to take Jacky trick-or-treating the following night. They didn't talk very long, as she wanted to get back on the road.

He called Jacky's phone, and when Jacky answered he said, "Hi, Daddy. Mommy's sick."

"What do you mean when you say she's sick?"

"She didn't get out of bed today, and she looks all white."

"Jacky, when I tell you to, I want you to hang up the phone and call nine-one-one. When they answer, you tell them that your mother is very sick and tell them your address. Do you understand, Jacky?"

"Yes, sir."

"Okay, now hang up and call like I said. Nine-one-one."

Jack didn't wait for Jacky to call back. He called the airlines and booked an early morning flight out of Spokane to Houston. He called Juliette's phone, let it ring twice, hung up, and sent the same signal two more times. Two minutes later a panicked Juliette called him.

"What's the emergency?" she asked.

"Are you parked in a safe place?"

"Yes, Daddy. Why the emergency call?"

"Your mother is ill. I told Jacky to call nine-one-one. How far are you from home?"

"I'm still about an hour away."

"If they get her into an ambulance right away, you may not get there until after she's gone. Go ahead. I'll try to find out from Jacky where she's going and call you back. I love you, Juli."

Jack called Jacky's phone. "Jacky, it's your father. How is your mother? Did you call nine-one-one?"

"Yes, Daddy. The lady said that an ambulance is on its way. Mommy is sitting up saying she don't want to go."

"Let me talk to her."

"Hellooo." Yvette dragged out the word.

"Evie, it's Jack, are you okay?"

He heard the phone hit the floor. Jacky came on the line again. "Daddy, she can't hold the phone. She dropped it."

"That's okay, Jacky. You stay on the phone with me until the people from the ambulance get there."

For a tortured twenty minutes Jack hung on the line before Jacky told him the ambulance had arrived. Jack told Jacky to give the phone to one of the people there. "Hello," came a strong female voice. "The little boy says you're his father?"

"Yes, that's right. What hospital are you taking my wife to?"

"Christus Jasper Memorial Hospital. We need to get her stable now, sir."

"Wait!" Jack pleaded. "My son will be alone there unless you take him in the ambulance with his mother. Can you do that?"

"Yes, sir, we'll do that."

"Thank you very much."

Jack dialed the emergency signal to Juliette's phone then waited for her to pull over and call him back.

"Yes, Daddy, I'm in a safe place. What's the latest?"

"They are taking her to Christus Jasper Memorial. You will probably be there before they get there. I suggest you just go to the emergency waiting room. Jacky did really well. They are letting him ride with your mother in the ambulance. Juli, honey, keep me informed. I have a flight out of Spokane at four a.m. I'll be in the air for a while. I'll call you as soon as I'm back on the ground. I love you, honey."

"I love you too."

Jack drove the Honda into the parking garage across from the terminal at Spokane International Airport. He parked in long-term parking, emptied the saddle bags into his duffel bag, and crossed on the pedestrian bridge to the terminal. His flight was on time, and in a worried three hours and thirty minutes, he was deplaning at George Bush International Airport in Houston. There was a long line at all of the car rental desks, so Jack just hurried past them and out to the waiting taxis. He walked down the line until he spotted a new, obviously well-maintained cab.

"Can you take me to Jasper?" he asked the young man standing by the driver-side door.

"If you can afford it."

Jack climbed into the back as the driver climbed into the front. "Off the meter, how much?" Jack asked.

"One fifty!"

"I'll give you four hundred to get me there safe and in the fastest possible time."

"Yes, sir!"

"I want to go to Christus Memorial."

As they sped along, Jack called Juli's phone and told her he was on his way. He forgot to ask for Yvette's room number. Juli didn't give him much information except to say the hospital was taking very good care of her mother. In just over two hours the taxi pulled up in front of the hospital. Jack paid the driver the promised amount, thanked him, and headed toward the entry.

Jack stopped at the reception desk and inquired for the room number of Mrs. Lockhart. The volunteer receptionist said they had no one by that name.

"They brought her into emergency last night!"

"No, sir, I'm sorry."

Jack started to turn away to go outside and see if Juli's BMW was in the parking lot then remembered. "Oh, do you have a Ms. DuBoise?"

The volunteer checked her computer again. "Yes, sir. She's in room three-thirty three."

The hospital florist was right next to the reception desk, and Jack went in to pick out a flower. He got a box of three purple orchids to take with him and asked that a vase of purple gladiolas be sent to room 333.

Then, bypassing the elevators, Jack ran up the stairs, taking them two at a time. He hurried down the third floor corridor to room 333. He paused just outside the door, took a deep breath, put on his best smile, and pushed the door open.

Jack was not prepared for what he saw. The gaunt, pale face, the sunken eyes, the frail-looking arms and hands with veins and bones barely hidden by pale skin. An IV was hanging near her head. A monitor gave her heart rate and blood pressure. A bag hung from the side of her bed to catch her urine. Jack's knees almost failed him. He would have believed he was in the wrong room had he not seen Juliette sitting in a chair by the bed.

Yvette's eyes were open, and she looked his way. He forced his legs forward until he was at her bedside. He took one of her cold, bony hands in his and smiling down at her, he said, "Hi, Evie."

Her smile was barely recognizable. Her voice was soft and weak. "Jack, you came."

Juli came over to where her father was standing. As Jack turned to hug her she whispered, "Jacky's in the waiting room. I'm going to go check on him."

"Okay, honey, tell him I'll be out shortly."

Jack stood holding Yvette's hand and looking into her eyes. Her hand was so cold. He began to rub it softly, trying to bring some warmth to it. Her other hand had an IV stuck into a vein in the back of it and he couldn't rub it, but he held her fingers to transfer his warmth to them. As they looked at each other, a tear appeared in the corner of her eye. Jack took a tissue and wiped it away. They remained like this for a long time, just looking at each other and not speaking, Jack tenderly rubbing her hand. A nurse appeared and asked if he was family.

"Yes, Jack told her. "I'm her husband."

"Well, Mr. DuBoise, I need you to step out for a minute."

Jack stooped and kissed the hand he was holding then went to find his children. He hugged Jacky and told him how proud he was of him. They sat in the waiting room, and Juli explained what she had learned from the doctors.

"They told me the technical medical term is Takotsubo cardiomyopathy," she said, "which means basically she is dying from a broken heart. When someone suffers a great emotional trauma, the brain gives off chemicals that cause damage to the organs. In older people, it often results in a heart attack. In much younger people it can result in psychological disorders. In Mom's case, she has been so nauseated from the emotional pain and the chemicals given off by the brain that she has not eaten since the nineteenth or twentieth. She also starved her body of moisture and that caused a partial failure of her kidneys. She's very sick, Daddy."

"Can she ever recover?"

"Yes, but it will take a long time. Her body won't heal unless her emotional problems are eliminated. It's a long road back they told me."

Jack was beside himself. "God, Juli, it took her less than two weeks to get to this point physically. You would think she would be back to normal in two weeks! Why did I let this thing happen? I should have stomped a mud hole in that Rex as soon as I learned about him! This is all my fault. I didn't protect the one person I love and care about the most!"

"Calm down, Daddy!" Juliette said, gripping her father's hand. "I've never seen you this upset."

"Can't you see, Juli," he said in a quieter but still urgent voice, "I can't do anything to fix this. It's out of my hands. I need to be able to fix this." He paused, hugged each of his children, then said, "I need to be alone."

Jack left the third floor the same way he had come in, by the stairway. He walked around the hospital grounds and down the street for more than a mile, not realizing how much ground he was covering. Meanwhile, his mind was busy trying to find a way to fix Yvette. *I could smother her with affection*, he thought. *But she doesn't want mine.* He wondered what had happened with her and Rex to cause her to pine away like this. He could never ask her, as that might cause the pain to return. All he really could do—and this would be extremely hard to do—was to stand by silently and be there when or if she needed him for anything. He did an about-face and headed back to the hospital.

The doctor told Jack that they had stabilized Mrs. DuBoise. Her body had begun to replenish her muscle tissue, and they had averted any permanent kidney damage. He told Jack that now it was up to her psychologically if she wanted to get better. He recommended regular visits to a psychiatrist after she was released.

"Full recovery is possible if that is what she wants. Your wife is still very young," he told Jack. "She has that going for her. Whatever the cause of her emotional collapse, and we have not been able to determine that, it must be removed if it's at all possible. She should be able to leave the hospital in another two or three weeks. She will need constant care for a while to see she doesn't have a relapse."

Each day Jack spent every available visiting hour beside Yvette's bed. Each day she got better and soon began to eat regularly. Her body began to fill out and color returned to her cheeks. Eventually Jack noticed she even smiled at him when he came in. Their conversation became less strained. Jack never mentioned how much he loved her. He just tried to show it in every way he could.

When the day finally came that she could go home, he suddenly realized she would be going to her home, which is far away from his nearby room. As the three of them climbed into Juliette's car, it was Yvette who broached the question. "Aren't you coming with us Jack?"

"Sure," he said. "Move over, Jacky."

Jack moved into the guest room and resumed many of his old duties. The one he loved most was taking care of Yvette's every need. Every day she seemed to grow stronger and Jack was able to once again bask in her beautiful smile several times a day. Not once in the weeks leading up to Thanksgiving and now almost Christmas did he ever attempt to verbalize his love for her. On Jacky's ninth birthday, the fifteenth of December, she even planned and pulled off a small party. Jack watched and praised her recovery efforts. He drove her to her therapy sessions and waited outside in the waiting room. Gradually things began to look almost as rosy as before, with two very obvious differences.

Jack and Yvette never said I love you to one another and Jack still occupied the guest room.

During the Thanksgiving holidays, Rolf accompanied Juliette from school and spent the time at the Lockharts. During his four-day stay both Jack and Yvette became very found of him. Everyone got a big laugh out of Jack's attempt to talk with a Norwegian accent while they were seated at the Thanksgiving meal and even a bigger laugh when Rolf impersonated Jack's Texas drawl. Rolf did a very good impersonation. It was obvious to anyone who took the time to notice that Rolf and Juliette were more than just fond of each other.

After observing what the two of them thought was a secret kiss, Jack took Rolf aside. "What are your intentions regarding my daughter?" he asked.

"She's the most special lady," Rolf said. "I adore her. But we have not made any future plans."

"Don't take this the wrong way, Rolf, but if you hurt her in any way, I'll be forced to hurt you. As her father, everything that affects her affects me."

Rolf smiled broadly. "Please believe me I have the most honorable of intentions, sir. If I ever do anything to hurt her, I hope you do hurt me badly!"

They shook hands, and Jack patted him on the back, saying, "Let's go join the ladies, shall we?"

Between Jacky's birthday and Christmas, Juliette came home from school on Christmas break while Rolf went to spend Christmas with his family in Trondheim. With Juliette home to look after her mother's needs and with Yvette's recovery coming along so well, Jack decided he could go get his car and motorcycle.

He asked Arty to drive him to the airport in Houston where he told him he had a ticket to Spokane. He didn't tell Arty that the ticket allowed for a six-hour layover in Shreveport.

Jack's plane landed in Shreveport just after 8:00 a.m. Jack took a taxi and was in front of the building housing the Rex Colt

Enterprises just before nine. He entered the building and rode the elevator to the top floor, where he found a receptionist just outside a set of very large double doors on which he saw in large gold lettering, Rex Colt, President.

"He in?" Jack asked as he stepped past the receptionist.

"Sir, you can't go in without an appointment!"

"He'll see me!"

Jack shoved one of the big doors open.

"I'm Jack Lockhart," he announced. "We need to talk!"

Rex leaned back in his ornate office chair with a grin on his face. "It's all right, Millie, you can go."

Millie left and closed the door behind her.

"Jack Lockhart," Rex said condescendingly with a smirk on his face. "So you're the dumb cowboy who's wife I've been screwing. Well, she really was a great piece of tail, but now I'm through with her. You can have her back. In fact, I've already sent her crawling back to you." His grin was now slowly turning into a sneer.

Jack took off his Stetson and laid it on the desk. As he pulled on his deerskin gloves, he took a long look at Rex, who was sitting behind his spacious desk in his thousand-dollar suit. He was much more handsome than Jack; he was taller than Jack; he was more muscular than Jack; he appeared more athletic than Jack, and he was fifteen years younger than Jack. In fact, Rex had an advantage over Jack in every category except one. Rex had hurt someone Jack loved.

Jack didn't hold anything back as he stepped around the desk and pulled Rex to his feet. His first punch landed squarely on Rex's perfectly sculptured nose, smashing it all over his handsome face. Rex brought both of his hands up to protect his face, and Jack kicked him severely in the groin. Rex dropped his hands to protect his genitals, and Jack landed three more quick punches to his face. Rex dropped to his knees, pleading. His lips were swollen and bleeding, an upper front tooth was missing, one eye was closing, and he had a broken nose. Jack picked up the box of tissues from the corner of the desk and threw it at Rex. "Stop whimpering and wipe your nose, sonny boy." He put his hat back on, turned, and walked out the door.

As Jack walked past the receptionist, he told her, "You better call for first aid. Your boss just tripped over his mouth!"

Jack flew from Shreveport to Spokane, where he picked up the Honda and headed home. It took only three days for Jack to get to the house in central Texas. He loaded the Honda on its trailer, took the Expedition off its jacks, hooked up the trailer, and continued toward home. He arrived at the entrance of Pine Tree Lane just past noon on the fourth day. Jack was exhausted from riding and driving. He needed a shave and a shower. As he entered the door quietly, he was surprised by a big hug and happy greeting from Yvette.

"Oh, Jack, I've missed you so much. Don't ever go away and leave me again," she scolded.

He pushed her away and headed for the shower. "I must smell like a goat," he told her. "Let me get this road dirt and these whiskers off of me."

Later, after he'd cleaned up and they had all had a good meal, Jacky was in bed, and Juliette was in her room on the phone with Rolf, he found Yvette very talkative. He was overjoyed that she was feeling so well and wanting to share everything with him again. They were sitting in the den in front of a slowly dying fire. Jack had just complimented her on how beautifully she had decorated the house for Christmas, both inside and out. She was on the couch, legs drawn up under her. Jack got up from his chair, stirred the fire, and put another log on it. Then, without thinking, instead of going back to his chair, he sat down on the couch beside her. Without missing a word she shifted her position so she could lean against him in that old familiar way. Without a thought he placed his arm around her. She took his hand and pulled his arm tighter around her. Suddenly she stopped talking and realized how they were sitting. For a second she stiffened up, turned to look at Jack, then slowly relaxed.

"Is this how things were meant to be?" she asked Jack seriously.

"Yes, Evie. This is how God intended it to be for you and me!"

She had stopped talking. Jack took her hand, and they sat close together holding hands like adolescents, occasionally looking at each other, until the fire died. As the room grew cold he stood up, took her other hand, and helped her to her feet. As she hurried off to her warm bed Jack called after her, "Good night, Evie."

The following morning, Christmas Eve, Jack and Yvette found themselves alone in the house. Juliette had taken her little brother to town for some last-minute Christmas shopping. Jack and Yvette were both in the den, sipping on eggnog and staring at the beautifully decorated tree.

Suddenly, Yvette addressed him. "Jack," she said quietly, "my therapist tells me I will never be completely well until I can forgive myself. I can't seem to do that because of how much I've hurt you and the children. You'll never forgive me, will you, Jack?"

Jack set his mug of eggnog down on the coffee table, got up, and walked over to where she was sitting. He knelt down in front of her and took her hands in his. "Look at me, Evie," he said. "I told you this before, a long time ago, and I'm going to tell you again. Look straight into my eyes so you can tell if I'm lying to you." He paused long enough for their eyes to lock on each other. "I love you, Evie," he said. "Unconditionally. I have never stopped loving you."

She stared at him for a while. The sincerity was evident in his eyes. Finally she stated, "I believe you, Jack, but the question is, can you ever forgive me?"

"I forgave you a long time ago, honey, but if you need to hear me say it, then yes, Evie, I forgive you."

"Oh, thank you, Jack," she said as she began to cry softly.

He got up off of his knees and sat close beside her, putting his arm around her, allowing her to cry into his shoulder.

"Will we ever have what we had before?" she sobbed.

"I don't know, but it's my wish for this year's Christmas miracle."

He sat with his arm around her for a long time. She dried her eyes and both sat silently engrossed in their own thoughts. Finally, Jack thinking to himself, finished his thought out loud. "Tomorrow is Saturday and Christmas, but what about Sunday?"

"What about Sunday?" she asked with a puzzled look on her face.

"Oh, I'm sorry. I guess I was thinking out loud."

He slid off the couch, again kneeling in front of her. He took her hands in his again, kissed them, and said, "Let's get married Sunday!"

Yvette sat starring at him, her mouth slightly open, a question forming on her lips. "You-you would want me like that again? Just like nothing ever happened? Are you sure, Jack? I think you'll change your mind before Sunday."

"I'll never change my mind. You and I were meant to be together forever."

"I need to sleep on it, Jack. I'll give you my answer tomorrow."

It seldom snowed in the piney woods of southeast Texas, but this Christmas was different. As the Lockhart home came to life, they were greeted with a crisp blanket of pristine new snow.

Yvette announced that she would cook breakfast for everyone before they sat down to open their Christmas gifts. As she completed her morning toilette and entered the kitchen, she found Jack seated at the table with an empty plate in front of him, a fork in one hand and a knife in the other in mock impatience. She kissed him on his bald spot as she walked behind him. Jack was pleased but didn't know just how to react.

He had already made coffee. He arose from his chair, fixed her a cup just like she liked it, and handed it to her. This had been a routine during their marriage. As she stood at the stove sipping her coffee, dressed in a neat slacks and blouse outfit, it seemed to Jack that she looked completely well. Except for a few strands of silver hairs that now streaked her otherwise raven locks, she looked just like the Yvette he had wooed and married over ten years ago.

The noise of their children broke into his thoughts. "Do we have to wait until after breakfast to open our presents?" Jacky asked.

"Yes," his mother said. "This year you're old enough to wait."

They ate hurriedly, Jacky pushing them to get to the den so he could see what Santa had brought him. Like all the past Christmases, Jack passed out the gifts and they watched as each one opened their treasures. Finally it was Yvette's turn. Jack had rewrapped the anniversary gifts in Christmas wrap and thrown the sentimental anniversary card away.

"The evening gown is lovely, Jack, but where will I ever wear something like this?"

When she opened the box containing the necklace with the entwined hearts, he saw a little tear run down her cheek. She wiped it away and said in a voice just above a whisper, "Please help me with the clasp, Jack."

When all the gifts had been removed from under the tree and all the papers cleaned up, Jack was relaxing in the den with a mug of eggnog. Yvette walked over and sat down on the arm of his chair. "There was one more gift for you," she said, giving him a small box about three inches square and a half inch deep. He opened it and found a single sheet of her lavender memo paper. On it she had written one word: "Yes."

Jack knew there was a seventy-two-hour waiting period between purchase of a marriage license and the marriage ceremony in both Texas and Louisiana. He hadn't even thought of purchasing a marriage license until yesterday. Still, he was determined to end this long nightmare and return to his rightful place beside the woman he loved.

At 9:05 a.m. Sunday morning, all four of the Lockharts were on a flight out of George Bush International Airport in Houston, to Las Vegas, Nevada, where there was no waiting period and licenses could be purchased 365 days out of the year. You could even hire an Elvis impersonator for your one required witness. Their one required witness however, was Juliette, who also had the honored position of maid of honor. Jacky played the part of best man, standing tall in a new suit beside his father. Jack purchased a single, simple gold band from one of the many vendors along the street.

Two hours after their plane landed in Las Vegas, Jack and Yvette were once again happily united as one. The plane ride back and the two-hour time difference put them back at home late Sunday night. Soon Jacky was in bed asleep. Juliette said good night to her parents, and Jack and Yvette were alone.

Yvette looked down at the small gold band and decided it would only bring them sad memories. She slid it off and put it in the very bottom of her jewelry chest. She then put on the wedding set that Jack had given her at their first wedding. "There," she said, "now things are right again. I'll never again take these off."

Jack made the familiar bath for his new bride, using her favorite bath crystals, then went to shower in the guest bedroom, where his clothes were. He shaved and brushed his teeth before entering the shower. Jack stepped out of the shower, dried, and put on his pajama bottoms. He was just finishing combing his hair when Yvette entered his bathroom, dressed only in a towel. "Could you do my back for me, Jack?"

She turned with her back to him. He took the towel and gently dried her back. He put the towel down and touched her arms and took her hands as she slowly turned to face him. He moved his hands and eyes up her arms to her neck. He let his fingers touch her skin so softly that she felt goose bumps. He traced the outline of her lips with a fingertip, touched her cheeks, then tenderly traced the outline of each ear. "Are you cold?" he whispered as he noticed the goose bumps.

"No," she whispered to him, hoping he would never stop.

Jack led her to her bed and continued his exploration. He scrutinized her face, looking deep into her violet-blue, passion-filled eyes, touching her brow lightly with his fingers. He lightly touched each eyebrow, her nose, her lips. He smoothed her hair. He let his palms and eyes follow the contour of her neck and shoulders, her throat and breasts, and the remainder of her abdomen. Completing his examination, he returned to her face, softly touching her lips again with his finger tip before kissing her tenderly and easing himself down on the bed beside her. He had satisfied himself that she was whole, she was well, and now she was safe beside him. He reached for her hand and held it tightly against his chest, just over his heart. They lay there quietly side by side.

After a few minutes Jack asked, "Are you happy, Evie?"

"Ecstatically!" she replied in a voice barely audible yet dripping with emotion.

He smiled contentedly with a feeling of pride and a grand sense of accomplishment, having at last fixed this, his most treasured and difficult project.

After a few moments Yvette rolled over, partially on top of his chest, and kissed him long and tenderly. As she removed her lips from his she spoke to him softly and sincerely. "I thought I loved you at one time, Jack, back some ten years ago. I guess I did in my own way. But I didn't know what love was at that time. The past two months you have shown me what it really means to love someone unconditionally. Thank you for loving me and not giving up on me, Jack. I love you so very much right now! I want to show you every day from this day on just how much your love means to me."

"Together," Jack whispered, "we can conquer anything as long as we stay together."

He wrapped his arms around her, pulled the blankets up over her bare shoulders, and held her close to him. They lay like this, quietly, close together for the remainder of the night. Yvette, feeling warm and safe inside Jack's arms, finally realized the unambiguous difference between love and sexual desire. She preferred the former.

Early the next morning, as Jack built a fire in the fireplace, he used the divorce decree as kindling to get it started. Jack and Yvette continued to celebrate their wedding anniversary on September 18, never mentioning the December 26 date or the traumatic few months of their separation. As far as Jack was concerned, they had never been divorced.

FOUR

With Jack and Yvette now happy and comfortable in their mutual love and respect for one another, Jack turned his worries to his lovely daughter and his rapidly growing son.

Juliette's newly found love should have caused him some paternal jealously, but he genuinely liked Rolf and enjoyed the company of this exceptionally intelligent young man.

Rolf, who was just two years older than Juliette, had just spent the Easter weekend with them and now wanted Juliette to accompany him to Norway for two weeks in May so she could meet his parents and enjoy the Norwegian celebration of Constitution Day on May 17. Both Jack and Yvette had reservations about a young, nineteen-year-old single girl traveling in the company of a single man and spending that much time alone with him. Jack confronted Rolf about his concerns.

"Please be assured you have nothing to worry about, Mr. Lockhart, eh, Jack," Rolf said. "I have the greatest respect for Juliette. I would never do anything to bring her shame. In fact," he said, holding up his left ring finger to show an engraved ring, "I have taken a vow of celibacy and purity until my wedding day!"

"I appreciate your candor, Rolf, but I'm also realistic. Juliette, is, shall we say, ripe for the picking, and I know if I was a young man in her company I'd have a whale of a time keeping my hands off of her!"

"I agree she is the most lovely woman I have ever known, but I am telling you, sir, she will be in the best possible hands with me. Would you be more comfortable if my parents called you? We will be staying in their home."

"Yes, I would like that. Do your parents speak English as well as you?"

"Probably better." He smiled. "My father also attended a university in the United States. He's on staff at the Norwegian University of Science and Technology in Trondheim. My mother is a medical doctor there at St. Olav's Hospital."

"That's very impressive, and let me say that I believe they raised a very responsible son. Okay, Rolf, she can go, with my blessing."

Rolf went to find Juliette to tell her of her father's consent, while Jack went to find Yvette and tell her he had relented.

"Evie, honey, I told Rolf he had my blessing to take Juli to Norway. Sometimes I have to take my own advice. When the time comes, I've always said, we have to believe Juli will make the right decisions."

"But we don't have to be a partner to putting temptation in her path."

"Are you talking about Rolf or their spending so much time alone in each other's company?" Jack joked.

"Both, actually," she said. "He is very attractive!"

"Come here," Jack said, pulling her into his arms, showing his boyish grin. "I was just as tall and handsome as he is when I was his age."

"Really, Jack?" She smiled up at him, kissing him tenderly. "What in the world happened to you?"

Juliette found them just then. "Is that all you guys ever do?" she teased. "Give it a rest, Dad! Rolf just told me you have consented to let me go with him to Norway! Thank you both so much. I'll take lots of pictures and call you as often as I can."

A few days later Jack received a call from a Professor Bernt Olsen of the Norwegian University of Science and Technology in Trondheim. "Mr Lockhart, this is Professor Olsen. My son, Rolf, has asked me to call you in regard to the upcoming visit to our home by your daughter, Juliette. Maybe I can alleviate some of your concerns."

"Please, Professor Olsen, call me Jack. Yes, we are naturally concerned about our daughter traveling that distance and staying in a foreign country. But I wouldn't go so far as to say we are overly concerned. Rolf has assured me he will take the best care of her. But as a father I always worry when my children are out of my sight."

"Then please, Jack, call me Bernt. My wife, Linnea, and I are looking forward to Juliette's visit. Rolf has told us so much about her. Our home is quite large and we could let her have a suite of her own, but for the sake of propriety, Linnea has decided she should stay in the same suite as our daughter, Janne. Janne is Rolf's older sister."

"Well, Bernt, may I complement you on raising a tremendous son? My wife, Yvette, and I both think the world of Rolf."

"I'm glad to hear that, Jack, because from the way Rolf speaks about Juliette, I would not be surprised if we hear wedding bells some time in the future."

"You may be right. I have even more evidence along those lines. I've seen the way they look at one other."

"Now I am even more anxious to meet this young woman who has turned my son's head. I hope to meet you and Yvette, some time in the future. Feel free to call me here at my office, Jack."

He gave Jack his personal restricted number before terminating the call.

Juliette started immediately getting things ready for the trip. She got her passport and purchased clothing suitable for the cooler temperatures of Norway. Rolf told her the high temperature in May was usually in the mid fifties, dropping down to around forty at night. A big difference from the high eighties and low seventies of Dallas. She and Rolf bought roundtrip tickets from Dallas/Fort Worth International to Trondheim Airport, Vaernes.

Their plan was to leave Dallas on Sunday May 8 and be back on Sunday May 22.

As their plane came in low over the Trondheimsfjord, heading for the landing strip that extended a long way out into the fjord near Stjordal, Juliette was amazed at the total differences from what she was used to in Texas. So much green. So much water.

Soon they were on the ground and went to claim their luggage. As they stood by the carousel awaiting their bags, she heard an announcement that was totally in Scandinavian. The only words she understood were Rolf and Olsen.

"I have been summoned to a courtesy phone," he told her. "Come with me while I find one. I don't want you out of my sight."

They found a phone. "God dag!" Rolf said into the phone. Juliette recognized the greeting as hello, but she didn't understand his next sentence. Then he changed to English. "Oh, hello, Father. Yes, we will meet you by the luggage carousel."

As they pulled their bags from the carousel they were joined by a tall, very distinguished-looking well-dressed gentleman in his late forties. Rolf introduced Juliette to his father with an air of pride.

Professor Olsen took her hand and kissed it in a gentlemanly fashion. Juliette gave him her adorable smile. "Rolf has been understating your loveliness," he said.

Juliette blushed. "Thank you, Professor Olsen."

"This way, my car is just outside."

At the home of the Olsens, Juliette was introduced to Rolf's mother, Dr. Linnea Olsen, and his sister, Janne. Within minutes Juliette and Janne were fast friends. Janne was planning to walk in the parade on Constitution Day and had a brightly colored dress for Juliette to wear in the parade.

"You're going to walk with us also, aren't you, Rolf?" Janne asked.

"Yes, of course. I should have warned you about this, Juliette. Someone from the Olsen family has participated in the parade every year as far back as I can remember."

"Oh, it sounds like fun!" Juliette told him.

Both Professor Olsen and his wife became fond of Juliette, who, because of her Texas rearing and time spent growing up in a café, was very outgoing and always at ease with any new people she met. She found herself to be very comfortable in their home.

On the seventeenth, as they gathered at the starting place and prepared to walk in the parade, they were joined by other youth familiar to Janne and Rolf. Janne was busy introducing Juliette to her friends when suddenly a strikingly pretty blond-haired girl a year or two older than Juliette rushed up to Rolf and hugging him, said, "Hei, Rolf," as she kissed his cheek.

"Hei, Astrid, I thought I might see you here today. May I introduce you to my friend from the United States? This is my close friend Juliette Lockhart. Juliette, meet Astrid Severson, a classmate of mine from high school."

"Hallo," Astrid said, smiling. "Rolf hasn't told you, but we were more than classmates. Tell her, Rolf!"

"It's true, we dated some in high school."

"More than some," Janne said. "They were voted the couple most apt!"

Rolf's ears were beginning to turn just a little red. Juliette herself was becoming jealous and noticed his embarrassment and quickly came to his defense.

"Well, Rolf and I are also more than just close friends." She took his arm and stood close to him. "We are planning a future together."

"This is exciting news!" Janne said. "I can hardly wait to tell Mother and Father!"

As they all walked in the parade, Juliette on Rolf's left, Janne to the left of Juliette, Astrid positioned herself on Rolf's right, smiling brightly and occasionally bumping his arm with her shoulder in a flirtatious way. Rolf pretended to not be aware.

Later, at the Olsen home, Astrid was a guest of the Olsens for the remainder of the evening. Her flirting with Rolf was so evident that Juliette felt her jealously heighten. She wanted to test Rolf's unspoken commitment to her, but instead she held her tongue and acted like a lady.

The following day Juliette and Rolf took a sightseeing tour of Trondheim. Juliette was so impressed by the old Nidaros Cathedral that she told Rolf she thought it would be the perfect place for a wedding ceremony.

"Can't you just see a bride with a long white train entering here? And look at the long aisle! It would take forever for her to get to the altar. It would give the groom plenty of time to back out," she teased.

"For that reason alone, I agree with you," Rolf countered. "It would be the perfect place to be married."

As she looked up at him, smiling, Rolf took the opportunity to kiss her tenderly, completely unaware of the crowd of visitors around them.

Their two weeks had gone by too rapidly. Soon they would have to say good-bye to the Olsens. The day before they were to leave, Mrs. Olsen called Rolf into her bedroom and closed the door.

"Sit down, Rolf," she instructed. "It's become apparent to your father and me that you are deeply in love with Juliette."

"Yes, Mother, that is true. I do so adore her!"

"I assume that someday soon you will want to ask her to be your wife. That is why I wanted to talk to you. Here, I want you to have this ring. It belonged to your great-grandmother Dahl, my father's mother. When you do ask her, I would be honored if she would wear this ring."

"She might turn me down, Mother. Have you thought of that?"

"She won't. I've watched her during the past two weeks. She would marry you today if you just asked her. Your father and I have discussed it, and we would both be thrilled if Juliette is your choice for a mate."

"Thank you, Mother. This ring is beautiful. Was your grandmother Dahl happy when she wore it?"

"Three girls and four boys! Judge for yourself."

"If happiness is measured in the number of children one has, then I suppose she was very happy."

"Here, now take it and go find your lovely Juliette."

The young couple returned to the University of Texas and working over the weekends, were able to complete the makeup work for the time lost during the two weeks in Norway. They completed and turned in their term papers. When the semester ended in mid-June and they both received excellent grade point averages, they decided to celebrate with a night out.

Rolf made reservations at the Sawadika Thai Zone, a five-star restaurant not too far from the campus. Juliette was dressed in a deep blue frock accenting her violet-blue eyes. Rolf was handsomely dressed in a summer suit. The atmosphere in the restaurant was quiet and restful.

During an after-dinner, non-alcoholic Thai fruit juice drink, Rolf reached across the table and took Juliette's hand. "Do I need to get down on one knee to ask you what's been on my mind for weeks now?"

"Yes," Juliette said, smiling. "It won't be right unless you are totally humiliated."

Rolf brought out his great-grandmother's ring and dropped down on one knee beside Juliette's chair. Somewhere in the restaurant someone struck a large cymbal and everyone turned to see what was going on. Rolf could only see Juliette, as his love for her had caused a sort of tunnel vision and at the end of the tunnel he saw an angel.

"Juliette," he began, holding the ring out toward her.

"Yes, of course I'll marry you, Rolf!" she blurted out, saving him from any more time kneeling.

They kissed tenderly and he returned to his seat. Rolf had hardly sat down when a waiter arrived, pushing a cart with wineglasses and two ice buckets. In one bucket was champagne and in the other a non-alcoholic wine. "Congratulations! Compliments of the house," he said. "Which do you prefer?" the waiter asked as he set a wineglass in front of Juliette.

"The non-alcoholic wine," she said.

He opened the bottle and filled her glass with her choice. "And for you, sir?"

"I'll have the same." Rolf smiled.

As the waiter rolled his cart away, the young lovers toasted one another then entwined their arms as they the drank the toast. Juliette then asked if he would mind if she made a quick phone call. "Not at all," he said.

Jack was in the den relaxing and listening to some Buckaroo Instrumentals when he heard the phone ring. He went to turn off the CD player before picking up the phone. In the kitchen Yvette had already picked up the phone.

"Jack," she called, "it's Juli. She wants you to pick up the extension."

Jack picked up the extension phone and greeted Juliette. "Hi, honey. How are you?"

"Mom, Dad," she said excitedly, "I have some wonderful news! Rolf just asked me to marry him!"

"Congratulations!" Jack said. "I'm happy for you and for Rolf."

"Yes, dear, congratulations!" Yvette told her daughter.

"Wait! Don't you want to hear what I said?"

"If it was anything other than yes," Jack said, "then no! I don't want to hear it."

"You're spoiling all my fun!" Juliette said. "Yes! That's what I said—yes! The ring he gave me is an heirloom. It's the engagement ring that was given to his great-grandmother. It's beautiful, Mom. I can't wait for you to see it."

When Juliette was through bubbling on about her engagement to Rolf and the remarkably exquisite engagement ring, Jack said, "Put Rolf on."

"Yes, sir?" Rolf asked.

"When were you going to ask me about this? Aren't you supposed to get the father's permission?"

"Yes, sir, I thought about that, but then I decided to try to do things the American way."

"Just joking with you, son. Congratulations. I don't know anyone I'd rather see my Juli marry than you. Have you told your parents yet?"

"No, sir, I'm about to do that now."

"Rolf?" Yvette's voice came on the line. "Congratulations! I wish you both all the happiness in the world."

"Thank you, Mrs. Lockhart."

Juliette came back on the line. "We hope to be in Bon Weir in a couple of days. The next semester doesn't start until August twenty-third. We will probably try to make another trip to Trondheim before school starts. Love you, Mom. Love you, Dad. Ha det!"

"Good-bye," Yvette told her.

Yvette went into the den to find Jack. She sat down on the arm of his chair, and he noticed she had tears in her eyes. Jack pulled her down on his lap and kissed her tenderly. "What's the matter, Evie, honey?"

"My little girl isn't a little girl anymore."

"You just now noticing that?" he teased.

"Don't, Jack! I'm really hurting here. Don't you feel a sense of loss?"

"Yes, of course."

"Next she'll marry; then she'll graduate; and then they'll go off to Norway to have my grandbabies. Things will never be the same!"

Jack knew that anything he said would only get in the way of her feelings. He held her on his lap tenderly, smoothing her hair and patting her shoulder until she finished her cry.

"Well," she said, wiping her eyes and standing up, "I have a wedding to plan!"

Jack looked at her with amazement and love in his eyes. One moment she was pathetic and the next she was superwoman.

Jacky came into the house and noticing his mother had been crying, asked Jack about it.

"Why is Mommy crying?"

"She's crying because she's happy!" Jack told him.

"Women are so weird!" Jacky said as he skipped off to his room.

Jack almost laughed out loud, hearing this coming from a nine-year-old. *But,* he thought, *yes, sometimes they do what we men consider to be weird things! But somehow we love them anyway!*

When Juliette and Rolf arrived two days later, they had discussed and come up with a plan for marriage. At first they had thought they would wait until June of next year, giving them a long engagement and time to plan for the perfect wedding. But once they had agreed to marriage, Rolf wanted to elope. "Let's do it now," he had suggested.

Juliette had nixed that, stating that as her mother's only daughter, she thought it only right that she and her mother get to plan the perfect wedding. "Next June will give us sufficient time."

Rolf couldn't imagine waiting another year, so they had compromised.

"If we can get everything done in time for an early August wedding," Juliette told her mother, "we will both be happy. We want to have the ceremony in the Nidaros Cathedral in Trondheim."

"We need to book that first!" Yvette told her. "I wonder how one goes about doing that?"

"I'll call my father and see if he can book it," Rolf told Yvette.

Professor Olsen was able to get the cathedral for four hours on Sunday August 7.

"That gives us just seven weeks to get everything done," Yvette stated.

"And just two weeks for the honeymoon before classes start again in August," Rolf said, smiling at Juliette.

Jack did not want to get in the way of the whirlwind planning session going on in the house, so he took his guitar to the homemade wooden settee on the front patio and was running through some chords when the shiny new car drove into his driveway. He put his guitar down and took notice of the occupants. As the car stopped, he recognized the very pretty tall blond woman. He leaped to his feet and hurried to meet her.

"Shannon honey," he said, "you look great! How are you?"

"Hi, Daddy Jack!" she said, as she hugged him.

Greg was busy pulling a small two-year-old from the car seat in the rear. He cradled her in his left arm as he shook hands with Jack. "This is Kathryn," Greg said.

"Aren't you just a doll?" Jack said as he took her from Greg. He smiled at the little blond-headed brown-eyed girl. "I'm your granddaddy Jack. Y'all come on in. Evie," he called from the door, "look what I have!"

Yvette looked up from her wedding books, saw Shannon, and jumped up to hug her and Greg before taking Kathryn away from Jack.

Juliette, seeing Shannon, also came to hug her and Greg.

Rolf was standing in the room wondering what was going on.

Jack, having just been relieved of his desire to hold and love on Kathryn some more, decided to make some mischief.

"Rolf," he said, "I want you to meet Greg Wilson, one of Juli's old flames. This is Greg's wife, my assumed daughter Shannon. This is Rolf Olsen, Juli's fiancé."

"Pleased to meet you," Rolf said, shaking hands with both of them.

"Fiancé?" Shannon asked. "Juliette, when did this happen? Let me see your ring! Oh, congratulations you two. When is the wedding?"

The girls withdrew to Juliette's old room to catch up on everything.

Jack, observing the strained looks between Rolf and Greg, decided he should break the tension he had caused. "I was teasing you, Rolf," he said. "Juli did have a crush on Greg back when she was a sophomore in high school, but Greg here only had eyes for Shannon."

Greg and Shannon were also between semesters at college, and the four young people found many common subjects to discuss. With Yvette now busy with wedding plans and the two young couples busy socializing, Jack saw his opportunity to spoil Kathryn some more. He put her on his foot and played horsey. Then he and Jacky took her to the corral to see the real horses. He sat her up on Blacky and held her tight while Blacky took her for a ride around the yard. Jacky rode along with them on Apollo. He took her on the swings with him, holding her on his lap. Finally he took her back to her mother and went into the kitchen to start supper.

When Greg, Shannon, and Kathryn took the guest room, Rolf was demoted to the foldout couch in the den.

Two days later Sean and Rebecca arrived with their two children. They were on their summer vacation and were towing a camping trailer. When Rebecca heard the news about Juliette's upcoming wedding, Yvette suddenly had another woman excited about planning it and spending Jack's money.

Juliette asked Shannon to be her maid of honor, Rebecca to be a bridesmaid, and she said she planned to ask Janne, Rolf's sister, to also be in the wedding as a bridesmaid.

By the end of the week they had decided on almost everything and all of the orders had been submitted. Now it was time to pick out gowns.

According to the women, this could only be done in person at a bridal shop, completely out of the view of anyone of the male gender. So on Monday, Yvette, Juliette, Shannon, and Rebecca all piled into Jack's Expedition and headed for a bridal shop in Beaumont. They were sure their purchases would not fit in Yvette's sedan.

Jack, Sean, Greg, and Rolf took the children on a boat trip up the Sabine River for a couple of miles then floated back down while Jacky and Kevin took turns trying to steer with an oar over the stern of the boat. Jack took this opportunity to teach them a lesson from his days in the Navy.

"You see, boys," he said, "it's much harder to steer a straight course in following seas than when you are heading into the seas or waves."

Kathryn, seated on her daddy's lap, soon fell asleep. Jack started the motor and they soon put in at the boathouse.

When the ladies returned that evening from their exhaustive search for the perfect gown, they were quieter than usual. Jack was just completing his cooking chores and the tables were set. The eight grownups and Kathryn would be at the dining room table and the three older children at a card table.

Juliette came into the kitchen, hugged her father, and said, "It's the most gorgeous bridal gown ever! Thank you, Daddy!"

"You're welcome, I think. When do I get a look at this investment?"

"About thirty minutes before Rolf sees it," Yvette answered for her as she stood up on her toes and kissed Jack lovingly.

At the table that night Yvette told him, "Jack, we have the date, the church, invitations ordered, gowns and tuxedos ordered, cakes ordered, and with what Professor and Doctor Olsen are providing, I think we have a wedding planned."

"I'm buying roundtrip tickets for everybody who is here tonight," Jack announced. "We'll see all of you at the cathedral in Trondheim at three p.m. on Sunday August seventh. Start making your plans now."

"I'm not sure my schedule allows for me to be there on that date and at that time." Rolf grinned as he looked at Juliette.

Juliette made a pouty face. "And what would be on your schedule to keep you away on that day? A date with Astrid?"

"Oops," Jack said, "low blow! Now you kids play nice!"

"Who's Astrid?" Shannon wanted to know.

Rolf blushed, "Just an old high school friend. Like Greg and Juliette."

"Touché," Juliette said.

During the rest of the meal the conversation touched on many subjects. Afterward, Rolf and Juliette went for a walk down to the river in the almost full moon. Shannon and Rebecca pushed everyone else out of the kitchen. Jack picked up Kathryn and carried her out to the patio and sat down beside Yvette on the patio swing. The rest were in the backyard.

Yvette reached over and lovingly brushed a wisp of hair from Jack's face. "You seem very happy tonight, with all your girls around you."

"I am," he said. "All the people I love are right here in one place. My lovely wife, my three daughters, my son and grandchildren, my sons-in-law. How could a man have it any better?"

Yvette wrapped her arm around his arm and snuggled up close to him. "I love you, old man," she whispered.

A few days later, Rolf flew to Norway to spend some time with his parents before the big event. Juliette was to join him there to spend some time with his parents after the final fitting of her gown. The Lockharts would bring the gown with them when they flew in on the Friday before the ceremony.

Gradually Yvette was able to pull everything together. Jack purchased and sent out all of the roundtrip tickets. There was even a pair of tickets for Arty and Mable.

The day finally arrived. The church was filled to capacity. The Olsens had made sure it was beautifully decorated. When the Wedding March started, Juliette appeared in the archway of the main hall. The congregation stood and faced her, many drawing in their breath at the sight of her total beauty. Jack waited for her at the last row of seats. As he took her hand to escort her down the aisle, Wagner's Wedding Chorus echoed throughout the castle-sized cathedral. He stood tall and proud beside Juliette as they took that long walk down the long, marble aisle together. Juliette's smile was radiant. Her hand rested on Jack's arm, and he could feel a slight tremble in her hand. They looked at each other and smiled. Jack, trying to reassure her, whispered, "I love you!" Although it was a long, slow walk to the altar, it was over too soon for Jack. As they reached Rolf he took his hand and gave him Juliette's hand.

Jack returned to his seat. He took Yvette's hand. She clutched his tightly. As he listened to the minister going through the ritual readings, he began to have flashbacks, bits and pieces of memories of his times with Juliette. The tiny, darling little girl he first saw on a stool in that café; his courting of both her and her mother; his wedding to Yvette where he presented Juliette with her own wedding band; her sweet sixteen dance with him; her high school graduation day; and now the mature and beautiful bride. She was not blood of his blood, but he could not possibly love her more. As the minister spoke the words, "Do you, Juliette Anne Lockhart, take this man, Rolf Linne Olsen…" Jack felt a tear roll down his face.